# THE RUSE

## EDEN FALLS ACADEMY

# the *ruse*

## JUDY CORRY

# ALSO BY JUDY CORRY

## **<u>Eden Falls Academy Series:</u>**

The Charade (Ava and Carter)

The Facade (Cambrielle and Mack)

The Ruse (Elyse and Asher)

The Confidant (Scarlett and Hunter)

The Confession (Kiara and Nash)

## **<u>Kings of Eden Falls:</u>**

Hide Away With You (Addie and Evan)

Say You Remember Me (Maddie and Ian)

Wish You Were Mine (Lucy and Owen)

## **<u>Rich and Famous Series:</u>**

Assisting My Brother's Best Friend (Kate and Drew)

Hollywood and Ivy (Ivy and Justin)

Her Football Star Ex (Emerson and Vincent)

Friend Zone to End Zone (Arianna and Cole)

Stolen Kisses from a Rock Star (Maya and Landon)

## **<u>Ridgewater High Series:</u>**

When We Began (Cassie and Liam)

Meet Me There (Ashlyn and Luke)

Don't Forget Me (Eliana and Jess)

It Was Always You (Lexi and Noah)

My Second Chance (Juliette and Easton)

My Mistletoe Mix-Up (Raven and Logan)

Forever Yours (Alyssa and Jace)

### **<u>Standalones:</u>**

Protect My Heart (Emma and Arie)

Kissing The Boy Next Door (Lauren and Wes)

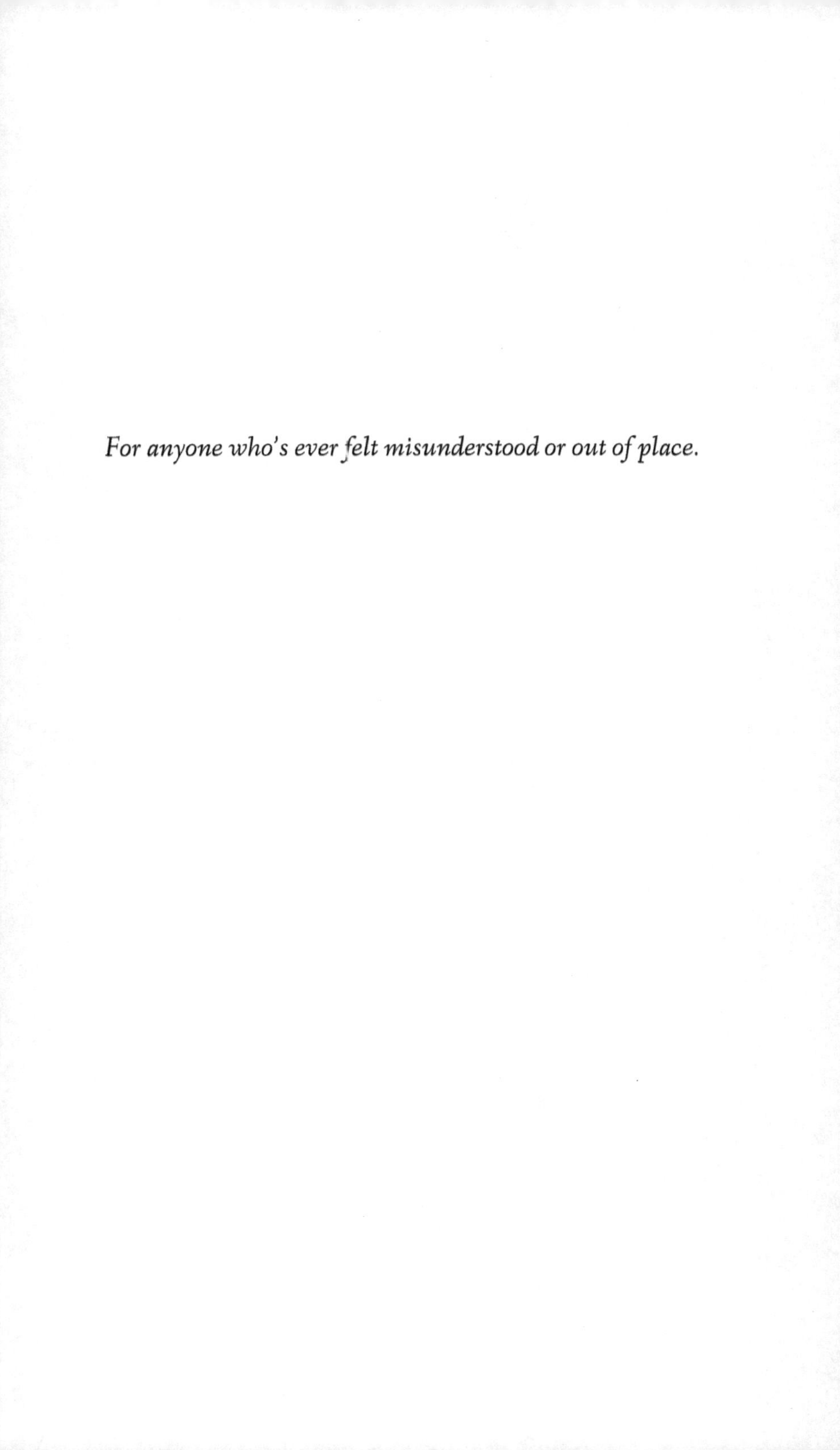

*For anyone who's ever felt misunderstood or out of place.*

# PLAYLIST

"bad ones" by Tate McRae
"Unseen" by Katie Armiger
"Think of Me" by David Archuleta
"Wondering" by Olivia Rodrigo & Julia Lester
"Just a Dream" by Nelly
"Perfect" by One Direction
"All I Ask of You" by Andrew Lloyd Webber, Patrick Wilson
and Emmy Rossum
"Somebody Else" by Ill-Advised Poetry
"How To Lose A Friend" by Wafia
"Slow Dance" by AJ Mitchell (feat. Ava Max)
"Mr. Brightside" by The Killers
"I Miss Being in Love" by Ian McConnell
"Heaven Help Me" by Conor Matthews
"Burn" by AJ Mitchell

1
——————

ELYSE

"READY FOR YOUR first Thanksgiving with your father?" Mom asked when we stood on the doorstep of the Hastings' family estate, hesitating just a moment before we rang the doorbell.

"I guess," I said, even though a kaleidoscope of butterflies fluttered in my chest. "At least, I guess I'd better be since it's happening right now."

Mom stepped closer and put an arm around my shoulder, pulling me close. "It will be great."

But even as she said it, a look of apprehension filled her dark-brown eyes.

Which should have been expected.

While Ava, my identical twin sister, and I were still getting used to the idea of Dr. Brendon Aarden, a world renown neuro-surgeon, being our father—after not knowing who he was for the first seventeen years of our lives—my mom was probably a little more nervous than I was right now. She'd be eating dinner with not only one of her high school exes but two—Joel Hastings, Brendon's neighbor and best friend, was hosting the meal with his wife Dawn.

"Should we ring the doorbell then?" I asked, glancing down at my mom who was several inches shorter than my five-foot-nine-inch height.

"Let me just take another deep breath." Mom inhaled through her nose and released it slowly. Then she pulled her shoulders back and stood a little straighter in her black Jimmy Choos, the skirt of her navy-blue dress swishing around her knees. "Okay. Let's do this."

I transferred the apple pie we'd brought to my left hand and reached out to press the doorbell.

While we waited for someone to answer the door, I looked up at the gigantic stone country house that my friends Cambrielle, Nash, and Carter Hastings lived in.

When I'd first come to the Hastings' mansion in September after starting my senior year at Eden Falls Academy, I'd been in awe of the house. My grandparents, who were very well-to-do in Israel, had a pretty-good-sized house that I'd visited during a few summer vacations growing up, but it had nothing on this place with its gray stone exterior, dozens of windows with white shutters, and tall white columns that held up the portico above us.

Did I mention that Mr. and Mrs. Hastings were billion-aires? And that their home and grounds could fit right in with Mr. Darcy's estate in *Pride and Prejudice*?

Yeah. They were crazy rich.

And even though hanging out with the top one percent in the country was becoming more normal since most of the kids at my private school came from money, it hadn't always been that way for us. My mom's career as a fashion designer hadn't taken off until this past year.

The door opened, bringing my attention back to what was

in front of me. In the entryway stood a woman with dark-brown hair and brown eyes: Mrs. Dawn Hastings.

I'd expected one of the many staff members to answer the door, since they usually answered it whenever Ava and I came by, but the Hastings must have given all their staff the holiday off.

"Welcome," Mrs. Hastings said, stepping back and gesturing for my mom and me to come in. "I'm so glad you could make it."

"Thanks," Mom said, nodding her head slightly at the woman who had married her high school sweetheart. "We appreciate you inviting us."

And if Mrs. Hastings felt any sort of threat at having her husband's old girlfriend joining them for Thanksgiving dinner, it didn't show. She just smiled warmly at us and said, "Any family of Brendon and Mack is our family, too."

*Family.*

It was still so weird to have Brendon and Mack as part of what had always just been my mom, Ava, and me.

"If you'd like to hang your coat in the closet, it's just right there." Mrs. Hastings pointed to the closet door to our right.

"Thank you," Mom said, already slipping out of the fitted wool coat she'd gotten on a recent trip to Paris. She hung her coat inside, and then I handed her the apple pie box so I could hang mine beside hers in the closet.

"Anyway, if you wanted to join the adults in the kitchen, we're still waiting on the turkey," Mrs. Hastings said to my mom. Then looking at me, she said, "And I think most of the kids are upstairs, if you want to go up and find them."

"Sounds good," I said.

I glanced back at my mom to make sure she was fine with me leaving her with the people she hadn't been close to since high school.

"Go ahead and find your friends and sister," Mom said with a look that told me she was going to be fine.

"Okay," I said. The two women disappeared around the corner, my mom carrying the pie with her.

I was about to head up the grand staircase to find my friends when the sound of a piano playing a familiar tune caught my attention. I stopped with one foot on the bottom stair and listened, picking out the melody of "Think of Me" from *The Phantom of the Opera* musical.

Was that Nash playing the piano?

I hadn't heard of him being a pianist, but if anyone in this house would know that specific song, it would be him, since he was set to play the Phantom in our school's upcoming winter musical. He had been immersing himself in the music for the past few months leading up to auditions.

When the drama teacher posted the cast list for the musical two days ago, I'd been nervous that my being new to the school might hurt my chances of being cast as the female lead, since she hadn't seen me in the productions at my old school in Ridgewater, New York. The part of Christine was such a demanding role, and so casting someone she hadn't seen perform in front of an audience could be considered a big risk.

But Miss Crawley had apparently been okay with taking a risk on the new girl, because when my eyes scanned down the list Tuesday afternoon, my name was next to the role of Christine Daaé.

I had been so relieved and happy. Because while I hadn't dressed up like the character for Halloween the way Nash had dressed up like the Phantom, I had wanted that part just as badly.

I'd dreamed of playing Christine on Broadway ever since I watched the 2004 movie version with my mom in our tiny living room in Ridgewater. And while the stage at Eden Falls

Academy was an hour-long train ride from Broadway, it felt almost as cool to get the part.

The music continued to drift down the hallway to my right, so I decided to follow it to see if it was Nash playing the piano in his family's music room.

I'd gotten a little bit of a crush on my blond-haired, blue-eyed friend as we'd hung out the past few weeks. There was nothing more attractive than a musician to me. I wanted to catch a glimpse of him playing so I could add it to my little mental file of moments when Nash was looking extra hot.

The music grew louder as I approached. After glancing around to make sure no one was around to watch me spy on Nash, I leaned closer to the small opening in the door and peeked my head inside to take a look.

Only, instead of finding Nash like I'd expected, it was a guy with jet-black hair and broad shoulders sitting on the piano bench with his back to me.

Who was this? A cousin of the Hastings, perhaps? Someone from Mrs. Hastings' side since she had the dark hair, maybe?

I hadn't heard of them inviting their extended family today, but it was Thanksgiving, so it made sense that they would, I guess.

I was about to head back the way I'd come—I didn't want to be the creepy stalker girl who spied on strangers—when the melody shifted into something much more complex. Instead of continuing to follow the tune of "Think of Me," it evolved into "All I Ask of You."

I paused and listened to the guy at the piano play the elaborate arrangement, and as cold chills raced up my arms, all I could think of was, *wow.* As the music swelled at my favorite part of the melody—the part where Raoul and Christine sing about wanting to always go where the other went—another wave of chills flowed from the crown of my head and all the way down to my toes.

Who was this guy playing the piano? And where had he found this arrangement? I'd never heard anything so beautiful —I felt like it was speaking to my soul.

The music came down from the big crescendo, softened, and then slowed, becoming more simplified as it returned to the original melody. As I waited for his fingers to play the last long note, I found myself holding my breath.

It wasn't until the stranger at the piano lifted his hands from the keyboard of the grand piano that I realized where I was. The music had temporarily transported me away from reality.

But when he started to swivel his body around on the piano bench, I knew that if I didn't move away from the crack in the door in the next instant, I would be caught spying on him.

I quickly pulled away from the opening in the doorway and took a few steps back. I was just turning around to run back the way I'd come when my butt bumped against a fancy side table along the wall. I watched in horror as a vase of fresh flowers wobbled, but my reflexes were quick, and I stopped it just before it could tip over.

Crisis averted, I sighed with relief. The relief only lasted a split second though, because just when I was about to dart down the hall like a kid who'd just stolen some chocolate from her grandma's candy jar, I heard the sound of someone stepping onto the marble floor behind me.

*So much for not getting caught and looking like a creeper.*

Even though I knew I'd been seen, I still considered running down the hall anyway. I could just pretend it was my identical twin sister who had been doing the creeping, if this guy were to ask around later, right?

But before I could flee, a deep voice behind me said, "I see they sent the new girl to spy on the enemy."

*Busted.*

Then I processed what he'd said.

Had he just called himself the enemy? And hinted that my friends had sent me to spy on him? So did that mean the Hastings' siblings weren't friends with this cousin of theirs?

I planned to ask the guy what he meant by his statement... right up until I turned around and saw his face.

And suddenly, all I could think was, *Holy heck, this guy is hot.*

I mean, he'd looked pretty good from behind while playing the piano. He had broad shoulders, a muscular build, a long torso that made me assume he was taller than average for a guy —always a bonus for a tall girl like me. And his black hair was slightly curly and tousled in a way that I loved.

But from the front... From the front, he was basically the kind of guy who every girl from the ages of twelve to sixty would leave their boyfriend or husbands for if he asked.

I swallowed as I took him in, momentarily wondering if he was even real because I had never seen anyone so physically attractive in my entire life.

Which was saying something, since Eden Falls seemed to be a breeding ground for the world's most beautiful people.

This guy had a jawline that could cut glass; his light tan skin was smooth and almost glowed. His eyebrows were dark, bold, and defined.

Everything about him was gorgeous.

But it was his large, hooded eyes that made me lose all coherent thoughts when they locked with mine. Because while his eyes were dark brown—a completely normal color for eyes— there was something in them that instantly drew me in. There was almost a dangerous quality to them.

Something that made me think he had secrets.

But that was a strange thought to have about a complete stranger, wasn't it? To assume someone had secrets from one look in their hypnotizing eyes.

*Stop staring at him, Elyse,* I told myself.

I pressed my eyes closed for a moment. Forcing my brain to remember that it knew how to say words, I said, "S-sorry if it looked like I was spying on you. I wasn't. I just heard the music and I had to see who was playing..." I shrugged. "You're really good."

"Oh, that?" He glanced behind him at the music room, and then back at me. "I was just playing around."

"That was 'playing around?'"

If that was the case, what did it sound like when he was being serious?

"Yeah." He narrowed his eyes like he was uncomfortable. "Just testing out the Hastings' piano while I wait for dinner. Is there something wrong with that?"

"N-no. I'm sure it's fine," I hurried to say, even though I really didn't know if the Hastings had rules on who could and couldn't touch their piano. "I-I'm Elyse, by the way."

I held my hand out for him to shake, but he just stared at it like he was confused about what to do with it. He lifted his gaze to meet my eyes, and with a frown on his perfectly shaped lips, he said, "I thought you said your name was Ava. Now you're Elyse?"

Ohhhh. Okay. So that was why he looked confused. He thought I was my twin.

Ava had come over early to hang out with her boyfriend Carter, while my mom and I had opted for a slower morning in my mom's hotel suite. This guy must have met Ava already. And since we looked identical—even our own mother sometimes got confused about who was who when we dressed and did our hair alike—I could see how it could be confusing.

Especially if he didn't know Ava had a twin.

"Ava is my sister. I'm her twin, Elyse Cohen."

"Oh." The guy whose name I still didn't know nodded his head slowly. "That makes sense, I guess. I thought it was weird that you changed outfits." His gaze slowly ran up and down my body, taking in my clothes.

And not for the first time, I wished that I'd taken more after my fashion-savvy mother. Instead of wearing an amazing dress like Ava had worn when she'd left with Carter this morning, I'd gone for the comfortable route with a simple sage-green T-shirt and plain jeans.

But I couldn't magically snap my fingers and have a better outfit appear, so I shrugged and said, "Nah, I like to keep things simple."

He seemed to study me for a moment, as if trying to compare me with whatever opinion he'd formed of my sister earlier. Then he said, "So, if you're not the girl I met earlier, I'm guessing this means Carter and Nash didn't send you to spy on me and report back." He arched a dark eyebrow.

"No?" I frowned, remembering his initial greeting when he'd assumed I was spying on the enemy. "W-why would you think that?"

He rolled his broad shoulders back and sighed. "Ah, it's nothing."

But it didn't seem like nothing.

Who was this guy, and why did he think Carter and Nash would have it out for him when he was at their house for Thanksgiving?

Didn't people usually spend the holidays with people they liked?

But then again, he was downstairs all by himself while the rest of the people our age were upstairs.

"Are you related to the Hastings?" I asked. "Is that why you're visiting today?"

"Naw, we're not related," he said. "My brother is buddies with Ian and got me an invite."

"Your brother is Mr. Park?" I asked, knowing my AP Chemistry teacher was close friends with the oldest Hastings' sibling after seeing them hang out on a few occasions.

"Yeah, I'm Asher." He nodded. "Asher Park."

And even though I'd never met him in person and hadn't known what he looked like before this afternoon, this was not the first time I'd heard his name.

I swallowed. The short conversation I'd had with Nash after the cast list had been posted came to mind. Nash told me that the guy our drama instructor had cast as Raoul was someone I should be careful around. Someone who didn't have a reputation for being a *good* guy.

Asher's eyes tightened when he saw my reaction to hearing his name. With a slow nod, he said, "So, you have heard of me then."

"Y-yes," I said. And when his expression fell further, I hurried to add, "Not much though. Just, um, well, Miss Crawley said you're coming back to the school and playing Raoul."

Which was true. She had said that.

In fact, she'd given such a glowing review of Asher, saying that he was a talented genius when it came to acting, that her description of him had basically been the opposite of the few things Nash had mentioned.

"Miss Crawley was talking to you about me?" Asher's dark eyebrows knitted together. "Why?"

"Because I saw your name on the cast list she posted and asked who you were."

"You're in the musical, too?"

"Yes." I nodded, my cheeks warming. "I-I'll be playing Christine."

Something seemed to flicker in his eyes at my mention of playing the female lead who also happened to be Raoul's love interest. I didn't have a chance to decide whether it was a disappointed look or not, because in the next moment, Nash came around the corner. And when Nash's blue eyes caught on Asher and me standing together, a scowl instantly formed on his face.

Okay, so maybe they really were enemies.

Instead of acknowledging Asher like I expected, Nash just looked at me and said, "I was wondering when you'd show up. How long have you been here?"

"Just a few minutes," I said. Then, to acknowledge the elephant in the room, I glanced back at the boy behind me and said, "I, um, ran into Asher and we were just getting to know each other."

Only then did Nash's gaze go to Asher. When their gazes locked, Asher folded his arms across his chest and stood to his full height, which had to be somewhere in the neighborhood of six-foot-two—an inch or two taller than Nash.

And from that one move, I knew that Nash was not the only one of these two guys who didn't like the other.

Which was so strange. Nash was like the sweetest, friendliest guy, and everyone at school liked him as far as I could tell. But it looked like these two had some serious beef with each other.

I really didn't want to get caught in the middle of their rivalry, so I turned to Nash and asked, "You said everyone was upstairs?"

He turned his bright blue eyes back to me. "Yes. We were just starting a new round of Secret Hitler and hoping you were here to join us."

"I love that game," I said with a smile. Secret Hitler was a board game where each player had a hidden identity, and the goal was to figure out who the good and bad guys were—kind of like Mafia. As someone who usually abided by the rules and always tried to make good choices, it was fun to pretend to be the bad guy and trick everyone for once. The actress in me thrived on these types of games because then I could let my walls come down.

"That's why I came to find you," Nash said with his signature charming smile—the smile that had been making my heart do somersaults in my chest more often than not lately.

I was about to follow Nash down the hall to join everyone upstairs when I noticed a slight slump in Asher's shoulders. "Do you want to play Secret Hitler with us?" I offered. Even though it wasn't my house or my game, it seemed like the appropriate thing to do.

"I don't think that's such a good idea." His gaze went to Nash who had already turned and started toward the staircase. "I was just going to see where my brother and Ian were anyway."

I was pretty sure this had more to do with whatever issues he and Nash had, but I decided to let it drop—I was new to Eden Falls and I really had no idea what was going on between these two guys.

So I gave Asher a half-smile and said, "I guess I'll see you later then."

He nodded, his brown eyes seeming to take me in for a moment before he said, "It was nice to meet you, *Elyse*." He emphasized my name in a way that told me he was making a note to remember that I was a twin and different from my sister whom he'd mistaken me for earlier.

"It was nice to meet you too, Asher."

"Glad to hear I made a good first impression," he said. He paused, as if he wasn't sure he wanted to say his next words, pressing his lips together. Then he added, "We'll see whether you think it was nice to meet me or not after your friends fill you in."

"O-okay." I frowned as I studied him once more, wondering what this guy's story must be.

But since it was weird to keep standing there staring at this guy who didn't seem interested in expounding on his cryptic comments, I turned and followed in the direction Nash had gone. As I walked up the marble staircase to the second story, I couldn't help but wonder who this Asher Park guy was and why he expected me to automatically dislike him.

## 2

## ELYSE

"DO you know the story behind Nash and Asher?" I asked Nash's sister, Cambrielle Hastings, as we put the game pieces for Secret Hitler back in the box. We'd played two rounds, and it had been loud and fun and everything I loved about the game. But Mrs. Hastings had just announced through the intercom system that dinner was ready, so we decided to clean up before heading down.

"Did they have another run-in before you came up?" she asked, glancing down the hall to where Carter, Nash, Ava, and Mack were already on their way to join our parents downstairs in the formal dining room.

"Not a run-in, per se," I said. "I was just introducing myself to Asher when Nash came downstairs to get me, and they acted really weird around each other."

Cambrielle put the last stack of cards in the box. "That doesn't surprise me." She pursed her lips, as if considering telling me her thoughts on the dark-haired boy who played the piano.

"Is there something wrong with Asher then?" I handed her the lid to the box.

Cambrielle was Nash's younger sister—a year younger than the rest of us in our friend group—and aside from Ava, she was probably my best friend. And though her brother obviously wasn't a fan of Asher, I figured Cambrielle would give me neutral feedback on the boy I'd met downstairs. Cambrielle was level-headed and stayed out of the drama her more dramatic brother often found himself caught up in.

Aside from the passive-aggressive interaction between Asher and Nash, and the cryptic comment from Asher at the end, our interaction had gone okay.

At least I thought it had. Though, I did have a history of seeing interactions with really cute guys through rose-colored glasses sometimes.

"It's kind of hard to say." Cambrielle placed the orange lid over the game. "Like, I always thought he was cool—smart and mysterious with a bit of that bad-boy vibe us nice girls tend to fall for." She winked, telling me she remembered our conversation from a few weeks ago about how I'd had a weakness for bad boys at my old school. "He was pretty well liked by most people." A half-smile slipped on her lips. "Most people aside from Nash anyway, since they've been rivals for years. But then there was the whole thing with Bailee last spring..." She drifted off, as if not sure she should say her next words.

"A thing with Bailee?" I asked, having no idea who she was talking about.

Was Bailee a girl that Nash and Asher had both liked? Someone they'd fought over?

"Well..." Cambrielle chewed on her lip, her blue eyes wary. "I don't want to spread rumors, since I know everyone deserves a second chance and nothing was ever proven..."

*Nothing was ever proven?*

"What happened?" I asked, a foreboding feeling welling up in my chest as I realized whatever happened was probably more serious than fighting over a girl.

Cambrielle looked toward the hallway again, checking to make sure no one was coming back to overhear our conversation. She turned back to me and said in a hushed tone, "Asher's girlfriend disappeared last April, and the police thought for a while that he was responsible for it."

"What?" My heart started pounding so hard it thundered in my ears. "The police thought he did something to his girlfriend? Something *bad*?" I whispered the last word.

"Yeah." She looked at me carefully, in a way that told me she was uncomfortable with the subject. "I guess someone said they saw Asher and Bailee arguing at The Italian Amigos the night she disappeared, and the rumor was that he did something to her."

"Do they think he killed her?" I whispered, my eyes going wide with shock.

She swallowed. Then she picked up the game box to put it in a closet nearby. "That's what the police were looking into. But they never found her body or really any other evidence to say what happened to Bailee that night, so they had to drop the charges."

"That's crazy." I thought back to my interaction with Asher earlier and how I never would have guessed I could have been talking to a possible murderer.

*He wasn't charged with murder,* I told myself before I could get too creeped out.

You can't have a murder case without a body.

*But just because they didn't find the body doesn't mean she's still alive,* the devil on my shoulder reminded me.

And I had to do a play with him? How could Miss Crawley do this to me?

"Do you think he did it?" I asked Cambrielle before my imagination could run too far off.

"I don't know." She put the game on a shelf and shut the closet door. She walked back toward me. "I've been trying to give him the benefit of the doubt, since I don't want to think that he could do that. But you never really know."

"Is that why he didn't come back to school earlier this year?" I asked. Miss Crawley had said that Asher had decided to go online after some stuff happened last spring—the stuff that I now knew was a possible murder investigation.

*Yikes!*

"I'm sure it was. The rumors were crazy. Reporters were coming to the school grounds. It was all over the local news. He had to stay in town at first since he was a person of interest and leaving right then would have made him look even more suspicious," Cambrielle said. "But after things died down, I think he went to live with his aunt and uncle somewhere in New York."

"Was he from Eden Falls originally?" I asked.

Most of the kids at Eden Falls Academy who boarded like Ava and me came from all over the U.S.—some from other countries. But maybe he was just a day student back then and had to leave home because the gossip around town was too much for his family to deal with.

Cambrielle nodded. "He grew up here, but his dad died a few years ago and then some stuff went down with his mom, so the older brother got custody of Asher."

I'd heard that one of the science teachers at our school— Mr. Park—was Asher's brother. But he seemed too young to be a teenager's legal guardian. He was like twenty-three—just barely out of college and in his first year of teaching from what he'd told our class.

I wanted to ask what happened to Asher's mom, but Mrs.

Hastings' voice sounded over the intercom system, "*Cambrielle. Elyse. Are you coming?*"

"We better head down before they send someone up," Cambrielle said. "My dad doesn't like waiting for his turkey."

"But do you think Asher did something to his girlfriend?" I asked, unable to ignore the tightness in my chest. I really didn't want to think that the guy I'd be playing opposite in the play could be a killer.

"I don't know. He and Bailee were always so good together. I mean, they were the ultimate couple goals. Prom King and Queen right before she disappeared. And from my point of view, he always seemed so in love with her."

"But you said someone saw them arguing right before she disappeared?" I asked, trying to piece together the details.

"Yeah, so maybe he did do it." She shrugged.

Why had I brought this up?

I looked down the hall, wondering what I was supposed to do with this information. Like, should I be afraid of Asher?

Should I be scared that I was supposed to play Christine and he was Raoul?

If he was actually dangerous, did that mean I needed to drop out of the play and keep my distance in order to stay safe?

To stay alive?

But the headmistress wouldn't have allowed him to come back, and Miss Crawley wouldn't have cast him if he was actually a bad guy.

They wouldn't put the rest of us in danger, would they?

Cambrielle must have sensed my anxiety because she touched my arm, bringing me back to the present. "I don't think he did it. I don't know what happened to Bailee that night. But I don't think Asher would have hurt her. He loved her too much."

*He loved her too much.* The words echoed in my head.

Joe had loved Beck in *You*—the Netflix show I was watching—and look what happened to her.

I shook the images that came with those thoughts away.

I was just jumping to the worst-case scenario. Asher wasn't a serial killer like Joe. He wouldn't have come back if he were. He was just a teenage guy who had been at the wrong place at the wrong time and had been a victim of his circumstances. He'd lost someone he apparently loved.

"You shouldn't worry about Asher," Cambrielle said, her blue eyes sincere when she met my anxious gaze. "Nash may not like him very much, but that rivalry was there long before Bailee disappeared. I really don't think you have anything to worry about."

"You sure?" I asked. "Because I'll be spending a lot of time with him over the next two months."

"I'm sure." She looped her arm through mine. "Now let's get downstairs and eat some food."

———

I FOLLOWED Cambrielle downstairs and into her family's formal dining room. The room was gorgeous—like what you'd find on the cover of an interior design magazine. Tall windows lined the far wall, the luxurious curtains opened to reveal the back terrace. The large table that everyone was seated at had been decorated to perfection for the holiday. Orange, yellow, and red leafy garlands ran down the center and antique candelabras added to the elegant ambiance.

Cambrielle slid into the chair next to Mack whom she'd recently started dating. The seat on the other side of her was full, and there were none available beside Ava and my mom.

I bit my lip as I glanced around the table full of people, wondering where I was supposed to sit.

*Please don't let the only open seat be next to Asher.*

My heart pounded as I looked at everywhere but the new boy I was now afraid of. I was about to force my gaze toward Asher, figuring I wasn't seeing the empty seat because I was avoiding looking his way, when a movement in my periphery brought my attention to Nash. He was across from Asher, and when I looked more closely, I was surprised to see that there was an empty high-backed chair to his left that I'd somehow missed.

"You're right here, Elyse," Nash called when our gazes met. And when he patted the padded chair, a whoosh of relief flooded me.

I smiled and took my seat, thankful that I didn't have to sit next to Asher.

"Thank you all for joining us," Mr. Hastings said from his spot at the head of the table. "It's so great to have all of you here to celebrate with us today. And if you're ready to get this meal started, I'd love to make a toast."

We all grabbed our glasses—the adults with their wine while the teens had sparkling cider.

"I know this year has been full of its challenges," Mr. Hastings started his toast. "We've been through a lot together. We've rekindled some friendships—" He glanced at my mom. "—met new friends and family—" He looked at Ava and me briefly. "—and suffered a loss that will change us forever." He nodded at Brendon and Mack who had just lost their wife and mom to a brain tumor less than two weeks ago.

He continued, "It's been a year of change and unexpected curveballs. But even though so many things look different today than they did a year ago, one thing remains: the love we have for each other. And so that's what I want to focus on today. That's what I'm the most grateful for this Thanksgiving. For all of you and the light each and every one of you brings to my life.

May we all continue to be there for each other during the good times and the bad, and remember that no matter what comes our way, as long as we have each other, we can get through anything."

He tipped his glass toward the center of the table, an indication for everyone to call out their "Cheers!" After everyone clinked glasses, we started passing the dishes around and loading our plates with the feast that had been provided for us.

"What were you and Cambrielle doing before you came down here?" Nash asked in a low voice after handing me the basket with dinner rolls. "I thought you were right behind me."

"We were just talking," I said, feeling my cheeks color because at that exact moment, Asher's gaze turned toward me from across the table.

Could he hear Nash and me? Was he listening to find out if Cambrielle had told me about him?

"Yeah?" Nash asked, seemingly oblivious to the extra ears on us. "What about?"

"Um, just stuff," I said, feeling my blush deepen because I couldn't come up with anything better.

"Just stuff, huh." Nash's eyes sparked with intrigue. "Would that have anything to do with our plans for tomorrow night?"

Our plans for tomorrow night being the date he'd asked me out on.

Yes, after weeks of beating around the bush and making me wonder if he was ever going to ask me out, Nash had finally done it.

Sure, it was a triple date. A date where my twin sister and half-brother would be joining us with their significant others... who happened to be Nash's siblings. But it was a "date" instead of a hang-out, so I was excited about it.

Though I technically hadn't been talking with Cambrielle

about the date, I decided to let Nash believe I had since it was better than having Asher know that I'd been gossiping about him.

I cleared my throat and set a roll on my plate. "I just asked Cambrielle what outfit she thought I should wear."

"You did?" Nash asked, his gaze going down to the T-shirt I currently wore. "And did you decide?"

"Not yet." I handed the basket of rolls to Brendon who sat on my other side. Then, slipping what I hoped looked like a coy smile on my lips, I whispered, "But even if I did, I wouldn't want to spoil it for you since it's a surprise."

I was simply trying to evade a conversation that would be awkward to have in front of Asher, but the way Nash's eyes lit up over the possibility of me wearing something special for our date made my stomach flutter. Because finally, after a year of liking all the wrong guys, I had a nice, good guy looking forward to spending quality time with me.

"Well, I can't wait to see this surprise outfit of yours." Nash dished some stuffing onto his plate. "Though, I'm sure you could wear a garbage bag and I'd still think you were beautiful."

I was ninety-nine percent sure he hadn't planned to say any of that based on the way his cheeks flushed an adorable shade of rosy pink right then. But I kind of loved that he had, since it told me the feelings I had for him might be mutual.

He cleared his throat. "Um, I guess I just said that out loud, didn't I?"

"Yeah," was all I could think to say before I blushed right back.

Man, weren't we quite the pair. So awkward and bashful. Did we even have a chance at acting normal on our date tomorrow?

Maybe I should be thankful we'd have two other couples

with us. If I got tongue-tied, I could just turn to Ava or Cambrielle and they could help me out.

Nash looked like he wanted to say something else, but then his mom asked him to grab the butter that they'd forgotten to bring to the table, and so he scooted away from the table.

---

I WAS JUST GRABBING my jacket from the entryway closet to ride four-wheelers with everyone after dinner when Asher walked up behind me.

Before I could decide if I needed to act like I hadn't been told anything about what happened last year with his girl-friend, or to bolt, he was grabbing his black jacket from the closet and saying, "So, I'm guessing from the way you avoided looking in my direction all throughout dinner, it means you're afraid of me now."

"What?" I startled, not expecting him to be standing so close behind me. Close enough that he could stab me in the back with a knife and no one would see.

*Okay...maybe I should hold off on the serial killer TV shows for a while.*

But since it was better to keep an eye on a threat, I took a step back and turned to face him more fully.

"You think I did it then, don't you?" he asked, his dark eyes searching my face in a way that was both vulnerable and intimi-dating at the same time.

I hadn't expected to address the subject outright. Hadn't planned to ask him for his side of the story, since it wasn't exactly the type of friendly conversation you had with a stranger.

But he was the one who brought it up, so I asked bluntly, "Well, did you?"

"Kill my girlfriend?" he asked, his tone indignant. "No. Of course I didn't kill her."

"Well, th-that's good," I said, my voice shaking slightly.

He must have sensed my fear because he narrowed his gaze again and leaned closer. Then he whispered, "But that's what all the bad guys say, don't they? Claim to be innocent before they find their next victim."

*What the heck?*

Chills raced down my spine and a sense of dread gripped me.

"Sorry, bad joke," he said with a chuckle when he saw that I was on the verge of screaming.

"Yeah..." I brushed some hair away from my face, wondering why he'd even said it in the first place.

Did he want to seem guilty?

He pulled his jacket over his shoulders. "I think I've gotten so used to everyone in Eden Falls believing I did it that I figured I might as well play into it."

"Do you think she's dead?" I asked before I could stop myself.

He went still momentarily, as if I'd shocked him with my bluntness. "Maybe." He zipped up his jacket. "Or maybe she just doesn't want to be found."

"Do you think she ran away?" I asked, not having considered that as an option from what Cambrielle had told me.

A look that I couldn't interpret crossed his face, but before he could respond, his brother stepped into the entryway, already wearing a jacket like he was on his way out.

"Ready to get back to the school?" Mr. Park asked Asher. "We have about an hour before the Dragons' game starts, and I'd like to get you settled before then."

"Sure," Asher said, lazily pulling his gaze away from me to

look at his older brother. "Might as well get settled in my new prison cell."

Mr. Park shook his head and chuckled at Asher's dramatic statement before turning to me. "Have a great rest of your day, Elyse."

"I will," I said. Now that I saw my AP Chemistry teacher next to his brother, I could definitely see the family resemblance.

"Make sure you fit in some time to study for the test on Monday," Mr. Park added. "I know you've been top of the class all year, but I think you're going to have a little more competition now that Asher is rejoining us." He shot Asher a smirk.

Asher rolled his eyes. "What my brother means is that you really have nothing to worry about, since I've never been the science nerd he is."

"Or so he says," Mr. Park said. "I think it's that he was always more interested in testing out the chemistry he had with the female population at our school instead of the actual science." He chuckled.

Did that mean Asher had been a player before he started dating Bailee?

I guess I could see it.

He certainly had the looks of someone who played the field. And though I was slightly terrified of him, I still found myself drawn to him on a level that didn't make sense given what I knew about him.

Which meant I needed to be all the more careful around Asher. Sure, he'd said he didn't know what happened to Bailee.

But that could all be a lie.

Miss Crawley said he was an amazing actor, so the less involvement I had with him, the safer I'd probably be.

3

—————

ASHER

"YOU WEREN'T able to get me a single room?" I asked Owen when we made it to my new room at the far end of the boys' dorms. Eden Falls Academy, the school I'd gotten a scholarship to since my freshman year, was a few miles outside of the city limits and looked like it could fit in right next to the Hogwarts castle in *Harry Potter*.

I'd grown up in Eden Falls and always thought it would be cool to go to school in the castle outside of town. We'd had more money back then and Owen had been accepted and had bragged about how much better it was than the local public high school. But after my dad died and all the stuff went down with my mom, I knew there was little chance of actually getting to attend such an expensive school.

We ended up not being able to afford it—spoiler alert—but Owen had heard about a scholarship opportunity from his best friend, Ian Hastings, and so I'd applied. Amazingly enough, I won the scholarship.

It ended up being just the right timing, too, since right before school was supposed to start during my freshman year, my mom got sent to prison. The only thing that kept me out of the foster care system was the fact that Owen agreed to be my guardian while still a sophomore in college, and my school scholarship covered my room and board.

"Believe it or not, all the single rooms were taken back in September." Owen patted my shoulder before setting the garment bag with all my school uniforms on top of the twin bed that would be mine for the next seven months. "You're lucky Hunter didn't mind getting a roommate almost three months into his senior year."

"I guess." I just hoped Hunter didn't snore. I was a light sleeper and staying at my Aunt Vivian's huge house the past few months had probably made me even more sensitive to sounds in the night, since I hadn't had to share a room while I was there.

"You could always stay in the Hastings' pool house with Ian and me if this is beneath you," Owen said. "The couch is pretty comfy."

Owen had moved in with his best friend Ian after they'd finished college and he'd gotten a position as the AP Biology and AP Chemistry teacher at my school. But as nice as their pool house was, I didn't feel comfortable mooching off the Hastings' generosity. I'd already secured my position on Nash's bad side after winning the part of Jean Valjean in last year's musical production of *Les Misérables*. I really didn't need him to think I was trying to take over his family's estate, too.

"Naw, I'm sure this will be fine." I set my suitcase on the floor and looked around at the various posters of NBA players Hunter had tacked on his side of the room. "Hunter's pretty chill. I'm sure it'll work out."

While we'd never been buddies and he was actually close friends with Nash, Hunter had always been nice to me. He didn't get involved in the drama that a lot of the kids at our school got into, so if I were to have a roommate, he was prob-ably the best option.

Owen helped me bring up the second load of my things. Afterwards, he gave me a hug where I probably clung onto him a little too tight—signaling that I was more anxious about being back at school than I tried to let on. Then my brother took my shoulders in his hands, looked me in the eyes, and said, "It's going to be fine, Asher." He gave me a sympathetic smile. "I know last year was bad and that we still don't have the answers we'd like about what happened to Bailee. But you didn't do anything wrong."

"I know." I sighed and let out the breath I'd probably been holding ever since Elyse asked me if I'd killed my girlfriend. "I just wish Bailee was here, you know?"

Wished that even though I knew I was innocent, I'd done things differently.

"We all wish Bailee was here." Owen sighed and ran a hand through his raven hair that was just slightly shorter than mine. "But it's been seven months. And as much as we wish she'd walk through the school doors and tell everyone where she's been, we can't just stop living because she isn't here. You have to try to move on, Asher."

"I know." I nodded, unable to meet his eyes because the thought of moving on while Bailee was who knows where just seemed wrong.

"It's a different school year," Owen said. "Just focus on school and the musical, and before you know it, you'll be off to college and all of this will be a distant memory."

He said it like it should be simple. Moving on and living a normal life when I'd just been suspected of murder a few months ago.

But what else could I do? I'd already searched for answers all summer and came up with nothing. Who knows how long it would be before the truth came out—if we ever did find out what happened that night on the twenty-fifth of April.

Owen watched me for a second, as if waiting for some sign that it was okay for him to leave and go back to his football game.

So I forced a smile on my face and said, "I'm sure once I get settled and through the first few days, I'll get back to normal."

I didn't really believe my own words. I was pretty sure the rest of my senior year would be misery, but that was my problem to worry about. Owen already had enough on his shoulders.

He was supposed to be living his best bachelor life right now. Being responsible for his seventeen-year-old brother probably wasn't how he envisioned life after college.

Not that I'd planned to be where I was right now, either. But at least I'd deliberately chosen to get involved with Bailee and all of her drama. Owen had gotten stuck with me by default for being my closest relative who wasn't currently serving time in jail.

"You sure you don't want to watch the game with us?" Owen asked on his way out.

"Naw, it's fine," I said. It was probably pathetic to hang out by myself on the night of Thanksgiving while everyone else was spending time with their families. But I had a room to put together, so I wouldn't be a burden on my brother and his friends tonight.

"Just let me know if you need anything, okay?" Owen said.

"Will do."

He left, shutting the door behind him.

Instead of unpacking, I spent the rest of the night going over the lines I needed to memorize for my part in *The Phantom of the Opera*. Getting a drama scholarship was my only ticket to a good college since my grades were sub-par. If I was going to impress the scouts Miss Crawley had set up to come watch me in the musical, I needed to put on the performance of a lifetime.

One that was better than the performance I'd been putting on since last year.

4

---

## ASHER

"TABLE SEVEN'S ORDER IS READY," Rosa, the owner of The Italian Amigos, told me after I'd come back from dropping off drinks at table six.

The Italian Amigos was a one-of-a-kind type of restaurant that served authentic Mexican and Italian cuisine. The owners, Rosa and Lucca, had opened it together, blending both of their cultures into one.

It was one of the busiest places in Eden Falls. People initially came because they were curious why a restaurant would be called The Italian Amigos when the word *amigos* was Spanish and not Italian. But they kept coming back because the food was the best and the atmosphere was something you couldn't find anywhere else.

I had a job here before I left last spring, mostly working on the weekends so I could set aside some money for college if the theatre scholarship didn't pan out. I wasn't an official employee again—not yet, anyway—because I'd be busy focusing on school and the musical for the next few months. But Rosa had heard from Owen that I was coming back to town this week, so she offered to give me a few shifts to keep me busy during the holiday weekend while her regular employees were off visiting family for Thanksgiving.

I took the plate of steaming food to table seven, checked on table five, and then headed back to the kitchen to check on the progress of table four's orders.

For being the day after Thanksgiving, it sure was a busy night. But I'd guess most people could only handle so many meals of leftover turkey before they wanted their pizza and enchilada fix.

The bell on the entry door rang, and I turned to see who was coming in. If it was a small party, they'd probably get placed in Reagan's section. But if it was a bigger party, they'd be placed in mine, since the family in the corner booth was getting ready to leave.

The statue of Michelangelo's *David* wearing a sombrero was blocking my view, but after another second, I saw that the people walking in were none other than the classmates I'd eaten Thanksgiving with the day before.

*Oh joy...*

Was it too early to take my break?

Maybe I should offer the family at the booth a dessert on my tab just to get them to stay a little longer and force the Hastings' trio and company into Reagan or Troy's section.

But when I looked back at the booth, the two dads had already grabbed their to-go boxes and were in the process of corralling their three elementary-aged children down the aisle and toward the exit.

*So much for getting out of serving their royal highnesses tonight.*

Okay, maybe I was being dramatic. For being the children of the seventh richest man in the U.S., Carter and Cambrielle actually weren't that bad. They were down-to-earth for the most part and didn't think the sun shone out their butts like a lot of the other rich kids at our school did.

But Nash...

Well, he might not act like the sun shone out of his butt, either, but he was annoying as heck. And the mere fact that he got the part of the Phantom and was probably going to rub it in my face every chance he got was enough to make me never want to be within ten feet of the guy.

Some people didn't like each other, and that was just how it was with Nash and me. It had been that way since elementary school, and I'd accepted long ago that it would be that way until we graduated.

Even though our rivalry could be petty at times, it was reliable at least. Everything else in my life could change, but I could always count on Nash to glare at me.

My schoolmates all sat down on the bench in the waiting area. Since it was pointless to put off the inevitable, I got busy cleaning up the mess the family of five had left at the booth. I pocketed my tip, wiped down the table, and then took the stack of dishes to the back so the hostess could seat the new party of six.

"Is that Carter and his new girlfriend?" Rosa asked in an excited tone as we watched the group scoot into the booth.

"Yep," I said, not feeling nearly as enthusiastic about seeing them again as she was.

"They haven't been here for a couple of weeks." She wiped her hands on her apron. "I'm going to go say hi."

Since she was probably going to chat with Carter in Spanish for a few minutes, I decided to check on another table.

As I refilled drinks for the elderly couple visiting from Australia, I found myself watching my classmates in the booth as Rosa chatted them all up. Carter sat on one end next to the twin who must be Ava, based on the fact that he had his arm draped around her shoulder. I'd guessed they were dating from the way they'd flirted endlessly at dinner yesterday. Carter had always been a bit of a grump. Not exactly the type of guy to make easy conversation with. But Ava seemed like the bubbly and fun type, which was probably perfect to balance out Carter's standoffish tendencies.

Beside them were Mack and Cambrielle. Yesterday, I'd been curious about their relationship status because Mack was a serial dater who never settled down with one girl for more than the weekend. But from the way he was looking at Cambrielle tonight, I was pretty sure they were a thing, too. I'd heard Mack's mom had passed recently, so it was probably good for him to have stability and someone to lean on right now, and Cambrielle was a sweetheart.

Next to them on the other end of the booth were Elyse and Nash. They'd blushed and seemed somewhat awkward all through Thanksgiving dinner, so I would guess that them being out together like this was a pretty recent development. I'd always been good at reading people, so I could tell that they were both into each other and it wasn't another one-sided thing like Nash's infatuation with Bailee last winter. But from the way they still sat with a few more inches of space between them compared to the other couples, I would bet tonight was more of a first-date type of situation for them both.

Which would make tonight something like a triple date.

AKA: a safe first date.

If they ran out of things to say to each other, they had the other couples to bounce off of and ease the awkwardness.

It was exactly the kind of date I hated. I'd always been a more private person—a *loner*, as the kids at school had labeled me before I'd started dating Bailee. But if I were going to ask someone on a date, I would want to get to know them without all the distractions.

Rosa left their table just as I was delivering the drink refills to the Australian couple. After giving them a few extra napkins, I headed to the corner booth with my notepad and pen to get this over with.

"Hello," I said. Deciding it would be weird to introduce myself to people I'd known since kindergarten, I just jumped in by asking them what drinks they'd like to order.

"Dr Pepper for me," Ava said.

"Me too," Cambrielle added.

Carter and Mack both asked for water—probably trying to be at their health peak since it was basketball season.

Nash glanced at the drink menu for a second before saying, "I'll take a horchata with no ice."

I looked at Elyse, waiting for her drink order. I didn't know what to expect after our short interaction yesterday, but I really must have scared her because you'd think I was the boogie man from how obviously she was trying not to make eye contact.

"Do you know what you'd like to drink, Elyse?" I asked when she still didn't say anything.

Did she think I was going to poison her food and drink or something and figured it was safer not to order anything? I guess that joke I'd made yesterday about claiming to be innocent before I found my next victim had gone a little too far.

I tended to make light of situations to ease the tension sometimes, but I supposed joking about being guilty of murdering your missing ex-girlfriend wasn't exactly the best thing to break the ice with.

After looking the menu over again, she finally said, "I'll just have water."

"You sure you don't want anything else?" Nash asked, like he thought she might have ordered water because it was a date and he was paying.

But she said, "I don't like carbonation, so I really just want water."

She didn't like carbonation?

Interesting.

Bailee had basically lived off diet coke.

I pushed the thought away. I really didn't need to be thinking about Bailee right now. Just because this restaurant was the last place I'd been with her, didn't mean I needed to think about her or any of the time from when we'd dated.

I wrote Elyse's order down and was about to leave to get their drinks when Carter cleared his throat and said, "Actually, I think we're ready to order, too."

*Fine by me. The fewer times I needed to come back here, the better.*

Instead of saying any of that aloud, I just pasted a smile on my lips and said, "Great. What can I get for you?"

I went around the table, jotting down the orders. Most everyone had been here enough times that they knew what they wanted without looking at the menu—something that happens when you're from a small town with very few dining-out options.

Cambrielle ordered fajitas, and so I moved on to Elyse who was actually looking at the menu.

"Sorry, I'm not quite ready," she said, her cheeks flushing slightly under the pressure of the moment. "Can you come back to me?"

"Of course." I turned to Nash who was at the end of the booth.

"I'll take the grilled chicken enchiladas," Nash said.

"Would you like sour cream with that?" I asked.

"Sure." He handed me his menu in a manner that was very civil.

In fact, our whole exchange so far tonight had been quite civil. Mature.

Maybe we were finally growing up.

But then I noticed the slight clench in Nash's jaw, and I knew he was simply just on his best behavior for his date. Which made me tempted to sabotage his night somehow. Perhaps I should slip some hot sauce in his horchata as a 'Did you miss me?' gesture.

"Chicken enchiladas actually sound really good," Elyse said, breaking into my thoughts of payback for Nash. "Can I get that as well?"

"With sour cream?" I asked, even though I was pretty sure a girl like her would turn it down. Bailee always had.

Hold the butter. Hold the cheese. Hold the tortilla strips on her sweet pork salad.

I was so sure Elyse would turn down the sour cream that I actually slipped my pen back into my apron, but then she said, "Is it possible to get two sides of sour cream?"

"Um," I said, slightly shocked by the request. "Sure. We can do that."

So maybe this new girl was nothing like Bailee.

Which, even though I couldn't tell anyone, was a refreshing thought.

I told them I'd be back with their complimentary chips and salsa then headed to the computer in the back corner to put in their orders.

As I filled their drinks, I found myself watching my classmates again. The Cohen twins had piqued my curiosity, and though ordering sour cream was a small surprise, I was intrigued by Elyse.

When I'd first met her in the hall before dinner yesterday, she'd seemed friendly—possibly a little shy, like she took time to warm up to people. But then, she also had no problem asking me outright if I'd killed my girlfriend, which told me she could be upfront as well.

She was an identical twin, which was interesting. I didn't have experience being a twin myself, but after living with my cousins Jace and Logan, who were identical twins, for the past several months, I had noticed that while they enjoyed the ability to confuse their parents and friends about who was who from time to time, they always seemed to secretly hope that they couldn't pull off the switcheroo—that the people who loved them most would always know them well enough that they couldn't be tricked.

Which was why I'd made a point to make sure Elyse knew I was separating her from her sister when I'd found out she was a twin yesterday.

Physically, I couldn't tell Elyse apart from Ava yet, since I'd only met them a day ago. I had only guessed who they were based on who they were sitting by tonight. So I was curious how everyone else was keeping them straight at school. With their long, nut-brown hair down and curled in the same way, they really did look identical—the only noticeable difference was that Ava wore a pink off-the-shoulder sweater with jeans while Elyse had a floral blouse on and a necklace with a tiny gold letter E.

Without the necklace, would Nash be able to tell the two apart? Did he know Elyse well enough—had he studied her enough to pick out the little details that made her unique?

Or did he just like the novelty of dating a twin? Would he have gone after Ava just as easily if she wasn't already dating his brother?

"The twins are beautiful, aren't they?" Rosa walked up beside me, nodding toward the cup that I was filling with Dr Pepper and hadn't realized it had started to overflow.

"What?" I asked, stopping the soda machine and pretending like I hadn't just been caught staring at Elyse.

Rosa handed me a wet cloth to clean up my mess. "Elyse is a nice girl."

"I-I'm sure she is," I said, wiping off the cup before setting it on the counter and rinsing off my hands.

"So you weren't just admiring her?" Rosa leaned against the open doorframe that led into the kitchen. "You were simply meditating and not at all staring at the girl sitting by Nash?"

"She's on a date. With the son of a billionaire, I might add." I dried my hands on a paper towel. "I wasn't having one of those romantic fantasies you think all guys my age have when a pretty girl walks into the restaurant."

"But you do think she's pretty, though." Rosa smirked, mischief in her brown eyes.

"Sure, she's pretty." I shrugged. Only an idiot would pretend not to find a girl who looked like she could be a doppelgänger for Nina Dobrev attractive. For all I knew, Elyse had every guy at our private school wrapped around her finger.

"I hear she's playing Christine in your school play," Rosa said, like it should mean something to me. "And you're playing Raoul."

"Yes, that's what I'm told." I started filling another glass with Dr Pepper. "Nash is in the play as well, as you've probably heard. And as you can see, *he* is the one Elyse is on a date with tonight."

"Yes, they're on a date *tonight*." Rosa lifted her shoulder in a shrug. "But just because someone is on a date doesn't mean they're *dating*. Lucca was dating someone when we met in culinary school. That didn't stop me."

"I know you love playing matchmaker." I grabbed the glass for Nash's drink and took it over to the horchata machine. "But

I'm actually not looking to date anyone right now. Especially not someone Nash is into."

I didn't need to give him another reason to hate me.

I was already on unsteady ground with the people in Eden Falls. If I started dating the first girl I met when I was supposed to be mourning my missing girlfriend, it wouldn't exactly make me look that great.

I had to be careful. Play everything just right. Because even the slightest mess-up would put me right back at the top of the police's people-of-interest list in Bailee's case.

Having a mother who was already in prison wasn't exactly making me look like the golden boy I wish they'd see me to be, either.

Nope, I needed to stick with my plan. Keep my head down. Stay out of trouble and do what I could to keep a low profile.

Then after the school year finished, I could finally escape this small town for good and put as much distance between me and my past as possible.

5

———

ELYSE

"HOW DID YOU LIKE THE MOVIE?" Nash asked me as we drove down Main Street toward the school.

We were at the end of our date, and it was getting closer to the time when I would find out if he was going to kiss me or not.

I hoped he would.

We'd been dancing around this thing growing between us for weeks now. There was only so much anticipation I could take before I made myself crazy.

He'd been giving me all the clues that he liked me, though. He'd held me close as we danced at the Halloween dance a few weeks ago. He always found an excuse to sit next to me when we were watching a movie with our friends. I often caught him looking at me across the way on the occasions when we weren't sitting by each other.

All throughout dinner and the movie tonight, I'd felt a charge of electricity buzzing between us. And when his fingers had brushed against mine when we reached for popcorn at the same time, it seemed like he'd felt something too, from the way he had looked at me.

We hadn't actually held hands yet, but it seemed like a goodnight kiss might be the logical next step. Something to finally propel our relationship into something more.

Heaven knows I was dying for him to kiss me.

It had been so long since I'd been kissed by a guy that I felt literal withdrawal symptoms—cravings and the inability to concentrate on anything else during our study sessions.

I was more cautious on the outside. Didn't ever make the first move. But in my head, Nash and I had been kissing for a long time. In my daydreams, we would sneak off to the back of the library stacks where he would trap me between himself and a bookshelf. And then he would tell me how he couldn't stop thinking about me before cupping my face in his hands and kissing me.

In my fantasies, his kisses were what brought me to life. The things I looked forward to reliving when I closed my eyes at the end of a long day of school and homework.

But so far, they were just daydreams.

I wanted it to become reality tonight.

"The movie was good," I said before I could start having one of my daydreams while he was sitting right next to me in his dimly lit BMW. "I'm used to seeing Justin Banks play in more serious roles, so it was fun watching him do a comedy."

"I know!" Nash said, glancing toward me in the dark car with a smile on his face. "He did great. That's the kind of career I want to have. One where I can play all sorts of roles and never be typecast."

"Are you hoping to do movies someday?" I asked.

We'd talked a lot about our mutual love of the theater and how we hoped to make acting into a career after graduating.

But I'd always imagined Nash on a Broadway stage more than the big screen.

Though, I supposed that with his talent and dedication, along with the connections and resources that his family had, Nash could do anything.

"I think it would be cool to have a career like Hugh Jackman." He turned on the windshield wipers as a few snowflakes hit the windshield of his BMW. "Start on Broadway, and then hope it propels me on to Hollywood. What about you?"

"I don't know," I said, watching the wipers swish back and forth. "I think I like the idea of doing movies or television and getting to film in cool places, but I'm also such a homebody that I'd probably prefer staying on the east coast and Broadway could do that." I glanced at him. "But really, just getting a part is the first goal."

"You'll get a part," Nash said. "There's no way you won't be a star with your talent."

"I hope so." My cheeks warmed at his compliment. I'd read a book over the summer about the different love languages we had as humans: physical touch, words of affirmation, acts of service, gifts, and quality time. And while I saw value in all five, I'd scored highest in the "words of affirmation" and "quality time" love languages.

I was pretty sure that one of the things that had drawn me to Nash was how well he filled my need for real and meaningful compliments when we were together.

I always felt better about myself after spending time with him.

A minute later, we made it to the wrought-iron gates with the words *Eden Falls Academy* arching over the top. Nash pressed the intercom button.

The gates swung wide. As we drove down the road and onto the cobblestone drive at the front of the school that looked like a medieval castle in the moonlight, I tried to mentally prepare myself for the doorstep scene we were about to have.

One part of the reason why Nash and I hadn't kissed yet was probably due to the fact that I could be super awkward around guys. If being smooth around guys was a talent someone could be born with, I was pretty sure Ava had received all of that ability when our egg had split. She was a natural and could basically turn any guy she wanted into her boyfriend—hence the reason why she was currently dating one of the most wanted guys at Eden Falls Academy.

But as for me, I just wasn't as good at dating because I took it too seriously. Dating was what you did to find your person— your soulmate—and so I overthought everything, which some- times would paralyze me.

Ava and I always joked that I needed a guy who would just take charge and make things happen, which was probably why I'd always had a thing for bad boys.

Bad boys took what they wanted without asking.

Okay, so that sounded bad. I didn't want a guy who was forceful or disrespectful or anything like that.

But one of the things that I really liked about my Nash daydreams was how he always took charge in them. "Fantasy Nash" always sensed when I wanted him to kiss me without having to ask or step too lightly to figure it out. "Fantasy Nash" was the ultimate Casanova who oozed confidence and expertise when it came to that kind of thing.

I did know that fantasies weren't real and I'd be setting myself up for failure if I believed a guy would just magically be able to read my mind and know what I wanted when I wanted it. So far, the only thing Nash lacked from the list of qualities my dream guy would have was impulsiveness. Real-life Nash was also cautious like me.

But I was determined to make that change tonight.

"Do you think Carter and Ava are right behind us?" I asked Nash, realizing that we might have company on the school's front steps.

"I think Carter said he and Ava were going to make another stop before he brought her here."

Which meant they were probably parked on the side of the road right now making out in his truck.

But that was good. I didn't need an audience for what I hoped would be our first kiss.

Nash pulled his car to a stop in front of the school, put it in park, and then pushed the button to turn it off. As he walked to my side of the car, I couldn't help but smile a little. Turning off his car instead of leaving it running while he walked me to the door could mean that he might be hoping for a prolonged goodbye.

Nash opened my door like the gentleman he was, and with a flourish of his arm, he gestured for me to step out. We walked side by side up the school steps, our hands swinging close by and brushing once.

We stopped under the light at the top of the stairs, and when I turned to look up at Nash, my heart hammered harder because he really was so handsome. He had these amazing, brilliant blue eyes that somehow caught me off guard every time I looked at him.

"I had a really great time tonight." Nash rubbed the back of his neck. He was just over six feet tall, so our faces were only inches apart. "Thanks for coming with me."

"Thanks for asking me out," I said, snowflakes falling onto my cheeks as I gazed up at him. "I had a good time, too."

"You did?" he asked, like he wasn't completely sure I had enjoyed myself.

"Of course." Had I done something that would make him think I hadn't had a good time?

It was definitely possible. We got our signals crossed often enough that I sometimes wondered if Nash and I spoke different languages.

We stood there for another long moment, and I was wondering what type of signal I needed to send to let him know that I wouldn't stop him if he tried to kiss me. But then his gaze fell on my lips, and he took a step closer.

*It's happening.*

Nash was going to do it.

I licked my lips as my toes and fingers tingled with anticipation.

But then, something flashed across his face, and instead of pressing his lips to mine, he asked, "Mind if I get a hug?"

*He's asking for a hug?*

"Uh, of course," I stammered. "A hug would be great."

I tried not to let my disappointment show.

He leaned close and wrapped me in his arms. While it felt nice to be close to him—and he smelled amazing—all I could wonder about was if I had a popcorn kernel stuck in my teeth that he'd decided to avoid at the last minute.

He bent his face close to my neck, his breath hot on my skin, and for a second, I wondered if he was working up the courage to go in for the kiss. That maybe he liked to warm up with a hug before moving on to the kissing...

But instead of trailing kisses along my neck and jaw like he'd done so many times in my fantasies, he pulled away and said, "Thanks again for saying yes to a date. We'll have to do this again soon."

Though I was disappointed about not getting that kiss, I smiled and said, "I'd like that."

Because I would. Even if things were taking a little longer than I wanted, I still liked him. And we had finally gone on a date, so that was progress.

I really didn't need to get caught up on a stupid kiss when the real goal was to spend more time with a guy I liked and who seemed to like me back. We were further along than we'd been yesterday. And the hug really had been nice, now that I thought about it again. He was a few inches taller than me, and while not quite as muscular as Carter and Mack, he was strong and had a great physique. Even through the jacket he was wearing right now, I could tell he'd look amazing without his shirt on.

*Get your mind back to reality, Elyse,* I chided myself before I could start imagining him climbing out of his family's swimming pool and slicking his blond hair back as water droplets drizzled across his broad shoulders and down his six-pack abs.

Okay, so maybe I was imagining that exact thing right now.

My imagination was such a traitor sometimes.

"...should be fun," Nash said, bringing me out of my daze.

*What should be fun?*

"Sorry, what did you just say?" I asked.

He gave me a half-smile, his blue eyes patient. "I was just saying that I'm excited to start our rehearsals on Monday. It'll be fun having so many scenes together."

"Oh yes, I'm excited." Nervous too, since playing Christine was slightly overwhelming.

But definitely excited as well. Cambrielle and Nash would both be there during rehearsals, so having my friends with me would make it fun.

Plus, there was that scene near the end where Christine kisses the Phantom...so if we couldn't get there on our own, we'd at least be kissing each other before too long.

In fact, maybe I should try convincing Miss Crawley to have us work on that particular scene first—suggest it as a good way to break the ice...

"Anyway." Nash took a step down the stairs, slipping a hand into his jacket. "I better head back home before this turns into a blizzard." He gestured at the snow that was falling faster around us.

I'd been so caught up in the moment that I hadn't even noticed how fast it was coming down.

"Drive safe," I said.

"I will." He shot me his dazzling smile that I loved and took another step down. "Sweet dreams, Elyse."

*Yeah, you have no idea how sweet my dreams will probably be tonight.*

6

———

ELYSE

THE COMMON ROOM was empty when I stepped inside. Most everyone was still visiting their families for Thanksgiving and there were only a handful of students who'd stayed on campus.

If my mom hadn't had to head back to make sure the Black Friday sale on her brand's website went well, we would've had an extended vacation with her. But such was the life of a newly discovered fashion designer. She had to put in the grunt work now to get the machine rolling well before she could move into a more hands-off role.

I looked at the time on the grandfather clock in the corner of the traditionally decorated room. It was close to eleven. Our curfew in the dorms was ten o'clock on weeknights, but because it was a weekend and a holiday, Ava had until midnight before she had to be back. And since she and Carter had less time to spend together these days, thanks to both of them being on the varsity basketball teams, I would bet that they planned to spend every last second together that they could tonight.

I didn't really feel like going to bed quite yet, so after

changing into the new pajamas my mom had bought me—a red set with little white stars on it—I went back downstairs to sit in front of the fire and catch up on the latest season of *You.*

Ava thought I was a weirdo for enjoying a show about a serial killer, but despite being slightly disturbing, I actually loved it. Joe was the most likable and sympathetic serial killer I knew of, and even though he found himself in some really bad situations, you couldn't help but root for him since he really was *trying* so hard to be good and not fall into his old habits.

I chuckled as I put my fuzzy gray blanket over my legs and settled into the big leather couch. Since when did I watch shows like this?

*Since I discovered what a hottie Penn Badgley was. That's when.*

If you'd asked me a couple of months ago who my celebrity crush was, I'd immediately say it was Joshua Basset or Kai from Exo. But after binging the first two seasons of *You* over the past week, I was certain that Penn Badgley, the actor who played Joe Goldberg, was my new celebrity crush.

He was a bit too old for me, sure. But there was something about his tousled curls, strong jawline, and smile with the slightest gap between his front teeth that had me hooked on watching him.

I'd even gotten so curious about him that last night, after my mom, Ava, and I had gotten back to my mom's hotel suite, I ended up watching a bunch of his old *Gossip Girl* interviews. And man, can I just say that Penn had pulled off the role of a studious prep-school boy *very* well? I was pretty sure that if we had someone like Dan Humphrey at Eden Falls Academy, I just might have someone else starring in my daydreams right alongside Nash.

I mean, wasn't it every girl's dream to have not just one but two super hot guys in private-school uniforms fighting for her heart?

I shook the thought away. I could barely get any momentum going with one guy. There was no way I'd know how to handle two.

Deciding to leave the love triangles to Joe, I hit the play arrow on my screen and got lost in the scene where Joe was pretending to browse through books at the library while he secretly spied on his latest obsession.

I was about halfway through the episode when I heard footsteps on the staircase behind me. Startled, I turned to see who was coming down from the boys' dorms and found Asher.

He'd changed out of the clothes he'd been wearing at The Italian Amigos earlier and now wore plaid pajama pants and a fitted white T-shirt that showed off his muscular physique.

And even though I had a crush on Nash, I could appreciate a guy who looked this good in his pajamas.

My gaze went to his biceps. Wow, Asher had nice arms. And they were tan and big and sculpted...

I made my eyes move away from them, though, since he didn't need to notice me checking out his biceps that peeked out from his pajama shirt sleeves.

When I first moved into the dorms last September, it had been weird seeing my classmates in their pajamas. But now it was becoming more and more normal and even made us feel somewhat like a big, diverse family.

Asher made it to the bottom of the stairs. Not wanting a suspected murderer to get any ideas from the show I was watching, I quickly locked my iPad's screen and shoved it in between the couch cushions.

"Hello," I said, my voice coming out higher pitched than normal with my nerves.

"Hi." He gave a slight wave before walking behind my

couch and heading toward the kitchenette in the corner of the room.

Should I say something else to him? Make small talk?

Or should I just go back to my show since making small talk was the worst?

Asher started opening various drawers in the kitchenette, like he was looking for something specific. After opening the third one, he bent over with one hand on the counter as if he was studying the contents of the drawer.

Was he hungry? He'd been working the dinner shift at the restaurant tonight. Had he not eaten anything while he was there?

He studied the drawer for another few seconds before turning to look at me and asking, "Do you know much about tea?"

"What?" I perked up, hoping he hadn't noticed that I'd been watching him.

He stood a little straighter and put his hands on his hips as he looked over at me. "My aunt was big into drinking tea when she had a sore throat. I think I might be coming down with something and want to see if I can stop it before it gets bad."

And he thought I would know how to help with that?

I frowned. I was super comfy on the couch and didn't want to leave my spot, but I figured that he would leave me to watch my show sooner if I helped him. So I stood and walked over to see what he was looking at.

"Cambrielle knows a lot more about tea than I do," I said when I reached him. "The only thing I really know about tea is that herbal tea doesn't have caffeine."

"Well, that's a good thing to know if I want to get some sleep tonight, huh?" His lip quirked up at the corner, and when our gazes locked, my heart flipped.

Which was stupid because since when did my heart flip over a random guy's half-smile?

It was probably because I'd been watching my new celebrity crush on my iPad a minute ago and Asher had dark, curly hair like Penn.

"So I know it's probably bad to have to ask this, after knowing who you are for all of a day," Asher said as he leafed through the various packets of tea. "But which Cohen twin are you?"

"What?" I asked, feigning offense. "You haven't figured out how to tell us apart after one day?"

"Not quite." He scrunched up his nose. "I'm basically the worst, aren't I?"

"Basically," I said. But then again, most of the people at our school still couldn't tell Ava and me apart after a few months. "I'm Elyse."

"Cool, I kind of thought so," he said. "But I didn't see any jewelry with the letter E on it, so I wasn't sure."

He'd noticed my necklace at the restaurant earlier?

I'd barely been able to make eye contact with him while he was serving us because I felt stupid for asking him just the day before if he had killed his girlfriend.

Like, of course he hadn't done it. Just because I'd watched a few too many episodes of *You* right before meeting a guy who had been a suspect in his girlfriend's disappearance, didn't mean I'd suddenly entered the fictional world I'd been immersing myself in.

"I don't usually wear my necklace to bed," I said. "But yeah, Ava and I try to make things easier on our friends and family by using jewelry or other monogrammed things."

"I bet they appreciate it," he said.

"We think so."

*At least it helps ward off my insecurity of not being seen for who I was apart from Ava.*

I looked at the tea drawer, noticing that he still seemed to be having a difficult time deciding what to choose. My eyes caught on a packet of a fizzy vitamin C drink powder. "This would probably be good for heading off a cold or sore throat." I lifted it from the drawer and offered it to him.

"Oh, yeah, of course." He took the packet of raspberry-flavored powder from my hand. "Thanks."

While he was grabbing a cup from the cupboard to make his drink, I decided I wasn't needed anymore and I went back to the couch. Hopefully, Asher would head upstairs again so I could get back to finishing my episode. It was a pretty intense part, and I wanted to know how Joe would get out of his latest pickle.

I got myself all cozy under my blanket again and was just reaching for my tablet when Asher took a seat on the chair a few feet away in front of the fire.

Was he planning to sit there for a while? Because this might get a little awkward.

Maybe I should just head to my room so I could finish my show. But then, that would probably make it look like I was trying to avoid him.

I checked the grandfather clock again. It was eleven thirty-five. Only twenty-five minutes until we had to be in our rooms. Which meant, there were like twenty-four minutes before Ava snuck through the door to beat curfew by the skin of her nose.

Should I pretend to be watching TikTok videos before sneaking away? I didn't bring my AirPods down and *You* wasn't exactly a show I wanted to watch with someone I didn't know very well.

Asher took a sip of his drink as he watched the flames from

the fire, and I couldn't help but wonder how he felt about being back in Eden Falls again.

From what Cambrielle had told me, last spring had been pretty intense and crazy for him.

Had he wanted to come back to this small town with all its gossip? Or had he been forced back here?

Cambrielle had said he went to live with his aunt and uncle in New York for a while. Had they sent him back here since his brother was his actual guardian?

I didn't get a chance to ask him any of my questions, though, because the doors opened behind us and Ava stepped into the room with a flurry of excited energy.

"I made it." Her cheeks were flushed, probably from a mixture of the cold weather and her rush to get here.

"With twenty-three minutes to spare even." I laughed at my sister's antics.

"Take that, Heather and Headmistress Sutton," Ava said with a smirk.

Ava was on shaky ground with our dorm mom and the headmistress of the school after missing curfew a few times this month. After plenty of warnings, she'd been threatened with house arrest if she was late again.

Apparently, the threat of not going to her boyfriend's house on the weekends was a good incentive to get her back here in time.

Ava glanced at Asher, as if noticing for the first time that he was in the room. "Did I just interrupt something?" Ava asked, glancing between the two of us.

"No," I said. Lifting my iPad for her to see, I added, "I was just watching my show while I waited for you to get back."

"Oh, that weird serial killer show you've been watching?" Ava asked.

Why did she have to describe it like that? It made me look sketchy.

"It's not all about him killing people," I hurried to say before Asher could think I was into weird stuff. "It's just an interesting story." I peeked sideways at Asher. "I-I don't like the actual violence."

I had always been more sensitive to gore and violence in fact, so I usually fast-forwarded or closed my eyes during those parts.

"I like the psychology of it," I added when they didn't say anything. "Joe's internal monologues are entertaining...you know, in a creepy sort of way..." I let my words drift off when I realized my rambling was not helping my case.

I probably should have told them about the parts that the hopeless romantic in me liked. The part where the underdog jumped through all sorts of hoops in order to get the girl.

You know...until the girl had to die...

*Wow. Maybe I am messed up for enjoying this show.*

Ava looked at Asher who was listening to our conversation, and with a smirk, she said, "It's always the quiet ones you need to worry about, isn't it?"

I was pretty sure she'd meant it as a joke, but from the uncomfortable expression on Asher's face, it was obvious he thought Ava was referring to him being the quiet, murdering type.

I should have told her about the conversation I'd had with Cambrielle yesterday. Then she'd know that she was talking to someone who'd been labeled the loner type whose girlfriend had suddenly disappeared after last being seen in an argument with him.

"Anyway..." I cleared my throat before Ava could say anything else that might upset Asher. "It's getting late, and we should probably get to bed."

"Yeah," Ava said. "Heather wanted me to check in when I got here."

"You better hurry up then," I said.

Ava rushed up the staircase that was on the opposite end of the room from the one Asher had used to come down earlier. The common room was a sort of middle ground between the boys' dorms and the girls' dorms, and the only way through the locked doors was with the ID badges we'd been given by the school.

The locks weren't foolproof. I'd heard of a couple of guys getting caught in their girlfriends' rooms after curfew a few times since school had started, but they did work better than I thought they would when I'd first moved in.

I picked up my blanket and iPad and was planning to follow Ava up the stairs when Asher nodded toward the screen of my tablet which showed the still frame of Joe talking to Love. "Did you decide to watch that show after learning about my police investigation?" he asked. "Trying to get inside the mind of a serial killer so you'll know what to watch for?"

"N-No," I stammered, my cheeks flushing hot.

"It's okay if you did. I know after my joke and what you heard..." He sighed and ran a hand through his wavy locks. "I guess I wouldn't blame you for being scared of me."

"I-I'm not scared of you," I said, even though I really wasn't sure whether I was afraid of him or not.

"So the reason why you weren't meeting my gaze at dinner tonight was because you were embarrassed to see someone from this rich school working for his college money?"

*He thought that's why I couldn't meet his eyes?*

"No," I said. "I-I'm not like that."

Did he think I was some entitled snob who thought everyone without a rich parent was beneath her?

When he didn't seem convinced, I added, "I grew up in a

two-bedroom home with a single mom who could barely afford to take us to the dentist more than three times before we were sixteen. My mom didn't have her 'big break,'" —I did air quotes when I said the last two words— "until last year. It was us against the world until very recently."

"So your world-renowned neurosurgeon father wasn't paying child support during that time?" Asher narrowed his eyes skeptically, like he didn't believe Brendon would do something like that.

Which, now that I knew Brendon better, I knew he wouldn't. He would have done everything he could have for Ava and me—my mom even.

He would have found a way to come to our school plays and basketball games. He would have taught me how to drive and been there to grill Logan Carmichael before he took me on my first date. He would have been there like the dad I'd always dreamed about having as a little girl...if he'd known Ava and I existed before this past October.

It still hurt to think about all we'd missed out on because of the choices my mom made based on her and Brendon's circumstances at the time.

"I don't know how much you've heard about my family situation," I said, knowing Asher hadn't been in Eden Falls when all the stuff came out about my mom and Brendon's fling at their five-year high school reunion. "But my mom raised Ava and me on her own, and we're only just now getting to know Brendon. My sister and I didn't know about him, and he also didn't know about us, until very recently."

My mom had her reasons for telling Brendon that she'd had a miscarriage. Things had been crazy back then for Brendon when Mack's mom was diagnosed with her first brain tumor. And while I still struggled to accept that my mom's lie had kept me from such a good man for all these years, I was trying to make peace with the fact that I couldn't go back in time and force her to do things differently.

"Oh." Asher blinked a few times, as if stunned. "Sorry to assume."

"It's okay." I hugged my blanket and tablet to my chest. "Most of the kids at our school have always had money, so it was the normal thing to assume. I mean, I probably would've assumed the same things about you if—"

"If I hadn't been your waiter on your date tonight," he finished for me.

"Yeah."

"What would you say if I told you I'm also the son of a billionaire, but I just like to moonlight as the scholarship kid who buys all his clothes from the clearance rack at the department store?"

"I'd probably be intrigued." I drew in a breath. "But even if you were just the regular Joe who got a scholarship to a private school, I'd probably still be intrigued."

Which was true. I was curious about Asher Park. He seemed different from everyone else that I'd met at school. And it wasn't simply because of his mysterious past. There was just something about him that drew me in. I was interested in his story.

Which was crazy, because I barely knew anything about the guy. Didn't know enough to even know what I should be curious about.

"Well." He stood from his seat and the delicious scent of his deodorant or body wash hit my nose. "I guess we'll have an interesting time getting to know each other, Elyse."

"I guess we will." I angled my face back to look at him, my heart beating fast for some reason. And even in his pajamas with his hair smashed to the side of his head like he'd been lying on a pillow before coming down here, I found something strangely fascinating about him.

"*Heather wants to lock up and go to bed,*" Ava's voice called from the top of the stairs, making me jump and drop my blanket.

"I guess you better go," Asher said, glancing up at Ava who had poked her head through the door that would lock all the boys out for the night.

"Yeah." I tucked some hair behind my ear and was just bending over to pick up my blanket when Asher grabbed it first.

"You might want this." He offered the blanket to me.

"Yes, th-thank you." When our fingers brushed gently in the exchange, a spark of electricity flashed up my arm. Our gazes locked for a second.

Clearing his throat first, Asher nodded toward the boys' dormitory. "I better get back to my room, too."

I nodded. "Good night, Asher."

"Good night, Elyse," he said, and I couldn't help but think that I liked the way he said my name.

I stood there for a second longer. And then, deciding that I probably looked stupid just standing there all glassy-eyed, I gave Asher a nod goodbye and headed up to my room.

---

"SO, how were things with Nash tonight?" Ava asked as soon as I made it into our room. We had one of the bigger rooms at the end of the girls' hall, with two twin beds, two dressers, and two desks where we could study.

Ava's was always the messier side, with various clothes strewn around the bed and floor. Mine reflected more of my minimalistic nature.

I dropped my things on my bed before turning back to my sister. "It was all right." Then I added, "It was good."

"Yeah?" Her smile was wide as she pulled her pajamas that matched mine out of a drawer. "Did he finally kiss you?" She bounced her eyebrows suggestively. "You know, that's why Carter and I waited behind. So you could have some time alone when he dropped you off."

"You weren't having a little goodnight kiss of your own in Carter's truck?" I said with a smirk, evading her question for a second.

"Maaaaybe." Her huge smile told me that was exactly what they'd done.

"I knew it." I laughed.

"Carter is addicting, what can I say?" She turned her back to me while she changed into her pajamas.

"At least one of us got to kiss a Hastings brother tonight," I said.

"What?" Ava turned around after pulling her top over her head. "Nash still didn't kiss you?"

"No." I dropped down to sit on my mattress with a sigh. "Do you think I've been reading everything wrong? Like, maybe I've just been seeing all these signs that he likes me just because I want it to be true so badly."

"You're not imagining it," Ava said. "Like, he asked you out, didn't he?"

"Well, yeah..." I said. "But I guess part of me wonders if he's just hanging out with me because I'm here and the only one of our friends who isn't paired off with anyone yet."

"Scarlett and Hunter aren't dating anyone." They were the other fourth of our group who had gone home for Thanksgiving.

"They might as well be dating each other, though," I said. "They say they're just friends, but I sometimes wonder if they're actually making out during all those extra study sessions they have together."

Scarlett had said that she and her best friend Hunter had dated for a short time last year before deciding to just be friends. And Hunter was always looking at her like he was in love with her.

"No, they're actually studying," Ava said matter-of-factly. "You know how anal Scarlett is about her grades. She's determined to beat Carter for valedictorian."

"You don't think they've ever slipped up?" I asked, unconvinced. "They're together all the time."

But Ava shook her head. "I asked Scarlett about it after practice last week, and she said that she and Hunter really aren't together." Ava picked her dirty clothes off the floor and threw them into her laundry hamper. "In fact, she just texted me tonight that her dad is trying to set her up with someone back home. Some older guy."

"Someone she likes?" I asked.

"I don't know." Ava shrugged. Then waving the subject away, she said, "But back to you and Nash, I really do think that he likes you. I was watching you two during dinner and I think he's just nervous."

"You do?" I asked, hope daring to blossom in my chest.

She nodded, her eyes meeting mine. "You're just kind of intimidating."

"Intimidating?"

"You just need to lighten up. Let loose," Ava hurried to say, her twin senses kicking in and telling her that I was taking offense to her comment. "Just try not to take everything so seriously."

I sighed. Ava had always been the fun twin. I was the serious one.

"Who knows, maybe I'm wrong." She raised her hands at her sides.

"No, I do take everything seriously."

It was a problem. Seeing my mom raise us by herself had made me cautious when it came to love.

I wanted to get it right.

I wanted to end up with the right guy—someone I could have a *happily ever after* with.

Or at least a *happy for now*. I wasn't delusional enough to think I could find my forever in high school.

But I didn't want to go on dates here and there just for the fun of it. That was exhausting to me, having to put yourself out there over and over again.

I just wanted to find the person where things clicked, and then we could cuddle up in our own little love bubble the same way Ava and Carter did when they were together.

I knew it made me sound like a middle-aged lady to have those kinds of thoughts, but that was just how I was wired. I couldn't just go out and have fun on a date without wondering how the future would be with the guy I was with.

"That Asher guy is pretty cute though, right?" Ava said, breaking me from my thoughts.

"What?"

"I saw him checking you out a few times." She wiggled her eyebrows, taunting me for a reaction.

"No, you didn't."

"I totally did," she said with a smile that lit up her golden-brown eyes. "I had a view of the back, and he was watching you while he was filling up our drinks."

"He was probably just glaring at Nash," I said. "I'm pretty sure they hate each other."

"Well, wouldn't that be exciting," Ava said. "Having two

guys who hate each other fighting over you. Especially when you're all in the play together."

"Sounds stressful." I stood and pulled my covers back on my bed. "It would be like the Phantom and Raoul fighting over Christine." I considered the interesting connection for a second as I climbed under the covers. But then, I shook the thought away. "Asher doesn't even know me well enough to like me."

"Well, Nash does," Ava said. "Maybe he just needs you to make the first move."

"Maybe he does..." I lay back on my pillow and thought about it. I'd never made the first move before.

Never even asked a guy on a date.

"The cast is supposed to have a retreat at Miss Crawley's cabin next weekend, right?" Ava asked as she climbed into her bed. "If Nash doesn't kiss you by then, you should make your move."

## 7

## ASHER

WELL, *that was a crappy first day,* I thought to myself as I walked toward the auditorium for the first play rehearsal.

My first day of classes sucked.

No one talked to me.

No one told me they were happy to see me back at school again.

In fact, people barely even made eye contact with me in the halls.

And for the few freshmen who hadn't known who I was when I first came down for breakfast in the great hall this morning, they were well informed about my history by the time I filled my tray with food and sat by myself at a table in the back.

Had I been delusional to think that I could come back here? To hope that the rumors from last year would die once the police stopped investigating me?

Apparently, I had been delusional, because everywhere I went, people stared and whispered.

And they didn't even try to disguise it. That was the weirdest thing.

Last year, they'd at least spread their gossip through a text chain. Sent me their threatening messages through blocked numbers.

But apparently, this year they wanted me to overhear all the gossip so that I'd know they remembered last spring and that they were going to be keeping an eye on me.

I didn't even try to eat lunch in the great hall with everyone. Back then, I used to sit with Bailee and all of her friends. But after what happened, since her friends thought I'd offed their queen bee, I opted to just eat with Owen in his classroom.

A huge part of me was tempted to just call Aunt Vivian right now to ask if I could finish my senior year with my cousins in Ridgewater. But here I was, walking toward the auditorium after school anyway.

*If rehearsal sucks, then I'll quit,* I told myself as I opened the door to the backstage. *I'll tell Owen that I tried but Eden Falls just wasn't for me.*

I was putting my drop-out speech together in my head, lining up all the reasons for why Miss Crawley would need to find a different guy to play Raoul, when a petite, twenty-nine-year-old woman with wavy blonde hair looked up from where she was adding chairs to a circle on the stage.

"Asher!" Miss Crawley said, a huge smile spreading across her face when she saw me.

And before I knew what was happening, she was striding across the floor in her heels.

There were probably rules against teachers hugging their students at school, but she must have forgotten the proper protocol in that moment because she wrapped her arms around me in a tight embrace. "Welcome back! I'm so happy to see you again."

I didn't know what it was about those few words, but I found myself getting choked up. Because for the first time in the four days that I'd been back in Eden Falls, someone besides Owen and Rosa was happy to see me.

I forced my emotion down my throat—I didn't need everyone in the room to know I was a wreck—and patted my drama teacher on the back. "It's good to see you, too."

She stepped away a second later, seeming to remember herself and that she could be reported to the school board for hugging a student. But when she looked up at me after clearing her throat, her green eyes were smiling.

"It looks like you've grown a couple inches taller since I saw you last spring," she said, inspecting my appearance.

"Probably an inch or two," I agreed. I'd been about six feet last year, and when my aunt's tailor had measured me and my cousins for the tuxedos we were supposed to wear to this fancy event in Manhattan over Christmas break, the tailor had said I was six-foot-two.

"Well, just don't get too much taller, okay?" she said.

"I'll try not to."

Not that I could really control it.

A few more students came backstage. Miss Crawley seemed to remember that she had things to get ready before our first rehearsal because she said, "Anyway, it's so good to have you back, Asher. Just find a seat somewhere in the circle and we'll get started soon."

She went to greet the other students. After looking around the circle of chairs, I decided the one in front of me was as good as any and sat down.

*Now we'll see if anyone dares sit less than four chairs away from me.*

A few minutes went by, and just as expected, the chairs immediately surrounding me did not get filled. One girl, who was probably a freshman or sophomore, almost sat two chairs to my left, but just as she was hovering over her seat, she seemed to recognize me and sat in another seat farther away.

The room got more and more crowded with cast members and crew. I noticed a few students hesitating at the back of the stage, glancing over at me every so often like they knew they were going to have to sit close to me but were putting it off for as long as they could.

It was one minute before Miss Crawley had said we'd be starting our first rehearsal when someone in a blue plaid skirt and white collared shirt sat down a seat away.

I lifted my gaze to see who had dared sit so close to the school pariah and was surprised to find Elyse.

My mouth hung open for a second as I watched her tuck her light-brown book bag beneath her seat. And she must have felt my stare because when she sat up straighter, she glanced my way and asked, "Sorry, um, were you saving this seat for someone?"

"N-no..." I shook my head, slightly in shock. "I, well—" I cleared my throat. "—I just assumed everyone must have gotten the message about my leprosy."

"Your leprosy?" She furrowed her brow. "What are you talking about?"

"Well..." I gestured to the empty chairs surrounding me. "So far, it seems like everyone thinks I have some sort of contagious disease."

She seemed to notice the invisible forcefield around me for the first time. Then with a shrug, she said, "Well, I guess I'm going to just take my chances."

So maybe she wasn't as scared of me as I'd thought.

Nash, who had just finished chatting up Miss Crawley, took the seat on the other side of Elyse. He leaned back in his chair, draping his arm across the back of Elyse's like it belonged there, and then his gaze flicked to me.

In the brief moment that our eyes caught, his expression tensed and the hand currently sitting behind Elyse's back flexed, as if the thought of me being here caused violent feelings to rise in him.

I just chuckled and looked away. It was kind of nice seeing that small reaction from Nash, because the opposite of love wasn't hate but apathy. It was nice to see someone having some sort of emotional response to seeing me.

Would I have preferred to have more people greet me like Miss Crawley had?

Yes.

But this rivalry with Nash might just make up for all the crap it had taken for me to get back here.

"Can you all take your seats?" Miss Crawley said, looking at the people hovering in the back. "It's time to start."

The last few stragglers sat in the three empty seats to my left. Someone came running through the back doors at the last minute. Cambrielle Hastings rushed in and sat in the seat between Elyse and me, saying, "Sorry, for some reason, I thought we were meeting in your classroom."

"It's okay." Miss Crawley gave Cambrielle an understanding expression. "You got here just in time."

Cambrielle sighed with relief. Peeking over at me, she whispered, "Hi, Asher."

"Hi," I said.

And if there was any person in the room whom I had to sit by, I was glad it was Cambrielle. Because even though her brother had always been obvious about not liking me, Cambrielle had never seemed to hop on his "*Asher is the worst*" bandwagon. She had always thought for herself and seemed to stay on neutral ground in our war.

"I know some of you are joining us for the first time," Miss Crawley said once everyone was settled in. "In this stack of papers, you'll find the list of expectations that I have for each of you, a packing list for our little retreat this weekend, along with the schedule for the next two months."

Miss Crawley handed a tall stack of papers to a girl at the opposite end of the circle and indicated for her to take one and pass it down.

"I want each of you to go through the expectations form and bring it back to tomorrow's rehearsal with your signature," Miss Crawley explained. "I'll be emailing your parents and guardians a few forms for them to sign as well." She locked her fingers together behind her waist as she paced around the circle. "The main criteria that I wanted to point out is the attendance policy. *The Phantom of the Opera* is a very complicated musical—in fact, most of my colleagues think I'm crazy for attempting this with a group of high school students. But I know how talented you are and how hard you are willing to work. And I believe that if we each put forth our best effort, we'll have an amazing production to show our family, friends, and community by the end of January."

The pile of papers had made its way to me at this point, so I took a stapled packet from the top and handed the rest to Cambrielle.

As Miss Crawley went over the rest of her expectations, I scanned over the schedule. Tomorrow was the last day of November, and with two weeks of winter break, that gave us seven weeks to put together a good show.

"We've had some very generous donors donate an unprecedented amount of resources to our set and costume budget, which we are so thankful for," Miss Crawley said, probably referencing the Hastings as one of those benevolent families. "And I know all of you are going to do your best to help us have an amazing show. Ever since I started teaching at this school, I've dreamed of having a class that I believed could pull off this particular musical, and this is the year. You're the most talented group I've ever had, and I can't wait to see the magic that we can create together."

A few cheers erupted, along with applause.

"Thank you." Miss Crawley smiled at everyone. "With that said, let's start our very first read-through."

WE OPENED our scripts to the first scene: an auction where Raoul and Madam Giry bid on The Phantom's music box years after the main story had taken place. Since I'd had a lot of time to myself over the weekend, I'd memorized my lines easily enough from the script Miss Crawley had mailed to me before auditions. If I hadn't needed to keep track of everyone else's lines, I would have been completely off book.

Raoul's part wasn't huge compared to the roles of Christine and The Phantom, but I was determined to make the most of this opportunity to impress the scouts Miss Crawley had arranged to come watch our performance.

I'd saved a little for college, but if I was going to cover the tuition to one of my top three schools, I'd need a scholarship or a miracle to do it.

I sang my little part in that first scene, accompanied by the rehearsal track Miss Crawley had, and was able to relax until the students who were playing the new opera house owners, Andre and Firmin, introduced my character le Vicomte Raoul de Changy as their new patron. Everything went smoothly for the first few scenes. I could tell that my fellow castmates were taking their roles seriously because it was apparent that I wasn't the only one who had been practicing on his own time.

We went through the scene where Christine was chosen to take Carlotta's role in that evening's performance, and then the introduction to the song "Think of Me" was playing through Miss Crawley's speaker.

Out of the corner of my eye, I noticed Elyse sit up a little straighter, and after glancing around at our peers with a nervous expression, she started to sing the first verse of the song.

I didn't know what to expect of the new girl who had so far seemed pretty timid and shy, but I had not expected such a strong soprano singing voice to come out of her. She— well...I would mock anyone for saying the phrase that was coming to my mind since it was super cheesy and exactly the kind of thing that Nash would say—but all I could think of to describe Elyse's voice was as the voice of an angel.

Yes...I hated that it was the only description that came to my mind.

But this girl had some serious pipes and was hitting all the notes just right, making it sound effortless in only the way that someone with true musical talent could.

I kind of got it now. Nash and I had always been drawn to the same girls. The ones who were a bit understated until they surprised you with something. The girls that snuck up behind you.

I could see why Nash had been looking at her all throughout their date and in the classes we'd had together today. Because even after just a few lines of music, I could tell that Elyse had been made to play this role. And while I'd initially thought Nash would be my biggest competition in wowing the scouts who came to watch us, it was obvious that Elyse was the one I'd really have to outperform.

If such a thing was possible.

I got so caught up listening to the perfect pitch of Elyse's voice that I totally missed the first few notes that Raoul was supposed to sing.

Nash snickered at my mistake, of course, but I tried to ignore his smirk and focus on singing my small part in Elyse's song. I turned in my seat to face Elyse as I sang the lyrics where Raoul talked about how he and Christine had been close many years earlier, and how even though Christine might not remember him, he remembered her.

Elyse picked up the melody from there. Acting her part perfectly, she kept eye contact with me until she got to the complicated run. There was a beat where her voice cracked and she had to pause to catch her breath, but then she was able to hit the last note. By the time she was done, everyone in the whole room sat in awe for a moment before bursting into applause.

We made it through the first hour of the script, and then Miss Crawley told us to take a ten-minute break.

"Weren't expecting that, were you?" Nash said to me once Cambrielle and Elyse had left the circle together.

"What?" I furrowed my brow at my blond-haired, blue-eyed nemesis.

"For Elyse to sound like that," he said. "I saw how you reacted to hearing her voice."

"Yeah, she's really good." I ran my hands across my knees before standing. My legs could use a good stretch after sitting for so long.

Nash stood as well, and after stepping closer, he lowered his voice and said, "I know you've been away for a while, so it makes sense that you're a little rusty, but—"

"I'm not rusty," I cut him off before he could add whatever insult or threat he had planned. "Sure, I stumbled during that first song, but at least I'm off book."

"You have way less lines than I do," he said.

"I could do your part, too," I said.

"Too bad you're just my understudy, though."

"This time." I gritted my teeth, hating that Nash had the upper hand right now. I sighed. "Miss Crawley probably knew she couldn't cast me for both Jean Valjean *and* The Phantom without people accusing her of favoritism. That's why she gifted the role to the guy whose parents were subsidizing the show."

"You think I got the part because my parents made a donation?" Nash scoffed.

"I don't know, but it would make sense, right?" I shrugged, knowing it would only rile Nash up further.

And just like I'd hoped, anger flared in his expression. Nash hated it when people assumed he got perks because his parents were the town billionaires. Hated that he was always having to prove himself and in competition with some other force—be it me, his half-brother Carter who was in the same grade, or his parents' money—to prove he was good enough on his own merit.

It was a weakness that I enjoyed exploiting whenever I could.

Nash looked around the room briefly before saying, "I got the part because I was the best person for the job."

"If you say so."

His jaw clenched. "I did."

"I'm sure you did." I patted his shoulder in a placating gesture that I knew he would hate.

Nash thrived on the approval of others, and the fact that I was making it sound like he hadn't actually *earned* this role would drive him mad.

In fact, I was pretty sure he was considering dragging me over to Miss Crawley right now so she could tell me that he'd won the role fair and square.

He didn't need to do that, of course. I would never admit it to him, but I knew he was a good actor—a good singer, too. He and I had always been neck and neck in things like this for a reason.

He was a *worthy opponent,* as some might say.

And if I hadn't also auditioned for his part, I might have even told him as much. But since he'd never let me live it down if I admitted to losing the part to him fair and square, I would keep that little bit of information to myself.

"Getting to play Raoul does have its perks, though," I said instead, unable to help myself.

"It does?"

"Yeah." I pushed my hands into the pockets of my school-issued slacks. "A very *attractive* perk, I might say."

"Elyse isn't going to fall for you, if that's what you're trying to suggest," Nash said, catching on.

"No?" I tilted my head to the side. "And why's that?"

"Because she and I are..." He sighed, like he wanted to say they were an item but couldn't.

Which answered the question I'd been wondering about the past few days about the status of their relationship.

"Is she your girlfriend?" I arched an eyebrow. "Is that why she'd never be interested in someone like me?"

He clenched his jaw. I could tell he wanted to say that she was indeed his girlfriend, but he sighed and said, "No, she's not my girlfriend." He checked the area around us as if making sure Elyse wasn't in hearing range. Then he added, "Yet."

"Not yet, you say?" I asked, unable to resist the grin sneaking up my face over the plans formulating in my head. "Then I suppose I should say, challenge accepted."

8

———

ELYSE

"TALK ABOUT STEALING the show during the first read-through," a deep voice said when I walked backstage after the five-minute break Miss Crawley had given us.

I turned to see who had said those words, not sure who was talking to me, and saw Asher leaning against the black wall.

"Are you talking to me?" I put a hand on my chest, frowning at him.

"Of course." His tall form stepped away from the wall and he sidled up beside me. "When you said you were playing Christine, I had no idea I'd be playing opposite someone so talented."

"Oh." My cheeks filled with heat. "Th-thank you."

He pushed his hands into his pockets as we walked behind the curtains backstage, toward the circle of chairs. "I know I messed up during that first song, but I promise I'll do better the rest of the day." He peeked sideways at me with a half-smile on his lips. "I definitely don't want to look like the fool singing with a professional."

"Y-you did just fine," I said, my heart fluttering a little from the way he was looking at me. "It's normal not to be perfect on the first day."

I certainly hadn't done my part perfectly, either. Those high notes at the end of the song I sang with Nash just before the break were going to be a killer. I was a soprano, so I had a higher range, but even then, I'd found myself reaching to hit those high notes.

"Well, you're just making me look bad," Asher said when we made it to the end of the maroon curtains.

"Says the guy who is already off book and sounds like he's been singing these songs for years."

I knew he was just being nice and complimenting me, but seriously, he was good. His voice was warm and smooth—having a rich quality that I hadn't expected—and if he thought I was a professional vocalist, I could say the same for him.

Asher and I were hovering by the thick curtains when I noticed Nash walking through the stage doors. And even though he smiled when our gazes met, I caught the slight scowl he got when he realized I was talking to Asher.

Why did he dislike Asher so much? Aside from having rumors spread about him, all my interactions with Asher so far had been mostly positive. Did Nash believe Asher had something to do with the disappearance of his girlfriend?

Or was theirs a rivalry that had been going on for much longer than that?

"I think we're starting now," Nash said when he reached me, briefly touching my elbow to draw my attention.

"Okay, I'll be right there," I said, my skin warming where his fingers touched.

Nash's blue eyes searched mine for a second, like he was trying to figure out what my level of interest was with Asher. Which was nothing he should be worried about, of course, since I was team Nash all the way.

As Nash continued on to where our chairs were, I turned to look at Asher again.

"I better let you get back to your boyfriend." Asher slid his gaze back to me. "He looks like he's missed you in the past five minutes."

And instead of saying, "Yes, I better go," I found myself stupidly telling him, "Oh, he's not my boyfriend."

Why had I said it like that?

"He's not?" Asher arched a dark eyebrow.

"No, um—" I briefly glanced at Nash, worried he might be listening. Then in a lower voice, I said, "We're just friends right now."

Big emphasis on the *right now* part since I hoped that status was temporary.

"So that wasn't a date on Friday night?"

"Well, it was..." I tucked some hair behind my ear, feeling my whole face flush with awkwardness. "It was a first date."

"Okay, gotcha." Asher nodded like he understood. He glanced at Nash again briefly before saying, "Though, it looks like my buddy Nash thinks you're his girlfriend from the way he's glaring at me."

"What?" My eyes widened.

Asher nodded toward the circle, and when I turned my head, I saw that Nash was indeed watching us.

Did Nash think I was into Asher? Because if he did, that would definitely not be helpful. He wouldn't kiss me if he thought I was interested in someone else.

My hands felt sweaty, and I tried to think of something to say, but then Asher said, "Looks like Nash isn't the only one of you hoping for a second date."

Was I supposed to respond to that?

Asher leaned close and whispered, "Which, in my opinion, is kind of too bad."

"Too bad?" I frowned, wondering why he'd think it was bad that Nash and I both wanted a second date with each other.

Nash was great.

The best, in fact.

Asher bent closer, and I detected the slightest hint of that body wash or deodorant wafting off him again.

Dang, he smelled good.

"I was just thinking about how hard it's going to be for him to watch *us* on stage if you two are a thing."

"What?" I asked, not sure if I'd heard him right.

"Well," he said in the kind of voice that would make any girl feel weak in the knees. "You do understand that if I'm playing Raoul and you're playing Christine, we're going to have to act like we're in love, right?"

"Yes," I said. "F-for the play."

He knew what *acting* was, right?

"Yes..." he said it slowly, like there was something I should be reading into.

I frowned.

"Nothing against Nash." Asher's brown eyes searched mine. "But he gets a bit jealous when I spend time with the girls he likes."

"And why's that?" I crossed my arms.

He leaned even closer, and with his minty breath hot on my cheek, he whispered, "Because they always pick me in the end."

*What?*

He lingered for a moment, as if expecting me to swoon right then and there, but when he did step away, all I could wonder was: *What the heck is going on?*

Did he really think all he had to do was pay me a compliment and whisper a few words in my ear and I'd fall at his feet?

He barely even knew me.

Plus, who was he to assume that he was even my type?

Sure, guys who looked like he did were *every* girl's type. But for all he knew, I could be into shy, homely-looking guys with great personalities.

I wanted to correct his cocky assumption that I'd even be interested in him, but then Miss Crawley called for everyone to come back for the second half of our read-through.

"Sounds like it's time to start." I straightened my shoulders and met his gaze. "As much as I want to stay and chat with someone as *attractive* and *charming* as you," I said, hoping he'd catch on to how unimpressed I was by his arrogance. "I better get back to my seat."

Then I walked away without giving him the chance to say anything else.

9

———

ASHER

WELL...THAT hadn't gone to plan.

It was true that I hadn't exactly had the best welcome back to Eden Falls, but I'd thought for sure that if I turned up the charm a little with Elyse, she'd just lap it up like other girls had in the past.

I mean, that's how it usually worked for me.

But something must really be off with me today because instead of looking interested, she'd only been annoyed. Even while we sang what many people would consider to be one of the most romantic duets of all time, "All I Ask of You," she was stone-faced—barely even looking my way as we sang together.

Which I guess just showed that she was either really, really interested in dating Nash in a way that she couldn't even look at another guy...or she just wasn't interested in *me*.

For my pride's sake, I hoped it was the former. I didn't know what I'd do if I couldn't rely on my looks or flirting skills anymore.

*Not that my usual charm was working so great when everyone believed that I killed my girlfriend.*

But even if Elyse only had eyes for Nash, my new plan could still work since she didn't necessarily need to be interested in me. I just needed Nash to *think* I was a threat.

And let's face it, Nash was bound to get riled up over any amount of time I spent with Elyse.

So when Miss Crawley ended our rehearsal by giving us a few more details about this weekend's retreat, I formulated version number two of *Operation Annoy the Crap Out of Nash*.

The first step of that plan would be to apologize to Elyse for acting like an egotistical jerk who thought every girl bowed down at his feet. And after I'd groveled a little, I would simply try to befriend her.

Would me being friends with Elyse drive Nash bonkers?

Yes. I was one-hundred percent certain that Nash's blood would boil if he saw Elyse and me spending any amount of time together outside of rehearsal.

But that was just a secondary perk, because it really would be nice to have at least one friend at this school.

As everyone chatted excitedly about their plans for the retreat as they walked toward the wing where the dormitories were located, I followed closely behind Elyse.

She said goodbye to Cambrielle and Nash in the school's lobby—they would be heading home for dinner with their perfect family. And just before she opened the door to the common room of our house, I said, "Hey, Elyse, can I talk to you for a second?"

She turned around, and when she saw it was me, Elyse furrowed her brow in confusion.

I looked at the painting of one of the old headmasters on the wall behind Elyse, trying to figure out exactly what I was going to say since I hadn't rehearsed this particular speech.

I cleared my throat. "Um, I just wanted to apologize for earlier. I don't know what got into me."

"Yeah, what was that about, anyway?" she asked.

"Well..." I adjusted the strap of my backpack on my shoulder. Then, deciding to just go with the truth, I said, "I guess I saw Nash watching us and I wanted to see what he'd do if he saw me flirting with you."

"So you were just messing with me to annoy Nash?" she asked, a hint of irritation in her tone.

"I think my common sense goes out the door when I'm in competition mode with Nash."

"Competition mode?"

"Yeah..." I ran my hand through my hair. "He wants something, so I go for it, too, and vice versa."

Which, now that I was explaining it out loud, sounded really stupid. Like two toddlers fighting over a toy they didn't even necessarily want.

Her eyebrows knitted together. "Am I like a pawn in a war between you two?"

"No..." I tried to deny at first, but deciding that honesty was the best policy, I switched gears and said, "Well, I guess you were for a minute. But now that I've realized how stupid that is, I'm not going to do that anymore."

"So you aren't actually interested in dating me?" she asked, more direct than I ever would have guessed she'd be.

It took me a minute to respond, but I said, "We just met a couple days ago, so...um...no, I'm not." When she looked like she wasn't sure if she should be offended, I added, "I'm not really looking to date anyone." And then, to make it even more believable, I said, "After everything that happened last year, I just don't think I'm in the place for something like that."

"Oh, of course." Her face blanched, looking like she felt bad for having just brought up painful memories for me.

Since that was what I needed everyone to believe, I said, "It's just a little soon, I think."

I needed everyone to believe I was truly heartbroken over losing Bailee so they wouldn't find out what had really gone on between us last spring. I'd slipped up a little by flirting with Elyse earlier, but hopefully, not too many people had noticed.

"Anyway." I swallowed. "I just wanted to apologize. I know we're going to be spending a lot of time together over the next couple of months—you, me, and Nash—and I don't want there to be any hard feelings or drama."

"Well, that's good." She sighed like she was relieved. "Because I don't want there to be drama, either. The play is already going to be hard enough without you two in *competition mode* as you called it."

I nodded my agreement. Miss Crawley might have been confident in the cast's abilities, but it was still going to be a lot of hard work. If I let my rivalry with Nash get too out of hand, it could ruin the whole production and I could say goodbye to any scholarship opportunities coming my way.

Elyse looked like she was ready to leave, but before I let her go, I needed to clear up one more thing.

"I know our whole conversation during the break is probably tainted now in your mind, but I did mean what I said about your talent. You really are going to make for an amazing Christine."

"Oh," she said, seemingly caught off guard in the same way she'd been when I'd complimented her earlier. "Th-thank you."

Did she really not know how good she was?

"It's the truth," I said, looking more earnestly into her amber-colored eyes. "Miss Crawley is probably thrilled that you came to our school. I don't know of anyone else who could have done that part."

Not even Bailee, who had starred in *Les Misérables* alongside me last year.

"Well, I appreciate you saying that," Elyse said. After

glancing down the hall, she added, "It's nice to know that at least that part hadn't been a lie."

"I don't usually make a habit of lying."

*Not unless lying was necessary to keep me out of jail.*

"Cool, well..." She glanced behind her at the large double doors that led to the common room. "I'm gonna put my stuff in my room so I can get dinner."

"Ah yes, I won't keep you from that."

I stepped around to open the door for her like the gentleman Bailee had trained me to be. Elyse seemed surprised that I actually knew how to do gentlemanly things.

I followed her into the common room, and as I headed up the boys' staircase, I mentally prepared myself to eat in the great hall with a bunch of classmates who were scared of me.

---

I LEFT my backpack in my room, changed out of my school uniform and into a much more comfortable T-shirt and jeans, and then went back down for dinner.

Dinners at the school were a little more relaxed than lunches. Many of the day students went home to eat with their families, the teachers were gone for the day, and only a few staff members were there to supervise us and make sure we were following the rules.

Even though there would be less students to stare at me, a huge part of me wished I could still eat my meal with Owen in his classroom. But since I was pretty sure I'd be sticking with Eden Falls Academy for the long haul, I got in the cafeteria line and resigned myself to another meal where my classmates just gawked at me.

Once everyone got used to me being back and they saw that

no other female students were suddenly disappearing, they'd eventually trust me again, right?

I filled my tray with chicken fried steak and mashed potatoes then found a table with some freshmen and asked if I could sit with them. They looked at me like I had blood dripping from my hands, but they did reluctantly scoot closer together to make room.

So I sat down to eat my meal and tried not to take too personally how quickly my tablemates started shoveling their food into their mouths.

But when I started cutting into my meat and all eyes were on my plate, as if they were watching to see how I'd handle a knife, the impulsive side of me wanted to make a big spectacle of it.

I wanted to say something about how juicy and tender the steak was before stabbing my fork into it and chewing it in a way that would be horrifying to my aunt Vivian.

But I didn't. Instead, I tried to eat in as friendly and non-threatening of a manner as I could.

Not everything in my life needed to be a big show.

As I took a bite of the creamy potatoes with country gravy, I couldn't help but think that putting on a show was exactly how this problem had started in the first place: the chance to put on the show of a lifetime.

I'd known that dating Bailee Vanderbilt would bring me a certain level of attention. I mean, how could it not with her family basically being royalty with money so old no one was really sure where it came from?

Bailee had always been the queen of this school. The rest of us her loyal subjects.

Of course everyone would think I'd done something to her. That I was somehow jealous of her for always stealing the spotlight.

They just didn't know that when it came to Bailee, I really didn't feel what they thought. I'd always seen through her act, never been a part of her fan club.

Which was why our arrangement had been so perfect. I mean, could you really have a healthy relationship if one person was always putting the other on a pedestal?

It just didn't work.

And Bailee knew it, too. Knew that no one else at school could be the boyfriend she needed. So I'd gone along with her little plan.

*The ruse*, as Bailee had called it.

I'd done everything she asked. Played my part perfectly—even got us the title of Prom King and Queen.

And then, in true Bailee fashion, she left me to pay for her sins.

I was the one being punished for the mess she'd created.

But I'd played my part well. So well that if I told the police the truth of our arrangement, they would never believe me—the truth of what happened the night she disappeared would only make me look more guilty.

So I continued to play her game even when she wasn't here. Because playing it was the only way to survive now.

And so, even though the impulsive part of me wanted to play into everyone's fears and have a little fun with them, I decided that now was probably the time to give the speech I'd been rehearsing ever since I came back to this school.

I set my utensils down and said, "Can I have everyone's attention? I have something to say." I stepped back over the bench seat so I could stand. When I saw that I had most everyone's attention, I continued, "I know there's been a lot of talk about me today. That a lot of you are worried that the school has put you all in danger by allowing a suspected killer in your midst." I paused for dramatic effect, looking around the room and seeing that I really did have all eyes on me. "And I get it. I really do." I shrugged in a helpless gesture. "It's always the boyfriend, right?"

I looked down and swallowed, knowing that this was probably my one chance to convince people that they didn't need to be afraid of me.

It was my one last chance to convince everyone that I wasn't guilty and was actually devastated by Bailee's disappearance.

I looked back up, and putting as much emotion and anguish into my voice as I could muster, I said, "But I didn't kill Bailee." I put a fist to my mouth like I was trying to hold back a wave of emotion brought on by those words. "I didn't know she was gone until everyone else did, and I've been just as confused and desperate to find out what happened to her as all of you." I sighed. Then with a shrug, I added, "I've been working with the police and spent the past seven months searching for clues for what might have happened to her that night. Where she might have run away to, or who might have wanted to hurt her. Because I loved her. I truly did love Bailee." My voice cracked and the tears pricked at my eyes right on cue. "I really thought we would have a future together. Not knowing what happened to her still keeps me up late at night." I let out a gasp, as if I was all choked up and having a hard time breathing. "Not knowing if she's alive, or somewhere being tortured by someone. It's just…" I drifted off and wiped at my eyes again. "It's just hard wondering what she might be going through right now."

I sighed heavily, and then turned my gaze back to the crowd again.

Was anyone buying this?

Had I delivered the performance I needed to get back in their good graces again?

I looked over the faces of my classmates and saw a few

compassionate expressions. Even Scarlett Caldwell, who had been on the journalism team with Bailee, had tears in her eyes. And she had never seemed like the emotional type to me.

So this was a good sign.

Their guards were coming down.

Which really, they should. Even if my tears were forced right now, everything I'd said was true...

Well, okay, so *almost* everything. I'd allowed myself one little lie since that lie was the thing I needed to sell this.

"Anyway." I cleared my throat. "I just wanted to say all of that because I don't want anyone feeling unsafe around me. Also, if anyone has any information about what might have happened to Bailee that night, if you remember seeing her with anyone suspicious, or if she might have said anything to you that seemed off, I would love to know. I know it's been seven months, but part of the reason why I came back to this school is to help the police find out what happened to Bailee. And the more people we have looking for clues, the more likely we'll find something."

Deciding that I'd made enough of a scene for the night, I sat back down and went back to my dinner.

# 10

## ELYSE

"YOU COMING to study with us in the library?" my friend Scarlett asked me as we cleaned off our trays after dinner. Scarlett was one of my best friends who boarded in the room next to Ava's and mine. With dark auburn hair, high cheekbones, and brown eyes, I'd always thought she looked like a teenage Lily Collins.

She was on the volleyball team, the basketball team, student council, wrote for the school newspaper, and was enrolled in about every honors class the school offered.

I'd thought I was a high achiever compared to students at my last school, living by my to-do list and always aiming for straight A's. But that was nothing compared to Scarlett. She was involved in *everything,* and somehow, she was also the best at everything she did. I didn't know how she pulled it off while still also having time to hang out with all of us.

Sometimes I wondered if she secretly had an identical twin, too. Because with everything she was able to do in a day and at the level she was able to do it, there just had to be a "Scarlett clone" hiding in the room next to Ava's and mine.

I set my tray on the stack of used trays beside us. "I'll just have to grab my books from my room, and I'll meet you guys there."

"Cool." She set her cleared-off tray on top of mine. "We'll just be sitting at our usual table."

We were leaving the great hall together when I noticed Asher was still sitting at his table by himself—the freshmen had skittered away a while ago. As I looked at his slumped-over shoulders, I couldn't help but think how lonely he must feel at the school.

Cambrielle had said that he and his girlfriend had been close—everyone's "couple goals," as she'd worded it. It had to be hard being back here without her and seeing all the places they'd hung out together as they'd fallen in love.

"Hey, I'm gonna talk to Asher real quick," I told Scarlett before we reached his table. "See you in a little bit."

"Okay..." Her dark eyebrows knitted together like she was curious why I'd want to stop and talk to Asher. But then she shrugged and said, "See you in the library."

After she left, I took a deep breath to calm my nerves and give me the courage to do what I planned to do.

"Hey, Asher," I said, my voice coming out a lot quieter than planned.

He turned his head back and his face registered surprise, as if he hadn't really expected anyone to come up and talk to him after his speech during dinner.

"Hi?" he said.

*Okay, just do it, Elyse. Just invite him. If he says no, it doesn't matter.*

I counted down from five in my head, and then made myself say, "Hey. So, um, Scarlett just said that she, Hunter, and Ava are planning to study in the library after dinner, and since we're in so many of the same classes, I was wondering if you'd like to join us."

He looked stunned for a second. Like he wasn't sure I realized who I was talking to. But after blinking his dark-brown eyes a few times, he said, "Uh, sure." He slipped his phone into his back pocket. "That would actually be great."

"Yeah?" An unexpected fluttering of relief filled my chest over the fact that he hadn't turned me down.

"Yeah." He scooted back on the bench and started pulling his long legs out from under the table to stand. "I kept up okay when I was doing everything online, but it would be nice to work with the smart kids."

"The smart kids?" I chuckled.

He shrugged as he picked up his tray from the table. "Well, I already know Scarlett would have a panic attack if she ever got an A minus, and she wouldn't be best friends with Hunter if he couldn't keep up with her. So I just figured if you and your sister were studying with them, then it must mean you were one of them, too."

"I would probably have a panic attack if I got an A minus, too," I admitted.

"I knew it." A half-smile lifted his lips, and it was good to see it after noticing how lonely he'd looked during dinner and hearing how heartbroken he was after losing his girlfriend.

"Just don't tell Scarlett, okay?" I said, walking with him as he started carrying his tray to the back of the room. "As far as she knows, Carter is her only real competition for valedictorian. I don't want her to know that I'm going for it, too."

"She'd probably ban you from her study sessions if she knew." Asher chuckled, and it was such a nice sound that I couldn't keep a smile from my lips.

"That's why it's a secret," I said, liking the lighthearted

conversation way more than the awkward ones we'd had earlier today.

"Well, if there's anything I'm good at, it's keeping secrets. So your secret is safe with me." He made a show of pulling an imaginary zipper across his lips, drawing my attention to them. And I couldn't help but think that he had nice lips.

With lips like those, he was probably a good kisser.

I stumbled when I realized what had just passed through my mind.

Why in the world was I thinking about how good of a kisser Asher might be?

Weird.

I recovered my step, hoping he hadn't noticed any awkward vibes coming from me. After he'd left his tray stacked with the others, I said, "Anyway, I just have to grab my books from my room, so you can either just head to the library now or we can go together."

"I left my backpack in my room, too. I'll just walk there with you, if you don't mind," he said.

---

"SO, where did you move from, anyway?" Asher asked me as we headed down the main hall that led to the dorms.

"I'm from a small town in central New York called Ridgewater," I said, glancing up at him.

"Wait..." He stopped walking for a second, surprise in his tone. "You're from Ridgewater?" he asked, like he actually recognized the name. "You're actually from Ridgewater?"

"You've heard of it?" I asked. I was surprised, too, since no one else at our school had ever heard of it before we came here.

"Heard of it?" he asked, like it was the most recognizable town in the entire world. "I just came from there."

"What?"

He nodded. "That's where my aunt and uncle live."

"Really?" I stopped for a second. "You're not just saying that?"

"I'm being serious," he said. "In fact, they have twin boys our age. Maybe you know them."

No.

This was too much of a coincidence.

He couldn't be the Carmichael twins' cousin, could he?

I was just about to ask him what his cousins' names were when he said, "Jace and Logan Carmichael are my cousins."

"Seriously?" My jaw dropped open. "You're their cousin?"

"Yeah." He started walking again so I hurried to catch up. "I know I've got the whole half-Korean look going for me, so you probably wouldn't catch the family resemblance. But our moms are sisters. I moved in with them last June."

"We were in the same town over the summer?"

Had we run into each other before? I would have remembered him, wouldn't I?

"I guess?" he said. "I mean, we went to the Hamptons for a couple of weeks, but yeah, I was in Ridgewater for most of the summer."

"How is it that I never ran into you?" I asked, still shocked at this discovery. "I mean, I haven't been close friends with Logan and Jace since freshman year. But we went to some of the same bonfires over the summer. If you were hanging out with them, I should have seen you."

"I went to a couple of them." He shrugged. "But there were so many people there that we probably missed each other."

"Probably," I said.

I would have remembered if we'd met before. Asher didn't have one of those forgettable faces.

The first time we met, I had thought to myself that he had

the type of eyes that held secrets. And now that I knew a little more about him, I couldn't help but wonder how many secrets Asher Park was keeping.

He'd given his speech during dinner, where he pleaded for everyone to help him find the answers for his girlfriend's disappearance. But for some reason, I still felt the need to be cautious around him.

There was just something that told me he wasn't showing us all of his cards.

We walked through the gothic colonnade that attached the main part of the school to the dorms. When we made it to the common room, Asher opened one of the large, dark wooden doors for me to go through.

"Thank you," I said, grateful for the gentlemanly gesture.

The common room buzzed with the sounds of students winding down from the busy school day. There was a table in the corner where a few sophomores were playing what looked like Slapjack. A group of juniors and seniors were watching a movie on the big TV above the fireplace. And in the back corner, Megan Winters and Collin Daniels were playing tonsil hockey with each other.

"Um, I'll just grab my books from my room and meet you back here, okay?" I turned to Asher who seemed to notice Megan and Collin just then from the way his eyes went wide.

"Sounds good." He cleared his throat and looked back at me. "I'll grab my backpack, too."

I ran up the stairs and down to the very end of the girls' hall where mine and Ava's room was. I grabbed my brown leather shoulder bag from the corner where I'd stashed it earlier and caught a glimpse of myself in the mirror.

My ponytail was sagging a little, so I straightened it. I was also a little washed out, so I grabbed my blush and added a quick dash of color to my cheeks.

Much better.

I did a quick armpit sniff as well. It had been a long day and my new deodorant had yet to prove itself to last the full twenty-four hours it bragged about on the label. I still smelled okay, but I grabbed my perfume bottle anyway and sprayed a stream to twirl through.

I was about to swipe some lip gloss across my lips as well when I stopped myself.

What was I doing?

Asher was totally going to think I was primping for him.

Crap.

Earlier this afternoon, he'd totally bragged about getting all the girls Nash liked to fall for him, and here I was two hours later putting in extra effort to look better for a study session I'd invited him to.

I was an idiot.

I set the lip gloss back down on my dresser, not about to accidentally feed his ego. I considered changing out of my school uniform—because he'd probably notice the new perfume on my clothes. But I didn't want to look like I'd changed just for the study session, so I kept my freshly perfumed uniform on.

Though, I did grab my towel from its hook on the back of the door and wiped off whatever scent I could. Then I slung my bag over my shoulder and rushed back down the hall.

As expected, Asher was waiting at the bottom of the stairs in the common room.

Not looking like he'd changed a thing about his appearance in the past five minutes, since he was normal, unlike me.

"Ready?" he asked, standing up straighter.

"Yep."

He opened the door, and when I walked past him, he said, "Someone smells good."

"Oh..." I peeked up at him, willing my cheeks not to flush

from both embarrassment and pleasure over him noticing my perfume. "I, uh, it's a new one, and I just wanted to see how it smelled on this shirt."

*I wanted to see how it smelled on my shirt?* What kind of lame excuse was that?

Asher shot me a knowing smile. "Should I tell Nash he should be worried? 'Cause it kind of feels like you sprayed that perfume just for me."

"Well, I didn't." I held my chin higher. "So, that would be a lie."

He chuckled in the lighthearted way that all guys who were in love with themselves did when they thought a girl liked them. And even though he was being totally cocky, I hated that I kind of liked that he was.

Confidence had always been attractive to me.

"Well..." He followed me out the door. "Since you're testing how compatible your shirt and perfume are with each other—" He bent closer, sniffing the air around me. "—based on my scientific observations, I think they're a good match."

"Oh." I tucked some hair behind my ear, not used to having such an attractive guy stand so close to me. "That's good. I'll, um—" *Think of something, Elyse.* "I'll have to mark that down on my spreadsheet."

*Man, I was bad at this.*

"Yes, you better do that." He winked, like he knew I was totally making this whole perfume-and-blouse-testing thing up. "What's the name of this new perfume, anyway? You know, in case I want to get a bottle of my own to test on all my different shirts."

Ugh, why did I like that he was teasing me?

I was a feminist.

I wasn't supposed to like it when a guy teased me.

But then, I also had a huge weakness for bad boys, and so the teasing banter was kind of my kryptonite.

"I think it's called, Sweet Nothings," I said, ignoring my conflicting thoughts. "It's a new one. My mom just designed some flower girl dresses for Emma and Arie Blackwell's daughters, and they gave her a few samples from the new perfume line they're coming out with."

"Well, I have a feeling that the Blackwells are about to get even richer than they already are." Asher chuckled. "Especially if we get everyone to start doing experiments with it. Owen is always looking for new ways to keep his students interested in science. Maybe we should tell him about this experiment of yours."

"Okay, now you're just making fun of me," I said.

"I'm just seeing how far you're going to go in order to hide the fact that you wanted to smell nice for our study session."

"I didn't do it for you," I said.

"Is it for Hunter then?" he asked. "Because I know he and Scarlett say they're just friends, but I have a feeling that Scarlett would bring out the claws if anyone tried to steal him."

"Can't a girl just want to smell good for herself?" I asked.

"Sure..." He lifted a broad shoulder. "But I just prefer to think the world revolves around me."

We made it to the main part of the school, and I tried to change the subject to something that would make me blush less.

"You said you went to live with the Carmichaels in Ridgewater last summer, right?" I asked. "Where are you from originally?" He'd said he was half-Korean. Had he lived there before coming to school here? We did have quite a few international students.

"I'm from Eden Falls."

"Oh, that's right," I said, my memory triggered. "I think

Cambrielle mentioned something about that when I asked her about you."

"Ah yes, that was the conversation that made you assume I must be a serial killer since it went along with that show you were watching." He winked.

"Yeah..." I said, feeling my neck grow hot. "That was just a coincidence."

"So, do you still think I'm a serial killer?" he asked.

"No," I hurried to say. "I never thought that. I just, um..." I was feeling more flustered the more I tried to piece together a coherent sentence.

"It's fine, Elyse," he said. "I'm just being a butt. If you haven't noticed yet, I like to make other people feel uncomfortable so I don't have to be."

"Well, it's working," I said. "I don't think I've felt relaxed around you yet."

We were quiet as we walked past a few classrooms, and I worried that I might have said the wrong thing. But since it was true that I'd been on edge ever since meeting Asher, I couldn't exactly take it back and have it sound believable.

We walked past the glass displays outside of the auditorium where there were various trophies and photos from the academy's past, and I tried to think of something else to say. There was a framed newspaper clipping of my dad at age eighteen holding a state basketball trophy, and he was standing between Mr. Hastings and another guy. I had to do a double take, because the guy with slicked black hair looked surprisingly similar to Asher.

Asher said, "You can see where I got all my good looks from, can't you?"

"What?" I stumbled.

He nodded toward the photo I'd been looking at. "That's my dad."

"Your dad went to school with my dad and Mr. Hastings?" My mom, too, since she was in their graduating class as well.

"Yep. They were all friends when I was younger. My dad even worked for Mr. Hastings' company."

"Really?" I asked, surprised by this new information.

"Yeah, our families go way back." He glanced sideways at me. "Nash and I were actually best friends back in the day."

"What?" I asked, my jaw dropping.

"Surprising after what you've seen from us, huh?"

"You might say that..."

"I can't believe Cambrielle left out those details when she was filling you in." He chuckled, and we started walking toward the library again. He adjusted his backpack strap on his shoulder. "I actually grew up just down the street from their family. And before Mack's family built their house next door, and before the Hastings found Carter in Guatemala, it was just Nash and me terrorizing the neighborhood with our water guns all summer long."

"Really?" I asked, trying to imagine an elementary-aged Asher running around the Hastings' backyard with a cute, sun-bleached and blond-haired Nash as they soaked a younger Cambrielle and her friends with oversized water guns in the way little boys always did.

"Yeah." He ran a hand through his curly locks. "We called ourselves the water bandits. Cambrielle and Callie hated us back then."

"I bet they did."

I didn't know who Callie was, but I assumed she must have been one of Cambrielle's childhood friends.

The library came into view, and I found myself wishing it was farther away because I wanted to hear more about this past that I had no idea existed between the two guys. I'd assumed they'd always been enemies.

"So, what happened with you and Nash?" I asked before I lost the chance. "Why do you guys seem to hate each other so much?"

"Well, the first thing that divided us was when the girl we both liked asked me to be her valentine in second grade. Nash couldn't take the rejection."

"This rivalry is all because of a girl in second grade?" I didn't even try to hide the skepticism in my voice.

"She gave me a *really* good gift," Asher said, a wry smile on his lips. "I mean, you won't believe how many wars have been started over a box of chocolates."

"Okay, you have to be joking."

"So maybe that was only part of it." He sighed and ran a hand through his hair again, the sleeve of his T-shirt rising with the movement and showing off his muscular bicep.

*Daaang. That is a* very *nice-looking arm.*

He must have noticed me checking out his bicep, because he gave me a slightly cocky grin before he dropped his arm back down to his side.

"So, besides having an eight-year-old girl pick you over Nash, what else turned you against each other?"

"It wasn't just one thing," he said, a faraway look coming into his eyes. "But I think the first real issues started when Mack moved into the neighborhood, and I kind of ditched Nash for a while to be friends with him."

"Why'd you do that?"

"Because I was eight and dumb." He shrugged. "I wasn't exactly as cool as I am now, and so I wanted to be friends with the cool new kid." He said it lightly, but I caught a hint of regret in his voice.

"You couldn't *all* be friends?" I asked.

"Three's a crowd."

Which I guess was true. Growing up, I certainly had

enough experience of being the third wheel whenever Ava had a friend come over.

Asher continued, "Then I said something stupid when they found Carter and he moved into their mansion with them."

"What did you say?"

We had made it to the library by this point, but instead of going in to find my friends, Asher stopped just outside the door. He chewed on his lip for a second before saying, "I don't remember exactly, but I'm pretty sure I said something about how Carter was going to be his dad's new favorite kid and that everyone at school was going to want to be friends with the upgraded version of Nash."

I took a step back, somewhat shocked by his words. "You said that?"

"Something like that, anyway." And he had the decency to look like he felt bad about what the younger version of him had said to his one-time best friend.

"I can see why Nash resented you," I said. "He and Carter are in the same grade. They were already going to be competing in everything. Competition for the best grades, to be the best in sports, the best at making friends, the best at getting dates. Nash didn't need to think he'd be competing for his dad's love, too."

I suddenly felt a kinship I hadn't felt before with Nash. Because he and I were so similar, since I had always been compared to Ava.

She was the fun twin.

I was the serious twin.

She was good at sports.

I was the straight-A student.

She was the twin people called when they wanted to hang out.

I was the twin you wanted to do a group project with because I usually did all the work.

"It was a really stupid thing for me to say at the time," Asher interrupted my thoughts, probably picking up on my sudden agitation at the memories flitting through my mind. "Eight-year-old me was an idiot."

"Did you ever apologize?" I asked.

He scratched the back of his neck. "Probably not."

"So you've been at war ever since?"

"Basically."

"That's kind of sad."

"That's what my brother Owen tells me." He pushed away from the wall, and we walked through the library doors. "It's had one good side effect, though."

"And what's that?" I asked, curious how he could think a rivalry like theirs could have a good side.

"It's helped push us to be the best at our craft," he said. We walked past the checkout counter where the librarian looked up from her book to smile at us. "Miss Crawley probably wouldn't have done *The Phantom of the Opera* if Nash and I hadn't pushed each other so hard to be the best."

"You're saying I should thank you and Nash for fighting just enough to give me the opportunity to play Christine?" I glanced up to look at Asher's tall form.

"Sure," he said with a smile. "I'll take the credit for that."

I shook my head. "And here I thought I got it because I worked really hard and have been singing those songs since I was five."

"So maybe you earned some of it on your own." He winked.

We made it to the back of the library where the study tables were located, and after glancing around for a second, I spotted my friends at our usual table in the back.

But as we got closer, I realized it wasn't just Scarlett, Ava, and Hunter at the table.

No, sitting on the other side of Hunter with his back to us was Nash.

A flutter of excitement filled my stomach because I was excited to spend more time with him. But then I remembered who was standing next to me and how it would probably make Nash feel.

*Crap.*

Asher had noticed him as well because he mumbled under his breath, "I don't remember you mentioning that Nash would be part of the study group."

"That's because I didn't think he was," I mumbled back, my heart rate climbing. I thought he said he was going home for the night—not just dinner.

What should I do? Nash was *not* going to like that I'd invited Asher to join us.

Here I was just trying to be nice to Asher after seeing him look so lonely during dinner, but now I was looking like I had gone behind my crush's back to hang out with his enemy.

I was considering uninviting Asher and telling him he could join us another time when Nash swiveled around in his seat and looked right at us.

*Noooo!* was all I could think of when his gaze went from me to Asher.

And the betrayal in his blue eyes was instant when he real- ized I'd invited Asher here.

## 11

## ASHER

THINK, *Asher, think.*

If I could come up with a reason for why I just walked over here with Elyse, maybe she wouldn't look like she was going to puke.

"Oh, good. I'm glad you found us, Asher," Ava said, probably noticing the way Elyse and I were both panicking. "I saved you a spot right here next to me." She patted the empty seat beside her that she must have been saving for her sister.

"Perfect," I said, leaving Elyse's side to sit next to Ava. And then, since I figured Ava was trying to be Elyse's wing-woman and keep Nash from feeling like his territory was being threatened, I added, "I just got done talking to Owen about that question you had about our chemistry assignment, and I think I figured out the right chemical formula for us to use."

I was lying out of my butt, of course, since I hadn't talked to Ava today whatsoever, but it was the best I could come up with at the moment.

"I hope you don't mind that I invited Asher to join us," Ava addressed the rest of the table while I took the seat beside her.

"I saw how good he was at chemistry today and figured he'd be a good study partner for all of us."

"Fine with me." Scarlett barely lifted her gaze from the textbook page she was currently scanning.

"The more the merrier," my roommate Hunter added.

Nash's eyes darted between Ava and me and Elyse, a worry line between his eyebrows, like he thought something might be going on but wasn't sure what. But then he said, "I already finished our chemistry assignment, but who am I to say who can and can't study with us."

Since no one was running me out of the library with pitchforks, I unzipped my backpack and started pulling out my books.

"Were you and Asher rehearsing a scene together or something?" Nash asked Elyse in a hushed tone that he probably thought I couldn't hear. "Is that why you walked in together?"

I peeked at Elyse, curious what she would say. She looked startled for a second, like she hadn't expected him to flat out ask why we'd been together. But then she said, "We weren't rehearsing anything. We just ran into each other on the way here."

Which was kind of true, I guess. If you counted walking all the way from the great hall to the dorms and then over here as being "on the way here."

Nash visibly relaxed, the tension in his shoulders releasing as he leaned back in his chair, so I allowed myself to relax, too.

Because as much as I didn't like Nash or the way he seemed so obsessed with Elyse and how much time we may or may not have spent together this evening, I didn't want Elyse to feel more uncomfortable than she already did being around me.

I needed a friend, and I wasn't delusional enough to think that if put in the situation where she had to choose between Nash and me, she would pick me.

I seemed to have lost all my luck in winning my ongoing competition with Nash at the same time I'd lost my girlfriend.

———

THE REST of the study session was pretty uneventful, aside from getting a few side-eyed glances from Nash. I ended up spending most of the time working on the chemistry assignment with Ava. I wasn't a chemistry genius despite what she'd told everyone. But she didn't seem to care for the subject very much herself, so we just did what we could and joked our way through the assignment.

"Glad that's done," Ava said, closing her textbook with a sigh after we'd finished. "Thanks for helping me figure that out. I'm glad you agreed to join us."

"Of course," I said. "I appreciated the invite." I lifted the corner of my lip in a smirk and winked.

"Well, you know me. I'm just the thoughtful twin." She laughed lightly because we both knew she hadn't been the one to invite me at all.

But she had been thoughtful enough to jump in and save Elyse from dealing with an awkward situation--or from feeling like she had betrayed Nash somehow. So I said, "You are thoughtful." I lowered my voice. "And a good sister, too."

"Sometimes," she said. "Usually, it's Elyse who's watching out for me."

Her gaze went to Elyse who was listening to Nash talk about his vision for one of the scenes they would be doing for the play. And even though I'd never admit it to anyone else, I was impressed with how seriously he was taking his role of The Phantom.

I liked getting into character as much as the next guy, but with the way Nash was talking Elyse through the scene, it was obvious that he'd taken a deeper study of The Phantom. He seemed to have researched multiple sources besides the script to get a better grasp of The Phantom's background and wounds than I ever did when I played a role.

"So, what are your intentions with my sister?" Ava asked in a whisper, bringing my attention back to her.

"My intentions?" I frowned, not sure what she meant.

"Yeah." She folded her arms across her chest. When I studied her face, I was amazed at just how identical she and Elyse looked. They had the same amber-brown eyes with little gold flecks. The same long brown hair. The same pouty lips. Quite a few of their mannerisms were even the same. "I've caught you two alone twice, and it's making me wonder why you're interested in spending time with her."

"Don't you think it's possible for a guy to just want to make a friend?" I asked.

"Usually, I would think that," she said. "But Carter filled me in on the way you and Nash typically work, and I just want to make sure you aren't pretending to be friendly or interested in my sister just because you want to rile up Nash."

Had she read my mind earlier?

Because I'd planned to do that exact thing.

"Did Elyse say that's what I'm doing?" I asked, curious how much Elyse might have talked to Ava about me during dinner.

"No," she said. "That's just something I'm wondering. You're Elyse's type, but I don't want her getting her heart played with."

"I'm her type?" I asked, picking up on that one piece of information, an unexpected warmth filling my chest.

"Yes," Ava said.

"Then why is she interested in Nash?" I asked in a low voice, nodding toward them.

I knew Nash and I had always gone for the same type of

girl in the past, but we couldn't be more different from each other.

We'd never had a girl torn between the two of us before, since they either liked one of us or the other. It was always a cut-and-dry choice for the girl.

Did that mean Elyse was trying out a different brand of guy than her usual with hopes it would work out better?

"She's trying something new," Ava said, answering my unspoken question. "Because her *type* hasn't exactly been good to her."

"They haven't?" What did they do? Had she been hurt in the past?

Ava must have seen the concern in my expression because she shook her head and said, "It's not like that. It's just that she always goes for the *bad boys*." She put air quotes around those two words. "And they've taken advantage of how nice she is and never given much in return."

"So she's going for the nice guy this time," I said, understanding what she was getting at, even if I didn't agree with how she had lumped me into a category that I didn't feel I belonged in.

I might have an impulsive side that got the better of me when it came to my rivalry with Nash. And I would love to have someone care about me in the way I was sure a sweet girl like Elyse would care about her boyfriend.

But I wasn't always the "taker" in a relationship. When I really cared about someone, I gave in proportion to how much I took.

*I'd certainly given more than Bailee had in our little arrangement.*

"I just wanted to make sure you didn't get any ideas about stealing her from Nash just for the fun of it," Ava said, continuing her thought. "She deserves to end up with a good guy for a change."

"And I'm not a good guy?" I winced.

"I didn't mean it like that," Ava hurried to say, realizing that she'd ruffled my feelings. "Obviously, I don't know you well enough to make a judgement call."

"I would hope not," I said. "Because despite all the rumors, I'd always treated Bailee well."

It might have all been for show, but I'd been a great boyfriend. Exactly what Bailee had asked for.

I'd been so great at my job that people had even given us our own couple name: Ashlee.

And we'd reveled in the attention—laughed at how everyone was eating up the huge piece of imitation pie we were serving them.

"Of course." Ava covered her face with her hands, as if embarrassed to have said anything now that my missing girlfriend had been brought into the conversation. "Sorry. I obviously don't know what I'm talking about."

"It's okay." I decided to let her off, even if the judgment did burn. "You weren't here to see any of the good parts."

She'd only known what people were saying *after*.

It was interesting how quickly a narrative could turn when Bailee decided to go rogue.

But even so, Bailee and I had been good friends. That was what I'd started to believe we were, at least. I'd thought we were the type of friends who shared all their secrets with each other.

I would find out a little too late that I was the only one who had seen us that way since Bailee had taken all my secrets while giving none of hers in return.

Elyse laughed at something Nash said, bringing my attention back to them. And despite what Ava had said about Nash not being Elyse's typical type, there was nothing about the way they were interacting that would lead me to think he wasn't exactly what she was interested in.

Her eyes brightened as they talked, and she leaned closer to him as their voices lowered. She seemed genuinely interested in everything he had to say.

I'd even caught her peeking over at him several times as we'd studied, as if she truly liked looking at him and enjoyed the fact that he was sitting next to her.

Based on all of that, I doubted that she'd take the bait even if I was still trying to execute my plan from earlier this afternoon, which was to steal her away from Nash. She seemed all in on him at this point, so much so that I was actually embarrassed that I'd tried my little stunt in the first place.

I mean, just because one girl in second grade had chosen me over Nash didn't mean all girls would.

Yes, I knew I was attractive. Bailee herself said part of the reason she'd picked me to be her fill-in boyfriend was because I was one of the hottest guys at school—her words, not mine.

But looks weren't everything.

Ava lifted her books from the table and hugged them to her chest. "Wanna walk back to the dorms with me?"

Scarlett and Hunter were just packing up as well, so I guessed Ava was trying to give her sister some alone time with Nash.

"Sure." I picked up my books and dropped them into my backpack. "I'll make sure you get there safely since your boyfriend is elsewhere tonight."

It was something I had lots of practice with: filling in until the real love interest could come and take the place I'd kept warm for him.

## 12

## ELYSE

"THANKS FOR SAVING ME TONIGHT," I told Ava when I got back to our room after Nash walked me back to the dorms. "My mind went totally blank when I saw Nash sitting at the table with you guys. I literally thought I'd just ruined everything."

"What are sisters for?" Ava pulled a makeup wipe from the package she had on the corner of her desk that doubled as a vanity. "I saw the panic on your face and knew just what to do."

I set my book bag on my bed. "I thought Nash was staying home with Carter and Cambrielle tonight, so I didn't think inviting Asher to study with us would be an issue."

"Apparently, Nash wanted another excuse to spend more time with you." Ava waggled her eyebrows suggestively. "He's so smitten."

I felt the skin on my face tighten with a blush. "You think that's why he came?"

"Why else would he come?" She wiped off her eyeshadow. "If it was just to get his assignment done, he could have just done his homework with Carter since they have most of the same classes."

"I guess that's true." And studying with Carter would have probably been the smarter option—Carter was an actual tutor and really good at explaining complicated subjects in simpler terms.

Or so Ava told me, since Carter had been her math tutor when they first met.

"Nash just can't get enough of you." Ava giggled. "He's addicted."

I shook my head and laughed at how over the top those words were. "I'll be fine just thinking that he wanted to spend time with me."

"And how did things go after I left?" Ava tossed her makeup wipe in the nearby trashcan and squeezed a dollop of moisturizer on her finger. "Did Nash finally make a move? Did he pull you into one of the colonnades on the way here and kiss you until you couldn't breathe?"

"No." I sighed as I pulled a makeup wipe out of the package. "He just walked me to the common room doors and waved goodbye." I stared down at the moist wipe in my hands. "Do you think there's something about me that's making him move so slowly?" I looked at Ava. "I mean, back when we first moved here, Cambrielle made fun of him for going in for the kiss on his first date with Bree Peterson and getting her cheek. So it doesn't seem like he's always moved so slowly."

Had I just been interpreting all the signs wrong because I wanted him to want me like that?

"I don't know." Ava shrugged and looked at my reflection in the mirror on the wall above her desk. "But I'm pretty sure he likes you. I saw the way he looked at Asher when you walked in, and it was not the look of someone who had neutral feelings."

My chest warmed at the thought. "He did seem worried for a second before you swooped in."

Was it bad that I was comforted by his jealousy?

"See, he likes you." Ava patted my arm. "He's just prolonging the big moment until the anticipation of it makes for an even more explosive experience."

"Well, if that's his game, then I think I'm there." I wiped the mascara from my lashes. "I literally just watched his lips the whole time we were singing a duet at rehearsal today."

Seriously, I'd been watching them like I'd hoped that if I watched his lips for long enough, they'd find their way to mine.

I shook away the memory. Hopefully, not too many people had noticed that.

"If something doesn't happen soon, I'm probably going to push him into a corner myself and attack him," I said before I could stop myself.

Ava cracked up. Like the image of me being that aggressive was hilarious.

"I would pay to see you do that with a guy," she said between laughs. "It would totally shock him, but I bet he would loooooove that."

"You think he would?"

She nodded. "What guy doesn't want to be pushed up against a wall and kissed by the girl he likes?"

"I don't know. With my luck, Nash would probably run for the hills."

"Yeah right." Ava waved the thought away. "In fact, if something doesn't happen before your retreat this weekend, you should make a move."

"I should?" I asked, feeling my throat tighten with nerves.

"Yes."

"But what if it goes bad?" I asked, imagining him running

down a snowy hill as fast as he could to get away from me. "I'll be stuck in a cabin with him, feeling like a loser."

"But if it works, you could be staying at a cabin in the woods with your *boyfriend*," Ava said. "Sitting by the fire, drinking hot chocolate, and cuddling under a cozy blanket. Doesn't that sound nice?"

I imagined the scenario she was painting, and it did sound perfect. Like a scene from a book or a movie.

"Just keep that idea in your back pocket." Ava stood and grabbed her toothbrush and toothpaste like she was ready to head to the girls' bathroom to finish her bedtime routine. "You still have four days. Who knows, maybe he'll ask to practice that kiss between The Phantom and Christine before then."

Butterflies erupted in my stomach at the thought. I'd considered that scene before and it would be a good excuse to have a first kiss.

But did I really want our first kiss to be practice for the musical?

In front of the other cast members?

No, I wanted it to be special. Something that wasn't scripted. Something just between us.

But if something didn't happen soon, that might just be how it was going to happen.

*Why am I such a chicken?*

"What were you and Asher talking about in the library?" I asked Ava, changing the subject before I could make myself too anxious.

She smirked. "I was just telling him not to get in the way of you and Nash."

"What?" My eyes went wide. "You're joking."

But she just chuckled and said, "I'm not."

"Didn't you hear his speech at dinner?" I asked, feeling

hives race up my neck. "He's clearly still in love with his girlfriend."

Did Asher think I'd told Ava that I thought he might like me?

"Yeah, I got that *after* I told him to stay away."

I buried my face in my hands. "He's going to think I assume every guy at this school is bound to fall in love with me."

"He doesn't think that," Ava said, sounding sure. "I told him it was an honest mistake."

I lifted my head and looked into my sister's eyes. "He's going to think I'm a narcissist."

"No, he's not." Ava touched my arm in an attempt to calm me down.

I took in a deep breath and let it out slowly. "Well, I appreciate you trying to look out for me. But in the future, could we just not assume guys are falling in love with me everywhere I go?"

"Fine," she said. "Just make that kiss happen with Nash, and I'll stop meddling in your love life."

---

## 13

## ELYSE

THE NEXT FEW days were busy. I had three rehearsals, two tests, one quiz plus a book report, but shared zero kisses with Nash.

So, as Cambrielle and I sat on the bus that would take us to Miss Crawley's family cabin in the woods thirty minutes away from Eden Falls, we came up with a game plan.

"I think you should go for it after the campfire songs," Cambrielle said, pointing to the spot on the schedule just before *lights out.* "We'll be done with all the activities for the day. Everyone will be winding down and doing their own thing, and no one would notice if you pulled Nash outside for a moonlight rendezvous."

"You think I should kiss him outside?" I asked.

She lifted a petite shoulder. "It worked for me and Mack. Kisses under the moonlight are just more romantic than kisses elsewhere." She smiled. "Plus, it will be chilly, so it'll give you an excuse to get really close."

I glanced around the bus to make sure no one was listening. I caught Asher's gaze from a few rows behind us. He did the little head nod like he was saying hi, but it looked like he had earbuds in so he couldn't be listening to us.

Nash had been sitting on the seat just in front of Cambrielle and me, but he'd walked up to ask Miss Crawley a question a couple of minutes ago and they were still chatting.

Everyone else surrounding us seemed immersed in their own conversations, so I figured it was safe to continue.

"How do you think I should get him outside?" I asked in a voice just above a whisper. "Just ask him to go for a walk?"

"If you want."

But it didn't sound like she really thought it was the greatest idea. So I waited for her real thoughts to come out.

She turned in her seat to face me better, and after glancing around to make sure Nash was still talking to Miss Crawley, she said, "I was actually thinking that you should just kind of sneak up behind him and go for it."

"What?"

She nodded. "You're like me; you overthink everything. If you ask him to go on a moonlight stroll, you're going to start walking and your mind is going to start racing, and you're going to try to figure out the exact right moment for it to happen... But then an hour will go by and you'll be freezing your toes off, and then you'll come back to the girls' loft still wondering what it would be like to kiss my brother."

I wanted to argue. To tell her that the walk would be the perfect setup for a romantic kiss...but I knew she was right. Nash and I were really good at walking around and talking and then getting too nervous to take the next step.

"So what do you suggest?" I sighed. "How do you suggest I 'sneak up and go for it,' as you say? Because it sounds like some sort of sexual assault charge waiting to happen. And your parents are billionaires, so I'm sure you have lawyers on call to help with that kind of thing."

"Nash will not be pressing charges." Cambrielle chuckled. "More like he's going to be so happy that he won't be able to stop smiling for five days."

"Are you sure he won't run his hand across his lips and wipe my kiss back on my shirt?" I asked, referencing what had happened when she kissed Ben Barnett a while back.

She made a face. "I never should have told you about that."

I laughed. "At least I'll know I'm in good company if that does happen."

She glanced at the front of the bus and her eyes widened. "He's coming back."

We both turned to face forward again, not at all looking like we'd just been talking about Nash.

But when he got stopped by the guy playing Andre, one of the new opera house owners, Cambrielle whispered, "He'd probably kill me if I told you, but Nash has told me himself that he likes you. Like, a lot..." She gave me a meaningful look that made me believe what she was saying. "He's just too in his head and wants everything to be perfect."

Nash started walking toward us again, and my heart started beating faster with each step he took closer.

I really did like him.

So much.

I inhaled deeply. "Okay, I'm going to go for it," I said to Cambrielle under my breath.

"Good," she whispered back. "I'll get him outside, then you can do the rest."

I just hoped that when I took the leap, Nash would be ready to catch me.

"ARE you ready for me to send the text to Nash?" Cambrielle asked after we'd finished our last activity for the night.

We were upstairs in the loft where the girls would be sleeping, and all the other girls were chatting as they got ready to turn in for the night.

"Almost," I said, my heart racing at the thought that this was actually happening. Cambrielle was going to text Nash to ask him to meet her outside, but I was going to meet him instead. "I want to brush my teeth first."

A slow smile lifted my friend's lips. "You don't want your first kiss with Nash to taste like the Dutch-oven chicken and potatoes we had tonight?"

"I thought about it," I said. "But I think I'll stick with my trusty minty-fresh taste instead."

"I guess that's probably a good call."

We waited for a few of the other girls to leave the upstairs bathroom, and then Cambrielle and I went to the double sink to brush our teeth together.

"Are you having fun so far?" I asked Cambrielle as I put some toothpaste onto my toothbrush.

"Yeah, it's been super fun," Cambrielle said, her blue eyes bright. "I wasn't sure how I'd feel about all the games since I've only been a crew member before, but I can see why you and Nash like acting so much. It's actually really fun."

Cambrielle had initially only auditioned to be one of the dancers, not expecting a speaking role. But Miss Crawley had seen how gifted she was at not just dancing but also performing in front of a crowd and had asked if she'd play the part of Meg Giry, Christine Daaé's close friend in the play.

And I was so happy that she accepted the role because it was so fun having her here this weekend.

The whole afternoon and evening had been fun, actually.

We'd played games, had a great meal, and even though it

had only been a few hours, I felt a lot closer to my castmates than I had before.

I was usually pretty slow to warm up to people I didn't know very well. Took my time coming out of my shell, so it felt good to feel a camaraderie with the people I'd be spending most of my afternoons with for the next two months.

The fact that Nash and I had flirted and made hot eye contact all night didn't hurt, either.

Okay, so maybe those had been my favorite parts of the night, since it gave me hope that he'd want the kiss I had planned just as much as I did.

I looked at myself in the mirror as I brushed my teeth.

*Eek. I can't believe I'm going to do this.*

I never made the first move on a guy. Ever.

But then, I'd never liked a guy like Nash before. I'd always gone for the players. The bad boys. The alphas.

The guys who knew what they wanted and went after it.

The primal part of me had always craved a guy taking charge like that. But since it had never worked out with any of my last boyfriends, I hoped that things would turn out better with Nash.

After we were done, Cambrielle and I went back to the queen bed we'd be sharing tonight. Then I said, "Okay, I think I'm ready."

"Yeah?" she asked, pulling her phone from her back pocket.

I nodded. "It's now or never."

She typed on her phone, and a second later, a swoosh sound signaled that the text had gone out.

"You better get outside, Juliet," Cambrielle said. "Romeo will be waiting for you."

I walked down the stairs on semi-shaky legs, my heart already beating a million beats a minute. There were a few guys and girls standing in the kitchen when I passed them, using a kettle to make hot chocolate.

I didn't stop to say hi since I didn't know how quickly Nash would be coming up from the basement where the boys were sleeping. And instead of going to the front door where I assumed Nash would wait for Cambrielle, I made a beeline for the back door.

*Okay, you're almost there, Elyse. Just do it. Don't say anything. Don't stall. Just go for it. He's been waiting for this and will be happy to see you.*

I paced by the back door for a second, trying to get the nerve to go outside. I was considering taking a few more deep breaths to calm my nerves when I heard footsteps on the deck outside.

Nash was already there.

*It's now or never.*

There was no more time to waste. Just ten seconds of courage and I might have a boyfriend by the end of the night.

I quietly stepped out onto the porch. I'd expected to have to walk around the corner to see Nash waiting on the bench out front, but his tall figure was leaning against the outside corner of the cabin. He was facing the front porch light, his back to me.

He was wearing a beanie, which covered his short blond hair, but I was pretty sure it was Nash.

Who else would be on the porch in the freezing cold right now?

Nash slipped his phone into his back pocket—he was probably just checking Cambrielle's text to make sure he'd read it right. Then he stood up straighter, like he might be planning to wait for her inside instead.

*If I don't go now, I'll miss my chance.*

Instead of hesitating any more, I made myself rush forward,

my heart pounding in my ears. Before he could take another step toward the front door, I grabbed his arm and said, "Nash. Wait."

He turned around to face me. And before I could chicken out or even wait for my eyes to adjust to the darkness, I stood on my tiptoes and pressed my lips against his.

He didn't immediately respond to the kiss. He just stood still for a moment, as if unsure what was going on. For a terrifying moment, I was tempted to run away and hide before he could realize it was me.

But then I remembered Cambrielle saying that Nash liked me. I remembered how he'd been looking at me all night, and so I forced myself to hold the kiss. To give him a few more seconds to realize what was going on and to respond.

He was back lit, so I couldn't see his features, but if his eyes were open, he'd be able to see that it was me who had surprised him and not someone else.

"Elyse?" he asked, his surprise making his voice sound different than usual.

"Yes," I whispered, only then daring to open my eyes again.

It was still too dark for me to see the features of his face, but I really hoped he wasn't angry or offended that I'd just gone in for the kiss.

After a few excruciating seconds where he still wasn't saying anything, I whispered, "Did I interpret everything wrong and just mess everything up?"

"No," he said, like he was only just now realizing what was going on. He mumbled, "You didn't mess anything up." And then, just like he'd done in my fantasies so many times, Nash slipped one hand up the side of my neck until he was gently cupping my face. His hand was colder than I'd expected, but I loved it because it was the most intimate moment we'd had so far.

My eyes fluttered shut, and a second later, he was kissing me.

Nash Hastings, the guy I'd dreamed of kissing for a month, was finally kissing me. And it was amazing. His lips were soft but sure, and when he gently tugged on my bottom lip with his teeth, I had to hold onto him to stay upright.

I let my hand slip up his chest where his coat was open and across his neck until my thumb could trace along his jaw.

I'd expected his jawline to be smooth, since everyone always made fun of Nash for only needing to shave once a year, but my thumb chaffed against what felt like a five o'clock shadow.

So he did need to shave after all. I must not have noticed it before because of how light his facial hair was.

But I liked the feel of it. Liked that I was learning something new about him that I hadn't known before this moment.

He must have liked the sensation of my thumb running along his strong jawline because he pulled me closer against him and let his fingers comb through the hair at my nape. And it felt so good. So good that tingles raced all the way down to my toes.

"I was so scared," I whispered between kisses, feeling slightly breathless. "But I'm so glad I came outside."

He didn't say anything back. But he didn't need to, because the way his lips moved with mine—slow, unhurried, and in a rhythm that made my heart erratic—told me everything I needed to know.

He was glad I'd taken the step, too.

I never knew that ten seconds of courage could change your life. But this small moment might have changed everything for Nash and me.

I was just noticing his cologne and how it was different from the one he usually wore when I heard the front door creak open behind Nash, followed by footsteps on the wooden porch floor.

I opened my eyes to see who had joined us, and that was when I noticed a shock of blond hair under the light.

*Wait, what?*

I stumbled backward when I got a better look at the guy who'd just come outside. How was this possible?

"Who are you?" I asked the boy before me when I realized he couldn't be Nash since Nash had just come through the door.

"It's me, Asher," he said quietly, sounding genuinely confused. "Didn't you know it was me?"

I'd been kissing Asher?

I'd just been making out with the one guy in the drama department who Nash would never get over me kissing?

"Why would I kiss you?" I asked, panic causing my throat to constrict. But since I only had a split second before Nash would look our way and see that I'd been kissing his enemy, I didn't wait for Asher's answer. Instead, I ran for the back door.

I hurried up the stairs to the loft, not caring that people were giving me weird looks. I rushed to the bed where Cambrielle was on her phone, probably texting Mack.

"You need to go outside," I told her breathlessly. "I just messed up big time, and I need you to pretend like you actually did need to talk to Nash about something."

"What?" Cambrielle set her phone down, looking alarmed. "What happened?"

"I'll explain later. I just need you to go downstairs and pretend like you planned to meet Nash there all along."

"Okay..." She still looked confused, but being the awesome friend that she was, she slipped her feet into her boots and pulled on her coat.

As she hurried down the stairs, I moved to the railing of the loft so I could see what was going on. Cambrielle ran across the rug and made it to the front door just as Asher was coming inside.

He held the door open for her to go through, seeming surprised to see her right there. And when he turned back around after shutting the door behind him, his cheeks were flushed.

*His cheeks are just flushed from the cold and not from our kiss.*

His gaze lifted up to the loft, as if he was looking for me. And when our eyes caught, my heart throbbed and felt like it was going to beat out of my chest because I'd kissed him and he knew it.

And he also knew that I had liked it.

Why did I have to like it? Shouldn't the Universe have come to my rescue and made me hate it?

I wanted to step away from the rail so he couldn't just look up at me the way he was with his eyes all mysterious and his lips all pouty pink. But I wanted to make sure Cambrielle made it to Nash, so I gripped the railing for support and tried to ignore Asher.

Cambrielle's puffy pink coat appeared in one of the windows. I watched her pull Nash over to the bench in front of the next window over.

Was Nash okay?

Was he upset?

Had he seen Asher and me?

Or had Asher said something to him on his way in?

My grip tightened on the railing as I watched their profiles. It was hard to make out their expressions, since the porch light wasn't as bright as a spotlight. But from what I could see of their body language, Nash didn't seem upset. He seemed relaxed and happy.

So maybe they were just having a friendly brother-and-sister conversation.

Maybe everything would be okay.

Somewhat satisfied that everything was okay on the Nash front, I tried to look for Asher. I saw that he had moved to the kitchen area and was making himself a cup of hot chocolate.

He grabbed a plastic straw and swirled it around in his disposable coffee cup. Then he lifted the cup to his lips and blew on the hot liquid. He must have sensed my stare, because just as I was looking at the way his mouth was blowing on his drink, his eyes ticked up to me again.

And I hated that my stomach did a little flip when our gazes locked.

Why had he let me kiss him? And why had he kissed me back like that—like he could've spent hours kissing me on the porch if we hadn't been interrupted?

Had he believed that I had actually wanted to kiss *him*? Was that what had happened? I was pretty sure I'd called him Nash, but Nash and Asher did have a similar sound to them.

Or had he known what was going on all along and had seen it as an opportunity to get the upper hand in the never-ending battle he had going on with his rival?

There was movement in the window. Nash and Cambrielle stood from the bench, and he put his arm around her shoulders in a brotherly way, like they'd just had a special heart-to-heart.

I stepped back from the rail before they could come inside, and I tried to tell myself that everything would be fine.

Nash didn't know what I'd just done.

Cambrielle had covered up my disaster.

And Asher hadn't said anything to Nash.

*Oh, I really hope he wouldn't say something to Nash.*

They would be staying in the basement together. Was it too much to hope that Asher would keep this secret to himself?

He'd told me before that he was good at keeping secrets. Would he keep mine?

Probably not.

Which meant, I needed to do something quick.

A minute later, Cambrielle came back upstairs. After taking her coat off and slipping her boots off her feet, she said, "Okay, it's time for you to spill it. I saw Asher coming in when I was on my way out. Did something happen between you two?"

## 14

## ASHER

"FIVE MINUTES UNTIL LIGHTS OUT," Miss Crawley called from the center of the house so everyone on the main floor and the loft could hear her announcement.

I only had a few sips of hot chocolate left in my cup, so I quickly gulped them down and tossed the disposable cup into a garbage can nearby.

Miss Simmons, who was a math teacher at our school and had come with her husband to help cook and chaperone, led the remaining girls upstairs to the loft where they'd be spending the night. And while Miss Simmons took care of the girls, Miss Crawley, accompanied by Mr. Simmons, led the rest of the guys downstairs.

I was about to follow Henry Jenkins down the wooden staircase when Elyse suddenly appeared before me.

Had she just slipped out of the laundry room?

"Hey, can I talk to you for a quick sec?" she whispered, looking around to make sure we were alone.

And though I was pretty sure I knew what she wanted to

say—that she'd made a mistake and had most definitely not intended to kiss me outside fifteen minutes ago and that I better not get any ideas about it—I said, "Sure," and followed her back into the laundry room.

The laundry room was dark, with only the light from the kitchen filtering in through the open doorway. When she seemed satisfied that we were alone, she turned to me and said, "So I don't know what you think happened out on the porch, but I just want to make sure we're on the same page."

I could tell she was on edge, but the side of me that didn't like awkward conversations and always had to turn everything into a joke so no one would know what my true feelings were prevailed. I said teasingly, "Are you talking about the page where you enjoyed kissing me so much that you pulled me in here for round two?"

"What?" she said, sounding truly shocked. "O-of course not."

"Because it's okay if you liked it." I leaned closer. Close enough that I could smell the faint scent of her shampoo. And wow, she smelled good. "You can't help it when the chemistry is there."

"What are you even...?" She took a step back and shook her head, like she couldn't understand what I was talking about.

And it was kind of fun seeing her get all flustered like this.

Because even if I knew *now* that she hadn't meant that kiss for me, the way she was acting told me she'd still enjoyed it.

Even if she'd thought she was kissing Nash, she'd still enjoyed the kiss with *me*.

I stepped closer and twisted a lock of her hair around my finger. "Do you want to break the news to Nash?" I bent my head down to meet her gaze in the darkness. "Or should I?"

"Asher!" she scolded in a hushed voice before glancing at

the doorway behind me. I couldn't help but smile to myself because this was fun.

"Sorry," I said, pretending like I'd misunderstood. "Were you hoping to keep everything a secret? Did you really just pull me in here for another kiss? Because I know we barely know each other, but I'd be okay with kissing you again if you really want."

"Asher," she said, a little louder this time. "You need to stop. This is serious."

"I know," I whispered back. "My feelings for you are really serious. I didn't realize how strongly I could feel so early on, but..." I paused for dramatic effect.

Before I could finish my sentence and proclaim my unexpected love for her, she put her hand over my mouth and said, "Stop. Please. Someone is going to hear you and I need to talk."

I was tempted to lick her hand, just to make her squeal, but I reined myself in at the last second.

She watched me for a moment, as if checking to make sure I was going to cooperate with her. I must have looked repentant enough because she slowly lowered her hand and said, "Okay, so I'm going to do the talking and you are going to listen."

I pressed my lips together obediently and nodded.

She sighed and tried to take a step back but bumped against the washing machine. "Can I get just a little more space?" She made a "scoot back" motion with her hands.

And being the gentleman that I was not, I only scooted back three inches.

She looked like she wanted to comment on my inability to follow directions, but she shook her head instead. "Now that you have your listening ears on, I just wanted to make sure you understood that what happened tonight on the porch was a big misunderstanding." She looked up at me to make sure I really was paying attention. "I was supposed to meet Nash outside, but I made a mistake and confused you for him. What happened because of that was..."

"Mind blowing," I filled in for her when she paused, unable to help myself.

"No." She glared at me. "I was going to say it was unfortunate."

*Unfortunate?*

*Really?*

"Are you sure about that?" I asked. "Because I—"

She held up a finger to my lips, stopping me from finishing my rebuttal. "Yes, it was an unfortunate mistake, and I'm sorry if I confused you and made you think I kissed you on purpose."

Those words chaffed a little because yes, I had in fact thought she'd meant that kiss for me.

You know, right up until the moment she stepped away in horror and asked who I was.

Did I feel like an idiot for kissing her back, now that I was on this side of that kiss?

Yes.

A really big one.

But in that quiet moment when she had asked if she'd read all of the signs wrong, using that tender voice of hers, I couldn't turn her away.

I had to kiss her.

If for no other reason than to keep her from believing anyone wouldn't want to kiss her.

It didn't make sense since we'd only met a week ago, but apparently, I was still in love with myself *just enough* to believe that someone like Elyse could experience love—or in the very least, lust—at first sight with someone like me.

I mean, if no one else was going to love me, at least I could still love myself, right?

I'd simply missed the part where she hadn't known it was me at all.

She looked at me like she was expecting a response, and so I said, "I get it. You like Nash."

"Yes, I like Nash." She nodded. "And only Nash."

*AKA, I definitely don't have any feelings for you, Asher.*

Who knew that a girl so sweet could be so great at demolishing my ego.

I was about to leave before she could say anything to make it even more clear that she would never kiss me on purpose when she asked, "Why were you outside, anyway? Did you overhear Cambrielle and me on the bus and decided to interfere?"

I wished that was what had happened. I'd feel a lot less stupid and rejected right now if I had planned this whole thing out.

But too tired to lie, I pinched the bridge of my nose and said, "No, I didn't know about your plans. I got a call from my aunt who needed to confirm some plans for winter break and took the call outside." I reached for my phone in my back pocket. "I can show you my call log if you need proof."

"No, that's okay." She pushed my phone back when I tried to hand it to her. "I guess it was a wrong-place-at-the-wrong-time sort of thing."

In the moment I'd thought it was a wrong place at the right time, but I wouldn't tell her that now.

"I promise I wasn't trying to interfere with you and Nash," I said. "It was an honest mistake on my end, too." And since I knew she was waiting for it, I added, "Don't worry, I'm not planning to tell anyone about it. Not even Nash."

"Good." She sighed like the weight of the world had just been lifted off her shoulders. "I appreciate it."

"So now that we cleared that up, do you think we can still be friends?" I asked.

Even after the awkwardness of the past few minutes, I still wanted to be friends.

There was something about Elyse that made me feel at ease in a way I never had before. It was weird and something I couldn't explain, but she was easy to talk to, and I rarely found it easy to open up to anyone.

Bailee was probably the closest I'd ever been to being an open book with someone, but even that felt different than whatever this thing was with Elyse.

While she seemed to be considering whether we could be friends or not, I added, "I promise I won't trick you into kissing me again."

"I thought you said it wasn't a trick." A flash of betrayal covered her expression.

"It wasn't," I hurried to say. "I-I'm just saying that since now that you know how good of a kisser I am, it will probably be even more tempting to accidentally cross the line again."

I'd probably be thinking about that kiss tomorrow at least.

And the next day.

And probably the next.

Man, it had been too long since I'd kissed someone.

Elyse studied me in the dark, as if trying to decide whether two people who kissed the way we just had could still be friends.

So I gave her my most angelic look and said, "We'll just be buddies. I wouldn't let you kiss me again even if you begged me to."

She rolled her eyes, but then she said, "Fine. We can *try* to be friends."

"Good." I released the breath I'd been holding. "Buddies, it is."

I held my hand out for her to shake, and when she placed her hand in mine, I tried not to notice the pulse of electricity that shot up my arm.

It didn't mean anything. I was just starved for physical touch was all.

I was most definitely not catching feelings for the girl Nash liked—the girl who had just made it very clear that she wasn't into me.

15
———

## ASHER

"WHERE ARE NASH AND CAMBRIELLE?" I asked Elyse during lunch the next day. She'd been sitting at the far end of one of the long tables alone, so I figured now was my best chance to talk and make sure we were still good.

We'd had a morning full of workshops, but since Elyse and I had been put in different groups each hour, I hadn't spent any time with her yet.

It was kind of strange that we hadn't been paired together, especially when we were playing love interests in the play, but so far, the closest I'd been to interacting with her was when I'd briefly caught her gaze across the room at breakfast.

Had she asked Miss Crawley to keep me away from her after what happened last night?

Had she only pretended that we could be friends just to be nice in the moment?

"Nash and Cambrielle had to leave early for some family event," she said, surprising me by gesturing for me to sit in the chair beside her. "I think their great-grandma is celebrating her ninetieth birthday or something."

"Are they coming back tonight?" I scooted closer to the table.

"I think so." She tore off a piece of her roll. "I know we're just going to be watching the movie version of the play tonight, but Nash sounded like he really wanted to make it back for that."

"I bet he's hoping you'll save him a spot next to you on the couch," I said, wiggling my eyebrows. "Maybe even has plans to invite you out on the porch for a moonlight rendezvous himself."

"Asher," she scolded, putting her hands to her cheeks like she was trying to hide her blush. "You know you're not supposed to say things like that."

"But we're friends now, aren't we?" I asked, bumping shoulders with her.

"Yes..." Though she said it like she still wasn't sure we should be.

"Then as your *friend*, it's my job to tease you about your crush."

She let out a nervous sigh. "I'm just not used to my guy friends teasing me about my crushes."

"Probably because all your guy friends have always wanted to be the one you were crushing on," I said.

"Yeah right." She shook her head, like I was being ridiculous.

"I bet it's true," I wagered. "I bet you've never been able to be friends with a guy without it getting complicated."

She was beautiful, talented, and smart. And though she was quiet, she also had a surprisingly spunky side that guys loved.

It would be hard to want to stay just friends with someone like her.

"I'm friends with Hunter," she said. "Nothing has ever been complicated with him."

"Yeah." I picked up my water bottle and unscrewed the lid. "But that's only because he's too busy trying not to be in love with Scarlett."

She looked like she was trying to think of another friend she had who wasn't related to her or dating her sister already. After thinking for a few seconds and getting the cutest little pucker line between her eyebrows from such deep concentration, she shrugged and said, "I just haven't had that many guy friends, I guess."

"Even at your old school?" I asked. "Because I can text my cousins Jace and Logan to verify."

"Please don't." Her eyes widened with alarm when I pretended to reach for my phone.

"Do you have something you'd like to confess?" I took a pull from my water and set it back down on the table. "Because Logan is always more than happy to talk to me."

"Please don't talk to Logan about me," she rushed to say.

I couldn't keep a half-smile from my lips. "Now I *really* need to text Logan." From the way she seemed so against the idea of me texting him, I was almost sure he must have some sort of dirt on her.

"You better not text him," she said.

"Why?"

She looked at the other end of the table where a few other students were laughing about something. Then back at me, she said, "So maybe I've never been that successful at staying friends with guys for very long."

"I knew it." I grinned, genuinely proud of myself for being right about her.

"Not that I've had that many boyfriends," she hurried to say. "Only two that I'd really call a *boyfriend* boyfriend."

"Yeah?" I asked, suddenly curious about these ex-boyfriends of hers.

She nodded and poked at her veggies with her fork. "And those two didn't start as friends, either, so your theory isn't very valid."

"So you're saying that since *we're* friends now," —I pointed to her and then at myself— "it means we could never be boyfriend and girlfriend?"

"No," she said. "I mean yes." She shook her head, looking flustered. "I mean..." She sighed. "Ugh. You are annoying, did you know that?"

I laughed, enjoying this whole exchange way more than I'd enjoyed anything in a long time.

Well, aside from that kiss last night, I guess. I had certainly enjoyed that for the few moments that I'd thought it had been meant for me.

"So the guys who made it to boyfriend status, what were they like?" I asked, curious about what she'd been into before she'd moved here and met Nash.

Ava had said that I was Elyse's type—that she was into "bad boys." But I wasn't quite sure what she'd meant by that since I'd never seen myself as *bad*. Just morally grey sometimes.

The only thing that I could think of that would make me bad was if I had actually done something to Bailee to make her disappear.

Had all of Elyse's previous boyfriends been suspected of murdering their girlfriends?

Because that was a pretty specific trait to be attracted to.

"You want me to talk about my exes?" she asked, a skeptical look on her face.

"Sure." I shrugged. "This isn't a first date, so it's okay to talk about previous relationships."

"I know it's not a date," she said quickly.

"So what's the low-down on your exes?" I leaned back in my chair and folded my arms, ready for a long explanation.

She studied me for a moment, her brown eyes seeming to weigh whether she wanted to tell me or not. Then with a shrug, she said, "You actually already know one of them."

"I do?" I frowned.

She nodded. "My first boyfriend was your cousin Logan."

"Seriously?" I sat up straight. "When?" Because his family had moved away from Ridgewater for a couple of years, and I was pretty sure Logan started dating his current girlfriend, Raven, almost immediately after moving back.

"It was only for a few weeks during freshman year." She waved her hand like it had been nothing. "I was really into his bad-boy vibe and messy hair at the time."

There was that "bad boy" phrase again.

"What do you mean by *bad boy* vibe?" I asked, putting the phrase in air quotes. "I don't think I've ever heard of that term until Ava mentioned it on Monday."

"Oh, it's something I've read in books. Romance novels mostly," she said, her cheeks turning rosy pink. "I guess it's weird that I assumed it was a universal phrase."

"Maybe it is." I held up my hands. "Shame on me for not reading romance novels, I guess."

"They're definitely not for everyone." She shrugged. "Though, I have heard that they're great research material for guys since they really demonstrate what girls want."

"I'm sure they are," I said, filing that little tip into my memory for if I ever got to the point where I wanted to get serious about dating again. "So, what made my cousin a bad boy?"

"Well, you know, he was kind of broody and troubled at the time." She looked at me. "Always doing reckless things and not seeming to care about what anyone thought."

"And you were attracted to that?" I raised my eyebrows, surprised that this sweet girl next to me was interested in the qualities that my cousin had worked hard to change about himself over the past three years.

"I don't know. I guess I thought I could help him. Plus, he was, well—" She bit her lip as if uncertain whether to say the next part.

"He was what?" I prodded, super curious now.

"Um, never mind." She picked up her fork like she was suddenly hungry again. "I, uh, I didn't have anything else to add."

"Yes, you did," I said. "It's okay if you liked him because he's hot. I mean, we're cousins, so it makes sense that you'd think he was at least half as hot as you think I am."

"That's not it." She rolled her eyes. "Though, yes, Logan and Jace are very good-looking, and Ava and I did joke about how it would be fun to each marry one of the twins one day and have beautiful children that looked the same."

"Too bad they're both taken," I said.

"And Ava has Carter, of course."

"Ah, but you're going after Carter's brother..." I said. "So you're still trying to get that same look, aren't you?"

"No." She pulled her head back, like the idea actually surprised her. Her eyes widened further. "I-I never even considered that..."

"You didn't?"

"No..." She got an odd look on her face. "That would be really weird, actually. For Ava, Mack, *and* me to all end up with the Hastings' siblings."

"You're really just realizing that?" I asked since I'd made the connection almost immediately when I saw them all on that triple date together.

"Yeah..." She shook her head and seemed to mull the thought over.

While she was thinking over it, I picked up my fork and took my first bite of pasta. Somehow, I'd been so caught up in the conversation that I'd forgotten to start eating.

"Do you think other people would think it was weird if Nash and I started dating?" she asked.

I finished chewing my bite of salad and washed it down with a gulp of water. "I don't know. Maybe." I wiped my mouth with a napkin. "I mean, obviously I would think it's weird for anyone to pick Nash over myself..." I shot her a cocky grin, and she rolled her eyes. "But it's not like it's illegal or anything. So you might as well go after who you want, right?"

"Yeah..." she said thoughtfully. "That's actually the thing I liked about Logan. He wasn't afraid to go for what he wanted."

"What do you mean by that?" I frowned, genuinely not understanding.

"Okay, this is awkward." She shook her head and looked back at her plate. "I don't know why I brought it up again."

"It's fine. Logan and I are buds," I said, in case she was worried about sharing personal details with someone related to her ex.

"Well...I guess I liked how he wasn't scared of making the first move." She peeked over at me. "I, um, I guess I like it when a guy is assertive that way."

"So you're saying last night was an anomaly for you?" I asked. "That you don't usually surprise guys with your kisses?"

"No." She put her face in her hands. "That was me trying something new." She shifted her head in her hands to glance sideways at me. "Which is probably why it backfired big time, I might add."

"I don't know if it completely backfired," I said. "You seemed to enjoy it well enough."

And I couldn't help but remember the way her fingers had traced along my jawline, or how she'd pressed herself closer to me and sighed into each kiss.

I might not have kissed anyone for a long time, but I wasn't dumb enough that I couldn't recognize the signs of someone enjoying a stolen moment like that. She'd been into it as much as I had been.

"I can't believe you just said that." Her jaw dropped and she smacked my arm. "I thought you were someone else."

"Maybe you did." I rubbed my arm. Then leaning closer to her ear, I whispered, "But that still doesn't change the fact that it was me. Or that you got swept up in the moment just as much as I did."

She shivered, as if my hot breath on her neck made her feel whatever sensations she'd felt last night when she'd been in my arms.

I knew it was probably wrong of me to say those things when I'd agreed to just be her friend and when I really wasn't supposed to be flirting with anyone right now...but part of me just wanted her to admit that it had felt as good to her as it had to me.

That it wasn't just an "unfortunate mistake."

She breathed in slowly, like she needed to take time to say her next words just right. Then, leaning close with her voice just above a whisper, she said, "So maybe you're a good kisser." Her gaze fell to my lips, and I found myself licking them as if anticipating another kiss. "I'm sure any girl would have reacted the same way that I did." She lifted her gaze to mine. "Especially if she thought it was the guy she liked kissing her back like that."

*Well, that was sort of a compliment.*

She'd said I was a good kisser, at least.

I hadn't had anyone tell me that in a while. Hadn't kissed anyone like that in a long time.

Even my kisses with Bailee had never made me feel the way I felt when I kissed Elyse.

"I've been wondering something, though," she said. "Why did you kiss me back? The light was on my face, so you had to know it was me."

And suddenly, I was the one in the hot seat.

I looked away, not wanting to answer her question.

"Come on." She touched my arm. "I just told you a lot about myself and what I'm into when it comes to guys. It's only fair that you tell me why you kissed me back."

She had a point. She had told me some personal things. It was only fair that I reveal something about myself.

It wasn't like this would be the most revealing secret I had to tell.

I looked at her hand on my arm then lifted my gaze to meet hers, hoping she wouldn't know how much I craved the touch of another human. Then I swallowed and said, "I guess I thought you knew it was me, and I figured I might as well see how it felt to kiss someone new after so long."

"Oh." She removed her hand from my arm as if burned. "I didn't realize that was your first kiss since..." She drifted off like she didn't want to say the name of the ex I was supposed to be mourning.

"Yeah," I said, my voice huskier than usual. "It was the first time in a while."

"I guess I should probably say sorry then, huh?" she whispered, guilt reflected in her eyes. "I was only thinking about how it affected me and didn't even consider how it was for you."

"It's okay," I said, searching her eyes so she'd know I was sincere. "I could have stepped away if I didn't want it."

Her gaze darted back and forth, like she was wondering what I meant by my words. And then, I realized how it had sounded.

It sounded like I'd wanted that kiss in a way that was specific to her.

And while I hadn't necessarily been searching for it initially, I *had* wanted to kiss her in that moment—if only to see if I could still feel something for someone after being emotionally stunted for so long.

Turns out, I did still have those types of desires buried deep within me.

But since I didn't want her to worry that I had a secret crush on her or anything, I said, "What I mean is, I could have stepped away from the kiss if I wasn't up to it."

"Okay, good," she said slowly. "I just want to make sure I didn't stir up uncomfortable feelings."

I wanted to tell her that her worries over making me miss the relationship I'd had with Bailee were unnecessary, because it hadn't been the romantic connection she thought it was.

But I still needed to live by my lie, so I simply said, "I'm fine." And since I'd had enough vulnerability for one conversation, I added, "If anything, I'm just a little dumbfounded that you would only want to be friends with someone who's as good of a kisser as you say I am."

"Okay..." She chuckled and shook her head. "Now I really know you're going to be fine."

## ASHER

ELYSE and I kept the conversation lighthearted for the rest of lunch, which was nice. After we threw our paper plates and empty water bottles into the trash, Miss Crawley called everyone into the main living area to give us instructions for our next activity. We were supposed to pick a buddy and go on a scavenger hunt in the woods outside of the cabin.

We had two hours to get a photo of everything on the list, but the first people back would be the winners.

While Miss Crawley explained a few of the rules that I already knew from last year's scavenger hunt, I turned to Elyse and asked, "Wanna be my buddy?"

"Sure," she said with a shrug.

"Good choice," I said with a smile. "Because I'm the reigning scavenger hunt champion from last year and you'd hate to be pitted against me."

She laughed. "Good thing you asked me then, because I'm also an expert at scavenger hunting."

We took one of the printed scavenger hunt lists that Miss

Crawley had set on the coffee table, and then after grabbing our coats, scarves, and gloves, we headed outside.

"What's the first thing on the list?" I asked Elyse when we'd made it to the landing just outside of the cabin. The afternoon sun was high in the sky and reflecting off the snow in just the right way to make me wish I'd brought my sunglasses.

"It's a pinecone," she said, looking back at me with her eyes squinted against the sun. "But we don't have to go in order, right? Wouldn't it be faster to just keep our eyes open for everything?"

"Of course," I said. "I was just testing you to see if you really were a scavenger hunt expert."

"Sure you were." She gave me a knowing smile.

I scanned the area to decide which way I thought might give us the best results. "Wanna head that way?" I pointed to the woods west of the cabin, which was on a bit of a slope down from the cabin. We'd have to hike up a little on our way back, which is why it kept most people from going that way in previous years, but I'd had a lot of luck going that route with my partner last year so I figured it would probably produce similar results.

Elyse looked to where I was pointing. With a shrug of her shoulders, she said, "Sounds good to me."

And so we headed off down the hill in the direction of where the sun would be setting later tonight.

"ARE you sure this is the right way?" Elyse asked me.

It was a few hours after we'd started our scavenger hunt. Elyse and I had found the last item on our list over an hour ago, but it turned out that finding the cabin again was the hardest task of the day.

"I think so," I said. "I think I recognize that tree with the crooked trunk." I pointed to the tree about twenty feet away.

"I think you recognize it because we've already passed it three times," Elyse said, her voice showing signs of how tired she was.

Stomping around in the snow for three and a half hours was no joke.

"It has to be close," I said, knowing that giving up was not an option.

The sky had been sunny and blue, with just a few puffy white clouds when we'd started our afternoon adventure. But as the sun dipped lower in the sky, the clouds became darker and grayer and more like the kind you'd see right before a really big storm would hit.

The fact that the sun was also about to set was worrisome as well. I'd accidentally left my phone on my charger this morning and Elyse's phone was running low on battery life, so we'd only be able to use it as a flashlight for a short amount of time.

We'd already tried calling Miss Crawley, but the service was so spotty out here that it was hard to send a call through from anywhere besides the cabin.

"What time is it, anyway?" Elyse put a hand on her side as she stopped to catch her breath. "It seems like they should have sent someone to look for us by now."

You'd think so.

But then again, that would just put other people at risk of getting caught in a possible blizzard.

I checked the time on my watch. "It's four ten."

We were only an hour and a half late getting back, so they'd probably hold off on calling search and rescue for at least a little while.

"Hasn't the sun been setting at like four-thirty recently?" Elyse asked.

I nodded, a foreboding feeling washing over me. "But I really do think the cabin is at the top of this hill."

As long as I pretended like I had a handle on things and that the cabin was just behind the next hill, then it might keep Elyse from panicking or giving up.

Elyse narrowed her gaze at the hill we were going to climb, and I worried for a moment that she might tell me that it was too high to be the right one. But she drew in a deep breath and said, "Okay. Hopefully, this is the one."

We trudged up the hill, but instead of being greeted with a big cabin, with lights and people visible from the windows, we found more trees and snow.

Elyse looked like she might cry.

*Please don't cry,* I pleaded in my head. I never knew what to do when someone was crying.

"It's probably just a little farther south," I said. "We walked along that stream for a long time. Let's just go that way for a little while and see what we find."

"Okay," she said, quietly wiping at her eyes that glistened with tears. "L-let's go."

Her voice trembled, as if she was doing all she could to keep from sobbing. I wasn't sure if she was the type of person who liked to be hugged or left alone while she cried, so I just took her arm and looped it through mine.

"Let's just try going this way for a few minutes. If we don't see it before the sun goes down, then we can stop and make a game plan for what to do next."

"Okay." She nodded but didn't say anything else. And so we trekked through the trees toward a place where I hoped we'd find the cabin.

"IS THAT IT?" Elyse asked after a while. "That looks like it might be part of the roof. It was red, right?"

I looked at where she was pointing, and my heart did a little thud in my chest because it really did look like it could be the cabin's roof.

"I think it might be," I said.

We walked a little faster, and the closer we got to the patch of red in the distance, the more it started to resemble the features of a cabin.

I wasn't sure if it was Miss Crawley's family cabin, but at least it was something. Some form of shelter where we could stay in for the night.

We walked another twenty yards or so, and the trees finally cleared to reveal that it was indeed the right cabin.

"We found it!" Elyse said, relief filling her voice as she took in the two-story cabin with huge windows and a wrap-around porch. "We found the cabin."

And with a sudden burst of adrenaline, we both ran the rest of the way. We hurried up the porch steps, barely stomping the snow from our boots, and then I turned the door handle.

It was locked.

I frowned. That was weird.

I knocked on the door for someone to let us in, but no one answered. After waiting for a while, I turned to Elyse and asked, "Do you think this is the wrong cabin?"

We searched around the area until I realized the bus wasn't here. There were dozens of footprints in the snow that led from the cabin to the driveway. And yep, on the driveway were fresh tire tracks.

"Did they leave us?" Elyse asked, seeming to be on the same wavelength as me.

"I hope not." I jiggled the doorknob again then gestured for her to follow me. "Let's check the other doors."

We checked the back door and the one on the other side of the house, but they were both locked.

"Is there a door in the basement?" Elyse asked, shivering. We each wore our warm coats, gloves and boots, but the sun was basically gone from the sky now and the cold was setting in fast.

"I think I saw one down there last night."

We hurried back down the porch steps and around the side where there was a garage. And sure enough, next to the garage was another door.

But it was also locked.

"There has to be a spare key here somewhere, right?" Elyse asked, looking around. "People with cabins always leave one close by in case they forget theirs."

"Probably," I said, liking the idea of something helping us to get inside that wouldn't involve me having to break a window.

"How about you check here, and I'll go look at the back door," Elyse suggested.

"Sounds good."

While she walked away, I started rooting around for anywhere that might look like a good place to hide a key.

I was just about to dig through a pile of wood when Elyse's voice yelled, "Found it!"

By the time I made it to the back door, Elyse was already inside and turning on the lights.

The cabin was a mess. Looking like there had been a big rush to get out of there.

I didn't understand why they would leave when we were scheduled to be here until tomorrow morning, but they must have had some reason to go.

And quickly.

"Why do you think they left?" Elyse asked, stepping up beside me and taking in the empty cabin.

"I don't know," I said. "Should we see if our things are still here?"

"Yeah."

While Elyse headed upstairs to the loft where all the girls had slept last night, I went to the basement. Even though part of me had expected to find suitcases and duffel bags—like they'd just gone on a scenic drive or were out scouring the roads for us, there was nothing besides a bunch of rumpled bedding on the beds and my duffle bag in the back corner of the room where I'd left it this morning.

Where had they gone?

I grabbed my phone from where I'd left it on the charger this morning. When the screen lit up, there were about a dozen missed calls from Miss Crawley and my brother, in addition to several texts. I was just about to call Owen when my phone started ringing with Miss Crawley's name at the top of the phone screen.

*I guess I'll talk to her first.*

"Hello?"

"Oh, thank goodness you finally answered!" Miss Crawley's voice came through high-pitched and anxious. "Are you still at the cabin? Is Elyse with you?"

"Yeah," I said, starting to walk back up the stairs. "We just made it back from the scavenger hunt a minute ago. Where is everyone?"

"We left," she said. "We got an emergency notification that a blizzard was coming and that we were going to get snowed in. I don't know how we didn't realize you two weren't on the bus. I'm so sorry. It was chaos."

So, we'd been forgotten.

I mean, I understood them forgetting *me*, since that was kind of my M.O.

But they'd forgotten Elyse?

Miss Crawley continued, "Someone said they thought Elyse left with Cambrielle and Nash and—"

*And nobody even thought of me at all.*

"I'm so sorry, Asher," Miss Crawley said, sounding like she actually was. "I would drive there myself to come and get you two, but it's literally a whiteout right now and we can't see anything."

"It's okay," I said. I made it to the top of the stairs and almost bumped into Elyse who was just turning around the corner. "We're inside now and should be fine for the night."

"What's going on?" Elyse whispered, her eyebrows knitting together.

"They heard there was a blizzard coming and went back to Eden Falls," I whispered to her while our drama teacher went on about how there was food and blankets and lots of wood in the garage in case the furnace somehow went out.

"I mean, the furnace is new," Miss Crawley rambled on. "So it shouldn't go out. But just in case it does, do you know how to use a wood-burning stove?"

"I'm sure I can figure it out," I said just to get her to stop. "I can pull up a YouTube video if I need it."

"Okay." She sighed heavily, like she was only now taking a real breath. "I really am so sorry, Asher. I don't know how we didn't notice you weren't with us. I feel terrible and I hope you can forgive me."

"It's okay," I said. "I'm sure it was an honest mistake."

"It was, but that's still no excuse," she said. It sounded like she was going to hang up, but then at the last minute, she said, "Can you make sure to call your brother? I told him what happened, and he's been worried."

"Yeah, I'll call him."

"Okay, good," she said. "I'm hoping we can get some snow-mobiles up the road there tomorrow morning. But until then, just lock the doors and stay put. Don't try to go anywhere else."

"I won't."

Sometimes she acted like she was my mom. I was just the forgettable middle child today, apparently.

I heard what sounded like a sniffle through the phone and I immediately felt bad for thinking that. Because of all the other adults in my life, Miss Crawley was one of the few who actually cared about me.

She'd checked in on me all summer, and it was her who convinced me to come back to Eden Falls Academy, even though I hadn't wanted to.

It was an interesting dynamic since she was only my drama teacher. And yet, she cared more about me and my well-being than my own mother who hadn't tried calling me from prison in over a year.

After reassuring Miss Crawley that Elyse and I would be okay for a night or two in the cabin, we finally hung up.

## 17

## ELYSE

"SO, WHAT EXACTLY IS GOING ON?" I asked Asher when he hung up with Miss Crawley. "Did you say they left because of a blizzard warning?"

A blizzard that was apparently going to be so bad, they left here in such a rush and didn't even notice we were missing from the group.

How had Miss Crawley not done a head count?

"Yeah," he said, moving to look out the windows. "It must have started in town because it's only barely starting to snow here, and she said it was whiteout conditions there."

I stepped up beside him to look out the window. The storm clouds that had been taunting us over the past hour as we'd searched for the cabin had finally broken, and a soft flurry of snow was drifting to the ground.

I hadn't experienced winter in Connecticut yet—aside from the small amount of snow we'd received the night of my date with Nash—but I imagined it was similar to winter in Ridgewater.

Harsh and cold and long.

"Do you know when they realized we weren't with them?" I glanced up at Asher, trying not to feel hurt over being forgotten. "Was it not until just barely when she called?"

Because if they were already back in town, they had to have left about an hour ago.

"I didn't ask. But I had a bunch of texts and missed calls when I picked up my phone." He looked sideways at me. "I think they noticed you were missing first, since she mentioned there was confusion about you possibly heading back to town with Cambrielle and Nash earlier."

"I guess that makes sense," I said, feeling slightly better that they hadn't completely forgotten about me. I had stowed my suitcase under the bed Cambrielle and I had slept on last night, so it wouldn't have been visible if they'd done a quick sweep of the cabin.

"I'm not sure when they realized I was missing, though." He shrugged, his broad shoulders gently rubbing against mine with the movement. "Might not have been until everyone was back and Hunter pointed out that he was roommate-less."

Asher's jaw flexed, and I guessed that being forgotten was something he was taking personally.

Which I got. I was hurt myself.

"Either way," he said, stepping back from the window to head toward the leather couches. "You and I are stuck here for at least tonight."

And that was when it actually hit me. I was stranded in the cabin with Asher.

With a guy I was just barely getting to know and become friends with...who had also been under police investigation a few months ago.

A spine-chilling feeling wrapped around me.

Was I going to be snowed in with a murderer?

I looked over to where he was now texting someone from his phone. He seemed calm. Relaxed.

Was he too relaxed?

*It's cool. Stay cool.*

*He's not a wacko bad guy. He's normal. Fun. Just like every other guy at school. And he only made a couple of jokes about what serial killers do.*

Just because someone joked about something didn't mean they'd actually do the thing...

He was still texting on his phone. Who was he texting?

An accomplice?

Someone with the hookups to hide a body?

*Why did I agree to be his partner for the scavenger hunt?*

Had he somehow known this would happen and had planned all this in order to get me alone so I could be his next victim? Had he made a deal with someone else to tell Miss Crawley that I'd left with Nash and Cambrielle?

Why had I binge-watched a series about a serial killer last week? I was never going to sleep now.

Wasn't there an episode where Joe went to some cabin, or house in the country, and killed someone while he was there? Had Asher watched the show and taken notes?

Asher must have sensed the sudden shift in my mood because he looked up from his phone and asked, "Is something wrong?"

"Um, no," I said, tucking some hair behind my ear. "Everything is fine—great. Everything is great."

Why did I have to sound like I was scared? Didn't killers thrive off the fear of their victims?

Asher narrowed his dark-brown eyes, like he didn't believe me. And if he had a slight gap in between his two front teeth, he would have looked surprisingly similar to Penn Badgley.

They both had the dark wavy hair. The brown eyes. The self-deprecating humor.

*Was Asher obsessed with rare books, too? Did he like to wear a blue ball cap when he went outside?*

I didn't know how tall Penn was—probably not as tall as Asher, since Asher was in the six-foot-two or three range.

And he was also quite a bit more muscular.

Those things would come in handy if he needed to carry a dead body into the woods.

"Are you worried about being stuck here for a long time?" he asked. "Because Miss Crawley said she'd try to get a couple of snowmobiles out here tomorrow. And that there was plenty of food left up here for us to eat."

"They'll be here in the morning?" I asked, grasping onto that piece of information like it was a lifeline.

"She's going to try."

*And you're not going to try to kill me before then?*

"Well, that's good," I said, trying to sound as calm as I could manage. "One night up here shouldn't be so bad."

Plus, Miss Crawley knew I was here. Asher wouldn't do anything tonight if he knew everyone would suspect him.

Unless he pretended like I'd gotten lost in the woods during the scavenger hunt.

Maybe I should FaceTime Ava just so she'd have official proof that I was currently alive and alone with Asher.

"Yeah, we'll have the whole place to ourselves." Asher stretched one arm along the back of the couch. "Plenty of time to practice that kissing scene we'll have together."

"What?" I pulled my head back, completely caught off guard by his statement.

Had I missed something?

He set his phone on the cushion beside him. "The kiss

during 'All I Ask of You.'" He narrowed his gaze. "You did know about that kiss, right?"

"I, um..." I scratched the back of my neck. "I guess I hadn't thought about it yet."

*Somehow.*

I'd been so focused on wanting to kiss Nash before we kissed on stage that I'd completely forgotten all about the other guy I'd be kissing for the musical.

A kiss that was supposed to be pretty passionate—more passionate than the one between Christine and The Phantom, anyway.

"Well, it's all I've been thinking about since our kiss last night." He winked.

Okay, so now we were back to flirty Asher.

Which I guess was fine. Definitely better than the serial killer version of Asher that I'd been imagining.

But since I was too on edge to banter back right now, I just said, "I think we might wait to practice that one during rehearsal." I felt around my back pocket for my phone, only to remember that I'd left it upstairs on the charger. "Hey, I'm actually going to call Ava really quick just to let her know where I am."

"Okay," he said, not seeming to notice how weird I was being. "I'll start digging through the fridge to see what our options are for dinner."

---

I FINISHED my call with Ava and sent a quick text to my mom who was currently in London and probably already asleep for the night. Then, after giving myself a little pep talk, I headed back down to Asher.

Ava had reassured me that I would be fine. She'd even had

Carter get on the phone to reassure me as well since they were currently snowed in at his grandma's house together. Carter, who had known Asher for ten years, said that he was sure Asher had nothing to do with Bailee's disappearance and that the only thing I should worry about was the jealousy that Nash was sure to feel when he heard I was stuck in a cabin with his enemy. I felt a lot better.

I just needed to stay out of my head and try to relax. I was safe. I was warm. I had food.

I should be fine staying here for one night.

Down in the kitchen, I found Asher bent over, looking through the contents of the fridge. He stood up when he heard me. "Called your family to tell them you're alive?"

"Yep," I said. "So now I guess the only thing left to do is watch how high the snow gets tonight."

"That and eat," Asher said with a smile.

"Did you find anything good?" I asked, moving farther into the kitchen to take a look around.

"I found a bunch of ingredients that would make that stew Miss Simmons and her husband were bragging about making tonight," he said. "But since I've never made stew before and don't know if they left their recipe here, I was thinking of skipping over tonight's dinner and just have the breakfast burritos we were supposed to have tomorrow."

"Are those pretty easy to make?" I asked. I was taking a culinary arts class at school, but we hadn't made breakfast burritos yet.

"They're super simple," he said. "Especially since the bacon crumbles are already pre-cooked."

"Is there any salsa?" I took a few steps closer to look in the fridge. "I can't eat eggs unless they're drowned in salsa."

He rooted around the various condiments in the fridge door and pulled out a jar of red salsa. "Right here."

"Great. Breakfast burritos for dinner, it is." I took the salsa from him and set it on the counter while he grabbed a carton of eggs.

While he cracked the eggs in a bowl, I went and got the shredded cheese, bacon crumbles, and the Ziplock bag full of pre-chopped green peppers.

"Do you like your eggs cheesy and scrambled?" I asked, showing him the huge bag of shredded cheese that Miss Crawley had brought.

He looked over his shoulder at me as he tossed an eggshell into the garbage can. "The cheesier, the better."

"Great! That's how I like them, too." I set everything on the counter next to where he was working and went to find a skillet.

"Do you want me to mix these in right now, or do you want to add them separately?" Asher gestured at the ingredients as I turned on the stove to warm the skillet.

"Mixed in is my preference, if you're okay with that." Growing up, I'd never been a fan of eggs, but I had recently learned that if I could cover up the egg taste with all the extras, I could stomach them.

"Fine by me." A minute later, he poured the egg mixture into the prepared skillet.

With a wooden spoon, I started stirring the eggs. I was much calmer now than I'd been before my chat with Ava and Carter.

So far, Asher was acting as normal as ever. And we were even working to create a yummy meal together.

Since we didn't have to chop any of the ingredients up, I didn't witness him holding a sharp knife or anything. But none of my alarm bells were going off anymore, and the energy around him was laidback and calm.

I had always been pretty in-tune with other people's energy—

my mom had always called me her little empath. And now that I'd calmed some of my own anxiety, I was able to see that what I'd felt earlier had come purely from my own thoughts on things I'd been told and not from anything I'd actually experienced with Asher.

I was pretty embarrassed that I'd been so scared before, because if he'd really wished me harm, he could have just left me out in the snow this afternoon instead of being patient and encouraging when I was on the edge of giving up.

"So...I know we've talked all about your crush on Nash, and your amazing talent for the theater," Asher broke into my thoughts as he leaned against the counter beside the stove. "But I've been wondering something else ever since I met you."

"You have?" I looked up, curious about what he would want to know. I didn't think I was that interesting.

Hopefully, this wasn't another segue into how we had a kissing scene coming up—Asher had been all too happy to talk about that particular subject ever since my big mistake last night.

But instead of bringing that up, he said, "I've been curious about why you and Ava decided to come to Eden Falls for your senior year. Was it so you could be closer to Brendon and Mack? That first night we talked, you said that you only found out about each other recently."

Oh, so he wanted the family gossip. This was a slightly better topic than I'd anticipated. Though, I was pretty surprised that someone hadn't already filled him in on everything.

"You didn't ask Hunter to tell you all the details?" I scooped some of the eggs around so they wouldn't get stuck to the pan. "You guys are roommates, right?"

"Sure, we board together." He shrugged his broad shoulders, and I couldn't help but notice how nice his fitted black T-shirt looked on him. He definitely had nice forearms that were usually hidden under his school uniform.

I looked away before he could notice me admiring him.

He continued, "But as someone who's had his fair share of chatter circling him, I try to get my information from the source."

*Interesting.*

"You really don't know anything about Ava and me?" I asked.

"Nothing aside from what you've already told me," he said. "I know that your mom raised you and Ava on her own. That you weren't well off financially until this year. And that you didn't know who your dad was growing up."

"Huh." I leaned back on my heel as I stirred. "I'm actually really surprised that you haven't heard anything."

"I'm not exactly everyone's best friend at school," he said, his voice lowering. "You and Hunter are pretty much the only people who will really talk to me. Well, aside from Owen and Miss Crawley." He rubbed a spot on the counter, as if embarrassed by what he'd just admitted. When he looked back at me, his cheeks were ruddy. "But who wants to brag about teachers being their closest friends?"

I didn't know what it was about him, but my heart squeezed in my chest at the vulnerability in his voice.

How would it be to be Asher Park? To go from sitting at the cool table in the great hall where he was adored by everyone, to suddenly being the school outcast—the pariah that no one wanted to touch with a ten-foot pole?

To have people actually *fear* you.

From what I'd picked up from little whisperings here and there, Asher and Bailee had been *the* power couple of the school last year. They'd been Prom King and Queen. Both had the leading roles in *Les Misérables* last year—Bailee had played Jean Valjean's adopted daughter Cosette.

Bailee had been the queen bee, with all the freshmen and sophomore girls hoping to be her royal subjects. She'd ruled the social scene at the school, and Asher had been made popular by affiliation.

She'd taken him from loner boy to the hot, unobtainable guy that all the girls secretly wanted to date.

It had to be crazy to go from a beloved fellow student to the guy everyone was afraid of.

And the fact that his parents weren't even in the picture to help him out when all the chaos ensued—that he only had his barely-out-of-college older brother to lean on before his aunt and uncle swooped in...

It had to have been a nightmare.

I didn't know how he'd been strong enough to come back to Eden Falls Academy, knowing what kind of a welcome he'd be receiving.

If I'd gone through what he had, I probably would have just stayed at the Carmichael's big house on the hill and written off this place as a really bad memory.

Since I already knew about the skeletons he probably wanted locked in a closet, I found myself saying, "Ava and I actually didn't know who Brendon and Mack were until after we came to Eden Falls."

"Did your mom introduce you?" Asher asked. "Or did it come out some other way?"

"My mom didn't breathe a word about it." I sighed, remembering how little my mom had shared about our father while we were growing up. "She just enrolled us here because she'd gone to the academy when she was our age. She thought it would be a good place for us to live since her job started taking her out of town a lot."

She somehow hadn't considered how quickly the truth would come out.

I told him about how Ava and I had come across some photos of our mom and Nash's dad in the yearbook and how that had made me curious about their connection. How I'd thought for a little while that Mr. Hastings could be our dad since he and my mom had been very close, according to one of our teachers who had gone to school with them.

"My mom never really talked about her time at this school, so Ava and I had always assumed it just hadn't been very memorable." I grabbed the salt and pepper shakers and seasoned the eggs. "But then, we found out the real reason she didn't want to talk about it was because of some difficult memories and a huge secret she didn't want to get out." I put the salt and pepper back on the counter and looked at Asher through my lashes. "I guess she and Brendon dated before she dated Mr. Hastings back in high school, and though they'd only been friends after high school, when they met up again at their five-year reunion..." I drifted off, not wanting to say the words out loud.

"They slept together," Asher filled in for me. Apparently, he was not as shy about that subject as I was.

My cheeks heated. "Yeah."

"But Mack is older than you, right?" Asher said, putting the details together quickly.

I nodded. "By a couple of months."

"So he cheated on Mack's mom?" He frowned. "He always seemed like such a family man."

"They were broken up during that time," I hurried to say before Asher could get too bad of an impression of Brendon, or my mom for that matter. "He didn't know Mack's mom was pregnant, either." The eggs looked like they were done, so I switched off the stove and moved them to a different burner.

"Apparently, they were both drunk and on the rebound, and the spark they'd always had in high school just made for a really perfect tornado and—"

"And a little while later your mom found out she was expecting twins," Asher finished for me.

"Yeah."

"But she didn't tell your dad?"

"She did," I said. My mom definitely hadn't set out to raise twin girls by herself. "But he'd gotten back with Mack's mom by that point and found out she was expecting Mack at the same time she had her first brain tumor. He had a mental breakdown from all the stress of everything."

"Three babies at once would do that to you, I guess." Asher handed me a paper plate with a flour tortilla. "I heard he was also drafted to the NBA, or something like that?"

"Yeah, it was insane. He ended up in a mental hospital for a few days because everything was just too much for him to see a way through." I scooped some of the scrambled eggs onto my tortilla to make it into a breakfast burrito. "So when my mom found that out, she made the split-second decision to tell him that she miscarried."

"Really?" Asher's brown eyes widened. "And Mr. Aarden just believed her?"

I shrugged. "He feels really bad about it now. But at the time, it was just one less thing for him to worry about, and so I guess he didn't question it."

"And your mom never talked to him again?"

I set the wooden spoon back in the skillet. "Not until a month and a half ago when everything came out in the open."

"Wow."

"Yeah." I nodded and stepped away from the stove so he could fill up his tortillas. Yes, he was making two breakfast burritos for himself since apparently, it took a lot of food to fuel the kind of muscles that he had.

*Why did I just think that?*

I pushed the random thought away and tried not to watch the veins in his arm as he picked up the spoon.

"So, he'd just found out about his seventeen-year-old twin daughters, and then his wife died a month later?" He looked over at me as he dished his food up.

"Yep," I said, feeling so bad for Brendon.

"Talk about everything happening all at once for the guy." Asher plopped a big glob of the egg mixture onto his first tortilla.

"Yeah." I lifted a shoulder. "The Universe seems to think that's how it needs to be for him."

"The Universe is fun like that."

He said it like he had personal experience with the Universe's games.

I wanted to ask if he was referencing what Cambrielle had told me about his dad dying in a car accident at the same time his brother got custody of him, but before I could, he asked, "Are you guys close now?" Asher brought his plate back to the counter and started rolling up his burritos. "I mean, you're still in the dorms, so it sounds like you're taking things slow?"

"He invited Ava and me to move in with him and Mack after winter break..." I said, biting my lip.

"But you're not sure you want to," Asher guessed, probably from the hesitant look on my face.

I thought about it for a second, trying to get a good gauge on my feelings. Then with a sigh, I said, "It's just a lot so soon." I grabbed the salsa, deciding to add some to my plate to dip my burrito in. "We just met a few weeks ago. And he and Mack are dealing with their own grief right now." I looked back at Asher. "It's just kind of fast for me."

I liked to take things slow. Dip my toes in the water before I jumped in. Try things out before I fully committed to them.

Which was the opposite of how Ava did things. She preferred running at things full speed, and then thinking about them later.

Which was why she was all gung-ho about moving in and I was the one holding us back.

"Do you not get along with him?" Asher took the salsa from me, his fingers gently grazing against mine in the exchange and warming my skin.

"No, he's great," I said, tucking my fingers into the pocket of my jeans. "Really great. I guess I just...I'm not sure."

"It will make you next-door neighbors with Nash, though," Asher said with a teasing glint in his eyes. "Have you considered that?"

"That's actually one of the first things Ava pointed out to me when we started talking about it, if you can imagine." I chuckled. "You know, since she's all for living next door to Carter."

"Sounds about right from what I know about your sister." Asher grinned.

"Yeah, so it's basically a no-brainer for Ava."

"Naturally," Asher said. "Though, as someone who lived just down the street from them for a long time, I will say that it *is* possible to see too much of Nash."

"Because you two can barely stand to be in the same room for more than a few minutes at a time." I laughed, knowing I should have expected him to say something like that.

He shrugged and started carrying his plate to the other side of the counter. "I'm just saying that you'd probably prefer staying at the school. If only to have more opportunities to hang out in the common room with me."

"Since we're best buddies now, huh?" I raised an eyebrow.

He lifted a shoulder. "I mean, you have spent the last six hours with me and don't seem to be too sick of me yet." He pulled out a stool and sat on it.

Had I been scared to death about staying here with him half an hour ago? Definitely.

But now that I was out of panic mode, I had to admit that he was right. I wasn't sick of him. I wasn't in a hurry to chow down on my dinner and disappear into a faraway corner of the cabin.

As an introvert who usually needed time alone to recharge, it was kind of amazing that I was still having as good of a time with him tonight as I was.

"I guess I better tell Brendon that I can't move in with him because I have a new best bud who I'm in a musical with, and who I have several classes with, but also need to spend every other free moment of time with as well."

"Sounds like a good plan to me." He winked, and I didn't think he'd been trying to flirt with me right then, but my stomach did a little swoop anyway.

Which was dumb because I didn't even like Asher in that way. Sure he was super cute—okay, *drop dead gorgeous* was probably a better description—especially right now in his fitted black shirt that showed off how toned his upper body was. And his hair was tousled in just the way I liked after being in a beanie all afternoon.

But just because you thought someone was crazy hot didn't mean the attraction went any deeper than that.

It was more that my stomach was having weird reactions because I hadn't eaten anything since lunch and trekking around in the snow for three hours burned a ton of calories.

I definitely wasn't getting a crush on this beautiful, brown-haired, brown-eyed boy in front of me. And I definitely wasn't going to even think for a second about how much I'd enjoyed kissing him for those few stupid minutes last night.

I blinked my eyes shut and shook my head.

*What's happening to me?*

I was not supposed to be thinking any of these thoughts right now.

Hadn't I just been terrified of him a little while ago?

I picked up my burrito and dipped it in my salsa. Maybe getting some food in my system would help my brain function a little better.

We ate in silence for a little while. Him sitting on the stool. Me standing at the end of the counter. Usually, long silences made me feel uncomfortable, making me feel like I needed to think of something to say. But with Asher, it was fine. Nice, even. We could talk. We could be quiet. There was no pressure to really *do* anything with Asher.

Which was different from how things were with Nash. We got along well enough, but I was never this relaxed with him...

"Do you want something to drink?" Asher asked. He stood and started walking toward the cupboard where the plastic cups had been stored.

I swallowed the bite I'd just taken. "Sure." I cleared my throat. "I could use some water."

He filled two red cups with water from the fridge and set one in front of me before taking his seat again. As he started on his second burrito, I realized that I still didn't really know a whole lot about him.

"So, you said you grew up down the street from the Hastings?" I asked.

"Yeah." He grabbed a red napkin from a stack nearby and wiped his mouth.

"But since you board at the school, I'm guessing your mom moved away?"

"Um, kind of..."

"Kind of?" What did that mean?

"It's just, well..." An uncomfortable look crossed his face, like he didn't really want to talk about it. Then meeting my eyes, he said, "My family doesn't exactly have the kind of story that you can brag about."

"Yeah?" I asked, having no idea what he meant.

I'd already told him about the skeletons in my family's closet. I knew everyone had a few.

"We're not like the Hastings, or the Aardens." He shrugged and looked down at his plate. Then he rubbed his neck and said, "There's a reason why I had to go live with my aunt and uncle instead of living with my mom."

"There is?" I held my breath as I waited for him to continue.

"Yeah." He crumpled his napkin in his hand, taking his time, as if trying to decide if he was going to continue. He released a heavy sigh. "Did you know that my brother Owen actually has custody over me?"

"I had heard that..." Cambrielle had said something about his dad passing away and that something happened with his mom.

"Yeah. He, uh—" He tossed the napkin back on the counter. "—he got custody over me my freshman year after some stuff went down with my mom."

"Yeah?" I asked, not sure what else I should say.

"Yeah, so my dad and—"

My phone started ringing upstairs.

"Is that your phone?" Asher asked, looking somewhat relieved he'd been interrupted as his gaze went to the loft above us.

"It sounds like it," I said. "I left it up there to charge. It might be my mom calling from London."

It wasn't her specific ringtone—just the general one I had for my regular contacts and unfamiliar numbers—but she could have called me from the hotel phone.

"You should probably get it then." He gestured for me to go.

"You think so?" I asked, not really wanting to leave.

"Of course. I'm sure she's worried about you."

"Yeah, probably..." Though I really wanted to hear what he'd been about to tell me about his family, I hurried up the stairs to answer the call.

But when I picked up my phone, it was Nash's face on the screen. He'd probably heard from Ava that I was stuck at the cabin.

I considered sending his call to voicemail and just calling him later, so that I could get back to Asher's story. But I figured it would probably only take a minute.

"Hello?"

"Hey," Nash said, sounding somewhat anxious. "Ava just told me that you got left in the cabin with Asher, and I just wanted to see how you're doing."

"Oh." I took a seat on the edge of my bed. Then I lowered my voice to a level that Asher hopefully wouldn't hear from down below. "I'm doing good. We were lost in the woods for a while, so I was confused about what was going on at first. But I'm feeling a lot better now."

"That's good," he said with a sigh. "I can't believe they left you up there."

"I guess they thought I went back to Eden Falls with you guys for some reason."

I didn't know how that thought had come to be, since I didn't know their great-grandma and I wasn't Nash's girlfriend or anything official like Ava was to Carter...but apparently, I was tied to their hip enough that it had seemed believable.

"If I wasn't snowed in at my grandma's house right now, I'd totally try to save you from a night alone with Asher."

"I'm sure you would," I said, hoping that Asher couldn't somehow overhear us and know what Nash had just said.

"He hasn't done anything to make you uncomfortable, right?" Nash asked, like he really thought it was a possibility. "Because just say the word, and I'll ask one of our staff to drive a snowmobile up there to get you."

"No, it's been fine," I hurried to say before he could think anything was wrong. "You don't need to do anything like that. I don't want anyone else put in danger when I'm perfectly safe staying here."

"Are you sure?" Nash asked. "Because I know how creepy Asher can be. Bailee told me stories."

She did?

"What kind of stories?" I asked, my pulse suddenly pounding in my temples.

"Just how he was so obsessed with her," Nash said. "I know a lot of people thought they were *couple goals* and everything, but from what Bailee told me, it sounded like she wasn't as serious about him as it seemed."

"Really?" I asked. "Are you sure?"

"Yeah," Nash said. "I always kind of wondered if they were fighting that night because he was super controlling or something."

They had a fight the night Bailee disappeared?

I looked around the loft, suddenly afraid that Asher was going to come upstairs any moment and hear what Nash was telling me. I quickly dashed to the bathroom and shut the door for more privacy.

"Someone saw them fighting?" I whispered after locking the door.

"It was me. I actually saw the fight," he said. "I was grabbing some takeout from The Italian Amigos and saw them arguing in a booth."

"Did you overhear their conversation?" I asked, feeling that whatever he may have heard could be vital.

"I wasn't close enough to hear," he said. "But I could tell they were arguing about something. I'm pretty sure Bailee was crying. Which is why I told the police about it when she didn't show up at the school again."

Nash had told the police about it?

Was that why Asher had been under investigation? Because of something Nash had reported?

I mean, couples argued all the time, right? And even if they were breaking up, that didn't mean Asher hurt her.

I wanted to defend Asher, since what Nash was saying was purely speculation and I was pretty sure their ongoing feud could have clouded his judgement of the situation.

But since I wasn't there and hadn't seen what he'd seen, I just said, "Well, hopefully Bailee is all right. Hopefully, she's just, I don't know, hiding out somewhere and having a good laugh at everything."

"Hopefully." There was a beat of silence before Nash seemed to remember something and said, "Actually, I have something else that I wanted to ask you."

"You do?" I asked.

*Please don't give me another reason to be afraid of Asher.*

I was stuck in the cabin with him for the night and really didn't want to be on edge the whole time.

"Yes," Nash said. "I was actually hoping to ask you this when I got back to the cabin tonight but..."

Was he going to ask me to be his girlfriend?

Because, of course, my answer was yes.

He continued, "I got these really amazing tickets to *The Phantom of the Opera* on Broadway next Saturday, and I was wondering if you would want to go with me." He paused for a second before adding, "Like, on a date."

A date to my all-time favorite musical *on* Broadway? With the guy I had a huge crush on?

I didn't even need to think about that.

"I would love to go," I said. "I've always wanted to go to a Broadway show and that would be amazing."

"You would?" he asked, sounding relieved, as if he'd actually been uncertain of what my answer would be.

"Yes, of course."

"Awesome," he said. "We'll have our driver with us, too, since my parents don't want me to drive into New York by myself. But I promise it won't feel like he's there."

"I don't mind," I said.

"Awesome," Nash said, and I couldn't help but smile when I heard the excitement in his voice. "The plan is to leave here around three o'clock that afternoon so we can grab an early dinner first and then get to the theater."

"Perfect," I said. "I'm excited."

"Me too."

There was some chatter in the background that took Nash's attention away for a moment, like Cambrielle and Ava were making fun of Carter about something.

"Anyway," Nash said after their laughter died down. "I'm glad that you're doing okay at the cabin. But if anything happens that makes you want to get out of there, don't hesitate to let me know."

"I will," I said. "But I'm sure I'll be fine."

18
______

ELYSE

I PLUGGED my phone back into my charger after finishing my call. Nash and I had ended up talking a little longer until Cambrielle and Ava heard I was on the phone. They stole Nash's phone so we could talk about this debutante ball we were all planning to attend in New York over Christmas break. Apparently, my mom had finalized the designs for our gowns this morning.

Cambrielle and Ava told me that they had both already asked Mack and Carter to be their escorts for the ball and that Scarlett was going to ask Hunter tonight.

"Are you still planning to ask Nash?" Ava asked. "Because you know he's probably going to be expecting it now that everyone else is going together."

"I need to." I sighed as a swell of anxiety filled me. "I'm just trying to figure out how to do it."

I'd never asked a guy out before, and while I was pretty sure Nash would say yes—since he'd just asked me on a date a few minutes ago and he'd already be at the ball with his family —it was scary to put myself out there.

"Just don't wait too long," Ava said. "Guys like being chased too."

Ava then told me that Brendon had called to invite us to dinner and Yule-tree decorating with him and Mack the next evening. Before I knew it, an hour had ticked by.

I hoped Asher would still be waiting for me downstairs so we could finish the conversation we'd started about his family and the dynamics of it, but instead of finding him sitting at the counter where I'd left him, he was at the sink washing the last of the dishes.

"Hey," I said in as friendly of a tone as I could manage. "Sorry about that. I didn't expect them to want to talk for so long."

"Them?" he asked.

"Nash, Cambrielle, and Ava." When he looked confused, I explained, "It was Nash who called me. Not my mom like I'd thought."

"Oh." He went back to rinsing off the dirty skillet.

I watched him for a second as I finished the last few bites of my breakfast burrito, which had gone cold.

He seemed upset. Frustrated.

"Everything okay?" I took a sip of water. "Did I do something wrong?"

Had he somehow overheard my conversation with Nash and was mad about it?

Because even if Nash's talk of seeing Asher and Bailee fighting the night she'd disappeared had put me on edge for a moment, I was trying not to jump to conclusions.

Just because someone had an argument with someone didn't mean they wanted to make them disappear.

"No." He looked over his shoulder. "I'm just..." He sighed. "I'm just feeling a bit tired."

"Yeah?"

He turned off the water and set the skillet down on a towel to dry. "I think I'm just gonna head to bed."

"Really?" *So soon?*

I glanced at the clock on the wall. It was almost eight-thirty. Which was a time that some people went to bed, I'd guess, but it seemed a little too early to me.

He washed his hands and dried them on a towel. "It's been a long day, and I think all that walking around in the snow really tired me out."

"Okay," I said. "Th-that makes sense."

He switched off the light above the sink.

"Anyway, I'll see you in the morning." He looked back at me, and when our gazes met, I could tell his smile was forced. "Have a good night, Elyse."

"Thanks," I said, still so caught off guard by the unexpected shift of his mood.

Had I done something wrong?

Was he mad that I'd left my conversation with him to take that call from Nash? I had only gone upstairs because he'd told me to, and I had thought it might be my mom.

I wasn't trying to ignore him.

But then I remembered what he'd said about Hunter and me being the only people at school who talked to him. Had I just made him feel unseen by going upstairs for so long when he'd been about to tell me about his family?

Because I wasn't trying to make him feel that way. I still very much wanted to know about his past.

But when he turned his muscular back to me and headed down the stairs, I knew that I must have done something wrong.

I FINISHED MY COLD BURRITO, and because there wasn't anything else to do, I went around and made sure all of the doors and windows were locked. The snow had picked up speed since I'd last looked out the windows and there were already several inches of white powder clinging to the tree branches.

Hopefully, Miss Crawley would find a way up the mountain tomorrow, because if things continued to be as awkward between Asher and me as they'd been just before he headed to bed, it was going to be a long day.

I closed all the blinds since the thought of someone walking up to the cabin in the middle of the night and peeking in through the windows freaked me out. Then I turned off the lights on the main floor and hurried up to the loft to get ready for bed.

I changed in the bathroom and brushed my teeth, and then climbed into the bed that I'd shared with Cambrielle last night. As I turned off the lamp on the nightstand, I got the creepy feeling that someone was watching me.

I pulled the covers up to my chin. With my heart racing faster than a jackhammer, I turned onto my side as slowly and quietly as I could and tried to see through the darkness.

Had Asher come upstairs?

Or had someone been hiding in the cabin all along and was just coming out now that it was dark?

My heart pulsed faster, and heat flashed across my skin, but I tried to slow my breathing with hopes that it would help my heart calm down.

There was a creaking sound in the far wall, like the cabin was groaning against the storm outside and—

Was that a lumpy figure on the bed next to mine?

*Please don't kill me. Please don't kill me.*

I closed my eyes and held my breath, hoping that whatever

lay on the bed wouldn't care about me. Had the lump been there before I got in bed? Or had it somehow just appeared?

I waited for a long moment, but then, I had to know what was there. If someone was truly planning to kill me, they'd kill in the light just as much as they would in the dark. So I reached over and flicked on the lamp again.

And yep, the lump I'd been freaking out about was actually just a pile of pillows that the girls who'd slept there last night had left behind.

*Okay, so maybe I just have a really overactive imagination.*

But sleeping up here on the loft with no one else was so much scarier than it had been last night. I was so exposed. There wasn't a door up here to put a barrier between me or anything that might come inside the cabin. I could hear every little creak or tree branch that hit the cabin in the wind.

At least Asher could shut the door at the top of the stairs and hear it open as a warning that someone was coming.

There were those two bedrooms on the main floor that Miss Crawley and Mr. and Mrs. Simmons had used. Maybe I could sleep in one of those rooms.

It wasn't like they'd be needing them tonight.

Those doors probably even locked.

I quickly gathered my pillow that I'd brought with me, grabbed my phone and the charger, and rushed down the stairs.

I was just locking the door to Miss Crawley's room when there was a knock on the other side of the door.

I covered my mouth with my hand to stifle a scream.

*Who is it? Did someone follow me?*

I felt all the blood drain from my body and had to grip onto one of the posts of the four-poster bed.

The knock sounded again.

*I'm going to die!*

I looked around the small room, trying to figure out the best place to hide. The bed was high enough above the ground that I could probably crawl underneath it.

I was just bending down to slither under the bed when a deep voice called out, "Elyse, it's me."

*Asher?*

I stood up straight again and stepped closer to the door.

"Who is it?" I asked, just in case.

"It's me, Asher."

It sounded like it could be Asher, but you could never be too sure. "Tell me something that only you would know."

"Seriously?" There was a hint of annoyance in his tone. "I'm the only other person in the cabin."

That was still up for debate. I was hiding in this bedroom for a reason.

"Just tell me one thing," I said.

"Okay." I heard him sigh through the door. After a short pause, he said, "You were wearing vanilla-sugar-flavored lip gloss when you kissed me last night."

*What?*

"Now can you open the door?" he asked, seemingly unfazed by the fact that he'd just told me our kiss had registered enough in his mind for him to remember what kind of lip gloss I'd been wearing. "*Please.*"

I turned the lock on the doorknob and opened it. But instead of saying hi, or scolding him for scaring me, I asked, "Why did you choose that particular detail?"

He shrugged his broad shoulders as he stepped into the room. He was wearing a plain white T-shirt now and black-and-red plaid pajama bottoms. "I figured I was the only guy you kissed last night, so it seemed like something only I would know." He leaned his back against the wall and looked at me. "I was the only guy you kissed last night, right?"

"Of course you were!" I said indignantly.

"Sorry if I offended you." He held his hands up. "I was just trying to follow your instructions, and it really was the first thing I could think of that no one else would know."

"No, it's fine." I walked to the side of the bed where I'd dropped my pillow on the floor earlier, picking it up and setting it down at the head of the king-sized bed. "I'm just on edge right now. I thought you were coming to murder me."

His expression fell. "So you still believe those rumors about me?"

"No," I said, realizing that I'd just hurt his feelings. "I mean, I might have been worried for a little while when we first got stuck here, but since you haven't done anything yet, I'm telling myself that I'm safe."

"Nice to know you have so much faith in me," he said.

"Sorry." I sighed as I sat on the edge of the bed. "I just mistook a pillow for an intruder upstairs, so I'm not exactly functioning at my best."

"Well, if you want to give me a good pat-down to make sure I'm not hiding a butcher knife under my clothes, you have my permission." He held his hands above his head, like people did in the movies.

For a split second, I pictured myself running my hands along his chest and sides like I was doing a sexy pat-down, but then I came to my senses. "No, it's okay. I, um, I trust you."

"Okay, good." He lowered his hands, and my eyes lingered on the vein lines protruding from his forearms. All I could think of was how it was a shame he had to wear his long-sleeved school uniform so much because his arms were quite the works of art.

Seriously, Asher could have one of those social media accounts where all he had to do was stand and look into the camera with a sultry gaze, and he'd have millions of views and followers in a matter of hours.

He cleared his throat, and I realized I'd been staring at his arms for way longer than a normal person would.

"You done using your X-ray vision to see if I have any knives hiding beneath my shirt?" he asked.

"I wasn't looking for a knife."

"Oh, so you were just checking me out then." A cocky smirk lifted his lips.

My face burned instantly. "I wasn't checking you out."

"You don't think I know when someone is checking me out?" He arched an eyebrow. And of course, he would notice something like that. Hot guys thrived on their ability to turn heads and make people lose their train of thought.

"Anyway." I rolled my eyes. "Why did you knock on my door?"

"Oh, that." He rubbed his jawline with his fingers, as if suddenly embarrassed. "I just wanted to apologize for acting weird earlier." He moved his hand to rub the back of his head, and I hated that my eyes instantly went to his bicep as it flexed with the movement. "I kind of have this thing where I always assume people don't want to be around me, and so I got a little grouchy tonight when your call took so long."

"I wasn't trying to avoid you, if that's what you thought," I said.

In fact, it had been the opposite. If I hadn't thought it was my mom calling me, I never would have gone upstairs to get my phone—I had wanted to hear what he'd been about to say.

I was still interested in his story and wanted to ask him to tell me more, but sadly, that moment was gone.

Hopefully, I'd have another chance to ask him about it later.

"Well, I'm glad to hear that you weren't trying to avoid me." He let his hand drop back down to his side.

Since he really seemed to need to hear it, I said, "I really do like hanging out with you, Asher."

"You do?"

There was a vulnerability in his eyes that told me he wasn't sure he believed me. So I added, "I know we just met a little over a week ago, and I still don't really know a ton about you, but in a weird way, it kind of feels like I've known you for a really long time."

"Really?" He dipped his head down before looking at me through his dark lashes.

"Yeah." When our gazes locked, I felt breathless because gosh, he had the most beautiful eyes. They were dark brown with flecks of bright gold in the irises, and they seemed to hold secrets I very much wanted to know.

"It's interesting that you'd say that." His voice was so low and husky that it made my lower belly churn with heat. He pressed his lips together. "Because I've thought the same thing about you."

What was happening to me?

Why was I suddenly feeling like my whole body was buzzing with electricity?

Why did I feel so warm and alive, and yet, that I might faint at the same time?

What was it about this guy that had me lowering all of my walls and saying these things that I'd never say to anyone else?

We were both quiet for a moment as we just looked at each other. And usually, I would feel so uncomfortable being scrutinized because I was always worried that people would be disappointed when they saw the real me. But for some reason, I didn't feel any of that when Asher looked at me.

Instead, I felt safe and like I was at home.

Which was the strangest thing.

"Anyway," he said, breaking the silence that had fallen over us. "I guess I better get back downstairs."

"Do you have to?" I asked, another swell of nerves flooding me at the thought of sleeping alone in this unfamiliar place.

"Well, it's getting late, and you were heading to bed, weren't you?"

"Well, yeah..." I grabbed a lock of my hair and started mindlessly pulling it through my fingers. And since it was probably already obvious, I said, "I'm just a little on edge about sleeping alone tonight."

Growing up, Ava and I had always shared a bedroom. We'd always been together at night. And if there was the off chance that one of us was away at a school activity, we either had our mom nearby to make us feel safe or were sharing a room with a friend on a school trip like with Cambrielle last night.

I knew it was probably dumb for me to be so dependent on having another human close by when I was almost an adult, but since I hadn't ever needed to get used to sleeping on my own, I'd just never done it.

"What if someone sneaks into the cabin tonight and tries to kidnap me?" I whispered. "My mom is famous now. I could go for a high ransom."

"You think some wacko is going to come all the way up here in a blizzard to steal you away?" Asher narrowed his eyes skeptically.

"Maybe..."

"Well," he said, pushing away from the wall. "If you're worried about that, I guess you can come sleep in the basement with me. There's a bunch of extra beds. You could even sleep on the same bed Nash slept on last night." He wiggled his eyebrows teasingly. "Sleep on the same pillow. Breathe in his pheromones. Wouldn't that be fun?"

"This is serious," I said, realizing I never should have let him know about my crush on Nash since apparently, teasing me about it was one of his favorite pastimes. "And there isn't a lock on the basement door, so someone could still sneak down there."

He glanced behind him. "There's a lock on this door. So, if that's what you need, you should be set."

*You'd think so.*

I bit my lip, wanting to ask him something but not knowing how to say it.

He must be good at reading minds, though, because he said, "Are you trying to get up the nerve to ask me to stay up here with you? Is that why you were checking out my muscles earlier? Because you were hoping I could be your bodyguard for the night?"

"I wasn't trying to check out your muscles," I said. That part was accidental. "But yes." I tugged on my hair. "If you wouldn't mind, it would make me feel safer to have someone close by."

I mean, they did this kind of thing in the movies all the time. A guy and a girl who didn't know each other very well would get stranded somewhere together overnight. They would search and search for a place to sleep, only to find a run-down hotel to shelter in for the night.

They would request a room with two beds, of course, since they were basically strangers and most definitely didn't have romantic feelings for each other whatsoever. But when they got to their room—the very last room that the hotel had available— they would find that it only had one bed.

They'd stare awkwardly at the small bed for a moment, look at each other, then back at the bed, which would seem to get smaller and smaller the more that they stared at it.

And then the guy would graciously offer to sleep on the floor. Because even though there was an undercurrent of sparks flying between the two, deep down under his rough exterior, the guy was a gentleman. And offering to sleep on the floor was what gentlemen did.

Sure, we were in a cabin, and there were about fifteen other beds to choose from, but I figured the same rules would apply.

So while Asher shut the bedroom door and turned the lock as a safety precaution, I pulled the covers back on the left side of the bed and climbed in.

"That's the side you're taking?" Asher asked after turning around.

"Yes," I said with a frown, wondering why he was asking. "But you're sleeping on the floor, right?"

He scrunched up his nose. "Why would I want to sleep on the cold, hard floor when there's a perfectly good bed in front of me?"

"Well, because..." I started, trying to figure out how to say it.

"Because that's what they do in the movies?" He arched a dark eyebrow.

"Well, yes," I said, somewhat embarrassed since that was exactly what I'd been thinking about earlier.

He walked around to the other side of the bed and pulled the covers back. "Sorry to burst your bubble. But I'm not *that* much of a gentleman."

My eyes widened as he started to sit down like he was actually planning to share the bed with me.

"Are you really going to sleep in the same bed as me?" I gulped.

He swiveled to face me. "Unless you want me to go back downstairs."

"No!" I shrieked. I didn't want him to go back downstairs. "I, um, it's okay. Yeah, you can sleep in here, I guess."

I trusted him. Even if I'd waffled back and forth a lot on

whether I should feel safe around him, deep down I believed he was a good guy.

He simply wanted to be comfortable while he slept.

"Good." He climbed under the covers.

After hesitating for a second, I reached for the light switch on the wall beside the headboard, plunging the room in darkness.

We each shifted around in the dark to get comfortable. And I was ready to bolt if he tried to move onto my side of the bed. But even if he'd said he wasn't that much of a gentleman, he didn't move to cross the invisible barrier going down the center of the bed.

This would be fine.

We both would have enough space, and he would be close by if any danger came knocking on the door.

It was actually kind of nice in here. The room wasn't super big—it barely fit the king-sized bed, two nightstands, and a dresser—but it was a calming space. And the moonlight streaming through a break in the curtains was pretty. The sky was brighter tonight, thanks to the blanket of clouds hovering above us.

I lowered my hands from where they'd been crossed over my chest like a mummy and let them drop to my sides. Asher must have been moving at the same time, though, because as my left hand touched the mattress, my fingers accidentally brushed against his.

"Sorry!" I said at the same time Asher said, "Uh, my bad."

And we both yanked our hands away from the center of the bed.

He cleared his throat. "I take it this is your first time sharing a bed with a guy."

*Is it that obvious?* "Umm..."

There was an awkward pause before he hurried to say, "Sorry, I shouldn't have asked that."

"I-it's okay," I said. "And well, yeah, since I've never had a relationship get that serious so..."

"Got it," he said all too quickly, like he felt uncomfortable.

Did he feel awkward because he now knew that he was the first guy I'd ever shared a bed with?

But then he surprised me by saying, "If it makes you feel better, I've never shared a bed with a girl, either."

"Really?" I turned my head to the side to look at his dark form, not really believing him.

"Yep." He turned his whole body onto his side to face me. "So, um, you should feel pretty lucky that you're my first."

"You and Bailee didn't..." I stopped myself as soon as I realized how stupid it was to bring that up right now.

"No, um, we weren't like that."

They weren't like that?

What did that mean?

Then, almost as if a belated thought, he rushed to say, "I mean, the dorm parents are pretty good at keeping an eye on everything. Uh, we couldn't have even if we wanted to."

But his phrasing kind of sounded like they hadn't wanted to at all.

Was it possible they hadn't been as close as everyone said they were?

Had I romanticized their relationship a little more in my head since I hadn't known them back then?

"I heard you had a fight the night she disappeared," I said in a soft voice. "Was that a regular thing? Or just a bad night?"

Some couples thrived off the fighting. They loved the high emotions, the ups and the downs. Was that how he and Bailee had been?

"It was just a bad night." He propped his head up with his

arm. "We really did get along most of the time. Why do you ask?"

"I was just wondering," I said.

"Were you worried that was the reason she never showed up at the school again?" he asked in a gentle voice. "Because our argument got out of hand, and she got hurt?"

"No..." I swallowed and turned on my side the rest of the way to face him. "I mean, I don't want to think that. It's just interesting, the timing of it."

He let out a long sigh and rolled onto his back. He was quiet for a second, but then he asked, "Do you and your sister ever fight?"

"Yes." Of course we did. I was pretty sure all siblings fought.

He rolled back onto his side again to face me. "And have you ever wanted to take her out into the woods and murder her because of it?"

"No," I said, shocked by his bluntness.

He shrugged. "Bailee and I had a little argument. I was working my shift at The Italian Amigos when she came in and was on edge about something. So I took my break and we talked things over in one of the booths. She came there to talk about something I wasn't expecting, and then we both got upset and she left.

"I finished my shift, thinking that we would just continue the conversation back at the school, but when I texted her to meet me down in the common room, she never responded." He traced his finger along the sheet between us. "I went to bed when I got back, figuring she was already asleep, anyway. She'd been going to bed earlier than usual at that time and was always complaining that she needed more sleep. I really didn't think anything of it."

"And then you found out the next morning that she'd disappeared?" I finished for him.

"Yes." He stopped tracing his finger along the sheet. "She never made it home from the restaurant that night."

"So the last interaction you had with her was the fight?"

"Yeah." He rubbed the back of his neck. "It sucks, not only because that's the last memory I have with her but also because someone apparently saw our disagreement and decided to report it to the police."

That someone being Nash.

I could only imagine just how much worse the bad blood they had between each other would get if Asher knew that Nash was the reason he'd been under police investigation in the first place.

The reason why there was an invisible bubble around him everywhere he went at school because people were literally afraid of him.

Did I think what Nash did was wrong?

No, not exactly. Despite his feelings for Asher, I think he'd only reported it because he thought he was truly helping.

But it did suck for Asher.

His whole life had basically blown up at the same time that the girl he loved disappeared.

*Talk about traumatic.*

"Do you know who reported your argument?" I asked, curious if he'd seen Nash picking up his food that night.

"I never found that out," he said. "Someone from school is all I can guess."

"Well, I'm sorry you had to go through all of that," I said, truly meaning it. "It must have been so hard."

"It was." His gaze lifted to mine in the moonlight. "I just hope Bailee is okay, wherever she is."

And from the fondness in his voice, I could tell that he really must have loved her.

Was possibly still very much in love with her after all this time.

"Anyway," he said, rolling onto his back once again. "I should probably let you get some sleep. I'll try not to snore too much."

Which, I'd guess, was his way of signaling that the conversation was over.

So I maneuvered onto my back and said, "And I'll try not to say too many things in my sleep."

"Are you a sleep talker?" He sounded intrigued.

"Not really." I smiled. "Though, I bet you wish I was."

He chuckled. "I definitely wouldn't mind getting a little peek into what goes on in that lovely brain of yours."

I was glad that he couldn't. My brain was a really confusing place right now. Having lots of new strange thoughts about this intriguing boy beside me.

He rustled around again, this time turning on his side so his back was to me. After saying goodnight, it only took a couple of minutes for the rhythm of his breathing to change and convince me that he had fallen asleep.

I turned back on my side again, facing the center of the bed, and let my gaze run along the outline of his wavy hair in the darkness. He had great hair. So great that I kind of wished I'd taken the opportunity to slide my fingers through it last night when we'd kissed.

But then again, that probably would have tipped me off that it was him instead of Nash, and the kiss would have ended right away.

Which, though I'd never admit it to anyone, would have been a shame, since even though I shouldn't have, I had really enjoyed those few moments I'd been in his arms.

I might have thought he was someone else at the time, but that didn't change the fact that the kiss had been amazing—probably the best first kiss I'd ever had to be honest.

I let my gaze travel down Asher's neck and across his shoulders. He had the shoulders of an athlete—broad and toned. And the fabric of his shirt stretched tautly across his shoulder blades. It made me wonder if he was involved in any sports when he wasn't doing school musicals.

I looked at the rest of his sleeping form outlined by the comforter covering us both. And even though I should probably be freaking out that I was sleeping in the same bed as a guy as gorgeous as Asher was, I was surprisingly calm. He had such a soothing presence about him that I was really drawn to—you know, when he wasn't teasing me about the fact that I'd accidentally made out with him.

I watched his shoulders rise and fall, and it was kind of hypnotizing in a way—the steadiness of it.

I made my breathing match his, and soon my eyelids felt heavy. I drifted off to sleep.

## ELYSE

THE SOUND of a door closing jarred me awake.

When I opened my eyes, I was face to face with Asher.

He woke up a second later, and after looking at each other with surprised expressions, we both looked down and saw that we had somehow held each other's hands while we'd slept.

I quickly pulled my hand away at the same time that he said, "Sorry."

Then there was a knock on the door, and we heard the reason why we'd both woken up at the same time.

"Elyse? Asher? Are you in there?" Miss Crawley's voice sounded muffled on the other side of the door. "Owen—er, Mr. Park and I are here to pick you up."

*Crap!*

What should we do? Were we going to get in trouble for sleeping in the same bed?

Nothing happened of course, but from the way we'd both sunk into the middle of the bed, anyone who found us would assume we'd shared a bed in a non-platonic way.

Asher must have been better than I was at thinking fast

this early in the morning because he quickly grabbed a pillow and one of the blankets off the dresser and called, "We're in here."

He hurried and threw the pillow on the floor at the foot of the bed. And as he plopped himself down on the floor to lie down with the blanket like he'd been there all night, I whispered, "Oh, so you don't actually want to be a gentleman. You just want to *look* like you are one."

He made a face. But then he nodded toward the door, signaling that I should hurry up and open it and prove that no monkey business had been going on.

So I climbed out of the warm bed and padded toward the door. When I opened it, I found our drama teacher wearing a maroon parka with Asher's brother standing right behind her.

"Is Asher in there with you?" Miss Crawley stepped forward and peeked her head into the room suspiciously.

"Yeah, he's just there on the floor." I swung the door wider so she could see him. And right on cue, Asher made a show of stretching like he was just waking up and muttered something about how his back was sore from sleeping on the hard floor all night.

He was such a liar!

Our gazes caught briefly, and he shot me a wink when Miss Crawley and Mr. Park weren't looking.

Dang, this boy. He was trouble!

And yeah, he also looked super cute with his bedhead and rumpled T-shirt right now.

"Why were you sleeping on the floor, Asher?" Miss Crawley asked as he stood. "We have plenty of beds."

"Oh, that's my fault," I said, trying to keep my voice as non-guilty-sounding as possible. "I got scared last night. Asher was such a gentleman and offered to sleep on the floor, so I'd feel safe."

"Sounds like Asher." She beamed at him like he was the drama teacher's pet. "He's always been that way."

As Miss Crawley pulled me into her arms for a hug, I caught Mr. Park's face briefly, and his expression told me he wasn't quite buying our story but wasn't going to say anything because he found it entertaining that Miss Crawley was.

"I'm so sorry that we left you two up here." Miss Crawley squeezed me in a tight embrace. "I feel so bad that this happened." She stepped away and turned to Asher who was just hugging his brother. "I hope you two were okay and weren't too scared."

"We were fine," I said. Then, remembering I had a ruse to keep up, I added. "Once Asher offered to sleep on the floor, it actually wasn't so bad."

And it really hadn't been. Despite being scared for my life at a few points, it had overall been a positive experience.

Even if I was curious how Asher and I had ended up holding hands while we'd slept.

Man, things could get complicated if I started having feelings for him. I had a date with Nash next weekend. I couldn't start liking his rival at the same time I was trying to make something happen with him.

Was it even possible to like two guys at the same time?

"Well, I'm glad you both survived." Miss Crawley clapped her hands together, bringing my attention back to the present. "Now if you two can quickly pack your things, Owen and I have snowmobiles waiting outside to take you home."

---

MISS CRAWLEY HAD donuts and hot chocolate waiting at the truck that was parked on the recently plowed main road.

The treats were a "please forgive me for forgetting you" gesture.

And it was so sweet of her to do that.

It took us about an hour to make it back to the school, since we had to drive so slowly on the icy roads. I was glad to be back in the place I'd called home since September, and it was also kind of nice to see how many of our classmates were relieved to see Asher and me and hear how worried they'd been.

A few of the girls in our house even gave Asher a hug when we walked into the common room, which I could tell from the look on his face shocked him a little.

But he was sweet and hugged them back, and even told them he was happy to see them again when they told him how sad they'd been when they realized he wasn't with them.

I knew it was such a simple thing, but it was nice to see his countenance brighten more and more as each classmate gave him the warm welcome back that he should have received when he returned to the school a week and a half ago.

"So, how was it staying in the cabin all alone with Asher?" Ava asked when we made it up to our room a few minutes later. "I see you survived, at least."

"It was good," I said, chuckling. "I *might* have overreacted just a little when I FaceTimed you."

"So, do you have a major crush on him now?"

"What?" I asked, my voice going higher. "No, of course not."

"It's okay if you do." Ava sat on the foot of my bed next to where I'd set my suitcase down. "I mean, he's super hot, and I know you've always had a thing for guys like him."

*Why is she saying this?*

*Did I look weird when Asher and I walked into the common room together?*

I'd tried so hard to seem normal and not at all conflicted.

I pulled my dirty clothes out of my suitcase and threw them into the dirty laundry basket, hoping to seem unruffled. "Asher is good-looking," I said. "And I've liked guys like him in the past." I grabbed my pajamas and chucked them into the hamper. "But those guys never worked out for a reason." I paused for a second before adding, "Plus, I like Nash."

And I had a date with Nash next week.

A really *amazing* date, from what he'd told me of his plans.

"I know, I'm just teasing." Ava smirked. "Nash is great. And speaking of Nash...how did things go with him this weekend? Did you finally kiss him?"

"Well..." I started, not really sure how to explain.

"You did?" Ava sat up straighter.

"Um, well. How do I put this?" I scrunched up my nose. "I certainly *tried* to." I had tried to do the bold thing that she and Cambrielle had suggested I do.

"What do you mean you tried to?" Ava's eyebrows knitted together.

I sighed as I pulled my makeup bag from my suitcase. "Well, Cambrielle and I came up with this whole plan to get Nash and me alone on the deck on Friday night. So I went out there, and I saw him leaning against the wall. I couldn't really see his face, but I was pretty sure it was him, so I just went for it and kissed him."

"But it wasn't him?" Ava covered her mouth, her eyes growing wide with shock. "You kissed someone else?"

I nodded, feeling the guilt wash over me again. "And it wasn't like just a peck, either." I whispered, "I, like, went *all* in."

"You made out with someone?" Ava asked. "Who was it?"

"It was Asher." I covered my eyes, reliving the horror I'd felt when I realized I had kissed the wrong guy. "It was dark, and he was wearing a beanie, and I couldn't see his face."

"So you kissed Asher, and then got stuck spending the night with him?" Ava slapped her leg and laughed like I'd just told her the funniest story she'd ever heard. "That is amazing."

"It's not funny." I glared at her. "It's terrible."

Ava just kept on laughing. "I think this is my favorite story that you've ever told me."

I picked up my pillow and smacked her on the head with it to get her to shut up. But she just blocked it with her hands and tossed it to the other side of the room. She said, "I bet Asher was a good kisser." She wiggled her eyebrows. "I mean, you've noticed his lips, right?"

Had I noticed them?

Um, of course. I wasn't blind, and he had *really* nice lips. Somewhat pouty and a deeper pink that looked amazing against his light tan skin.

A memory of how they'd felt against mine flashed into my mind before I realized what Ava had said.

"Why were you looking at Asher's lips?" I asked, feeling somewhat territorial over them for some reason. "You already have a boyfriend."

"Just because I'm not *looking* doesn't mean I don't notice things."

"Well, I just hope Nash doesn't find out," I said. "He'd go nuts."

"Eh, he'd get over it." Ava waved the thought away like it would be nothing for Nash to find out that I'd kissed his mortal enemy. "Especially when he finds out it was a mistake meant for him."

"Maybe." I thought about it for a moment. Then I shook my head and said, "Just promise you won't tell Carter, okay? I already have Cambrielle sworn to secrecy, so I'd like to keep this just between us girls."

"And Asher, of course." Ava winked. "I bet he loved it."

Had he?

I'd had a hard time reading him. He was confusing in a way that I sometimes felt like I was getting whiplash.

One minute he was being all flirty and basically daring me to kiss him again. And then the next minute, he was talking about Bailee in a way that told me he had loved her so hard and might not get over her anytime soon.

But even with that confusion, he never said he'd hated our kiss.

I let my mind wander back to the kiss, and when the thought of him actually enjoying it fluttered across my mind, my stomach flipped.

I liked the idea of Asher liking our kiss and wanting to kiss me again.

I liked that thought way more than I should.

Ava's phone and mine dinged at the same time, bringing me out of my daydream. It was a text from Brendon.

Brendon: I'm about two minutes away from the school. See you soon.

"Looks like we better head downstairs," Ava said.

"Yeah," I agreed, slipping my phone into my back pocket.

I would just have to try to figure out later the mystery of how Asher really saw me. As for now, I would focus on decorating a Yule tree and having Sunday dinner with Brendon and Mack, and most definitely not think about the fact that I might have a crush on two guys I was in a musical with.

## 20

## ASHER

"IS THERE something going on between you and Elyse?" Miss Crawley pulled me to the side during our rehearsal on Friday afternoon. "Any tension that is making it hard to work together?"

Elyse and I had just finished running through the choreography for "All I Ask of You" for the fifth time this afternoon, and just like what had been happening all week, Elyse froze whenever we got to the part where Raoul and Christine were supposed to kiss on the rooftop.

There we'd be, singing all the right lyrics, hitting all the notes, and moving across the stage the way the choreographers had instructed us to. But then the music would crescendo, and as I would try to pull Elyse into my arms, a look of panic would suddenly fill her eyes. She'd get all anxious and freeze up, and before I could follow through with the kiss we were supposed to have, everything would go off the rails.

To anyone watching, they might assume she was simply nervous about kissing me for the first time...like she was a shy, seventeen-year-old girl about to have her first kiss on stage.

But I knew from personal experience that we had already put that initial kiss in the books and that she was in fact an excellent kisser and definitely had nothing to worry about in that arena. So I had to wonder if the reason for her sudden awkwardness was because her crush was watching our every move from behind the horse statue at the front corner of the stage.

"I don't think there's any weird tension between us," I told my drama teacher. "We get along well enough outside of rehearsal."

Sure, we'd been busy with classes and homework all week, so we hadn't hung out in the way we had at the cabin. But I assumed we were still friends. She hadn't told me otherwise, at least.

"Do you think Miss Cohen and Mr. Hastings' budding relationship is making it difficult for her to play the part with you?" Miss Crawley asked, of course knowing what was going on in the personal lives of her students.

"That might be a part of it." I sighed, glad she was the one to bring it up and not me. "As you know, Nash and I have, well…" I scratched my neck, not quite sure how to explain the dynamic between Nash and me. "Uh, I guess it's no mystery that we haven't always seen eye to eye."

"I was going to say that you two have always been great at pushing each other to be your best," Miss Crawley said with a sly smile. "But yes, your rivalry has never been a secret to me."

"Yeah." My cheeks warmed, and I was somewhat embarrassed by the childish nature of our feud. "Anyway, I think that Elyse might be uncomfortable fully getting into that particular scene with Nash watching us."

The Phantom was supposed to watch Christine and Raoul from behind the statue as they declared their love for each other. He stood behind a horse statue for most of the scene, and

Elyse's back was to him through the majority of the song, so I doubted she even saw his face.

But knowing her crush was right there watching us had to be intimidating—especially when they had a date coming up tomorrow.

An over-the-top, fancy dinner and Broadway musical date that I could never afford to take a girl to in a million years.

"I worried that might be what's happening." Miss Crawley sighed. "This is why I always discourage dating within the cast. It always makes things so messy."

"Yeah, I remember you telling Bailee and me last year that we better not let our relationship mess up the musical."

"And you two did a fabulous job," she said, patting my arm. "You were so good at keeping things professional. I don't think you even batted an eye during the romantic scenes between Cosette and Marius."

"The show must go on." I shrugged.

Sure, it had helped that we hadn't actually been in love with each other at the time—my feelings hadn't come until later. But who was I to pass up the chance to show how much more professional I was than Nash?

Miss Crawley was quiet for a second, like she just realized something. "I'm sorry you two didn't get the happy ending we hoped for."

"Me too," I replied. And since it was something I was expected to say, I added, "But hopefully, she'll be found soon and we can get our second chance."

My teacher gave me a gentle smile. "I hope that happens, too."

She looked at me with her big green eyes for another long moment, like she was feeling the pain I was supposed to be feeling anytime Bailee was brought up in a conversation. "Is it difficult for you to perform that romantic scene with Elyse as well? I didn't even think about how it might affect you when I gave you the part of Raoul."

"No, it's fine." I cleared my throat. I definitely didn't have any hang-ups in playing the lead's love interest. "In fact, I think it's good. I need to be able to do things like that again. Even if it's only acting at this point."

Mostly acting, anyway.

The weird bundle of nerves I got in the pit of my stomach each time I held Elyse in my arms was not something anyone needed to know about.

That was my own little problem to figure out.

"Okay, good." She looked over my shoulder to where Elyse and Nash were currently rehearsing "The Music of the Night." Then her face brightened, as if an idea had sparked in her brain.

"Do you think it would help if you two practiced that scene on your own?" she asked. "Perhaps arrange a time to get together this weekend, so you can work out all the kinks without the pressure of certain people watching?"

"That might help," I said, considering her suggestion. We could practice the scene without Nash hovering over us, get it just right so we know what we're doing, and then hopefully, it would become second nature when we got back on stage.

"Yes, I think that might be exactly what you two need." Miss Crawley clapped her hands like she was excited. "Would you like me to tell Miss Cohen about the private rehearsal, or do you want to do it since you know your schedule this weekend better than I do?"

"I can handle it," I said. Then as a second thought, I added, "But if Nash hears about it and thinks I'm trying to steal his girl, I'll need you to tell him this was your idea and not mine."

Miss Crawley laughed. "Just get that scene where it needs to be, and I'll gladly be the bad guy."

21

———

## ASHER

I FOUND Elyse sitting in the common room after dinner and decided to take the opportunity to talk to her about what Miss Crawley had spoken to me about during rehearsal.

"You didn't go to the basketball game with all your friends?" I asked as I sat in the stuffed chair beside her.

There was a boys' basketball game in New Haven, and since Hunter, Carter, and Mack were all on the basketball team, I assumed Elyse would be going with her dad or her other friends to watch it.

I'd heard them chatting about it in class earlier, anyway.

"I decided not to go." She looked up from the book she'd been reading. "It's been a long week and I have a pretty big day tomorrow, so I just wanted a little more of a chill night tonight."

"Is that book you're reading actually a big 'don't talk to me right now' sign that I didn't understand?" I glanced at the Jane Austen paperback she held, worried I might be interfering with her plans for peace and quiet.

"No." She laughed and placed her bookmark on a page before setting the book down on her lap. "I was just reading since I never have time for it these days. But I'm fine talking to you instead."

"Well, that's a relief." I glanced at the couple wearing regency-era clothes on the cover of her book. "Though, I'm sure Mr. Knightley and Emma have all sorts of fun banter for you to get back to."

"Wait—" Her eyes lit up. "You've read *Emma?*"

"Watched the movie." I chuckled. And before she could get any ideas that I was a closeted Jane Austen fan, I held up a finger and said, "But I only watched it because Jace and Logan were out on dates one Friday night and my aunt wanted someone to watch it with her."

"Well, aren't you a sweet nephew."

"Eh." I shrugged. "Just trying to stay on her good side so she'd have me back for winter break."

I meant it as a joke, but from the concern in Elyse's eyes, I could tell she worried there might be some truth behind what I said.

Which I guess there was. I hadn't exactly had a real home to go to for several years, and so I had tried to be as pleasant of a house guest as I could be while staying with my aunt and uncle.

Owen had always been great about me staying with him over the holidays and during summer breaks the first few years I was in high school, but I didn't like always tying him down when I knew he had his own life to live and girls to date.

"So..." Elyse cleared her throat. "Which version of *Emma* did you watch?"

"You mean which version did I suffer through?" I arched an eyebrow, trying to keep up my manly facade.

"Sure," she said, fighting a smile. And I liked that we could still be playful even if our rehearsals had been awkward this week.

"It was the Gwyneth Paltrow version."

"And you didn't like it?" Her jaw dropped, as if my dislike of the movie was a personal attack. "That's one of my all-time favorite movies. In fact, I picked this book off the reading list solely because I liked the movie so much."

"I bet you rewound that kiss under the tree about ten times, didn't you?" I asked.

"How did you...?" Her eyes went wide, and then her cheeks flushed an adorable shade of rosy pink.

I laughed. "My aunt rewatched that part over and over again, so I figured it must be a girl thing."

"It wasn't ten times," she said. "But yeah, that proposal is one of my favorite parts in the whole movie."

"Well..." I said, deciding that this was as good of a segue as ever. "Speaking of kissing scenes..." I cleared my throat, noticing the way she stiffened a little. "Miss Crawley pulled me aside during rehearsal today and asked if I could arrange for us to get together sometime this weekend and practice the rooftop scene."

"She did?" Elyse's face paled.

"She thinks that we might be having trouble because of the..." I searched for the right word. "Because of the *intimate* nature of the scene." I cringed as soon as the word was out of my mouth. *Intimate* was such a weird word to say to the girl you might be getting the slightest crush on. "And it might be easier for us to figure things out without everyone watching."

"You mean without Nash watching us?"

"Yeah..." And the fact that she mentioned Nash without me bringing up his name told me that Miss Crawley's and my assumptions had been correct about what was causing the problem.

"Well, I'm a bit embarrassed I did so bad that Miss Crawley had to ask you to do an intervention." She looked down at the book on her lap. "But since I don't want to ruin the play for everyone, I guess I should probably rehearse with you tonight instead of reading this book."

"You're not ruining the play," I hurried to say, hating that she assumed that was what I was suggesting. "We've only had two weeks of rehearsals. It's completely normal to have nerves, or you know, whatever... Kissing scenes are awkward to do in front of other people, anyway."

Awkward to talk about, too, as was apparent by the way my cheeks were currently on fire.

"Yeah." She looked down shyly. "But, um, we can be mature about it, right?" She glanced around the common room to make sure none of the other students hanging out in here were listening.

No one seemed to be paying us attention.

She lowered her voice. "I mean, it's not like I haven't kissed you before. So it should be fine."

"Yeah." I rubbed the back of my neck, hoping she wouldn't notice me blushing—my cheeks grew even hotter at the mention of our previous kiss. "We just need to work in what we've already done with the music and choreography, and it should be easy."

I mean, I'd relived that kiss in my mind so many times that it really should be easy to repeat.

"Okay." She bit her lip, her golden-brown eyes meeting mine. "Where should we rehearse?"

"We could practice in my room," I said. "Hunter should be out at the game for a while, so we won't be interrupted."

"You want to practice in your room?" Her voice raised an octave, like she was worried I had ulterior motives for getting her up there.

"Or your room," I said quickly. "I just figured it would be the best place to go and not have to worry about anyone interrupting us. I promise I'll be a complete gentleman."

"Kind of like how you were such a gentleman that you only *pretended* you'd slept on the floor at the cabin." A smirk lifted her lips.

"Hey." I held up my hands. "I stayed on my side of the bed. You can't blame me for wanting to be fully rested in case I needed to go all taekwondo on a burglar."

She chuckled. "Do you even know taekwondo?"

"No," I admitted. "But as a Korean-American, I'd only need to strike a convincing pose and a burglar would assume I knew what I was doing."

She laughed, and I liked the sound of it. It was the kind of laugh that just made you feel light and happy inside.

Happier than I'd been in a long time.

"What I'm trying to say is that we can rehearse anywhere you're comfortable, but my room is an option if you wanted to try it out."

She stared at me for a second, as if to make sure I was really trustworthy, and then said, "Just let me grab my notes from rehearsal, and I'll meet you there."

AS SOON AS Elyse headed up to the girls' dorms, I ran up to my room to make sure it looked decent. Hunter had a bunch of his sweaty gym clothes strewn all over his bed, like he'd dumped out his duffle bag before the game and ran. To try and get rid of the funky smell, I threw them all in the dirty laundry hamper he had stored in his closet and shut the door. I wanted to crack a window, but it was too cold for that right now. I spritzed the room instead with the air freshener I kept in my desk for the off chance that I ever had a girl in my room. Then I swung the door back and forth to hopefully get enough fresh air circulating.

I was sure she was almost here when I realized I hadn't brushed my teeth since before rehearsal. If we were going to be working on a kissing scene, I had better freshen my breath as well.

We didn't have a sink in our dorm room and the boys' bathroom was at the other end of the hall, so I just put some toothpaste on my toothbrush, dry-brushed my teeth, and swallowed.

Not ideal, but it was better than taco-salad breath.

Elyse's knock came a second later.

"Theo said we have to keep the door open," Elyse said as she walked into my room. "And that he'll be checking on us every twenty minutes. So he's got my back, in case you get any ideas about why I'm here."

She'd said it all like it was a joke, but I could tell there was a hint of nervous energy coming from her.

"Thanks for the warning."

"So, this is your place?" She stepped farther in and surveyed my room.

"Yep, this is it." I pushed my hands into my pockets, looking around the room myself and trying to see it from her eyes.

My side was pretty bare. I didn't have anything on the walls. My dresser didn't have anything on top of it besides a couple of framed photos. My bed had a striped gray and blue comforter that Aunt Vivian had bought me before I came here, with a single pillow at the top.

Overall, the only thing she could probably guess about me from my living area was that I didn't have a lot of clutter and knew how to make my bed.

Which contrasted with Hunter's side. Even with my quick tidy-up job, he still had books and papers strewn about.

"Did you clean up before I came in here?" she asked, a wry smile on her lips.

"Just Hunter's stuff." I shrugged. "And unlike how you

sprayed that perfume on yourself just so you could smell good for that study session you invited me to, I only used that air freshener because Hunter's gym bag makes our room smell like butt."

"Ew." She made a face. "Maybe we should have gone to my room instead."

I chuckled. "Sorry…that wasn't the most appropriate thing to say."

"Eh." She lifted a shoulder. "You're a guy. It's probably something I should get used to if Ava and I move in with Brendon and Mack."

"So you've decided you're going to do that, then?" I asked.

"I'm considering it." She walked toward my dresser and bent over to look at the photo of Owen and me. "We had dinner there on Sunday, and I think it could work." She nodded at me. "Plus, my mom said she wants to sell our house in Ridgewater since she spends so much time in Manhattan with her team or traveling to other places these days."

"How do you feel about your mom selling the home you grew up in?" I asked, curious.

Losing the house I'd grown up in had been devastating for me.

"It's kind of sad." She glanced at my backpack sitting on the floor before looking back at me. "But Ava and I are both going off to college next year and don't have plans to move back again, so it seems kind of pointless to keep it when we'd just be visiting our mom at her condo in Manhattan, or Brendon at his house for holidays. It doesn't make sense for her to keep a house that no one lives in."

"That's probably true," I said, seeing her point. "I guess with that being the plan, moving in with Brendon and Mack might actually be a great idea. You can make it your new home and get to know them better before you graduate."

That was kind of how this summer had been for me at my Aunt Vivian's. It was the first place that actually felt like home in a long time. A place that I wouldn't mind actually calling "home" if they kept inviting me back.

Owen had done his best to take care of me the last few years, but barely an adult and trying to get through college himself, it had been hard for him to do everything.

So even though I was so thankful my brother had stepped in when I needed him, it had been nice to have a stable environment to come back to each night. And while Aunt Vivian's family wasn't perfect, I appreciated having adults who were already established in their lives to help me get my feet under me and process some of the trauma I'd experienced in losing so much of my family—including all the stuff that happened with Bailee.

I hadn't realized just how much I had craved the security they gave me until I'd been there a few weeks and actually experienced what I'd been missing all along.

*You can't miss what you never had, I guess.*

Not that I'd *never* had it.

The first fourteen years of my life had been pretty idyllic.

Elyse finished her inspection of my room. She turned to me and said, "I guess we should probably get started, huh?"

A thrill of nerves went through me when I saw the anxiety in her eyes about what we were about to do.

But since the show had to go on, and I needed her to be comfortable kissing me in order for our performance to go off without a hitch, I said, "Yes. Let's do this."

## 22

## ELYSE

"AM I DOING SOMETHING WRONG?" Asher asked, stopping the rehearsal track for "All I Ask of You" on his phone. "Because you can just tell me what you need me to do to make this more comfortable, and I'll do it."

"It's not you." I leaned against his desk, feeling so frustrated with myself for messing up the scene yet again. "Really. I just —" I sighed and held my hands out at my sides. "I don't know why I'm having such a hard time."

It was just like the rehearsals we'd had all week all over again.

Nash wasn't even here to watch us, and I was still stumbling my way through the scene.

And the dumb thing was, it wasn't even *that* complicated of a scene. Not choreography-wise, anyway. All we really had to do was sing the song I'd been singing since elementary while looking at each other, hold hands and walk to the other side of the room, hug for a little while, walk around some more, and then have him stand behind me and hold me before we kissed.

Simple.

Easy.

But for some reason, every time I had to turn around and sing about Christine asking Raoul to tell her he loves her, my heart would race, my face would get all flushed, and I would find it impossible to remember what lyrics I was supposed to sing next.

"Would it help if we broke the scene down in smaller chunks?" Asher asked, tossing his phone back onto his bed. "That's what I do when I'm learning a new song on the piano. Break it down page by page and practice the rough sections over and over until they flow."

"That would probably work," I said.

If that was how he learned to play the song I'd heard him playing the first day we met, it sounded like a technique worth trying—especially because he played the piano like a master.

Though, if I were honest with myself, there was really only one part that was causing my mind to get scrambled.

The part near the end of the song when the music swelled, and Raoul and Christine declared their love for each other before coming together for an epic kiss.

But I wasn't about to just flat-out say that we needed to practice kissing. That would be super awkward.

I said, "How about we start from the beginning one more time, and as soon as the scene starts to get rocky, we can stop and just go over that part?" Over and over and over again until I stopped overthinking it.

Until I stopped stressing out over the fact that I might like kissing him again too much and it could make my life really complicated really fast.

"Sounds like a good plan to me." He said it so calmly, as if he wasn't the least bit nervous about kissing me again.

Which he most likely wasn't.

This was probably just another stage kiss to him. He probably saw me in the same way he'd seen all the other girls he'd kissed and not fallen in love with during his previous musicals.

This was definitely not the kind of moment that might make him face the fact that he had feelings for me. Because *he* didn't see me that way.

No, the only person trying to smother her confusing feelings for her co-actor was me.

All because I had tried to kiss Nash and kissed him instead.

Asher picked up his phone again, and soon the music was playing through the Bluetooth speaker. And as he sang the first few lines where Raoul tells Christine there would be no more talk of darkness and to let go of the fears she was having regarding The Phantom, I tried to quiet my mind and told myself to become Christine.

To forget Nash and how he'd be staring daggers at Asher right now if he could see us.

To forget how it felt a little like betrayal to kiss someone who wasn't the guy I had a date planned with the next day—the guy I was planning to ask to be my escort to a ball in a few weeks.

Yes, I would forget about what was going on in real life right now and immerse myself fully in this scene and this moment alone with the guy who was playing Raoul.

I would stop thinking of Asher as himself, stop thinking of how he made my heart race every time he smiled at me, and only picture him as the person my character was in love with.

Asher walked toward me and held out his hands in the way he'd been instructed to by Miss Crawley and the choreographer. And when I placed my hands in his, I ignored the tingling sensations running up my arms and just looked in his deep brown eyes, letting the lyrics he sang fill my mind.

He really did have an amazing voice—the kind of voice that

could make whatever song he was singing become your new favorite.

In fact, I was pretty sure he could sing the dictionary in his rich, tenor voice and it would still sound amazing.

It had actually surprised me the first time I'd heard him sing in rehearsal, because for whatever reason, I hadn't expected him to sound so good. I'd been sure that there was no way Eden Falls Academy could have that much talent in one drama program.

But now that I'd been listening to him for a couple of weeks, his voice was soothing and familiar—just the perfect type of voice to soothe a worried Christine.

He continued singing. Raoul tells Christine that nothing will harm her and his words will warm and calm her. And just like in the movie, which I'd watched a hundred times, Asher lifted his hand and ran his thumb across my cheekbone like he was wiping away a tear. It was a gentle caress, a seemingly small gesture, yet my whole body glowed with warmth from his delicate touch.

He finished his verse, and it was my turn. I looked up into his face with a soft gaze and sang. Christine asks Raoul to tell her that he'd love her every moment and talk to her about summertime. Then she requests that he promises everything he says is true. At this point, we transitioned from facing each other to the next phase of the choreography where Asher would hug me as he sang his verse. He pulled me against his chest, singing about becoming my shelter as he held me protectively against him. Then pulling away, he led me around the room until we came to stand by Hunter's messy desk. He stepped behind me with his chest pressed against my back and just held me there as we sang.

He let his fingers comb through the hair resting over my shoulder, his fingers gentle, sending goosebumps racing across my skin the way they did every time we rehearsed this part. And as I started singing again, his arms wrapped around my waist, and he pressed a gentle kiss to my brow.

It was such a romantic scene, and even though my whole body was feeling like a live wire, it was going better than it had during any of our other practices...

But when we came to the part where I had to turn in his arms and face him again, where Christine asks Raoul to love her so he could tell her that he already did, I felt my presence in the moment slipping. When Asher slipped his hand behind my neck to transition us into the kiss that was supposed to happen as the orchestra swelled, a surge of anticipation filled my veins, making me lightheaded.

And here we were again. At the place where I took the scene off the rails every single time, because the thought of kissing Asher again was overwhelming. I was afraid of what it might make me feel—afraid that anyone watching us would sense how much I enjoyed kissing him despite also liking someone else...

Because even though it had been a mistake to kiss him at the cabin a week ago, I had thought about that kiss more times than I should have.

I'd had Asher's face slip into my mind at night when I was supposed to be dreaming about my Broadway date with Nash.

Asher must have sensed that I was about to ruin the moment like I had all week because he whispered, "It's going so well. Please stay with me." He traced his thumb across my jawline. "Just do what you did last weekend at the cabin. Pretend you're kissing Nash if you need to. Kiss him in your mind instead of me."

And I didn't know if it was the desperation I saw in his eyes as he willed me to just follow through with the scene. Or if it was his permission for me to close my eyes and take myself away from reality and to another place and time. But I nodded and said, "Okay."

"We can continue?" Asher asked, like he wanted to make sure I was actually okay with him making the move.

"Yes," I said breathlessly.

Apparently, that was all the invitation he needed. As the orchestra solo played through the speaker, he used the hand behind my neck to pull me closer and pressed his lips to mine. He kissed me once, twice, and then gave me another lingering kiss with his soft lips before spinning me around in his arms the way Raoul did with Christine during their kiss.

My leg bumped against Hunter's desk chair during the spin, since this room was a lot smaller than the stage. We both laughed, and he set me back on my feet. Then, just as we were supposed to, we looked into each other's eyes before leaning in for another kiss. And instead of hesitating like I had before, I closed my eyes and just let myself feel what Christine was supposed to feel for her fiancé.

I wrapped my arms behind Asher's neck and kissed him. His lips were slow, and now that I wasn't messing everything up, he seemed to allow himself to become more immersed in the scene as well. His hands slid up my back, his palms pressing into me as he pulled me tighter against him.

The last time we'd kissed, we'd both been wearing bulky coats, so I hadn't had the privilege of feeling his strong chest pressed against mine, or the tightly corded muscles of his back beneath my hands.

But tonight, wearing only a thin gray T-shirt, he felt amazing. So amazing that I had the briefest thought that it was too bad Raoul wore a thick tuxedo for most of the play.

I let my hands trace their way along his shoulders and down his biceps, and then smoothing them down his sides. And the thought came to me that we might need to rehearse this scene a lot more.

Just to make sure we got it right.

He slipped his hands into the hair at the nape of my neck and coaxed my lips to move with his in a rhythm much slower than the tempo of the music. And when he deepened the kiss, electricity pulsed from a place low in my stomach and all throughout my body.

As my mind started to drift off to a faraway place, all I could think of was that I wanted to practice this scene all night.

That maybe I should keep messing it up just so I'd have an excuse to kiss Asher like this again and again.

"Is this the part where we're supposed to sing again?" Asher broke away a moment later, sounding as breathless as I felt.

"I don't know, is it?" I asked, my gaze darting back and forth between his hypnotizing eyes as I tried to catch my breath.

We'd only started the kiss a few seconds ago, right? It seemed like there should be at least a few measures before we had to sing again. Though, I'd stopped paying attention to the music the moment our lips touched for the second kiss.

But a beat later, the music registered in my mind, and I realized that Asher was right. It was time for us to pull away from the kiss and sing the last two lines of the song.

So we stepped back a little, each drawing in a deep breath, and then looked in each other's eyes as we sang the grand finale of the song where Raoul and Christine declare their love for one another. I felt myself getting swept up in the moment, as if I were truly becoming one right then and there with Asher.

We were in sync in our performance in a way that I rarely ever found myself with someone else.

The music came down from the crescendo, and just like Miss Crawley had asked us to do, we came together again for one more kiss. As Asher took my bottom lip in his, I wrapped my arms behind his neck and completely melted into him.

The song ended, and I felt Asher's lips curl up into a smile before he pulled away and whispered, "We did it." He gently brushed some hair away from my forehead with his thumb. "We made it through the scene."

"I know." I leaned my forehead against his, feeling light with relief and happiness. "Finally."

It may have taken a full week where I'd completely bombed the kissing scene, but I'd finally been able to make it through.

"It wasn't even that bad, was it?" he asked.

"No." My cheeks warmed, suddenly shy to talk about how un-horrible it had been kissing him again. "It wasn't bad. I think I just got stuck in my head about it for some reason."

"Well, you did amazing." He pulled me into his arms for a hug.

"Thank you," I said, returning his embrace.

His hand rubbed along my back. "Just do what you just did next time, and Miss Crawley will be impressed."

"I'll do my best."

Now would probably be the time to step away from the hug and move on to the next thing. But he didn't step away and neither did I.

We just stood there for a long moment, holding each other as we rode the high of finally finishing the scene that had been stressing me out all week.

And I didn't know what it was about hugging Asher, but it just felt...nice. He was tall and strong and smelled really good. Not like he was wearing cologne or anything like that, but his shirt smelled clean—like he'd just done a load of laundry. And there was possibly a hint of aftershave on his face as well.

I liked it.

Liked that he was the kind of guy who had to shave.

A memory of the way his five o'clock shadow had felt under my fingertips the first time we'd kissed flashed through my mind, and I realized I should have known then that I couldn't have been kissing the person I'd set out to kiss.

I should have known the moment our lips touched that I was kissing someone with a different kind of energy to him.

The kind of energy that I'd never been able to resist.

"You're a good hugger," Asher whispered in a quiet voice next to my ear.

"Am I?" I asked, trying not to notice the way his hot breath sent chills racing from my head to my toes.

"Yeah." He tilted his head down so his cheek rested against mine. "I think that's part of why I kissed you back last week. Because it felt nice to be close to someone again."

"Yeah?" I asked, feeling breathless as he spoke about the moment that had crossed my mind way more than it should have. "H-have you thought about that kiss very much?"

"A few times..." He bent his face down closer to my neck, as if smelling the perfume I'd sprayed there this morning. He pressed a gentle kiss to my skin. "Have you?"

"Huh?" I asked, a little dazed. The way his lips felt against my skin was making me forget what we were talking about.

"Have you thought about it at all this week?" His lips gently grazed against the sensitive skin of my collarbone, muddling my thoughts even more.

What was he doing to me?

"Ummm." I drew in a shallow breath, suddenly finding it so hard to breathe.

Did he know what he was doing to me right now?

Did he know that every single nerve ending in my body was buzzing?

One of his hands smoothed up and down my side and

across my back. "Because it's okay if you thought about it," he whispered in my ear. "I won't tell anyone…"

Oh my heck, I was going to faint.

Could he tell that I'd been dreaming about that kiss all week?

Had he somehow hacked into my brain and seen all the times I'd fantasized about kissing him again in a way that was definitely not the type of kiss meant for others to watch on stage?

But since he'd admitted to thinking about it, I pulled back enough to meet his gaze and whispered, "I thought about it a few times."

His gaze fell to my lips, and I licked them as anticipation welled inside me. Was he thinking about kissing me again?

Did I want him to kiss me again?

To kiss me for a reason that had nothing to do with the extra rehearsal we were supposed to be having?

His eyes met mine, and he leaned slightly closer, as if gauging whether I was okay with him closing the distance between us or not.

And all I could think of was, *please, oh please, oh please just do it.*

*Don't ask permission. Just kiss me.*

His hand cradled my neck, and we were so close that my eyes fluttered shut.

His lips just barely grazed against mine, and I was in the middle of melting when the smoke detector above our heads started beeping.

We both jumped apart as the smoke detectors spoke in its robotic voice. *"Warning. Evacuate. Fire detected. Warning. Evacuate. Fire detected."*

# 23

## ELYSE

"DO YOU THINK THERE'S A FIRE?" I asked Asher.

Or had the smoke detectors somehow picked up on the fireworks sparking between us?

"I don't know," he said, looking at the smoke detector above us. "Last time this happened, it was just Rushil burning stuff in his room."

"What?"

"Rushil's room is next to mine, and he thinks it's cool to burn like five different incense sticks at the same time." Asher walked over to his closet and pulled out the coat he'd worn at the cabin. "Here, you can wear this." He handed it to me before turning back to the closet and pulling out another thick jacket. "We better head outside, just in case."

He grabbed his phone from his bed while I put his coat on, noticing the scent of the cologne I'd smelled on him when we'd kissed at the cabin. I caught a half-smile on his lips—as if he knew I'd just been savoring his intoxicating scent—but he didn't say anything. Instead, he led me out of his room and down the hall where several other boys and a few girls were leaving the other dorm rooms.

The emergency exit was already propped open at the end of the hall, and Asher took my hand in his as we went down the metal staircase.

The wind whipped at my face as soon as we stepped outside, the cold biting at me and reminding me why I didn't like to go outside during winter.

"How long do you think we're going to have to wait outside?" I asked through chattering teeth as our feet clanked down the metal steps.

He glanced at me over his shoulder. "Hopefully, not too long."

We made it to the cement pad below where a bunch of other students were gathering, their expressions ranging from annoyed to excited to anxious over the fact that we'd had to evacuate the dorms.

Another gust of wind whipped through the air. Asher let go of my hand so he could zip up his jacket.

"Good thinking to grab the coats," I said, pulling the hood over my head before digging my hands into the deep pockets.

"I learned my lesson last time this happened." He rubbed his hands over the sleeves of his jacket like it wasn't quite warm enough for the freezing weather. "It wasn't quite this cold last time, but we were out here for a really long time."

"I feel bad that I have your warm coat and you only have your jacket," I said, watching him as he shivered.

"It's fine," he said. "I'm tough."

"And a gentleman, too," I said.

He shrugged. "Gotta make up for last week when I didn't offer to sleep on the floor."

I couldn't stop the smile that curved my lips as I remembered our night in the cabin.

I wouldn't admit it to him now, but I kind of liked that he wasn't a completely selfless gentleman.

But he must be a mind reader because he leaned closer and said, "But then again, you do have a thing for bad boys, don't you?"

"Are you trying to say you're a bad boy?" I asked, my smile only growing bigger because he was so stinking cute and I kind of loved that he knew it, too.

"I don't know." He pursed his pouty lips. Then he shrugged and said, "Maybe."

"Maybe?" I raised an eyebrow.

"Yeah." An impish grin lifted his lips. "I mean, I know I've been pretty good at keeping my bad-boy side hidden from you so far, but I totally had all sorts of reckless plans for tonight before we decided to rehearse our scene instead."

"Really?" I asked, enjoying his playful side way too much. "And what would you be doing right now if Miss Crawley hadn't asked you to rehearse with me?"

"You really want to know?" He looked sideways at me like he was enjoying our back and forth as much as I was. "Because it's some pretty dangerous stuff."

"I think I need to know just what kind of a bad boy I'm working with."

"I don't know if you can handle hearing about the level of mischief I had planned, though."

"Try me," I said, loving that he'd just called it *mischief.*

"Well, if you must know." He glanced around, pretending like he was worried one of our classmates was listening. "I was going to do, like, lawbreaking type of stuff." He raised his eyebrows and made a face like I should be impressed.

"Oooh, lawbreaking stuff?" I said, playing along. "And what would that entail?"

"Only the baddest of things made it onto my night-of-mischief list, of course." He pushed his hands into his jacket pockets. "Things like doorbell-ditching, jaywalking..." He looked behind him again and lowered his voice so only I could hear. "Throwing pants at someone and yelling, 'You just got pantsed.'" He took a step back and shrugged. "You know, typical bad-boy stuff."

"Oh man, Asher," I said, unable to stop the giggle that bubbled up inside me. "I had no idea you were such a naughty boy."

*Throwing pants at someone and yelling "you just got pantsed"?*

How did he come up with this stuff so fast?

He leaned closer again and whispered, "You have no idea how naughty I can be, Elyse."

And though the activities he'd listed made him sound like the most harmless bad boy I'd ever met, with those few words and one flirtatious look, I was suddenly reminded of why I had always been helpless when it came to bad boys.

As someone who always followed the rules, there was something deep down within me that craved the freedom to throw caution to the wind and do the things I normally wouldn't dare do.

To be with someone who made life exciting and unpredictable.

And while none of the things Asher talked about were "bad," when his gaze fell to my lips, I had a feeling he still had all the qualities I really liked about bad boys.

That if he wanted something, he just went for it.

He didn't ask a girl if she wanted to kiss him. He already *knew* she did and made it happen.

*Unless a fire alarm went off, of course.*

Would we be kissing in his room right now if the smoke detector hadn't been set off?

I was pretty sure we would be. And it would have been much more like the kisses from my fantasies than the stage kiss we'd rehearsed.

I wrapped my arms around myself to fight the shiver those thoughts sent through me.

"You cold?" Asher asked, noticing the movement.

"Kind of," I said. And I was. But the cold wasn't the only reason why I'd shivered.

"Here, let me help," he said. He stepped behind me and wrapped his arms around my waist to share his body heat and protect me from the wind.

And dang, he felt so good right next to me.

I'd reveled in the feeling of him holding me like this during our rehearsals, but there was just something about him doing it when it wasn't part of the script that was intoxicating.

His hot breath crept over my neck as he rested his face next to mine. "Is this any better?" he asked in a husky voice.

"Much better," I whispered back. I was definitely not cold right now. Though, it had suddenly become a lot harder to breathe.

"Good."

We just stood there quietly as we watched the other students around us. Not everyone had brought a coat or jacket with them in their rush to get to safety, and so some were running up and down the sidewalk as if hoping to work up a sweat.

A few other students had a similar idea as us and were huddled together for warmth. Girls and guys. Girls and girls. Two girls with one guy.

My gaze caught on Addison Michaels and Evan Rodgers standing in a position very similar to the way Asher and I were standing.

"Now that's an interesting development," I said to Asher,

pointing in the direction of the couple standing on the outer edge of the group.

"Is that Addison and Evan?" Asher craned his neck over my shoulder, trying to get a better look. "Aren't they brother and sister?"

"Step-siblings," I said. "At least, that's what I thought, anyway..." I watched as Evan rubbed Addison's arms like he was trying to warm her up. He was probably six-foot-four with biceps even bigger than Asher's. When I'd seen him and Addison bringing their suitcases into the dorms the first day, I'd assumed Evan was just Addison's older brother who was dropping her off at school.

But despite looking a couple of years older than us, he was a senior.

A senior who was doing a very good job of keeping his stepsister from freezing right now.

"Maybe it's nothing," Asher said. "I mean, you have a date with another guy tomorrow, yet here you're with me right now."

*Right...*

It was probably a bad sign that I'd completely forgotten about my date with Nash until Asher brought it up.

A rush of guilt swept over me.

What was I doing?

"Um, I think I'm all warmed up." I took a step forward, making Asher drop his arms. "Th-thanks for your help."

He furrowed his brow in confusion as he inspected my face. "Did I do something wrong?"

"No," I said too quickly. "Of course not. I, um..." I chewed on my lip, trying to think of an excuse for why I was suddenly acting weird. "I just forgot about my date tomorrow and well..."

"And you wouldn't want anyone to tell Nash that we were hanging out tonight?" he asked, disappointment in his voice.

"Yes," I started, but then I saw hurt flash in his eyes and realized that was the exact wrong thing to say to a guy who already had a hard enough time believing people wanted to be around him. "I mean, no." I sighed, my cheeks burning. "I mean..."

What was I trying to say?

I didn't know.

Because I couldn't make sense of what was going on inside my brain right now.

It was like my heart was tied to a rope, and Nash and Asher were both tugging on opposite ends of it.

I'd been sure that I wanted something to happen with Nash just a week ago. He was amazing and I always had fun when we were together, and he was just a really great guy.

But the more time I spent with Asher—

Well, the more time I spent with Asher, the more torn I became.

"It's okay, Elyse," Asher murmured, seeming to sense that I didn't know what to say. "I know you like Nash. I think we just got caught up in our characters tonight and forgot to get back to best-buddy mode."

Was that what happened? Had that almost-kiss in his room only been a possibility because he'd still been in character?

It hadn't felt like that.

It had felt like it was real, and all I'd wanted in that moment was for Asher to kiss me.

*Me*...not Christine Daaé.

But that was insane, right? It shouldn't be possible to like two guys at once. Especially not two guys who were so different from each other.

I knew I should say something to Asher to explain why I was sending so many mixed signals, but just then, our dorm parents, Heather and Theo, came to tell all of us that there was no fire.

"It was a false alarm," Heather said. "Triggered by a chemistry experiment gone wrong in a dorm room." She sighed, like her job of taking care of thirty high school students was making her age faster than normal. "Anyway, everything should be fine now, and you can all head back inside."

Excited chatter started as soon as she finished, and our classmates all began pushing toward the doors to get back to the warmth inside the building.

The line up the fire escape was long, so Asher and I opted to go through the main doors under the colonnade to get back inside, the silence thick between us as we walked side by side.

I tried to think of something to say that would get us back to the laughing and joking around that we'd been doing when we'd first gone outside. But I couldn't come up with anything.

Asher opened one of the large doors that led to the common room, and I stepped inside.

What was I supposed to do now?

Were we done rehearsing the scene? Should I just go to my room and hide?

Asher glanced around the large living area filling with students before turning his brown-eyed gaze on me. "Well, I think I'm going to call it a night. It's been a long week and I'm more tired than I thought."

"No jaywalking or doorbell-ditching for you then?" I asked, hoping to bring back the lightness from earlier.

"No," he said flatly. "I don't think I'll be doing any of that."

Okay, I really must have messed things up somehow because he was not in his usual playful mood.

Not knowing what else to say, I muttered, "I'll probably just head to bed, too."

"You do have a big date tomorrow," he said.

And I hated how that one sentence from him made me feel like I was somehow betraying him by having plans to go on a date with Nash.

Why did I feel that way?

It wasn't like Asher and I were dating. We were just friends. Co-actors.

Co-actors who had insane chemistry, sure. But he'd said so himself that he was just interested in being friends. That his flirting was harmless because he was still getting over Bailee and not ready to even think about putting himself out there again.

That was what he'd said, right?

*Unless that has somehow changed in the past week...*

He stood there for a moment, as if waiting for me to say or do something more, and then I realized I was still wearing his coat. So I quickly pulled it off.

"Thanks for letting me use this," I said, offering it back to him.

"Of course." He took it from me and hugged it to himself.

We looked at each other for another awkward second. Then he said, "I hope you have a great time in New York tomorrow."

"Y-you do?" I asked, and my stomach fell with his words.

Was I disappointed that he was hoping I'd enjoy my date with Nash?

Shouldn't I *want* him to want me to have a great time?

That was what good friends did for each other, right? Hope for the best for each other.

"Well..." He looked away, as if debating what to say. Then he met my gaze again. "I'm hoping you'll have a good time because you enjoy the musical and the magic of New York. I never said I wanted you to have a good time with Nash. I'm still too petty to think he deserves someone as great as you."

And just like that, my chest warmed, and the world righted itself on its axis again.

Was I a terrible person for being relieved that his beef with Nash was still intact?

Had I turned into one of those girls who thrived on two guys fighting over her?

I might have. Because if Asher and Nash could just duke it out between themselves, I wouldn't have to decide which guy I liked more and then possibly regret my decision.

They could make the decision for me.

Not that Asher was even interested in me like that...

I sighed. Hopefully, my date with Nash would make things clearer.

"Have a good night, Elyse," Asher said, breaking me from my confusing thoughts. "I'll tell Miss Crawley that we made it through the scene."

"Th-thanks," I managed to say.

It seemed like he was about to leave, but then he said, "And since I'm going to try to be the better man, if it's what you want, I hope you have a great time with Nash as well."

"Thank you," I said, a huge wave of guilt crashing over me when I caught a glimpse of sadness in his dark eyes. "I hope you have a good day tomorrow, too."

## 24

## ASHER

"DID you try on the tux I sent over?" Aunt Vivian asked me through the earpiece of my phone.

It was Saturday afternoon, and my aunt had called me while I was walking into my dorm room after a homework session with Hunter and Scarlett.

"I was just about to do that," I said, looking at the large rectangular box that had been delivered to my room this morning.

I hadn't actually planned to try on the tux since my mind had been elsewhere this afternoon, but now that she'd reminded me, I was going to put it on.

"Okay, I just want to make sure it fits right," Aunt Vivian said. "Geraldo says that if we need him to do any more alterations, we'll have to get it back to him before the fifteenth since he'll be taking a few weeks off for the holidays."

"I'm sure it'll fit me just fine," I said.

"Please just try it on and let me know," she said. "I know this debutante ball probably seems silly to you, but as the chairman, I just want to make sure you boys look your best."

I didn't know why it mattered what I wore since I wasn't an escort like Jace and Logan would be—I'd simply be hanging out in the crowd, sitting at the table as my cousins did the dorky debutante dance with their girlfriends.

But my aunt was already stressed enough about the fancy event she was in charge of for the first time, so I said, "I'll try it on right now and let you know."

"Send me some photos, too," she said. "I want to see it for myself."

"Okay." I chuckled. "I'll send some photos, too." We hung up, and I went to open the box I'd stashed on my bed.

The Ralph Lauren black tuxedo with tails looked just like it had when we'd ordered it two months ago. I hadn't thought it needed any alterations then, but apparently, my aunt wanted it to fit my every angle and muscle just right, so off to Geraldo it had gone.

"Let's see if Geraldo is worth the price he charges," I mumbled to myself as I pulled off my T-shirt and slipped my arms into the white button-up shirt.

I stood in front of the full-length mirror on my closet door a minute later, so that I could tie the bowtie. I probably didn't need to do this, since the bowtie wouldn't need altering, but my aunt had wanted photos. I figured I'd be a good nephew and go the extra mile.

I looked at my reflection in the mirror, my mind wandering to other people who I knew had dressed up today.

Nash and Elyse.

They were on their date now. Nash had picked her up a couple of hours ago. I'd been sitting at a table with Hunter and Scarlett in the common room a few minutes before three when Elyse had come down the stairs from the girls' dorms.

Ever since our awkward goodbye last night, I'd been trying not to think about her and what she'd be doing with Nash today because I was trying very hard not to care. But then she'd come down the stairs looking amazing in a black dress that hit her mid-thigh, and I had found it impossible not to stare at her—to rake her in from head to toe.

She'd worn a white wool coat over the top of her dress, so I couldn't tell if the dress was strapless or had long sleeves. But because it was Elyse wearing it, I knew Nash would be drooling over her all night.

She usually only wore light makeup with her hair either in a ponytail or down and straight, but she'd really gone all out today with bold eye makeup and lipstick. Her hair had even been pulled up in an elegant updo that showed off her delicate neck.

*Man, I wanted to kiss her neck again.*

I'd had a small taste of her skin last night and had been on the verge of tasting her vanilla-sugar lips again when the stupid fire alarm had gone off.

Would she be on her date with Nash right now if I'd been able to kiss her the way I wanted?

Or would things have shifted enough that she'd want to choose me instead?

It was probably stupid to even think that I had a chance with her when she was on a date with a billionaire's son right now—when she'd gotten dressed up for him.

But even though I'd told her that we'd just gotten caught up in playing Raoul and Christine as a way to save face, something told me it had really just been us in that moment.

Just Asher and Elyse and the undeniable spark that had been growing ever since the first day we met.

I sighed and tried to focus back on tying my bowtie. I needed to stop thinking about the *what ifs* and *what could have beens.*

The fact was that she was on a date with Nash right now.

She'd gotten all dressed up for *Nash*.

Not me.

After I finished with the bowtie, I grabbed my phone and snapped a few photos for my aunt, making sure to get all the angles I thought she'd want. Then I sat down on my bed to text them to her.

> Me: It feels like it fits right. Here are the photos you requested.

I attached the photos to the text, pressed send, and then waited for her to respond. The three-piece tux took long enough to put on that I didn't want to change out of it until I was sure she had all the photos she wanted.

As I waited for her response, my eyes landed on the script that Elyse had left on my desk, and I couldn't help but wonder what she and Nash were doing right now.

I'd overheard Nash telling Hunter that they were eating at La Masseria before the show. I'd never eaten there before, but it sounded like a fancy Italian restaurant.

Were they sitting at a candlelit table right now?

Or were they still in the Escalade he'd picked her up in?

Yes, I'd watched them leave through one of the windows that overlooked the school's front drive. Nash had helped her step up into the back of a black Escalade before climbing in beside her. Since he was the son of the seventh richest man in the United States, of course he had a chauffeur on hand to drive them on their fancy date.

And unlike me who felt overdressed in this tuxedo, Nash had looked right at home in his navy-blue suit.

Elyse probably loved how he looked in it, too. Probably thought he was so cute with his blond hair and the blue eyes the Hastings' siblings were practically famous for.

Was that her type then? Dirty-blond hair, blue eyes, and

golden skin? She said she'd gone for bad boys before moving here, but there had to be a certain look she preferred.

And I was a complete opposite to Nash in that arena. He was the sun. I was the midnight sky.

My phone dinged with a text.

> Aunt Vivian: Those photos look great. If you say it fits right, I'll take your word for it. Just make sure you bring it with you when you come home for winter break.

My eyes snagged on the word *home*. Was she saying her house was my home? Or just calling it that because it was *her* home?

Not that it mattered.

I typed back a response.

> Me: I'll put it on top of my suitcase right now, so I don't forget.

Speaking of forgetting things, I still needed to book my bus ticket back to Ridgewater.

I was in the middle of doing that when my door beeped with the sound of Hunter unlocking it with his card. A second later, he walked into our room with Scarlett trailing right behind him.

"What are you all dressed up for?" Hunter asked, taking in my tuxedo.

"Oh this?" I looked down at my clothes. "I was just having one of my fancy-tux Saturdays where I sit in my room and sip tea while I look out on the veranda."

Scarlett and Hunter looked at each other like they weren't sure if I was serious or not.

"I'm kidding," I said. "I'm not weird like that. This was just delivered today, and I was making sure it fit."

"Is that your costume for the musical?" Scarlett asked.

"No." I stood and took the jacket off since it was getting hot. "It's for some fancy event my aunt is making me go to over winter break."

"That's so crazy," Hunter said. "Because I just got my first coat with tails for a party over Christmas break, too."

Scarlett narrowed her eyes at me. "What type of event are you going to?"

I ran a hand through my hair. "It's this debutante ball my aunt is in charge of."

"Wait, is it the debutante ball in Manhattan?" Scarlett's brown eyes widened. "The one on the twenty-eighth?"

"Uh, yeah..." I frowned, surprised that she'd heard of it.

Scarlett was from Manhattan, so maybe she was somehow up on all the things going on in that city. She was an over-achiever, after all.

But she and Hunter both exchanged a look and said, "We're going to be there, too."

"Really?"

"Yeah." Scarlett tucked some of her auburn hair behind her ear. "Cambrielle, Ava, Elyse, and I are all being presented as debutantes. Hunter is my escort."

Wait, Elyse was going to be there?

I glanced at the mirror on my closet door to catch my reflec-tion. I hadn't cared too much about how I looked in my tuxedo before, since I figured I'd just be around a bunch of strangers all night.

But if Elyse was going to be there and possibly see me...

I pushed the thought away. Cambrielle was going to be there, and since it was a family event, it meant Nash would be there, too. And Carter was probably going to be Ava's escort, so it would only make sense that Elyse would have asked Nash to be her escort for the night.

Even though I figured I already knew the answer, I found myself asking, "Do all of you already have escorts?"

"For the most part." Scarlett leaned against Hunter's desk. "Ava asked Carter, of course. And Cambrielle asked Mack. But I don't think Elyse has asked anyone yet."

"She didn't ask Nash?" I asked, hope filling my chest. I might not be able to afford to take her on the fancy kind of date she was currently on, but I had a tux and I'd already be at the ball...

My aunt had wanted me to look the part in case one of the debutante's escorts couldn't make it at the last minute. But if Elyse was having a hard time asking someone...maybe I could offer to be her prince charming for the night.

She'd said before that she liked it when guys went after what they wanted.

And the more I was around Elyse, the more I wanted her.

"I don't think she's asked Nash yet," Scarlett said. "Apparently, she's never asked a guy out before and is putting it off until the last minute."

"She's never asked a guy out?"

"That's what she said." Scarlett shrugged. "But who knows, maybe she just wanted to see how their date went today before she asked him."

*Oh.*

Of course...

"But that's cool that you're going to be there," Scarlett said. "Are you escorting someone you met while you were living with your aunt and uncle?"

"Uh, no," I said, suddenly realizing that I was going to look like a dork sitting in the audience when Elyse and all her friends had the spotlight on them all night. "Apparently, I'm the backup escort."

"Oh, that's cool," Scarlett said.

"Does Elyse know you're going to be there?" Hunter asked.

"I don't know why she would," I said. "This is the first I've heard of anyone else from our school going."

Why was he asking that, anyway?

Had he noticed the way I couldn't keep my eyes off Elyse as she'd left for her date today? Had I been way too obvious when I'd gone to stand by the window to watch her leave—using the excuse that I needed to stretch my legs?

He probably had. Hunter didn't usually say a ton, but he noticed *everything*.

Hunter studied my face for a moment, as if piecing together everything in his mind. Then with a slight smirk, he said, "Maybe you should offer to be Elyse's escort."

Scarlett's jaw dropped as Hunter's suggestion seemed to register in her mind. She looked at me. "Do you like Elyse?"

"No—" I hurried to say, my breath catching in my throat. "I —we're just friends."

But she didn't look like she believed me because she said, "I saw her script on your desk when I came to get Hunter this morning. Was Elyse even tired when she stayed home from the basketball game last night? Or was that just her excuse so she could have some alone time with you?"

"My side of the room *was* all cleaned up when I got back from the game," Hunter added. "I thought you were just being nice, but did you tidy up because you had a girl over?"

"Of course not. I mean, it's not in the way you're thinking." Panic filled my chest for some reason. "Elyse was reading a book in the common room last night, and we only ended up in here because Miss Crawley wanted us to work on a scene for the play."

"What kind of scene were you working on?" Hunter arched an eyebrow like he already knew.

And man, this looked bad.

"It was just a scene that was giving us some trouble during rehearsals this week." I scratched at a spot under my collar, hoping he'd let me leave it at that.

"It was a kissing scene, wasn't it?" Scarlett guessed, a huge smile on her lips.

My neck started to sweat, and I wanted to crack open a window.

"It was totally a kissing scene." Hunter looked at Scarlett, his green eyes lighting up. Then glancing at his bed, he asked, "Wait... You guys didn't, like, make out on my bed, did you?"

"No, of course not," I said. Even if we had started making out, I'd never subject Elyse to Hunter's bed. I was pretty sure he only washed his sheets once a month.

"But you *were* kissing in here, weren't you," Scarlett said.

"We only did what we were supposed to do for the scene." *The fire alarm had interrupted us before we could get any further.*

I stood, suddenly feeling amped up with pent-up energy.

"But you like her, don't you?" Scarlett prodded.

"You guys aren't going to let me off easy, are you?" I started taking the cuff links out of my dress shirt for something to do.

"You don't need to feel guilty for liking her, if that's what's going on," Scarlett said, a sudden tenderness in her voice that I hadn't expected. "Bailee would want you to move on and be happy."

I froze.

I'd been so caught up in my little Elyse bubble that I'd completely forgotten I was supposed to be mourning my ex.

But I couldn't just act like I was pining for Bailee for forever, could I? It had been seven and a half months since she'd disappeared, and we still hadn't found a single clue as to what had happened to her.

There had to be a point when I could believably move on without making people think I hurt her.

"Elyse is a sweetheart," Scarlett said. "Heck, if I was into girls, I'd probably be in love with her, too."

Hunter's eyes widened momentarily, like he worried that might be a possibility and he'd have to deal with both girls *and* guys stealing his best friend's attention from him. But he managed to wipe the look away before Scarlett saw it.

"Shouldn't you guys be siding with Nash, though?" I asked, deciding to stop trying to deny what my feelings were for Elyse. Apparently, it was written all over my face already. "He was your friend way before me."

"You're my friend, too," Hunter said quickly, as if worried I doubted the friendship we'd built over the last two weeks. "So don't try playing that card with me."

Was it needy of me to want to hear that?

Friends were a hard commodity to come by these days.

"And yes, we're Nash's friends," Scarlett said. "But we're also Elyse's friends as well, and..." Her words tapered off, like she wasn't sure she should continue.

"Well, what?" I asked, my heart pounding fast.

Scarlett shrugged. "I guess I've wondered if she started liking Nash just because he was available and showed interest in her first."

"You do?" I asked, a spark of hope flickering in my chest again. "Like a crush of convenience?"

"I mean, I think she does like him," Scarlett said. "I just—" She pressed her lips together, as if really considering her words. "I saw the way she was looking at you when you both got back from the cabin last weekend. And then, I watched her all week and caught her staring at you when she didn't think anyone was paying attention."

My stomach fluttered and tingles raced from my shoulders and down to my toes.

She bit her lip and added, "I guess I just wondered if she'd really be interested in Nash if she had met you first."

Her words and what she was suggesting hit me like a bucket of ice being poured over my head.

Could that be possible?

Would Elyse and I be together right now if Nash had never been a distraction?

"You're not just playing with me, are you?" I asked, my heart beating so fast with the possibility.

"No, of course not." Scarlett shook her head and frowned a little like she was worried she might have said something wrong. "But I mean, this is all just my opinion based on what I've seen from the outside. Elyse hasn't actually talked to me about any of this."

My chest deflated. Scarlett must have somehow picked up on the disappointment and confusion swirling through my mind because she said, "I know she's on a date with Nash right now. But if you like her, you should let her know."

"Offer to be her escort to the debutante ball," Hunter said. "Put the feelers out there when she gets back tonight and see if you can make it happen."

"You really think I should?" My hands felt sweaty at the thought of doing that. Scarlett had said Elyse had never asked a guy out, but it would probably surprise her that I'd never asked a girl out. Bailee had arranged everything between us, and I'd never cared enough about anyone else to put myself out there before.

Never felt like I ever had a chance with any of the high-society girls from our school when I didn't have a trust fund of my own.

Hunter shrugged. "It's fair game until she has a ring on her finger."

"Nash isn't going to propose." Scarlett swatted Hunter on the arm like he was ridiculous for saying that.

But I understood the sentiment. And from the look Hunter got in his eyes after the brief touch from Scarlett, I wondered if he was trying to tell himself the same thing.

He'd told me that Scarlett's dad was trying to set her up with some older guy who was a family friend. Was Hunter working up the courage to put himself out there again, too?

"We're watching a movie in the common room tonight," Scarlett said. "If you happen to be watching it with us, you'll be down there when she gets back and can pull her aside to ask her."

"You think I should just flat-out ask her if I can be her escort?"

That was bold. Even for me.

"Or you could just return her script to her room," Hunter said with a shrug. "That's probably what I'd do."

"Okay..." I sighed, considering this plan they were making for me. "Guess I'll be watching the movie with you then."

# 25

## ELYSE

"DO you have any fun plans for winter break?" Nash asked me after the server brought our plates to the table.

We were sitting at a table on the indoor balcony of a fancy Italian restaurant in the heart of New York, and he was looking like a male model just fresh off the runway in his navy-blue suit.

When Nash told me he wanted to go all out and dress up for our night out on the town, I'd assumed he'd show up looking dashing in a suit, since he always dressed well.

But I had not expected to be stricken speechless when he walked up the steps to the school to escort me to the Escalade. Or to suddenly be tongue-tied when I realized he'd dressed up like this solely for me.

Even now, sitting across from him, I found it hard to concentrate on what he was saying because I was so into how good he looked.

But he'd asked me a question just barely, right?

Oh yeah. He was wondering about my plans for winter break.

"I'm going to be celebrating Winter Solstice with my dad, Mack, and Ava on the twenty-first," I said, focusing on spinning some of the fettuccini from my *scialatielli alla siciliana* onto my fork so he wouldn't realize how much I liked staring at him. "And then, Ava and I will head to my mom's place here in Manhattan to celebrate Christmas with our mom before the debutante ball."

There I did it. I made it through a sentence without losing my train of thought.

"Oh that sounds fun." Nash cut into his pork chop covered in black truffle sauce. "I think it's cool the Aardens celebrate Winter Solstice like they do."

"Yeah." I tucked a strand of hair that had fallen from my updo behind my ear. "I've never celebrated it before, so I'm not sure what to expect. But I guess it's a tradition Mack's mom started a long time ago and they wanted to keep the tradition alive."

"Yeah, Mrs. Aarden was cool like that. Always having fun little celebrations for the change of seasons."

It was also convenient, too. Now that I had two parents to celebrate holidays with, it worked out that Brendon celebrated Winter Solstice and my mom celebrated Christmas. Ava and I could spend time with each parent on their special holiday and not have to miss out on anything.

"What about you?" I asked. "Any fun plans?"

"I think we're just hanging out around Eden Falls for Christmas this year," Nash said picking up his sparkling mineral water. "And then we'll be coming here to New York to stay at our penthouse for a few days while Cambrielle does all her debutante stuff."

Of course the Hastings had a New York penthouse. They probably had a house or condo in every big city around the world.

Nash took a sip and set his glass back on the table. "So, I haven't been to a debutante ball before." He tugged on his collar as if suddenly nervous. "But I, uh," –he swallowed– "I hear that you're supposed to all have escorts. Is that right?"

"I've never been to one before, either, but that's what I was told." My cheeks warmed, and I wondered if this was the moment I'd been putting off for weeks—the one where I went out on a limb and asked Nash to be my escort. I cleared my throat. "There was actually a bachelor's brunch or something like that last weekend where they have a bunch of guys come and spend time with the other debutantes so they can decide if they want to ask one of them to be their escort..."

"Really?" Nash raised his eyebrows, like he knew all about it but was trying to act surprised. "That's interesting."

"I thought so." I swirled my fork around in my pasta again.

*Just do it, Elyse. Just ask him to be your escort.*

"But you were at the cast retreat last weekend, so you didn't go."

"That's right."

He picked up his fork and poked at his food for a second before looking back at me. "Do you already have an escort?"

"Oh, no," I said, a jumble of nerves filling my stomach. "I haven't asked anyone yet." *AKA, I haven't gotten up the courage to ask you.* I took a sip of my water to drown the frog that had suddenly jumped into my throat. "I've just been so busy with the musical and school and everything that I haven't had time to figure out how to ask someone."

*Just spit out the words.*

The ball was two weeks away. I needed to have a date.

"Well," Nash said. "I don't want to assume anything..." His fingers twitched on the white tablecloth like he was nervous, too. "But I do have a tux for the event and will already be there..."

Was he saying what I thought he was?

"W-would you mind being my escort?" I asked, and then held my breath as I waited for him to answer. He might have helped me out a ton in asking him, but he could still say no.

But then, his aqua-blue eyes brightened and he got the cutest, happiest look on his face as he said, "It would be an honor to be your escort."

"Really?"

"Of course," he said, letting out a relieved laugh. "I've been hoping all week that you'd ask me."

He had?

*Awww.* My whole body warmed, because just the way he said it reminded me of exactly why I liked him so much. He was *so* sweet.

And suddenly, I didn't know why I'd put off asking him for so long because I should have done it a week ago when everyone else asked their guys.

Sure, I'd been a little distracted by that accidental kiss with Asher and all the confusing feelings I'd been experiencing all week. But now that I'd put it out there and Nash had accepted, it was so obvious that Nash was the right guy to ask all along.

"Are you okay to go to the events they have before the ball?" I asked, just so I didn't get ahead of myself. "There are a couple of practices for the dance all the debutantes and escorts will be doing that night. And I think there's a cocktail party the night before, too."

Now that I thought about it, being an escort was a pretty big ask.

But he smiled and said, "I'll already be in town since Cambrielle and Carter have to be at those things, too. So yes, I can make it to all those events."

"THAT WAS AMAZING," I whispered to Nash after the cast of *The Phantom of the Opera* had done their final bow and the curtains had closed. We were sitting in the front row and had just witnessed the show of a lifetime.

"I know." He turned to me, his eyes showing that he was just as in awe of the performance as I was. "I barely took a breath through the whole thing."

"Me either," I admitted. Although part of that had been because of him holding my hand the whole time.

It had been so long since I just sat through a show or movie with a guy, holding hands, that I'd forgotten how much I'd missed it.

"Did you get any ideas for things to add to our production?" he asked. "Because I have about a million ideas I want to talk to Miss Crawley about now."

"Just a few," I said. "Though after watching the way the actress played Christine, I have to admit that I'm a little intimidated now. She was phenomenal."

"She did a good job, didn't she?" Nash agreed, looking at the stage again. "But you're already so good with only two weeks of rehearsals. I wouldn't worry about it."

"Yeah?" I asked.

He nodded. "Of course. Plus, that actress has probably played that part hundreds of nights in a row. It's no wonder that she's so good at it."

A few people walked in front of us, and Nash checked the time on his expensive watch. "It's getting late," he said. "I'm going to tell Vaughn that we're ready for him to pick us up."

Vaughn was the Hastings' family driver who had driven us here in the expensive SUV.

I'd always thought it would be weird to have someone drive you around places, listening in on all of the private conversations. But the SUV had a partition between the front and back seats, so the ride here had actually been really nice. It felt like it was just the two of us.

Did I dare hope that the back of the Escalade might give us enough privacy to finally have our first kiss?

*You bet I'm hoping for one after such a magical night.*

Nash texted Vaughn, and then after we both stood, he offered to help me with my coat.

As he held my white coat out for me, we shared a long look at each other that made my stomach muscles flutter. He helped me slip my arms into the sleeves, and then he pulled his over-coat on. He held out his hand, which I took, and led me out of the theater.

The black Escalade was waiting for us out front, and Nash helped me up into the vehicle.

The lights of the city reflected on the dark windows as we drove through the busy streets.

"I'm really glad we got to do this," Nash said about a half-hour into our drive back to Eden Falls. "I've always wanted to do a Broadway date with someone, but it never felt right until you."

"Yeah?" I asked, flattered that he'd picked me for something so special.

He nodded. "I'm sure it's pretty obvious..." He reached over to take my hand in his. "But I really like you, Elyse."

"I like you too, Nash," I said, looking at the way he was drawing a swirly pattern on the palm of my hand.

"You really do?" His blue eyes searched mine in the dark vehicle.

I nodded, meeting his gaze. "I do."

And with my confirmation, he got the biggest smile on his face. "Well, isn't that just perfect?"

"I think so," I said. And the way his smile lit up his whole face in that moment made me feel so light and giddy.

"Well then...." He licked his lips as he looked down at our hands again. "If I like you, and you like me, I was wondering if you'd be up to trying something out."

"Yeah?" My chest felt tight with anticipation as I wondered what he was about to suggest.

He pursed his lips. "You see, I've been paying close attention to our rehearsal schedule and noticed that we're supposed to work on the 'Point of No Return' scene next week, as well as the 'Final Lair' where Christine and the Phantom are supposed to kiss and—" He rubbed the back of his neck like he was nervous again. "—I guess I was just thinking that I'd rather not have our first kiss be in front of everyone."

"Uh huh..." I nodded, my pulse throbbing in my neck as I waited for him to say what I thought he was going to say.

"And I guess I was wondering if it would be okay if I kissed you right now?"

"Oh," I said, somewhat caught off guard by how it felt to hear him say those words.

I mean, I'd guessed that was what he was planning to say, but it just felt a little different than I'd expected to have him actually ask to kiss me.

But that was just me being weird and awkward myself. Before too many seconds could pass, I said, "O-of course. I-I'd really like that."

Okay, that sounded awkward, too. But as long as this led to me kissing Nash, it would be worth fumbling our way through.

"Okay, cool." Nash sat up a little straighter. "I guess we should..." He leaned closer. And when I realized that we were doing this like *right now*, I leaned closer as well. After a little nose bumping and head bobbing where we tried to get the angle right, we finally kissed.

And it was nice.

Nash's lips were soft, and he was so gentle with me like he thought I was made of thin glass and might break if he wasn't careful.

When he slipped his fingers beneath my jaw to support the kiss, I noticed they were trembling slightly.

He was so nervous.

I was about to slip my hand behind his neck to signal that it was okay for him to treat me less like a china doll and more like a girl with raging hormones who had been waiting weeks and weeks for this moment to happen—but he pulled away from the kiss a second later.

"Wow," he said, releasing a big sigh and smiling like he'd just had the best first kiss of his life. "Did that actually just happen?"

"Yeah," I said.

It just did.

---

NASH KISSED me again when he dropped me off at the school, and it went a little better than our first kiss.

It was sweet.

Very sweet.

And I tried to get myself a little more into it. But for whatever reason, whether I was just having an off moment, or I was too tired to figure it out, the sparks that I'd been expecting just didn't come.

*Not like they had when I kissed Asher.*

I pushed the thought away.

I didn't need to compare the two guys.

They were very different from each other, so of course the way they kissed me was different.

Most likely, Nash and I just needed a little more practice to get used to each other. Two mediocre kisses didn't mean we couldn't have amazing chemistry later.

We could figure this out.

## 26

## ASHER

IS *Nash ever going to bring Elyse back?* My knee bounced as I looked at the grandfather clock in the corner for about the fiftieth time tonight. It was ten minutes to midnight, and I'd been watching a movie in the common room with Hunter, Scarlett, and a few other students.

Could I tell anyone what the plot was for the movie playing on the large TV in front of me?

No. I probably couldn't even name two characters since I'd been so distracted by what might be going on between Elyse and Nash.

Was she enjoying their date?

Had it been as romantic as it sounded when I'd heard Nash talk about it?

Had he kissed her?

Had she liked it?

Were they making out in the back of the Escalade right now in the way I had wanted to make out with Elyse last night?

It took about an hour and a half to drive here from the city, so if they'd left on time and didn't make any other stops, they should be back by now.

Curfew was in ten minutes. If she didn't get back soon, she'd be late.

But maybe she didn't care. Maybe spending some extra time with her crush was worth risking getting in trouble with Heather and the headmistress.

Unless she was staying at her dad's house. I'd heard Ava telling Scarlett that she was hanging out there tonight.

I hoped that wasn't the case, because I couldn't wait all the way until tomorrow to see her. I'd already been in my head all afternoon, trying to figure out how to bring up the debutante ball and how to offer to be her escort in just the right way.

I couldn't wait another eight hours or more to see her.

There was an explosion on the TV screen that broke me from my spiraling thoughts. I tried to focus on the movie again. Surely there was something about this movie that was more interesting than my worries about what Nash and Elyse might be doing together right now.

The camera panned in closer to the woman on the screen covered in smoke and ash. She was leaning over the man she was supposed to be falling in love with, tears streaming down her cheeks because she thought he might be dead.

I looked at the clock again.

How in the world had it only been a minute since I last checked?

I was just pulling out my phone to distract myself with mindless social media scrolling when one of the big doors pushed open.

I held my breath as I waited for someone to step through.

But it was only Addison and Evan.

My chest fell and I went back to reaching for my phone, but then another person walked through the door behind them.

A beautiful girl wearing a white wool coat and a black dress, her cheeks flushed from the cold.

Elyse.

She shut the door behind her and started tiptoeing toward the stairs like she was worried she was disrupting our movie.

As she started up the staircase that led to the girls' dorms, I quickly grabbed the script she'd left in my room from where I'd stowed it on the floor and then hurried to follow her.

She used her ID card to unlock the door, not seeming to notice that I was following her, and I managed to slip through the door behind her just before it clicked shut.

Usually, guys were supposed to check in with Heather so she would know they were in the land of the forbidden, but I didn't see her anywhere.

I'd just be a few minutes anyway, so instead of knocking on Heather's room and waiting for her to give me the go-ahead, I just followed Elyse down the first hall.

"Hey, Elyse," I said quietly, so no one in the surrounding dorm rooms would hear me. "Can I talk to you for a minute?"

She jumped a little, like she hadn't expected anyone to be so close behind her. She turned around and said, "Asher?"

"Yeah," I said. "Sorry to startle you. I just wanted to talk to you about something real quick."

She looked down the hall, like she was worried Heather might come around the corner to find me. And then she said, "Here, just come to my room and we can talk."

If I'd been more myself right now, I probably would have teased her about breaking the rules and letting her bad-girl side come out. But since I was a ball of nerves, I kept my mouth shut and quietly followed her down the hall.

As we walked past the doors, I realized that I had no idea which room was hers. I looked at the various doors and the different things the occupants had put on them to make them their own. One had a Christmas wreath. Another had strings of purple beads hanging down from the top of the door frame.

We kept walking down the long corridor, and only once we made it to the very end of the hall did she stop.

And when I looked at the number seven in the center of her door, a sense of déjà vu mixed with dread filled my stomach.

Because I'd been to this exact room many times before.

Because it was Bailee's room.

## 27

ASHER

"SO, WHAT DID YOU NEED?" Elyse asked after she closed the door behind us.

"Oh, I..." I reached for her script that I'd rolled up and put in my back pocket, trying to push away the flashbacks of Bailee and all the time we'd spent together in this very room. "I was just bringing you this."

"Oh, thanks." She took it from me. "I forgot I left it in your room."

"Yeah, the fire alarm kind of messed things up last night."

Her eyes widened, and I realized it probably sounded like I was suggesting the fire alarm had messed up the kiss I'd almost given her.

"I mean—" I cleared my throat. "—we left in such a hurry, so of course you couldn't grab it."

"Yeah. Safety first." She rocked back on her heels, and we stared at each other for an awkward moment. Was she thinking about that almost kiss? Or maybe the other kisses we'd actually had?

I shook my head. She probably wasn't thinking about any of

those things. She was probably wondering why the heck I was just standing in her room now that I'd delivered her script back to her.

Which meant that right now was probably the time to ask if I could be her escort.

But since it was awkward just bringing it up when we'd never even talked about the debutante ball before, I found myself asking her instead, "So, how was *The Phantom?*"

"The musical?"

"Uh, yeah..." Did she think I was referring to Nash as "The Phantom" since he was playing him? Because, sorry, I was still too petty to give him that title when I'd initially wanted that role for myself. "That's the show you went to tonight, right?"

"Yes, of course." She set her script on her desk.

*Bailee's desk.*

I forced the thought away. It was so weird being in here again.

"It was good," she said. "Really, really good actually."

"That's good." I swallowed the excess saliva in my mouth.

*Okay, just ask her and leave*, I told myself. *Just because you spent a lot of time in this room with a girl who might be dead doesn't mean you need to focus on it.*

My gaze caught on the top corner of her window. Was the moon-and-stars sticker still there? The one Bailee and I had stuck there the night we'd ordered pizza to her room, pigged out on candy, and played games all night.

The sticker that was supposed to symbolize that even when things were hard, we'd always be there for each other. Just like the moon and stars were always there even if you couldn't see them behind the clouds.

I tore my gaze away from the window. I didn't need to look for signs of Bailee in this room. It was Elyse and Ava's room now. It had their things in it.

Though, was that Bailee's same bed and dresser, too? Had they left all the same furniture in here when they'd cleaned her things out?

I rubbed the back of my neck. And I must have had a look of panic in my eyes or something because Elyse asked, "Is everything okay, Asher? You seem a little off right now."

*Yeah, I bet I am.*

Should I tell her? Or would that just make things weird?

I'd kept so much of Bailee's and my relationship a secret. Would it do any good to talk about it now?

But when I met Elyse's golden-brown eyes, I found myself wanting to talk about the things I'd never been able to talk about before.

"Sorry." I leaned my back against her closed door and ran a hand through my hair. "I'm just having a lot of memories hit me all at once."

"You are?" She furrowed her brow like she didn't understand why I'd suddenly go down memory lane.

"I just..." I let out a long breath. "I kind of spent a lot of time in this room last year."

The familiar pucker line formed between her eyebrows for a moment before she seemed to understand. "Was this..." Her eyes narrowed as they searched my face. "Was this Bailee's room then?"

"Yeah." I glanced around the room again. At the photos and art Elyse and Ava had hung on the walls. To the pink curtains that framed the two large windows. The string lights they had hung near the ceiling. "It looks completely different. But yeah, this was her room last year."

Bailee hadn't had a roommate, since she liked her privacy and her parents could afford the extra rate to turn what was meant to be a double room into a single. There had been a couch and a mini fridge in the place where Ava's bed now sat. And both closets were stocked to the brim with designer outfits.

I'd heard Ava was into fashion and design, taking after the twins' mom. But from what I could see of the closet that I assumed was hers, it had nothing on Bailee Vanderbilt's closet. Bailee had an outfit for every occasion and rarely wore the same thing twice.

Elyse gazed around the room as if seeing it with new eyes. With a frown, she asked, "Is it weird that no one told us this was her room?"

"I don't know." I shrugged. "The school likes to switch things up and put students in different halls every year, so the people staying in this hall now probably didn't even know it was hers."

Bailee had been very popular and had collected a lot of fans to her fan club, but she'd always kept them at a distance. I doubted she'd even invited many people besides me into her sanctuary.

"So...you said you spent a lot of time in here?" Elyse asked, sounding curious of what kinds of things we'd done together.

I'd told her at the cabin that I'd never shared a bed with a girl before, but that didn't mean we couldn't get up to mischief during the day if the door was closed and no one knew I was in here.

Since I didn't want Elyse to assume Bailee and I had been more intertwined than we really were, I said, "We mostly did homework or talked."

Bailee always found ways to sneak me in when Heather wasn't watching, and then we'd just talk and laugh about all the things we'd done that day to make people think we were so in love with each other.

"So I haven't been sleeping on a bed where you..." She

drifted off when she glanced at the bed behind her with a purple comforter.

"No." I shook my head. "Like I said at the cabin, we weren't like that." I cleared my throat and rubbed the back of my neck, deciding now was the time to come clean. "We, um, we were actually just friends."

"What?" Elyse looked confused. "What do you mean you were just friends?"

"Well..." I pressed my lips together, trying to figure out the best way to explain. Then with a shrug, I said, "We were just acting like we were a couple the whole time. Our relationship was all just a big ruse that Bailee came up with for her own entertainment."

She'd gotten such a huge kick out of it, like it filled some sort of need she had to always be on display and yet untouchable to everyone around her. She wanted people to think they knew her, without having them actually know anything.

She'd been especially delighted when the teachers bought it—loved it when the biology and chemistry professor Owen replaced, Mr. Hicks, would get after us for flirting too much in his class. It was like a little game to her, to see just how far she could push his buttons before he would split us up and make her sit in the front row and me in the back.

"Wait." Elyse sat down on the edge of her bed and started unbuttoning her wool coat. "Are you saying that you weren't actually boyfriend and girlfriend?"

"Not in the sense that everyone believed, no." I slid down the door so I could sit on the floor. "We were in what I guess most people would call a 'fake relationship.'"

"Seriously?" Her mouth hung open, and she looked like she was searching for words. "Are you saying that all this time I've been feeling bad that you lost this girl who you were madly in love with... All the times I felt so sorry that you were suspected of hurting the love of your life..." She scrunched up her nose, betrayal obvious in her expression. "And none of it was even real?" She scoffed in disgust. "Did you even miss her? Or was all of that just an act as well?"

And those questions right there were exactly why I hadn't told anyone about any of this. Because it made me look bad.

Really, really bad.

All the lies. All the pretending. The deceit.

Maybe Ava and Elyse had been right.

Maybe I really was a *bad boy*.

"It looks pretty bad, doesn't it?" I said.

She nodded. "Yeah." She pulled her coat off, revealing the rest of her dress that I'd been so curious about. It was sleeveless, with a high neckline that tapered in like an apron—only with scalloped edges and way sexier than an apron.

She stood and hung her coat on a hanger in the closet to my right. Then she kicked off the high-heeled black boots she'd been wearing.

She turned back to me and said, "So, has anything you've told me about yourself even been real?" She pursed her lips and seemed to mull over what she'd just said. Then with a contemplative look, she said, "Actually, now that I think about it, I don't know if you've told me that much about yourself. I know you're from Eden Falls and grew up on the same road as Nash, and that you lived with the Carmichaels in Ridgewater. But I still have no idea about your mom and why your brother has custody of you."

She was right. I hadn't told her a whole lot about myself and my past. Nothing super important, really.

None of the real dirt, anyway.

Because the real stuff was what made me isolate myself

from everyone else in the past. And for once...with meeting Elyse...I hadn't wanted to be judged by my baggage. I'd wanted Elyse to get to know just me the way I was today.

But I guess it was hard to get to know someone without understanding the things from their past that shaped them into who they were today.

I lifted my gaze to where she stood a few feet away, wondering if she'd even be willing to hear me out. If she'd listen with an open mind and be able to understand why I'd done the things that I'd done...even if they weren't always necessarily *good.*

She pulled the chair out from under her desk and sat down. Leaning forward, she asked in a whisper, "Do I even know you, Asher?"

When I saw the hurt reflected in her beautiful eyes, my stomach churned.

"I'd like to think that you know about the important parts," I said carefully, knowing I was currently sitting on very thin ice. "I may have pretended my relationship with Bailee was more serious than it actually was. But everything else was real." I lifted a shoulder. "And even then, I did—I still *do* miss Bailee. She might not have been in love with me like everyone thought, but she was the closest friend I had."

Elyse sighed, as if trying to decide whether she wanted to hear me out or not. She leaned back in her chair and was opening her mouth to say something when there was a soft knock on the door, followed by what sounded like Heather's voice. "Elyse? Are you in there?"

*Crap!*

I looked at Elyse with wide eyes, wondering what I was supposed to do. If I got caught in the girls' dorm after curfew, we'd both be in huge trouble.

Elyse looked around the room, and then pointing to her closet, she mouthed, "Climb in there."

I didn't say anything. I just crawled away from the door, got myself to a standing position as quietly as I could, and then pushed myself into her closet between the clothes that smelled like Elyse.

"Yes, I'm in here," Elyse called out to Heather as she slid the closet door shut for me. "Just a sec."

Darkness enveloped me, my heartbeat thudding in my ears as I waited for her to open the door and hopefully not rat me out to Heather.

I heard her door creak open a second later. "Sorry about that," Elyse said, somewhat breathlessly. "I was just about to change into my pajamas."

Did she sound guilty? Like there was a boy hiding in her closet?

"Okay, good." Heather's muffled voice drifted through the crack in the door. "Sorry to bug you so late, but you didn't check in, and I just wanted to make sure you made it back from your date."

"Oh yeah, sorry. I was a little distracted when I got back and completely forgot."

Had she been distracted because I'd followed after her? Or was it because she'd been in dreamland after her magical date with Nash?

She'd said the date was good, but I still didn't know exactly what that meant.

"That's okay," Heather said. "I'm just glad you made it back safely." There was a pause, and I wondered if Heather was peeking her head around the room.

Had I left anything on the floor?

Heather spoke again. "Anyway, it's after midnight, so if you could turn the lights out soon that would be great."

"Of course," Elyse said. "It's been a big day, and I'm definitely ready to get some sleep."

My phone vibrated in my pocket, making my already hammering heart skip a beat.

Had Heather just heard that?

I held my breath and waited for my hiding place to be discovered, but then it sounded like Heather and Elyse were saying goodbye so maybe they hadn't heard it.

Or maybe Heather just assumed it was Elyse's phone since Elyse's reputation for being a rule follower didn't exactly put off the "I'm secretly hiding a boy in my closet" vibe.

The door clicked shut, and I breathed a sigh of relief.

"She's gone," Elyse said, opening the closet door a little. "But, um, if you could actually just stay in there for another minute, I'm going to try to make at least some of what I just told Heather true and change into my pajamas."

"Uh, sure."

She closed the closet door again, and I pulled out my phone to see who had texted me. It was Hunter.

> Hunter: Theo just came to our room to make sure we were in bed. I told him you were having stomach issues from the fajitas tonight and were hanging out on the toilet. You're welcome. ;)

*You're welcome?*

Seriously? He couldn't come up with a less embarrassing excuse than that?

I was going to have a fun time meeting Theo's gaze tomorrow.

I texted him back.

> Me: Thanks for all that. I'm just with Elyse right now. Be back later.

Another text from him came through.

> Hunter: Good luck on asking her out.

Yeah, I'd definitely need a ton of luck there since right now, I wasn't sure she even thought I was a decent human anymore.

Hopefully, once I explained everything we'd be on okay terms.

I slipped my phone back into my pocket, expecting to be stuck in the closet for another minute or two, but then Elyse slid the closet door open a few inches wide.

"That was fas—" I started to say before noticing that she was still wearing the same dress from her date.

So maybe she wasn't changing after all?

"Hey, so this is probably going to sound really weird, but... um, I think my zipper is stuck and...well..." She looked down at the floor before meeting my gaze again. "And since Ava isn't going to be coming back tonight, I was wondering if you could help me get it unstuck."

"Oh," I said, my hands suddenly going tingly. "Y-you want me to unzip your dress?"

"Just like halfway," she said quickly, her cheeks noticeably pinker. "Just until it's unstuck. I can take it from there, of course."

"Of course." I cleared my throat. "I can help you with that."

She must have felt as awkward as I did because she didn't say anything else, just immediately turned her back to me.

After running my gaze across the black fabric of her dress, I could see what she was talking about. She'd managed to pull it down a few inches but now it was snagged on the fabric behind the zipper.

I started to reach for the zipper, but since it was awkward having all of her coats and other clothes from her closet pressing against my shoulders, I stepped out of the closet.

"Okay, let me just see if I can do this." I swallowed hard as I came closer, hoping I could stay professional. This was not the time to let the overwhelming attraction I had for her to come out.

But when I bent close to her neck to see what I was doing, her light perfume hit me. And man, she really did smell amazing.

Looked amazing, too. I couldn't recall if I'd ever seen her bare shoulders before, since she usually wore her school uniform or T-shirts.

She had really nice shoulders. Slender but strong and a beautiful light tan color.

I tried to gently tug the zipper down, but it didn't budge. So I braced one hand on her shoulder and tried to pull the zipper up first instead, thinking it would right itself that way. Still nothing.

"I think if you just, like, pull some of the fabric to the side, that might do it," Elyse said, her voice breathier than usual.

"Okay..." And since I knew my own voice would probably sound off if I said anything more, I slipped my fingers beneath the fabric at her back, keeping my thumb on the top side, and gently pulled the fabric away from the zipper.

She shivered, like the graze of my fingers against her skin surprised her. I briefly wondered if she liked it, but then I made my mind focus back on the task at hand. I was able to get the zipper to finally move up before I slowly pulled it down a few inches past the trouble area.

I stopped unzipping once the back of her semi-sheer black

bra came into view. And dang, I really didn't need to know what kind of underthings Elyse wore.

Until now, I'd never even thought about it, but now that I knew what the black strip of fabric looked like against her satiny, smooth skin—

I closed my eyes and gulped.

*Nothing like a new image to keep my mind busy when my head hits my pillow tonight.*

Once I was done, Elyse spun on her heel and thanked me for my assistance. "And if you could just go back into the closet for another minute, I'll hurry and change."

"Sure," I said, not realizing until that moment that my fingers were twitching from the feel of her skin.

I stepped back inside the closet, shut the door, and tried really, really hard not to picture what was happening on the other side.

When that didn't work so great, I pinched my eyes shut tight and forced myself to imagine her about a hundred years older with thousands of wrinkles and wearing a palm-tree-patterned muumuu.

There were some rustling sounds, and another minute later, she said, "Okay, I'm decent. You can come out now."

I slid the door open. But instead of the muumuu I'd been imagining, Elyse was wearing a silky black button-up pajama shirt with matching pants.

Was she still wearing that black bra underneath?

*Stop thinking about it, Asher!*

I must be craving Elyse really bad or something, because Bailee used to prance around her room wearing her skimpy workout clothes and I'd barely batted an eye. But one look at Elyse's back and my brain was buzzing.

How in the world was I going to keep from completely short-circuiting when she wore the corset dresses Christine wore for the musical? I mean, I'd never seen Elyse in anything with a low neckline before, but just from the shape of her body, I knew my eyes would have a hard time focusing on her face at all times.

*Grandma wearing a muumuu. Grandma wearing a muumuu.*

"What did you say?" Elyse asked.

"Uh, nothing."

Had I said that out loud?

She gave me a funny look like she thought I might be crazy, but then she shrugged and sat against a pile of pillows on her bed.

"So now that Heather thinks I'm headed to bed all alone in here tonight," she said. "I think it's time I hear this story about how you were never really in love with the girl everyone thought you adored."

"Okay..." I looked around for a place to sit. They didn't have a couch in here like Bailee used to have, and Ava probably wouldn't like me sitting on her bed. My gaze landed on the desk chair she'd pulled out earlier. I swiveled it around and pulled it close to the foot of Elyse's bed.

I was about to sit when she stopped me and said, "Actually, could you switch off the light real quick? Heather might notice the light coming from under my door."

"Sure."

I flipped the switch on the wall and was about to fumble my way back to my seat when the string lights above our heads turned on, bathing the room in a gentle glow.

"Okay, so I guess I should just start at the beginning?" I asked.

"That's usually a good place to start." She pulled a fuzzy gray blanket over her lap.

"Well..." I licked my lips. "I guess it all started last winter when we were doing *Les Misérables*. Bailee and I had been in the drama program together since freshman year but didn't really hang out outside of that. Anyway, she came to rehearsal one day last January with tears in her eyes. After trying to push through the scene we were supposed to be working on that day and failing, I asked her what was wrong."

I could still see the heartbreak in her blue eyes and the mascara smudges on her cheeks. She'd always been so put together before—never a hair out of place. So I knew something must be wrong for her to come to rehearsal looking like that.

"After crying on my shoulder for a long time, she told me that she'd broken up with this guy she'd been dating. I guess they'd been pretty serious and had been dating under the radar since summer break. I'd never seen her with him at school, so I had no idea who he was or when they'd had time to see each other. But from how torn up she seemed, I figured that they must have been really close."

I adjusted my position on the chair to get more comfortable. "Anyway, she stopped crying eventually, rehearsal ended, and I expected things to just go back to normal between us. She'd continue thriving in her popularity bubble. I'd continue to lie low while playing the occasional prank on Nash."

"So at least your rivalry with Nash has always been real." The corner of Elyse's lip quirked up.

"Yes," I said, daring a half-smile back. "I don't think that's something I'd brag about if it wasn't real."

Our feud really was stupid the more I thought about it. Childish.

"What happened next?" Elyse asked, bringing me back to my story. "I'm guessing that since you ended up with the whole school believing you were the ultimate high school relationship, things didn't go back to normal."

"That would be right," I said, my mind taking me back to

the year before. "Things were pretty normal the next few days. We got to know each other a little better. Became friends—not super close or anything—but we got along well enough. She was actually super funny, like in an almost manic sort of way." I smiled as I remembered some of the crazy antics she got up to. "Pretty soon we were hanging out after rehearsals, and she was inviting me to sit with her at lunch."

"Sounds like things were pretty good then," Elyse said.

"They were," I said. "And I guess I just kind of lapped it all up because for the first time, I felt like I belonged. I had friends that I actually hung out with on the weekends instead of just classmates that I sometimes said hi to in the hall."

Bailee had been magic that way. Even though she had her own motives for all the things she did, she really was great at making people happy.

"Anyway, a couple weeks before the musical wrapped, we saw one of the posters for the upcoming Valentine's Day dance and got this crazy idea. We joked about how funny it would be if we decided to go together and pretend like we were suddenly madly in love, just to see if we could get people to believe it.

"We went back to her room to watch a movie, and I didn't think anything of the Valentine's dance again until she brought it up the next day. She told me she'd been thinking about it all night and said she really wanted to go to the dance because she'd missed out on all of the other formal dances. I guess her older boyfriend hadn't wanted to go to a high school dance since he'd already graduated." I shrugged. "Then she said there weren't any other guys at school that she was interested in, and she knew that I wasn't interested in anyone, either... So I thought about it.

"I wasn't sure at first—I really didn't want to be anything more than friends. Plus, I knew there were tons of guys who would love to take her out. But she said I was the only one she could see herself going with, even going as far as telling me that I was the only guy hot enough to believably be her date."

The way Bailee could cater to anyone's ego was her superpower.

I glanced at Elyse, feeling my cheeks warm after saying how attractive Bailee said I was. But instead of looking like she disagreed, she just nodded and said, "She must have been really beautiful if you two matched."

"She was," I said.

*Though not as beautiful as you...*

Not to me, anyway.

"As you probably guessed, we ended up going to the dance together. We played it up so much that by the end of the night, everyone was tagging us in their social media posts as hashtag Ashlee—our new couple name, using the first three letters of my name and the last three of hers."

It would have been more fitting to put Bailee's name first since she was the mastermind behind the whole thing.

"Sounds like you guys were as epic as everyone made you sound," Elyse said. The room was too dark to see her face, but did I detect a hint of envy in her voice?

Was Elyse jealous of the fake relationship I'd had?

Was it wrong of me to hope that she was?

I shrugged. "We were pretty great together."

"I heard you guys were voted Prom King and Queen as well," Elyse said.

"That was another Bailee brainchild." I nodded. "After the notoriety that we gained from the Valentine's dance, she wanted to see how far we could take it, and so we really ramped things up after that. We came up with pet names for each other. We held hands everywhere we went. Sat close whenever we were in front of people. Sneak away from parties to pretend like we were finding a secluded place to make out."

"And did you?" Elyse asked.

"What? Make out?"

"Um, yeah...?" she said, and there was a strain in her voice that made me think she didn't want me to tell her that we had.

But since tonight was all about the truth, I said, "We were pretending to be obsessed with each other, so yeah, we kissed."

"A lot?" she asked.

Was this some kind of test? Because if she was going to tell me that I shouldn't have kissed someone I wasn't into, then I should probably tell her that she shouldn't have kissed me the way she had last night when she had plans to go on a date with another guy.

Not that I was complaining. I certainly hadn't minded how far into character we'd gotten last night.

"We made out a fair amount," I said.

More so at the beginning of things. That last month before she disappeared, she'd been more distracted, claiming she was tired and just wanted to go to bed instead of hang out.

"And is that normal for you?" Elyse asked. "Kissing girls you don't have feelings for?"

I narrowed my eyes, trying to figure out what she was trying to get at.

"I wouldn't say it's normal," I said. "But since we both knew it was just for fun, I didn't see any harm in it."

"Interesting..."

I studied her for a moment. What was going through her mind? But the female mind was too complicated for me to decode right now.

I said, "Anyway, we kept our little ruse going all the way through April, went to Prom together and were crowned Prom King and Queen. Everything was great on my side of things, and well..." I sighed, looking down at my hands in my lap. "I guess after over two months of pretending to be in love with her and doing all the things couples do together when they're in love..."

"It wasn't fake for you anymore?" Elyse finished for me, somehow guessing my exact words.

I nodded and lifted my head to look at her. "Somewhere along the way I started to catch feelings for Bailee, and yeah, I realized I wasn't acting anymore. It was real for me."

## 28

## ASHER

"SO DID YOU TELL HER?" Elyse asked. "Did she feel the same?"

"I didn't tell her right away," I said. "I wanted to feel things out before I said anything."

"What happened next then?" Elyse asked. "If you were already Prom King and Queen at this point, it means she had to disappear sometime shortly after you realized how you felt about her."

"This was just a few days before she vanished." I sighed again, taking myself back to that last week with Bailee. "We were both really busy that next week with school and the spring play. She missed school for a couple of days and went to visit her parents in New Haven."

At least that was what she'd told me. Who knew if any of the things she said she was doing were actually true.

"Then on the night she disappeared, she came to The Italian Amigos where I was working my shift. I could tell that something was wrong." She'd been a little more on edge than usual. "I asked to take my break. It was cold outside, so we went and sat in a corner booth.

"I asked her what was going on and she told me that she wanted to break up. She said that we had put on a great show and it had been fun, but she was ready to move on to the next adventure."

"The next adventure?" Elyse asked, like that should be some sort of clue.

"Something like that." I shrugged. "Anyway, I was obviously shocked since I thought things were going so well. And since I realized I had feelings for her, I was more than happy to keep everything going. I told her I didn't want to break up, that I actually liked her and hoped she might have some of the same feelings. But she told me she was sorry, that it had all been pretend on her side and just a way for her to try to get over her ex."

"So she was kissing you to get over her ex?" Elyse asked.

"I don't know. I guess...?" I held my hands out. "Anyway, I got kind of emotional because I was confused and sad, and then she got upset at me. She told me that she'd made it clear going into this that it was all just for show and I shouldn't have let any feelings get involved. I got defensive because she was basically scolding me for falling in love with her. I told her it wasn't my fault and that I couldn't control how I felt."

I shook my head. It had been a mess. And it was proof that you can't beg someone to love you back. No matter how much you care about someone, you can't force them to fall in love with you if they don't want to.

Especially if they were still in love with someone else.

Which would probably be a good thing for me to remember when it came to Elyse. Because if she was still in love with Nash after their date tonight, then it meant I should probably find a way to not like her.

I didn't need to learn that lesson again.

"Anyway, we broke up that night. She left the restaurant, and I finished my shift. I texted her when I got back to the school because I wanted a little more closure, and yeah, I also hoped I could convince her that being together was a better idea than breaking up."

It was pathetic. Trying to chase a girl who was just using me to get over another guy.

"She didn't respond to my texts, so I figured she'd just gone to bed early again and that I'd talk to her the next morning."

"Except the next morning you found out she never came back to the school," Elyse said, knowing that part of the story well enough.

I nodded. "I thought that she might have caught a train back to her parents' house since they lived in New York," I said. "But it became apparent pretty quickly that she was missing."

"Did anyone suspect that you had broken up?" Elyse asked.

I shook my head. "At first, I planned to tell everyone that we'd broken up—I didn't want to continue to lie about our relationship. But when the police called me in for the initial questioning, I realized that with her missing, the last thing I needed anyone to think was that we were having problems. So I just pretended like everything had been okay and we were still as in love as ever. And I thought it was going to work—"

"Except Nash had seen you two fighting at the restaurant," Elyse interrupted.

"Yeah." I started to nod before her actual words and what they meant hit me. "Wait—" My thoughts stuttered to a stop. "*Nash* was the one who reported me to the police?"

Her eyes widened, and she covered her mouth with her hands.

"How long have you known it was Nash who reported

me?" My heart raced as I realized that I wasn't the only one of us keeping secrets.

Elyse had been keeping secrets from me, too.

"H-he told me last week," she said, removing her hands from her mouth.

I raised my eyebrows and leaned toward her. "And you didn't think it was important to mention that to me?"

"You guys already hate each other." She sat up straighter and shook her head. "I didn't want to add fuel to the fire. Plus, I think he was just trying to do the right thing. He was watching out for Bailee."

She was siding with *him?*

She was siding with Nash?!

"Do you know what those accusations did to me?" I asked, feeling my entire body tremble as my temper flared. "Do you know how bad it was?" I shook my head and stood. "I had *death threats*, Elyse. I had people messaging me and telling me that I should just kill myself because of what they thought I did to Bailee. That I was no better than my mom and the apple must not have fallen too far from the tree."

"What?" She pulled her head back, looking so confused.

"Oh, that's right," I said, pushing her desk chair away from me with my foot. "You weren't in Eden Falls when my dad and sister died in a car accident caused by my mom. Or when my mom got sent to prison for ten years right after that because she'd been high as a kite when she'd gotten behind the wheel."

"What?" Elyse covered her mouth with her hand again. "You lost your sister too?"

"Yeah." I shook my head and wiped at my eyes that were suddenly wet. "I lost everything in that stupid accident. And then just a couple years later when I was finally starting to feel normal, everything went to crap all over again. Not only did the girl I was in love with disappear, but I basically lost all of my other friends and got ran out of the only home I had left because of what Nash reported." I took a deep breath and tried to will away the tears that were suddenly coming out of nowhere. *"It freaking sucked."*

I shoved her stupid chair that wouldn't get out of my freaking way and walked to Ava's side of the room to face the corner—I was too embarrassed to have Elyse see me angry cry.

I was supposed to be over this. It had been four years since my dad and Callie died. Three and a half years since my mom's sentencing. I'd gone to all the therapy the state had paid for. I'd stopped trying to run from the pain and started allowing myself to just feel it and let it flow through me so it could then go away.

But here I was again, getting hit with the feelings out of nowhere and having a breakdown in front of the girl I'd wanted to ask on a date earlier tonight.

*This is so stupid.*

I dropped my head, letting my forehead rest against the white painted wall and tried to will these emotions to go away. I could feel them again later when no one was around to watch me.

There was a rustling sound behind me, like Elyse was climbing off her bed.

Why had I chosen the corner? I should have just risked getting caught by Heather and run out the door.

"I'm sorry I didn't know about your family." Elyse's voice sounded closer behind me than I expected. "Or the death threats."

She touched my back, and I stiffened, not wanting to let myself be comforted by her because I knew if I did, I'd really lose it.

"I'm so sorry all of that happened, Asher," she whispered.

And before I knew it, two arms were wrapping around me

from behind and Elyse was pressing herself against my back in a hug.

Well, now I really felt like a big baby.

I sighed and turned around. Crying in a corner was actually more humiliating than crying in front of her. But instead of stepping away, she just hugged me even tighter, resting her head against my chest and not letting me go anywhere.

And even though everything in me wanted to run away, I wiped my eyes with the back of my hand, drew in a deep breath, and let my arms go around her.

I leaned back into the wall, pulling her with me, and a few more deep breaths later, I was able to calm back down.

"You gonna be okay?" she asked, inspecting my face.

"Yeah," I said, not really sure but hoping it was true.

She let her arms drop and stepped away. "Sorry I didn't tell you about Nash. I was just trying to keep you guys from hating each other even more."

"I know," I said. Then looking behind her, I added, "Sorry I kicked your chair. It was just really in my way right then."

"It's fine." She chuckled. "Sometimes you just gotta kick something."

She walked back to where it had fallen over and righted it before tucking it under her desk.

I drew in another deep breath, hoping to calm myself once and for all. "Anyway, that's basically my story. Thanks for hearing me out."

"Anytime," she said, looking like she actually meant it. "Thanks for telling me all that. I'm sure it wasn't easy."

"Yeah, talking about my past isn't something I'm very good at."

"Well..." She swallowed like she was nervous. "If you ever want to tell me anything else, I'm here."

"Thank you," I said. "I might take you up on that sometime."

"I hope you do."

I studied her for a long moment, wondering what she was thinking about me now. Did all of the romantic feelings I'd felt from her last night in my room disappear once she found out I'd been lying to everyone for the past year?

I hoped not.

I hoped that we could get back to that place we'd been before tonight. Hoped that she hadn't just written me off for good in her mind.

Falling in love with someone took a lot of trust, and with everything she now knew about me, it would probably take a lot for her to trust me again.

Especially since she already had golden-boy Nash wining and dining her.

I still had no idea how things stood between them after their date. For all I knew, they were boyfriend and girlfriend and planning their future after high school.

"Anyway," she said, breaking into my thoughts. "It's getting late. You should probably sneak back to your room now."

"You're right," I said. "It's probably close to one o' clock now."

"Should we check?" she asked, like it was a game.

She touched the screen of her phone that sat face up on her desk to look at the time, but my gaze landed on a text from Nash that said:

> Nash: Thanks again for tonight. Dinner, the musical…the car ride home. I'm already counting down the days until the debutante ball.

*Ouch.* I flinched when I wondered what might have happened on their car ride home.

Elyse must have realized I'd seen her text because she quickly turned her phone face down on her desk. "Looks like it's five to one."

"Yeah," I said, unable to say anything else right then because I was sure if I did, it would just come out sounding like I'd been kicked in the stomach by Nash.

*He was thanking her for the car ride home.*

They'd had a driver, and the backseat of his fancy Escalade was probably pretty big...

An image of them making out on the backseat came to mind.

Though, her hair hadn't seemed too much messier than it had when she'd left. And if I was going to make out with her, you bet I would be tangling my fingers in her hair...

Would it be weird if I asked her to just tell me what had happened so I could stop imagining things?

Yes.

Yes, it would be weird to ask her that.

So instead of saying anything about the text or her night with Nash, I said, "I should probably go."

"Yeah, you probably should."

I put my hand on the doorknob. Looking back at her once more, I wanted to ask what Nash had meant about the debutante ball. But deciding it probably meant what I thought it meant—that he was her escort—I simply said, "I'll see you later. Sleep well."

## 29

## ELYSE

I TRIED to fall asleep after Asher left my room, but instead of drifting off into a peaceful slumber, I lay there on my bed with my mind racing.

Had Asher actually confessed that his whole relationship with Bailee was just a big production? That they had simply been playing characters of themselves with Eden Falls as their stage?

It didn't seem like it could be real. People didn't do those kinds of things in real life.

Except, I knew it could actually happen in real life because that was exactly how Ava and Carter had gotten together. They'd started with a fake relationship.

Thankfully for them, they had both felt the same way about each other and it had worked out.

Asher hadn't been so lucky.

Was he still in love with her?

If Bailee were to come back today and tell him that she messed up and that she actually had feelings for him, too, would he want to be with her?

Ugh, I didn't want to think about it. Hearing about how much they'd kissed had already been enough for me.

Did that mean I was jealous? Jealous that they had such amazing chemistry that even when he knew it wasn't real, it made him *want* it to be real?

Was Bailee a better kisser than me?

I pushed the thought away. I didn't need to compare myself to a girl I'd never even met. I didn't even know what she looked like.

But Asher had said she was beautiful, so she was probably gorgeous. And fun and funny and all the things everyone had been saying about her since Asher came back to school and his missing ex was a hot topic again.

Was it bad that I hoped she wasn't actually as awesome as everyone had made her sound? That everyone was just viewing their memories of Bailee through rose-colored glasses because she was gone now?

Did that make me a bad person?

Yeah...it probably did.

I picked up my phone to do some research of my own. Everyone had social media these days—maybe Bailee did, and it was still up.

I typed in the name Bailee Vanderbilt in my Instagram app. A second later, my search page populated with a single account.

Really?

There was only one Bailee Vanderbilt in the world?

I guess that made my search easier, at least.

The profile showed a photo of a beautiful girl my age with dark-brown hair, a heart-shaped face, and a lean, athletic build. From the vibrant look in her dark-blue eyes, I knew this girl had to be Asher's Bailee.

Okay, not Asher's *Bailee*. I didn't want him to have a Bailee.

Not that I wanted her to not be alive. I just didn't want him to want her, because I wanted him to want me.

*Wait... Did I just think that I wanted Asher to want me? Is that what just happened?*

I shook my head and decided to ignore what my subconscious might be trying to tell me. I had just kissed Nash tonight and was going to the debutante ball with him.

Wanting to be with Asher right after I'd told Nash that I liked him would just make everything complicated.

I scrolled down the page to see what kinds of photos Bailee had liked enough to share with the world. There were lots of images of just herself. Her in front of the Eiffel tower with a Chloe bag over her shoulder. Pictures of her in what I guessed must be the costume she wore when she played Cosette.

Another of her sitting on the front steps of the academy in her school uniform with the caption: "Summer was a dream. Back to reality..."

And then there were the photos I was trying not to look too closely at. The ones with Asher.

My gaze stopped on a photo taken on what looked like my bed but with different bedding. His lips were pressed against her cheek, and she had a huge smile on her face.

They seemed so happy together. So playful and fun.

Next was of them at The Italian Amigos where he had his arms wrapped around her from behind and she was acting like she was going to cook something.

They had played their part so well. Even Bailee had a sparkle in her eye.

But I guess any heterosexual girl would have a hard time not swooning with arms like Asher's wrapped around her waist.

I glared at a few more photos of the happy couple before

scrolling back up to the top. The last image she'd posted was one of them dancing in the dimly lit great hall with crowns on their heads. The caption read: "So happy to be his Queen."

I noted the way he was looking at her. The softness in his gaze. The way he held her in his arms like there was no one he'd rather be with in the world.

And I could see what everyone else had talked about. Just from these photos, I could see the electric energy they'd had together.

Asher really did look like he was head-over-heels in love with Bailee.

Which I'd guess at that point, he had been.

I closed my phone and tossed it back onto my nightstand. I didn't need to see photos of Asher in love with another girl.

What I needed to do was pretend I wasn't insanely envious of this girl who had gotten Asher to fall in love with her when he wasn't supposed to. What I needed to do was get some sleep instead.

---

I SLEPT in late on Sunday, having been restless and awake until after two. When I went down for my late breakfast in the Great Hall, only a few students were left. I looked around to see if Asher might be there—if he'd slept in, too, and gotten a late start on his day—but I didn't find his wavy dark hair among those sitting at the tables.

When I got back to my room, Ava texted me, saying that she and Mack and our dad were going to come pick me up so we could test drive some cars this afternoon.

Brendon had decided to get us cars for our Yule gifts—a hugely extravagant gift in my opinion, since I hadn't grown up in the world of the rich and famous. But he'd told us that Mack had gotten a car for his sixteenth birthday, and insisted that, if anything, he was a year and a half late getting them for us.

So I changed into some comfortable clothes and was just adding a touch of blush to my cheeks when Scarlett knocked on my door.

"Hey," she said, stepping inside my room. She was wearing a pink floral-printed dress and dangly earrings, like she'd just gotten back from church.

"Hi." I let her in then shut the door behind her. I sat down on my bed to slip on my snow boots and asked, "What's up?"

"Not much," she said with a shrug as she looked around my room. "I was bored and thought I'd stop by to ask how your night was."

"My night?" I asked, unzipping one of my black boots. "Um... It was good." I shrugged, figuring she was asking about my date. "Dinner was super good and the musical was amazing."

I still wasn't quite sure about how it had ended. The two kisses at the end of the night hadn't quite gone like I'd been imagining the past several weeks. But they'd been good.

Fine.

Not horrible, at least.

"That's good," Scarlett said with a smile. "I know how excited Nash was about all of your plans."

"Yeah, it was really nice," I said. "Nash was sweet."

"I'd expect nothing less from Nash," Scarlett said. She was staring at the photo I had of my mom, Ava, and me that was sitting on my desk, like she was distracted or uncomfortable. I wondered if she was trying to get up the nerve to say something else.

I slipped my foot into my boot and zipped it up over my jeans for something to do while I waited.

"So, um..." She cleared her throat. "I was downstairs

watching a movie when you got back last night, and I, um, noticed Asher sneak up here behind you. What was that all about?"

She'd noticed that?

Had anyone else noticed Asher sneak into my room?

Did she think something had happened between us?

Was she fishing around to make sure I wasn't sneaking around with another guy behind Nash's back?

I picked up my other boot and unzipped it, trying to appear as innocent as I could. "He just came up to bring me my script," I said. "And then we just talked about some stuff."

Nothing to feel guilty about. I shouldn't feel guilty about just talking to a guy.

Talking to a guy I was insanely attracted to in my room after curfew...right after I'd gotten home from a magical date with another guy.

"What kind of stuff did you talk about?" she asked.

Why was she asking so many questions?

"Um, just how things were with him and Bailee," I answered honestly.

"Really?" Scarlett's dark eyebrows knitted together. "That's interesting that he would bring her up..."

Did she think I was lying? She seemed surprised that he and I would talk about his fake ex.

"I don't think he meant to bring her up, but I guess this was her room last year. And when he realized that, it kind of hit him with a bunch of memories all at once."

"Oh, this *was* Bailee's room." She nodded, looking around my room again like she was seeing it differently now that I'd mentioned it. "I can't believe I didn't even remember that."

"Anyway," I said. "We ended up just talking about how they got together and how close they were."

Best friends who pretended to be in love and made out all the time.

Which, even though I hadn't loved hearing about it, I couldn't really blame them for. If I was in a pretend relationship with Asher, I'd probably be okay making out with him all the time, too.

Probably find excuses for why we needed to keep practicing our fake girlfriend/boyfriend kissing skills.

"They were definitely something," Scarlett said. Then she looked at me like she was remembering something and quickly added, "But that was a long time ago. Long enough that I think he's actually ready to move on now."

Really?

She thought it was possible he was over Bailee enough to move on?

Wait, why was she mentioning this to me? Did she somehow know that I might have feelings for him?

I thought about asking why she'd brought it up, but then she said, "Did you guys talk about anything else? Maybe your plans for winter break?"

"No. Why?" I furrowed my brow, so confused with this whole conversation. It was so random and weird that she would be so interested in my conversation with Asher.

"Just wondering." She seemed to think for a second, and then said, "Oh, actually, Hunter and I were just talking about the debutante ball and all the things we'll be doing. So it made me wonder if you've decided who to ask to be your escort. You know, since it's just over a week away."

"I actually arranged that last night," I said, happy to be on a topic that made sense.

"You did?" she asked, seemingly excited. "Are you going with Asher?"

"No..." I shook my head, wondering how we were back to

Asher again. "I asked Nash. He brought it up at dinner. So that made it easy."

"Oh, of course." She nodded and gave me a smile that seemed forced. "That's awesome."

"Why did you think I asked Asher?"

Scarlett rubbed her arm. "I guess I just thought you might have been putting off asking Nash because you were thinking about asking Asher..."

"Why would you think that?"

Did she somehow know that I liked him, too? I didn't think I'd been too obvious. I'd tried not to make it too obvious, anyway.

"It's just something I thought about yesterday when Hunter and I were hanging out with Asher." She waved her hand like it was a silly idea. "But of course you asked Nash. So yay! That's exciting! You guys are going to be so cute together. I bet he's super excited."

"Yeah, it worked out great."

At least, I'd thought so until Scarlett brought it up.

And then I remembered the look on Asher's face when he'd seen the text from Nash. Had he seemed bothered by it?

Had he somehow known about the debutante ball and had been hoping I'd ask him?

Was that why he'd come to my room?

Scarlett said she'd been hanging out with Asher yesterday and that she and Hunter had also been discussing the debutante ball...

Did Scarlett know something that she wasn't telling me?

30

———

ELYSE

THE NEXT WEEK WAS CRAZY. It was the last week of the semester, so along with having a big week of rehearsals, I also had to study for and take all of my finals.

By Friday afternoon, my mind was basically mush and I was looking forward to the two weeks of winter break.

I'd be staying in town until Wednesday morning, since Ava and I would be celebrating Winter Solstice with Brendon and Mack before heading to New York to be with my mom. We'd also be moving all of our stuff from our dorm room and into the new rooms Brendon had been setting up for us at his house.

But before I could go to my room and finish packing the rest of my things into boxes, I had to make it through another rehearsal where we practiced the "The Point of No Return" and "The Final Lair" scenes.

"The Point of No Return" scene had been especially nerve-wracking to perform this week. It was the most provocative scene I'd ever done, so I was anxious about having to act the part of a newly engaged Christine being seduced by The Phantom—especially since my real-life relationship with Nash was way more timid than what we were supposed to act out for the audience.

But even though Nash had been so bashful and sweet when we'd kissed on Saturday night, his Phantom persona apparently had no trouble doing what we were instructed to do. There was nothing timid about the way he performed the choreography for that particular song.

In fact, it was almost like having Asher there watching us with gritted teeth gave him even more confidence, because when we got to the climax of the scene, he would turn into "Casanova Nash." He would bend his face close to my neck and let his hot breath send chills racing down my spine as he sang. And when his hands slid over mine as he held me from behind, moving them along my ribs and waist before slipping slowly up my arms above my head, I found it harder and harder to draw in decent breaths.

Yes, I was breathless during the entire scene...but not for the reasons I'd initially expected. Not because Nash was finally tapping into all the fantasies I'd had about us the past two months.

But because instead of looking forward to those moments, I found myself so conflicted and almost dreading them.

Dreading them because I knew Asher was right there, watching it all.

Watching the way Nash let his hands roam across my shoulders and down my arm.

Watching all the romantic moments that made Asher clench his hands into fists and look like he wanted to run on stage and tear Nash away from me.

It could all just be acting, since Raoul was supposed to feel jealous and hurt when he saw the way Christine and The Phantom sang the song together, but I wasn't so sure.

Because if he was simply acting, he wouldn't be in such a bad mood every time rehearsal ended, right?

The part of me that liked him—and had been looking for signs all week on whether or not he liked me back—hoped that he was at least partially wishing it was *us* doing that scene.

"Man, Asher, I've got to hand it to you," I overheard Nash tell Asher after rehearsal. "You're really spectacular at playing the part of a jealous Raoul."

We were the last people left in the auditorium and I was on the other side of the curtain from them, packing up my things, so Nash probably assumed they were alone.

"Just doing my job," Asher said, his voice more gruff than usual. Like he was annoyed at Nash for bringing it up.

"Well, you're nailing it," Nash said. "So well that during that last time through, I was starting to wonder if you might actually have real feelings."

"For Christine?"

"For Elyse," Nash said, a hint of taunting in his voice. "You don't have a crush on my girl, do you?"

"*Your* girl?" Asher asked.

My ears perked up, and I stepped closer to the curtain to hear them better.

Was Asher going to answer Nash's question? Did he have feelings for me?

We had barely spoken all week, so I really didn't know where things stood with us, aside from knowing how badly I was trying not to like him.

*I wasn't supposed to be falling for him.*

My heart pounded faster as I waited for him to say more.

But instead of answering Nash's question, Asher said, "Just enjoy this moment while you can."

"Enjoy this moment?" Nash asked, like he didn't know what Asher was talking about.

"Putting your hands all over Elyse," Asher said. "Having her sing that song to you and looking at you like she wants you to do the things you're singing about."

"Oh, I'm definitely enjoying it," Nash said. And then, after a short pause where I imagined a smirk lifting his lips, he added, "Elyse hasn't been complaining about it, either."

I gasped and had to cover my mouth to smother the sound.

*Is he actually saying all this?*

Was this how Nash talked about me when he didn't think I was around?

I stepped closer to the wall so I could look at the boys through a crack in the curtains. They were both facing each other in the center of the stage, Asher's few inches on Nash making him tower over him.

"That's because she's a great actress," Asher said, looking Nash up and down as if sizing him up.

"You think it's all just acting?" Nash scoffed.

"It could be," Asher said. "I know she likes you, but I've never seen her act like that around you outside of rehearsal."

Which I guess was true.

While things had seemingly heated up between Nash and me onstage, outside of rehearsals, we were still in relationship limbo where nothing had actually started.

It was like we were two people trying to have a conversation about our feelings, but instead of speaking the same language, he spoke Spanish and I spoke French.

And as the days went on and we continued to get our signals crossed, I also started to wonder if I really liked him as much as I'd thought. Or if I'd simply wanted to be with him because he was a great guy and I should want to be with someone like him.

That maybe I'd simply liked the idea of being with him more than actually being with him...

My conflicting feelings for Asher weren't exactly helping things on the Nash front either.

"Well..." Nash folded his arms across his chest. "If you'd been with us on our date last weekend, you might have a different opinion on what goes on when you aren't watching. She certainly wasn't acting when we kissed on Saturday night."

Was Nash trying to brag about the kiss he'd given me in his family's Escalade?

Because, um, I liked Nash and all, and the kiss had been sweet, but I doubted Asher would be jealous of it since the kisses *we'd* shared before that had been *very* different.

An image of us kissing in his room flitted through my mind.

"Just because someone lets you kiss them doesn't mean they have feelings for you," Asher said.

"I know," Nash said. "But when they tell you that they like you, it usually means that they do."

"So Elyse told you she likes you?" Asher asked.

"She did."

"Then you probably wouldn't like hearing that she kissed me the night before your big date."

My jaw dropped and I had to stifle a gasp. Had he actually just said that?

"You and Elyse were together Friday night?" Nash asked, sounding surprised.

"We were rehearsing together," Asher said. "But I could tell she wanted it."

Well, at least he was giving the context now.

"Ah, so it was for the play." Nash's shoulders relaxed. "She was probably just acting with you then. You did just say what an amazing actor she is."

*Should I do something?*

Before I could decide, Asher was saying, "You know Raoul

wins Christine in the end, right?" His jaw flexed. "That none of the theatrics from The Phantom actually win her over."

"Well," Nash said, seeming unbothered by Asher's passive-aggressive tone. "It's a good thing I'm not actually The Phantom then, isn't it? In fact, if anything, you're way more like The Phantom in real life and I'm more like Raoul."

"You think because you're rich and have the perfect family and can take her on fancy dates that she's going to choose you?" Asher scoffed. "You think those are the things Elyse cares about?"

"I don't see how they can hurt." Nash shrugged. "She seemed to enjoy our date well enough. And as far as I'm concerned, she's already picked me."

*Okay. This is just getting petty.*

If they kept talking like this, I was pretty sure I'd have no problem choosing between the two of them because I wouldn't want to pick either one.

They might both be super hot high school seniors, but they sounded like a couple of five-year-olds fighting over a toy.

I was just about to pull the curtain open and tell them as much when Asher said, "So if she was to pick me, would you call the police and blame me for some other crime that I didn't commit?"

*Oh no. This is not going to be good.*

Asher had not been happy when I'd told him that Nash had talked to the police. If he was even half as upset as he'd been after I told him, I didn't see this ending well.

He already didn't like Nash and might treat him like he'd treated my desk chair.

"What are you talking about?" Nash asked.

"I'm talking about the fact that you told the police Bailee and I had a fight the night she disappeared, and that it must mean I did something to her."

"Who told you I did that?" Nash asked, taking a step back.

"It doesn't matter," Asher said, thankfully not bringing me in to this part of their argument. "But just so you know, if you had asked me about it first instead of going straight to the police, you would have understood that we weren't having some big argument. The reason I was upset that night was because I had just told Bailee I was in love with her, but she decided to break up with me." He stopped, like he needed to take a deep breath. Then he added, "I would never hurt Bailee."

"Oh," Nash said, seeming like this was the first time he'd ever considered that Bailee might have been the one hurting Asher that night. He rubbed his cheek with his hand. "I-I didn't know."

"Yeah, well, maybe next time you should get your stupid biases out of the way before you jump to the kind of conclusions that could ruin someone's life."

"I'm really sorry. I thought I was doing the right thing," Nash said, regret in his voice.

They stared at each other for a moment, and Nash looked like he might be a little scared about what Asher would do next.

I held my breath as I waited, getting ready to jump in the middle if I needed to.

But then Asher shook his head and started walking toward my hiding place, and Nash went the other way to exit the stage.

I stepped back, hoping Asher wouldn't see me. But when he got behind the curtain, he looked my way, almost like he'd known I'd been there all along, and said, "Don't worry, I'm not going to punch your boyfriend's pretty face."

"He's not my boyfriend, we just..." I started to say.

"Seems like you've said that to me before," Asher said. He looked around the room. "In fact, I think you said it in this very spot a few weeks ago."

"I know." I sighed. "It's just complicated."

Everything was so complicated because I was trying to figure out my feelings for two boys who hated each other.

Two boys who were so different from each other, but magical in their own way.

I was torn between the bright summer day and the cool autumn night.

"It's complicated?" Asher scoffed and shook his head in disappointment. "Well, I'll make it less complicated for you." He took a step closer. "I'm not going to play a game where I fall in love with a girl who's already in love with someone else. I did that once before and it didn't turn out so well." He glanced at the now empty stage where he and Nash had been standing, before turning back to me and saying, "This is me tapping out."

He was tapping out?

So soon?

So easily?

Before even letting me know he had entered the match?

"I didn't even know until just now that you saw me like that," I said, my voice suddenly wobbly and sounding like I was on the verge of tears. "I thought it was you just teasing me."

Had I hoped that there was something behind all the looks and the flirting? That when he'd kissed me, some tiny part of that had been real? That when we sang the song where our characters declared their love for one another, maybe just a little bit of that had been him saying those things to me?

Yes, I'd hoped there was something real there and that I hadn't just been imagining it all.

But he'd never said or done anything to make me actually believe it could be real for him.

He stepped closer, so close that his chest pushed against mine. Then looking down at me with his big, hooded eyes, he said in a husky voice, "You say you don't know how I feel about you?" His gaze bobbed back and forth between my eyes. "That you didn't know that every time you caught me looking at you in class, I was hoping you could see me as something more than the boy you accidentally kissed one night?"

Was he saying what I thought he was saying?

That what had started as an accident had turned real for him?

I swallowed and tried to form a response, but the way he was towering over me and staring at me like I was the only thing he ever wanted in the world had me tongue-tied and feeling like I might burst into flames.

He slipped his hand behind my neck, tilted my head back, and whispered, "If you couldn't tell how much I've been wanting you the last few weeks from any of that, then I guess I better *show* you how I feel."

Before I knew what was happening, he was pulling me into his arms and pressing his lips to mine.

I went still, my brain needing a moment to catch on to what was happening.

"Let me show you just how much I want you, Elyse," Asher mumbled against my lips, letting his finger trace a line of fire along my jawline. "Let me show you how real everything is to me."

He pressed his lips to mine again, and this time I was ready for it. I wrapped my arms behind his neck, and when he backed me against the stage wall, I pulled him closer to me. Pulled him so close that there was no space between us, just his muscled torso against my body.

And it felt incredible.

His body pressed against mine.

The way his fingers tangled in my hair.

The way he kissed me like I was the only person in the whole world that he ever wanted to kiss.

His lips were so soft, softer than anything I'd ever known. Like the first fall of snow. Like biting into a cloud that tasted like cinnamon gum.

And I suddenly loved cinnamon gum. Cinnamon was my new favorite flavor in the whole world.

I might have kissed Asher twice before, but there was something different about the way he was kissing me this time. This was him laying everything on the line. That this was him and he was here, and that he wanted me and had wanted me for longer than I knew.

Maybe since we got snowed in at the cabin.

Or the night before that, when we had our first kiss.

Or maybe from the moment we first met.

He kissed me again and again, as if trying to memorize the feel of my lips against his. Like this might be the last time he'd ever kiss me, and he wanted to remember exactly how it felt and how I tasted.

And the more he kissed me, the more I wanted everything. His heart. His mind. His body. His soul. All of him.

I wanted him to be mine and for me to be his, and to have a lifetime of moments like this. Days and weeks and years where we were tucked away in our own little bubble, soaking up everything we had to give to each other.

I slipped my hands down his chest, beneath his jacket, and then along his sides. He felt so good. So strong. So perfect. So right.

I slid my hands to his back and was just about to pull him even closer when he broke the kiss and pulled himself away.

He stared at me, breathing hard, and searched my eyes for something. Like he was trying to figure out what I was thinking and if this was okay, and if I wanted him to keep going.

Like he wanted to make sure this was as real to me as it was to him before he fully exposed everything he usually kept locked deep inside his heart.

He didn't open up to people easily and wanted to know if I was a safe place for him to fall.

And as I gazed into his beautiful, deep brown eyes, trying to catch a decent breath of my own, all I could think was that I wanted to drown in him. I wanted him to show me everything that made him Asher Park and kiss me until I could no longer breathe.

So I pulled him back into me and told him with my kiss what I didn't dare say out loud.

That I wanted him. Wanted to know everything about him and for him to know everything about me.

That I was afraid that I wanted him more than I should.

More than he wanted me.

He came back to me and kissed me urgently, as if we were running out of time. His hands went to my hips, up my sides, and along my back like he was trying to learn my every angle and curve. He kissed down my neck and along my collarbone, and I frantically unbuttoned his sport jacket and pushed it down his shoulders because I needed to feel and squeeze and memorize his amazing arms that I'd been drooling over since we first met.

He helped me pull his jacket down and tossed it to the ground. Then he lifted me into the air and carried me to the couch that I'd always thought was a random thing to have back-stage until right now when Asher was taking me to it.

He sat down with my legs straddling his hips, and for a second, he rested his forehead against mine, needing to catch his breath. Then he looked up at me and whispered, "You're so beautiful, Elyse." He slipped his hands up and down my sides and said, "So incredibly beautiful."

## 31

## ASHER

HAD I somehow slipped into a daydream during rehearsal, or was this actually happening? Was I really sitting on the ugly orange couch backstage with Elyse on my lap?

Was she undoing my tie and unbuttoning the top few buttons of my dress shirt so she could kiss the crook of my neck and clavicle in the way that I loved?

In the way that made it hard to think clearly?

Because either I was dreaming, or Elyse was a lot less timid than I'd assumed.

That underneath the sweet and innocent facade she put on for the rest of the world, there was actually a girl who said she liked the bad boys who went after what they wanted because it helped her inner bad girl come out.

She kissed her way up my neck, under my chin, and across my jawline, causing a million nerve endings to spark to life. When she eventually made her way back to my mouth, she took my bottom lip between hers and sucked on it.

She took my face in her hands and let her tongue gently

graze against my lips, asking permission to deepen the kiss. I opened my mouth to hers and let her explore.

Her hair fell around us like a curtain, and the scent of her shampoo filled my senses. She smelled so good. Like apple and something else that made me think of crisp autumn nights and sipping wassail in front of the fire. I slipped my fingers into her hair as our tongues danced together. And when she quietly moaned into my mouth and pressed herself closer, my stomach muscles tightened so hard I wondered if they'd ever relax again.

She slipped one hand behind my neck, bracing herself against me, as she moved the other one down my shoulders to my left bicep. And after giving it a good squeeze and rubbing her hand all over it, she mumbled, "This is mine now, okay?"

A huge grin slipped onto my lips because I kind of loved that she'd just said that. With a slight chuckle, I said, "You can have the other arm, too, if you want."

A slow smile took shape on her lips. She took both of my forearms in her hands and put them behind her waist, saying, "If they're mine now, then they better hold me close."

So I wrapped them all the way around her and hugged her tighter against me. She let out a light giggle. We stared at each other for a moment, my heart swelling so big in my chest, and I wondered if I'd ever cared about someone as much as I cared about her. I pulled her lips back to mine and kissed her in a way that I hoped would tell her the things I was too afraid to say.

That I'd been falling in love with her since the moment we met. That she was everything I'd been searching for. She was funny and smart and beautiful and amazing...and falling for her had been inevitable.

As if it had been written in the stars long before we met.

*Please pick me.*

*Please choose me.*

Her lips met mine in a long, slow kiss. Without thinking, I lifted her off my lap, laid her down on the couch, and climbed down beside her.

She turned on her side to face me, and then we were kissing again. I was pressing her into the back of the couch, and she was arching into me.

I slipped my hand along her hip, smoothing it along the little bit of softness she had there. She pushed her hands into my hair, and when she gently combed her fingers through the wavy strands I never really knew what to do with, a shiver went down my back because it felt so good.

"I've been wanting to tangle my fingers in your hair since the first day we met," she said in a soft voice.

"Yeah?" I asked, meeting her gaze for a moment as my insides did a bunch of somersaults.

She nodded. "I love it."

And then we were kissing again. She kicked off her shoes and I kicked off mine, and we were tangling our legs together. She finished unbuttoning the front of my shirt, and when she pushed it open, I was glad I'd kept up my early morning workouts the past few weeks—she wasn't shy about the way her eyes were raking me all in, her hands feeling the contours of my chest and down the muscles over my ribcage.

She bent her head lower and pressed a kiss to my sternum before nuzzling her face against my skin like she was planning to stay there until we could both catch our breath.

And since we were snuggling now, I pulled her closer. I slid my hand along the hemline of her blouse, smoothing it over her hip. I lightly traced my fingers across the skin of her back that had tortured me so much when I'd helped her with her dress. And when she shivered with pleasure, I flattened my hand against her spine and pushed it a little higher.

My fingers barely grazed against the clasp of her bra, and I briefly wondered if she wore the black bra she'd been wearing last Saturday...

I stopped that thought. Thinking about it would only make me think of taking this to another level and we were not going to that other level with each other right now.

Right?

Not when she was still going to a stupid ball with another guy.

Plus, she was wearing a white blouse, and you didn't wear a black bra with a white blouse.

At least, I didn't think that was how it worked. I'd never had to worry about that myself, but I was pretty sure I would have noticed the hint of black beneath her blouse a long time ago if it was there since I'd basically been staring at her all afternoon.

She sighed, and it was such a sweet and contented sound that made me inexplicably happy for some reason. I kissed her forehead. When she looked up at me with those golden-brown eyes I could gaze into forever, I had the overwhelming feeling that for once in my life, I actually had a home.

That I'd been lost and always felt out of place because I hadn't known Elyse.

I tucked a lock of hair behind her ear, letting my fingers continue to trace along her shoulder and back up again along her cheek.

She closed her eyes and gently moaned, saying, "That feels so good."

And then we were kissing again. She rolled onto her back and pulled me on top of her. Any coherent thoughts that I might have been having before then went out the window, because I was lying down with the most beautiful girl in the world and it felt amazing.

Her curves against my edges.

And when her tongue flicked against mine, I literally couldn't think anymore.

COULD I just do this forever? Could I just lie here on the couch with Asher and kiss him until I died?

Could I forget about school, and the musical, and homework, and eating, and just stay right here and kiss him for the rest of my life?

Because if this was how it felt to kiss him, to really kiss him when I knew it was him and when we were just ourselves instead of acting for a play, I might just become an addict.

Could you be addicted to a person? Was that a thing?

I knew you could be addicted to substances. Addicted to getting the high you got from them.

But could you be addicted to a specific person? Because I had never felt this level of a high from kissing anyone else.

And I wanted more of it. More of his lips on mine. More of his body pressing into me. More of the way his skin felt beneath my hands.

Until this afternoon, I didn't think I even knew a guy could have so many muscles. Ava had bragged to me about how Carter had an eight pack, and how he basically had muscles everywhere, but I'd thought she was exaggerating because she was so obsessed with him.

But now that I'd seen Asher's impressive upper body and had the opportunity to slowly graze my fingertips across the ridges of his stomach muscles, I knew firsthand that such a thing did exist.

He was a work of art, and I was the girl who wanted to memorize every part of him.

"You still okay with this?" Asher asked breathlessly.

"Yes," I said. "I want this."

Way more than I dared tell him. Way more than I'd realized until we were here and doing this.

"And I'm not crushing you?" he asked, pulling back and lifting his weight off me a little.

I shook my head. "It's perfect."

He was heavy—muscles weighed a lot. But it felt amazing.

Seeming like he believed me, he lowered himself again and kissed his way along my jawline, down my neck, and nuzzled his face into the curve of my neck like he was breathing me in.

"You smell so good," he said into my skin, sending tingles racing across my neck. "Like apples and happiness."

*Like apples and happiness?*

I couldn't keep a smile from my lips because I'd never thought of happiness as having a smell before, but that was kind of the best thing a person could say to describe how you smelled, wasn't it?

Did I make Asher happy then?

Was that what it really was?

Because I suddenly wanted to make him happy all the time.

"You smell like happiness, too," I said, running my hands along his sides. "Hotness and happiness, that is."

He chuckled and pulled himself up to look at me again.

"I'm ninety-nine percent sure you're just making fun of me right now, but I'll take it."

"Not making fun of you at all," I said.

"Well, good."

I was just about to pull his lips to mine again when the sound of a stage door opening caught my attention, followed by footsteps.

*Who's here?* I wondered before turning my head to see who was about to discover Asher and me.

Did Nash come back? Or Miss Crawley? A feeling of dread washed over me, but then the person came into view a second later.

I sighed with relief. It was just Ava.

But when she saw Asher and me lying on the couch together, she stopped and said, "What the heck?" She shook her head like she wasn't sure she was seeing things right. "Elyse? And *Asher?*"

Yeah...probably not the guy she expected to see me cozied up with.

Asher looked at me with wide eyes, as if not sure what he was supposed to do. So I whispered, "I'll handle this."

Asher backed himself off me so I could sit up. I smoothed my hands over my hair and looked at Ava, saying, "Hey."

"Hi." She stared at Asher with wide eyes, watching him as he re-buttoned his shirt. "Um, this is quite the interesting discovery." She looked back at me. "Were you guys rehearsing a scene for the musical? Working on the chemistry Raoul and Christine have, by chance?"

"Um, sure... Something like that, anyway." I decided to go with it for now since my mind was still reeling from the past few minutes.

Had that actually just happened?

Had I just made out for who knows how long with Asher in a way that had definitely not been for the play?

I peeked over at Asher who had finished buttoning his dress shirt and was now reaching for the tie that I'd tossed to the floor earlier. And I was suddenly embarrassed that I'd done all of that.

I'd totally been undressing Asher!

I mean, I'd been doing that with my eyes for a while now since I'd been so curious about the kind of body he had hiding under the dress shirts and T-shirts that he usually wore.

But to literally unbutton his shirt, and then basically pull him on top of me?

I wanted to cover my face with my hands.

What was happening to me?

It was like I'd completely let go of my usual inhibitions the moment Asher kissed me, and it had released a side of me I usually kept under control.

"Anyway," Ava said when Asher started putting his shoes back on his feet. "I've been looking for you everywhere. You weren't answering my phone calls. Brendon and Mack will be here in a little while to take the first batch of boxes to their house."

"Oh, sorry, I completely forgot about that," I said.

"Yeah." Ava glanced at Asher again briefly, and then said, "Anyway, I guess I'll see you back up in our room?"

"Yes," I said quickly. "I'll grab my stuff and see you back there."

*And see if I could figure out what's going on with Asher and me.*

Ava left us, and Asher went to pick up his jacket that he'd thrown on the floor near my backpack. I put my shoes on and tried to figure out what to say.

But my mind was such a jumbled mess that I had no idea what I was supposed to say right now.

I obviously had strong feelings for Asher—probably way stronger than I'd realized before.

And he'd said before the kiss that he was going to show me how he felt about me. Which, from the explosiveness of that kiss, I was guessing—hoping—was pretty strongly.

Did that mean he wanted me then?

That he didn't want to just be "best buddies" like he'd labeled us before?

That he wanted to be something more serious than that?

Did I want that?

I was starting to think that I did.

But how could I do that when I was supposed to go to the debutante ball with Nash?

Part of me still liked Nash, right?

I tried to sift through my feelings to see where they stood. To see which guy was winning the game of tug of war they'd had on my heart.

A week ago, I probably would have said that it was Nash. He liked me. He'd been doing things all along that made me sure that he did and that he would be a great boyfriend.

But now that I knew Asher wanted something more with me, too... That it wasn't just me who had been feeling things the past few weeks...

I watched him as he pulled his jacket over his broad shoulders. Looked at his profile. His high cheekbones. His straight nose. His dark wavy hair that was more tousled than it usually was—thanks to me.

I'd thought the first time I saw him that he was one of the most beautiful humans I'd ever laid eyes on. And the more I got to know him, the more that became even more true because he was beautiful on the inside as well.

He was resilient and smart and funny and witty and made me laugh more than I'd ever laughed in my whole life.

He was a good person who felt things deeply and had become who he was despite having to do a lot of things on his own.

He was probably one of the strongest people I knew. Had been through things I couldn't even comprehend and managed to come back to the place that had basically ran him out and still was able to smile through it all.

He glanced my way, and when his beautiful eyes met mine, my heart swelled so big in my chest, because I knew that if I was forced to choose right here and now, I would choose him.

Asher was the guy I couldn't let go of.

Which meant, I needed to tell someone else that while he was amazing and had all the qualities I thought I wanted, I couldn't be his leading lady.

Asher finished buttoning his jacket and picked up his backpack that was stowed on the chair beside him. He slung it over his shoulder, and when I stood, he walked over to me.

After searching my gaze quietly for a moment, like he was trying to figure out where my feelings had landed after everything, he bent close and pressed a gentle kiss to my cheek. "I hope this helped clear up where I stand." He pulled back, and when our eyes locked, it felt like my heart might burst. "I guess I'm not ready to tap out quite yet."

Then before I could say anything, he left.

33

———

ELYSE

I HELPED AVA, Mack, and Brendon carry down the packed boxes to Brendon's truck that was in the parking lot closest to the dorms. Then, while they all headed to the house to unload, I went back upstairs to pack up a few more things.

Most of the students had already cleared out of the dorms for winter break, so the common room was basically empty when I walked back through it.

I'd heard Asher tell someone that he was headed to his aunt and uncle's house via bus tonight around six-thirty, so that meant he was probably in his room right now, packing his bag for the two-week vacation.

Part of me wanted to go up there to tell him what I hadn't told him backstage this afternoon, that I wanted to be with him. That he was the guy I chose, and how I felt dumb for not realizing it sooner.

But I knew I needed to have my conversation with Nash first. So I just looked longingly at the staircase that led to Asher's room before heading back up to my room.

I got to work taping together one of the moving boxes and

started emptying the contents of my desk. I put my pens and notebooks in the box, as well as the extra tape dispenser that I kept at the back of the middle drawer—the backup for when Ava stole mine.

I opened the top side drawer and put all my washi tape and stickers in the box. Once that was empty, I moved to the drawer just below that. But when I tried to open it, it didn't budge.

Had Ava borrowed my stapler again and just thrown it in there like she always did?

I looked through the small crack in it, and sure enough, my teal stapler had been haphazardly shoved in there and was blocking me from opening the drawer. I tried pushing on it with a ruler to get it loose. But it only moved a little way down. Why couldn't Ava just keep track of her own stapler?

I pushed on it again, and when that still didn't work, I started jiggling the door with hopes that it would make it come loose. When I heard things shift a little, I jiggled the drawer a little more and then yanked on it hard.

That seemed to do the trick, because not only did the drawer finally come out, but it came *all* of the way out, landing on the floor.

*Well, that's one way to do it, I guess.*

I brushed my hands off on my pants and bent down to pick the drawer back up. Then I saw something I hadn't noticed before.

The drawer had a false back to it—a piece of wood that from a regular viewpoint would look like the back of the drawer. But there was actually about two inches of space between that thin piece of wood and the actual back of the drawer.

And sitting in the secret slot was a book.

I reached in and pulled the book out, realizing it was actually a journal with butterflies and flowers embossed in the leather.

*Could this be?*

My fingers trembled and my heart raced as I realized what this might be.

*Who* the journal might belong to.

I unwrapped the leather strap around it and opened the front cover to see the first page.

And written in feminine handwriting was the name Bailee Vanderbilt, followed by a New York City address and phone number.

## 34

## ASHER

"ASHER, WAIT," Elyse called out from behind me.

I was just on my way out of the common room to meet Owen who was my ride to the bus stop when Elyse's voice came from the top of the stairs that led to the girls' dorms. I turned to look up at her. She still wore the same white blouse and navy-blue plaid skirt she had on earlier, but there was something different about her. She seemed frantic.

*Did something happen?*

"What's wrong?" I asked, dropping my duffle bag to the floor and rushing toward her.

"No, nothing's wrong," she said, sounding breathless. "It's just..." She sighed and held out a purple leather journal that I'd never seen before. "I found this in my desk when I was cleaning it out, and I opened it up and read it and...I think you need to read this."

I frowned and looked down at the book she was pushing toward me, taking it in my hand.

"It's Bailee's," she said.

"What?" My eyebrows knitted together as I looked at the journal then back to Elyse's face.

"There was a secret compartment in my desk," she said quickly. "I accidentally pulled the drawer all the way out. And I probably shouldn't have read it, but I did...and you really should read this, and then probably give it to her parents or the police or something."

I looked down at the journal again then opened the front cover. My heart stuttered in my chest when I saw Bailee's name written in her familiar, flowing cursive.

"Does this say where she went?" I asked, adrenaline pumping through my veins.

"Not exactly, but I think it gives enough clues that makes me think she's still alive and we might be able to find her."

"Really?" I licked my lips, suddenly feeling all jittery, like I needed to sit down.

This was Bailee's journal.

Elyse said she's probably still alive.

I wanted to sit down right there at the bottom of the stairs because I felt like passing out, and also because I wanted to rip the journal open and read everything Bailee had written. But then, my phone chimed with a text from Owen.

*Crap.* I was already running late before Elyse stopped me. I really needed to go.

I looked at Elyse. "I wish I could stay here and talk to you about this, but I'm going to miss my bus if I don't run."

"Of course. You should go."

I knew I should leave now, but before stepping away, I bent close and kissed her cheek. "I'll see you soon. Maybe we can hang out when you get to Ridgewater."

"I'd love that," she said. "But we'll be going to my mom's apartment in New York for Christmas. We won't be in Ridgewater until the twenty-ninth or thirtieth."

"Really?" I'd somehow assumed they'd be going to Ridgewater after celebrating Winter Solstice with their dad.

"Yeah, we have that ball in New York right after Christmas, and so she thought we should just go straight there."

So that meant the next time I'd be seeing Elyse was when I had to watch her dance with Nash at the debutante ball...

Had this afternoon really been my last chance to make something happen before she had her magical night with Nash?

Had that kiss been enough?

Probably not.

I should have done more. Done more to show her how much she meant to me. I should have told her how amazing and wonderful and beautiful and special I thought she was. Told her that it was so much more than physical, and even if she never kissed me again, I'd still want to spend all my free time with her because I just loved being around her.

The kiss had been amazing, but there was way more to a relationship than the physical side, and I probably should have led with that instead.

Ugh. Why hadn't I done more? Why had I waited until literally the last minute to make a move?

My phone started ringing. I knew I really needed to leave, or I was going to miss my bus.

I looked down at the journal again. "Thank you for this."

She nodded. "Just start from the beginning, and I think you'll understand what happened."

"Okay," I said. "Have fun celebrating the holidays with your family."

"Thank you." She bit her lip. "H-have a good break, Asher."

---

## 35

## ASHER

SINCE I WASN'T sure what the journal held, and I didn't want Owen asking me questions before I had answers, I tucked Bailee's journal into my duffel bag and made myself wait until I was settled on the bus before I pulled it out again.

My fingers trembled as I held it in my hands. What had Bailee written in here? Had she spelled out her whole disappearing plan?

Elyse said it held clues that might help us find Bailee. That what she'd written had made her believe that Bailee was still alive.

I sighed and leaned back against my seat as a wave of emotion poured over me.

*Bailee might be alive.*

I pressed my eyes closed and wiped away the tears that came.

*This nightmare might have a happy ending.*

I wanted to open it up to the last page, to see if Bailee had written the exact address and directions to wherever she'd disappeared. But since Elyse suggested I start at the beginning, and I had a four-hour bus ride to Ridgewater, I opened up to the first entry she'd written instead. It was dated mid-August from the year before.

The last few weeks of the summer before our junior year. I leaned back in my seat and settled in.

*August 16*

> *Welcome to my new journal. I finished my old one a couple weeks ago and found this at a cute little cart in Central Park and couldn't pass it up. Summer's been good. We went to Paris for a couple weeks last month and it was amazing as always. My dad was working on business most of the time so my mom, Alisha, and I did most of the exploring without him. I got some amazing clothes and shoes that I'm excited to take with me when I go back to school.*
>
> *After Paris, we just spent most of the rest of the summer in Manhattan. I went to a few parties with Alisha and her college friends. My favorite being last night when they snuck me into one of the clubs with them. I was scared they wouldn't let me through since I'm not even 17, but they let me through with the group.*
>
> *We ended up dancing and talking with a group of guys they know from NYU.*
>
> *They were all so hot and fun to hang out with. This is why I love older guys so much. They're just more fun and exciting to talk to.*
>
> *I ended up spending most of the night in the VIP lounge with this guy named Elijah. He just graduated from NYU in May and was so freaking hot. He had these amazing green eyes that I just wanted to get lost in. And he was tall. Like maybe 6'3" with the kind of body you'd find on a cover of a men's magazine.*
>
> *Seriously, his arms were as big as my thighs, he's so buff.*

*I was so nervous when he first started talking to me because I thought for sure he'd be able to tell I was only in high school and had totally snuck in.*

*I mean, I'll be 17 in a couple weeks tho. Everyone tells me I look like I could be in college—that Alisha and I look like twins. But the whole time I was just thinking he was going to notice something, or I was going to slip up and say something about being in high school and he'd realize I'm like 4 or 5 years younger than him.*

*But he didn't. He just talked to me like I was his age.*

*Anyway, we ended up talking all night and it was kind of amazing. Like one of those rare moments when you just have an instant connection with someone.*

*When it was time to go, I gave him my number and told him to call me. I've never given my number to an older guy before, but I really hope that he calls me. I'll be leaving for Eden Falls in a couple weeks so I know it can't go anywhere. But I don't know, it was just a magical night. I would love to see him again before I leave.*

I furrowed my brow as I looked over the entry again. Was this what Elyse thought I should be reading? Was there some sort of clue in here that I needed to remember?

Bailee had told me about sneaking into clubs with her sister and her friends over the summer, and I'd told the police about it when they'd interviewed me. But I really didn't think she'd run away to become a professional club hopper.

I shook my head. Maybe I was being too literal.

I turned the page to the next entry.

*August 21*

*The past few days have been so amazing!! Elijah texted me*

*the day after our night at the club and we went to a Yankee's game a couple days later. Normally I hate baseball games because they're so freaking long and boring, but it ended up being so fun. We just laughed the whole time because he was so hilarious. Anyway, I really wanted to kiss him because his lips are amazing. The universe must have heard my thoughts or something because during one of the timeouts near the end of the game, the kiss cam stopped on us and we were suddenly on the jumbotron.*

*I know I'm not usually super shy around guys but in that moment I kind of panicked and had no idea what to do. He's older and everyone was watching us. Like, what if my dad was watching the game and saw it? But Elijah just kind of looked at me as if asking if it was okay and I nodded yes, and he leaned over and gave me one of the sweetest first kisses I've ever had.*

*Ahhh!!!!!!*

*Like, I had hundreds of butterflies flapping in my stomach and thought everyone watching us would know how excited I was.*

*Anyway, he put his arm around me for the rest of the game. I could barely concentrate on the actual game because I literally felt like my whole body was full of little fireworks sparking.*

*We got on the subway together and he held my hand as he walked me the rest of the way home. It was totally like a date from a movie!*

*Anyway, I had him take me to Alisha's penthouse down the street from my parents' house, since I didn't want him to accidentally run into my mom or dad and figure out that I still live with them because I'm in high school.*

*I was planning to say good night on the front steps and*

*then go inside to wait for him to leave so I could sneak back home. But when I went to hug him, he ended up kissing me, and let's just say it was not the same kind of kiss he'd given me for the kiss cam.*

*It was so good!!!*

Okay, so she saw that guy from the club again. I looked up to find the guy's name.

Elijah.

Was he important to the mystery? I thought the older guy she'd dated before we became close had lived in Eden Falls and not New York.

But maybe I'd just assumed that?

I skimmed through the next few entries to see if this Elijah guy showed up again. And sure enough, he was the star of the next several entries since that date to the Yankee's game was just the first of many.

So maybe he was important to her story?

*September 8*

*Remember how I wrote in my last journal entry about how sad I was that Elijah was moving out of state for his new teaching job and that I wouldn't be able to visit him in New York during the school breaks?*

*Well...I guess I probably should have asked him more details about where he was going and what he would be doing with his science degree because I walked into my AP biology class this morning and found out that my new professor was none other than Elijah!!!*

Wait...

I stopped reading and shook my head.

Was Bailee's secret older boyfriend our biology teacher? Professor Hicks?

*Yeah, so that was a big surprise.*

*He didn't notice me when I first walked in, and I tried to hide in the back. But then he called roll and got to my name and...*

*Oh my gosh! It was so bad. The way he just stared at me in shock as I raised my hand.*

*Like, he looked so surprised to see me in his class. To realize that I was actually a high school junior and not the college student I'd led him to believe I was.*

*Anyway, he taught class, and I tried to figure out what I was going to do and how I was going to explain that I hadn't left New York to go to college in Connecticut like he assumed.*

*I mean, I'd been trying to come clean that last night together. To tell him that I was really in high school.*

*But when I brought up school in Connecticut, he somehow assumed I was going to Yale, and I decided that I might as well just let him continue to believe that and avoid him feeling all weird about dating a high schooler the past two weeks.*

*I thought it would be okay to leave it like that because I never expected to see him again.*

*But obviously, that wasn't how things turned out since karma is stupid.*

*So anyway, I stayed behind after the bell rang to try to explain everything. But he was so mad and looked so freaked out and told me I needed to leave.*

*So I left and went to lunch.*

*I don't know how I'm going to go back to his class on Thursday. I want to just drop the class and find a way to get my science credit some other way. But he's the only biology teacher at the school so I'll probably have to go back.*

*Ugh, this is such a disaster.*

*Why did I think I could get away with this?*

The next few entries were more of what a regular high school student might talk about. She complained about tests, talked about wanting to try out for the winter musical, and ranted about some drama with her friends.

She mentioned Professor Hicks AKA "Elijah" a few times, but it was mostly to say that he seemed to hate her now. Or how he barely ever looked her way during class. And how she was pretty sure he was going to fail her.

But then, as the entries went on, she started saying things like, *"Elijah looked really hot today. It was so hard to concentrate on what he was saying."* Or, *"I wish he wasn't my teacher. Every time he stands in front of the class, all I can think about is how much I want to kiss him again."* Or, *"Today I caught Elijah staring at me while we did our biology lab. I purposely wore my skirt shorter since I remembered how much he liked feeling my legs when we made out this summer. Then once I knew he was looking my way, I pretended to flirt with my lab partner just for fun. He looked so jealous. Finally he showed some kind of emotion! Might need to test some more things out to be sure."*

*October 20*

*I had to go into Elijah's class for some extra help today. Apparently, I daydream too much about him during class and it's gotten so bad I'm about to flunk biology.*

*When I first asked him for help, he thought I was just playing games with him and trying to find an excuse to spend some time alone with him—which is a special bonus, sure. But after looking over my assignment and seeing that I really had no idea what I was doing, he told me to pull up a chair and we went over some stuff.*

*To be honest, it wasn't helpful at all. The whole time he was helping me, all I could think about was how good he smelled and how much I'd missed sitting this close to him and how nice his hands are and how I wanted to trace my fingers along the veins in his forearms or slip my hand on his leg under the desk.*

*He soon realized I was distracted though, because he looked at me and asked me to repeat what he'd just said. But I couldn't remember anything aside from how his leg felt when he accidentally bumped it against mine.*

*Anyway, he said I should probably work with a tutor from now on if I keep having problems because it wouldn't be appropriate for us to spend any more time alone.*

*So looks like I need to find a tutor.*

*It's just so embarrassing because he knows how much I like him, but he wants nothing to do with me.*

October 25

*I went to a party at one of my friend's house this weekend. It was super dumb. Mostly a bunch of high school kids getting drunk and doing stupid stuff. So I left around eleven and decided to stop by the gas station on my way back to the school to grab a bag of Jalapeño Cheetos and a diet coke. I was just paying for my stuff when I saw Elijah outside, filling his car up with gas. He didn't see me.*

*And I guess I wasn't exactly thinking straight because when he started driving away, I followed him in my car. I guess I was curious about where he lived in Eden Falls or something. Anyway, he parked next to an apartment complex, and I pulled in behind him because I'm stupid.*

*I watched him go into his apartment and I should have left right then. But instead, I went up to his door and knocked.*

*He opened it and was shocked to see me. He looked like he*

*was going to send me away, but I told him I just needed to talk to him really quick and get all the drama ironed out, so I could be normal and we could stop acting all weird around each other all the time. If I'm going to be at this school for another year and a half and he's going to be my teacher, we needed to make things be okay.*

*He looked around to make sure no one was watching us then he let me come in so we could talk in his living room.*

*I apologized for lying about how old I was and making him think I was in college. I explained that I just had so much fun with him that I wanted to spend more time with him. I also told him how I hadn't thought it would be too big of a deal because I'd be leaving New York to come here in two weeks and then probably never see him again.*

*He said he kind of understood and agreed that we'd had a lot of fun together. He said if I hadn't ended up in his class the first day of school, he probably would have looked back on our time together as a fun summer fling.*

*But then he told me that he was my teacher now and if anyone found out he dated a student, even if it was before he knew I was his student, he could lose his job. That no matter how attracted he still was to me and how even though I acted and looked more like I'm 19 or 20 and not 17, he couldn't act on it.*

*Me being 17 and him being 22 was not okay.*

*I was bummed because I still really liked him, but I understood. He's a really good teacher and I don't want him to lose his job because of me.*

*Anyway, when we were saying goodbye, it was like we kind of went back in time to New York and we ended up hugging. It felt so nice to hug him again that I didn't want to let go.*

*He didn't seem to want to let go either, because he just*

held me against him and ran his hands along my back. I knew I should have stepped away and left his apartment. We'd already agreed we couldn't have a future together. But then he pulled away and rested his forehead against mine, and we just kind of stood there breathing each other's air. My heart was pounding so fast!! I was having a hard time breathing because I wanted him so badly.

I don't know who leaned in first but before I knew it, we were kissing! I pulled him closer to me and he pressed me against the wall, twisting his fingers in my hair. We were kissing like we were starving and that this was the only time we'd ever have to do this.

And before I knew it, it was two o'clock in the morning. We had been making out in his living room and on his couch and in his kitchen and against the wall by his bedroom door until our lips were swollen and my skin was chaffed from his scruffy beard.

When we finally realized what we'd just done, we both agreed that it could never happen again. This was just a one-time thing so we could get each other out of our systems.

So I grabbed my sweater that he'd thrown on the floor in the kitchen and he grabbed his T-shirt that had come off on the couch and we promised it would never happen again.

I fixed my hair into a ponytail so no one would see how messy it had gotten when he'd tangled his fingers in it and guess what I'd been up to tonight.

Then I snuck back to my car, vowing that I'd never come back to his apartment again. If I really cared about Elijah, I wouldn't do anything that would put him or his job in jeopardy.

I plan to keep that promise.

I'll be 18 in like 10 months. I could graduate early. I'll talk to my advisor tomorrow and see if it's possible.

*If we're really meant to be, we'll still both be around when a relationship between the two of us is legal...*

*So yeah...that's how my Saturday night went. Only like another 70 biology lessons to get through.*

The next few entries talked about school and how she was trying to stay away from Elijah—Professor Hicks. And it sounded like they were doing a good job of keeping their pact to stay away from each other and keep things the way a student/teacher relationship should be.

But a few weeks later, right before we had the auditions for the winter musical where she landed the role of Cosette, she mentioned how she'd gone to his office one day during lunch to ask him some questions and they'd slipped up and kissed before he pushed her away.

They didn't do anything else for another week, but then she saw him one evening when she was in town grabbing takeout from her favorite restaurant, and they ended up making out in his car.

After that, they tried to just date on the down low, visiting other small towns close by on Saturdays and Sundays so they could be out in public where no one would recognize them.

But a few days would go by, and they would break up again. He was paranoid that some people at school might be picking up on things.

I kept turning the pages and skimming through everything, wondering if this had just gone on the rest of the year.

Had they been secretly hooking up while she and I had been together?

Was our little ruse just a magician's trick where she was distracting everyone with what we were doing while her real forbidden relationship was happening in the dark corners of Eden Falls?

One entry dated January 2 talked about how they had met up at a New Year's Eve party in New York since they were both spending the holidays with their parents.

*It was such a magical night. We got all dressed up and went to this fancy party with a bunch of people who didn't know who we were. We ate delicious food, danced the night away, and really got to see what it would be like to be in a real relationship where we didn't have to hide. It was amazing and romantic and everything I'd dreamed it would be.*

*At the end of the night, we rang in the new year together and were able to kiss without worrying about who might see us because no one cared. The party ended and we knew it was time to go home and back to reality, but it had been so amazing that neither of us wanted to say goodnight.*

*So I booked a room at my grandpa's hotel and had Elijah sneak up a few minutes later. It was so amazing spending the night with the man I'm in love with for the first time. And I know some people's first time is scary or awkward or uncomfortable, but with Elijah, it was just so wonderful and everything I'd hoped it would be.*

*He was such a gentleman. He made me feel safe and loved and wanted. I've never felt so much love for someone in my whole life. I know that things have been tricky and that the rest of the school year is going to probably be no different since he's still my teacher and I won't graduate until June—yes, I forgot to say it earlier, but I was able to talk to my advisor and she said things were on track for me to graduate a year early.*

*But I love Elijah so much and can't imagine being with anyone else so I'm willing to continue what we've been doing for another five months. He's worth it and it's a small price to pay to get to be with him forever.*

*Anyway, this isn't how I imagined my junior year of high*

*school going. But I'm so happy!!! I can't wait to see what the*
*future holds for Elijah and me.*

I had to pause for a minute after reading that entry. Until
this point, they'd been flirting with danger. They'd been
spending time together. They'd been kissing. They'd been
doing lots of couple things. But they hadn't quite crossed the
line into illegal territory.

Was that why they'd broken up the next week? I wasn't
sure of the exact date that she'd come to rehearsal with tears in
her eyes, saying that her boyfriend had broken up with her. But
it had to be pretty soon after this.

I turned the page, and just like I'd expected, there was a
single sentence written for the 7th of January.

*Elijah broke up with me.*

It looked like little drops of water had fallen on the pages
based on the way the paper wrinkled in some spots—like she'd
been sobbing as she'd written that one sentence and couldn't
bring herself to write any more.

There were a couple weeks between journal entries after
that. Apparently, nothing noteworthy had happened during
that time in Bailee's life.

*January 24*

*It's been a couple weeks since I last wrote in here. Things*
*have been getting better. I'm still here at least.*

*I was really sad the first part of the month as I tried to get*
*over Elijah. I thought we might get back together, that he might*
*change his mind and try to continue what we had going, since*
*we'd broken up so many other times before. But I think it's*
*really over this time. He really meant it.*

*When we broke up, he asked that I respect his decision since he really thought it was what was best for us and our futures. That if we were caught in a student/teacher relationship, it could have repercussions that would haunt us for the rest of our lives.*

*I didn't want to accept it at first because I was so in love with him and thought we could be together forever. But now that it's been a couple weeks, I see that he was right. It's been hard seeing him every other day in his class, but I'm trying to move on because I know he deserves to keep his job. He's really good at it and loves what he does. Sometimes the best way to show someone that you love them is to let them go when they ask.*

*So instead of trying to get back with my teacher, I decided to try to have a more normal junior year and do all the things I probably should have been doing all along.*

*I started hanging out with Asher Park. He's a guy my age who I didn't know very well until recently. We were in the play together and he's actually really cool. He's super fun to be around and always makes me laugh. I know I've always said I don't like high school boys because they're all so immature, but Asher is surprisingly mature for a high school junior.*

Well, at least Bailee Vanderbilt had thought I was cool and fun and mature.

*January 30*

*Okay, so remember how in my last journal entry I said I was going to try to be the bigger person and let Elijah go?*

*Well...I think I spoke too soon.*

*You see, I was hanging out at The Italian Amigos with Asher and a few other friends on Friday night, when guess who walked in the door? It was Elijah...with a leggy blonde with big boobs on his arm!!*

*Yep. He was on a freaking date with silicone Barbie! And I had to watch the whole thing as they were seated at the table next to ours.*

*I don't know if he saw me though. His back was to me and he just stared at his date all through dinner. Yes, she was probably actually his age and gorgeous—so good job, Elijah, for finding someone you can legally date.*

*But yeah, that basically sucked.*

*Anyway, it put me in a weird mood. I've been trying so hard to move on and have a regular high school life while also trying to keep secret the fact that I'm being tortured by how hot my biology professor is.*

*I guess seeing him out on a date must have triggered something because as soon as we got back to the school and I saw a poster for the Valentine's Day dance, I decided that I wanted to give Elijah a taste of his own medicine. If he was going to start dating and flaunting it in my face, I was going to give him a show of his own. So Asher and I are going to start a fake relationship—The Ruse, as I so geniusly named it since every plan deserves to have a cool code name.*

*Asher knows it's fake and thinks it's just for fun and to practice our acting skills while tricking everyone at school. But yeah...it's really for Elijah.*


*February 21*

*I only have a second but I just wanted to say that the ruse is going so well. Everyone is buying it and Asher and I are having so much fun.*

*Elijah is even buying it, which is amazing. Asher and I have biology class together, which is basically perfect. Whenever we're in there, I really ramp up our flirting. It's so fun!*

*For me, at least.*

*Elijah doesn't seem to like it though, because he totally separated Asher and me during class this morning and made me sit in the front row with Asher in the back.*

*A normal high school student would probably be upset being separated from her boyfriend, but since it's not real, I totally didn't mind sitting just a little closer to Elijah as he was teaching us today. He might not let me touch him anymore, but at least I get to look at him and flirt with him with my eyes.*

*March 10*

*I decided to add kissing into the arrangement I have with Asher today. It's been too long since I actually kissed a guy. Plus, I figure it'll just make everything more believable if we get caught making out here and there.*

*No one needs to know that every time I kiss Asher, I'm picturing Elijah.*

I scoffed. *Every time she kissed me, she'd been picturing our teacher?*

If that didn't feel like a slap in the face, I didn't know what did.

*Well, most of the time anyway. Sometimes I do get lost in the moment because Asher is a spectacular kisser and has the body of a god. I mean, I did pick him to do this with me because he's the hottest guy at school.*

Well, that made my ego feel slightly better.

*Also, I think Asher and I should ramp things up even more so we can win Prom King and Queen. We could totally win.*

*April 3*

*I've been feeling kind of off lately. Really tired and pretty sick to my stomach in the mornings. I thought it was just me being depressed and missing Elijah, but then I realized it had been a while since I had my period.*

*So I took a pregnancy test.*

*And then another. And another.*

*They all came back positive.*

*I want to die.*

*April 9*

*I did the math and apparently, I'm like 16 weeks along. 16 weeks out of 40.*

*Who would have thought that the one time I had sex I would get pregnant? I don't know how it happened. Maybe the condom broke? Or expired? Or just failed somehow.*

*It had one job! To make me NOT get pregnant when I'm in high school. I wasn't supposed to get pregnant for like another ten years.*

*So that sucks.*

*But I was trying to pay better attention to my body today and felt little flutters in my stomach during first period so there is probably a real baby growing in there.*

*I'm trying to decide what to do. My parents will kill me if they find out I got pregnant. And then they'll press charges on Elijah and he'll get sent to jail.*

*This is a disaster.*

*April 14*

*I went to a clinic to get an abortion today. I figured it was the only way to protect Elijah. Plus, my parents made Alisha get an abortion when she got pregnant her freshman year of college, so I knew it's what they'd want me to do anyway.*

Becoming a mom at 17 is not in the life plan they mapped out for me.

But while I was waiting for the nurse to call me in, I realized that I couldn't go through with it. The baby is big enough to have a heartbeat and blink and we would be able to tell if it's a boy or a girl.

I know Alisha had a hard time after her abortion and sometimes wonders if it was the right thing. I just don't think I could live with myself for doing that to this baby. So I'm going to have to tell Elijah and try to figure out a way to tell my parents. I'm so scared.

PS: I won Prom Queen and Asher was Prom King. So yay for that, at least. I wonder if I should tell Asher that I'm pregnant... He's been such a good friend to me. He might understand.


*April 24*

It's been a week and a half and things have been a little better. Elijah didn't love the news at first but he got used to the idea and admitted that he hasn't been able to stop thinking about me. So we made some plans to disappear and go off the grid for a while. I'll stay at this cabin that his parents own about an hour away. They never go there anymore so it should be a safe place to hide out. I'm just starting to show and people are going to get suspicious if I stay in Eden Falls much longer.

Elijah will finish out the school year so no one suspects anything. And then he's going to try to get a job teaching in Alaska. They're always looking for teachers and it's so far away that we don't think anyone will notice us.

I know it's not the greatest plan, but my parents would never let me keep the baby and they would press charges against Elijah for statutory rape. I just know that's what they'd do.

*I don't want either of those things to happen.*

*I know it's complicated and everyone would think it's crazy, but we love each other and want to make this work and I want my baby to have his or her dad in his/her life. He can't do that if he's in prison. And he can't provide for us if he can't get a job.*

*Everything is all set. The only thing left is for me to break up with Asher. I wish I could tell him what's going on since I think he would understand. He has really become my best friend. But I don't want to risk anything, so I probably won't say anything.*

I turned the page, and the rest of the journal was blank. That was the last journal entry she made.

I looked back to the date at the top. It was the twenty-fourth of April.

Bailee disappeared the next day.

---

I SLIPPED Bailee's journal back into my duffel bag when I was done reading, and then pulled out my phone to text Elyse. I needed to talk to someone about this.

> Me: Just finished reading Bailee's journal.

Her text came through a few seconds later, like she'd been waiting for it ever since I left the school.

> Elyse: Yeah? How are you?

Bailee had always seemed so different in real life. Like
nothing could hurt her. Like she could rule the world someday.

The girl who'd written those journal entries was much
more human than the girl I thought I'd known.

The version of Bailee that I'd seen just laughed at everything. Hadn't seemed to take anything seriously. Life was just a
big game to her.

But this girl, who was the real Bailee, had felt things way
more intensely than I'd ever guess. This Bailee had feelings so
strong that she'd done crazy things to protect them from getting
out.

No wonder she always kept everyone at arm's length.



"Thought we were" being the keywords. We hadn't actually been close at all.

Not with the things that mattered, anyway.

And to think I'd thought that I loved her. I hadn't even
*known* her.



She had been able to stay off the radar because no one had
expected her to be with Professor Hicks. But now that we knew
who had helped her disappear, it would be easier to find her.

> Elyse: Are you going to give the journal to the police?

> Me: I'll mail it to her parents tomorrow and let them decide what to do with it.

Her parents had tons of connections. I'd leave it up to them on whether they wanted to get the police involved. On whether they were going to press charges like Bailee thought they would.

I just hoped that when all was said and done, Bailee and her baby would be okay.

---

## 36

# ELYSE

I FINISHED PACKING up my dorm room. After taking the rest of my things to my new bedroom on the second story of Brendon's house, I decided that now was probably the right time to talk to Nash and tell him what I'd realized this afternoon.

A huge part of me wanted to just text him and tell him I only wanted to be friends—hoping a text would suffice since we weren't officially girlfriend and boyfriend yet... But I wanted us to still be friends after this, so I needed to pull up my big-girl pants and do this in person.

After texting to make sure he was home, I walked next door and knocked.

When he answered the door, a hint of trepidation was written on his face—almost like he had an idea of what was coming.

"Wanna talk in the library?" Nash asked in a stilted voice after inviting me in. "I don't think anyone's in there."

"Sure," I said, my stomach twisting with nerves. "That would be great."

"Do you want anything to drink?" he asked as we walked down the large corridor with marble flooring and high ceilings.

"No thanks."

I'd only been to the library once—during the tour Cambrielle had given Ava and me the first time we'd come to the Hastings' estate. It was a beautiful room with floor-to-ceiling bookshelves, complete with one of those super cool ladders that could roll all around the room.

Nash flipped the switch on the gas fireplace and gestured for me to sit on one of the leather armchairs beside it as he took a seat in the chair across from it.

"So, what did you need to talk about?" he asked, looking as uncomfortable as I felt.

"Well..." I swallowed, trying to figure out the exact words I should say. I'd never had to break up with someone like this before.

All my other boyfriends had either just ghosted me, moved away, or we'd come to the realization together that we weren't a good fit.

None of them had been as kind and thoughtful and sweet as Nash.

"Well...?" Nash gently prodded when I didn't say anything.

I sighed. I needed to just rip off the Band-Aid. "I guess there isn't really a right way to do this." I twisted my fingers together in my lap. "But I, um, I wanted to come over and talk to you because I know that we've kind of had something growing between us the past several weeks. And well..." I looked down at my hands, unable to meet his gaze. "I just don't think it's the best idea for us to keep going on dates."

I stopped and kept staring at my hands, feeling my heart pounding everywhere as I waited for him to say something.

There was nothing but silence for a few agonizing moments,

and I wondered if I should have said things differently. Maybe given him more warning, since now that I thought about it, this probably seemed like it was coming out of nowhere to him.

But then he said, "I see."

I looked up at his face. His expression showed he was kind of stunned and still processing what I'd just said.

"I'm sorry," I said. "I didn't realize how I really felt until this afternoon and..." I shrugged helplessly. "And I just..." Did I really have to say this last part? Did I really need to bring another guy into this?

"You have stronger feelings for someone else," he guessed. "For Asher, right?"

I pressed my lips together and nodded, hating the pain that instantly flashed in his eyes. "I'm sorry, Nash."

"How long have you liked him?" He looked down and scratched at a spot on his jeans. "Before our date? He said you kissed the night before..."

"That was just for the play," I tried to explain. But since that kiss had probably been a little more involved than was necessary for that song, I said, "I mean, I guess I started having feelings before then. When I got to know him better at the cabin..."

"That long ago?"

"I was still hoping it would be you," I hurried to say, so he wouldn't think I'd just been stringing him along. "I really did like you so much and didn't expect for things to change."

"But it sounds like they did." His jaw flexed, like he was fighting a strong wave of disappointment.

"Yes," I admitted, hating that I was doing this to someone who was so awesome and had never done anything wrong.

He'd simply just not been my guy.

Nash focused his gaze on the fire. When I studied his

profile, I thought I saw moisture in his blue eyes before he wiped it away.

*Aw, Nash.*

He blew out a long breath before looking back at me and saying, "Well, this sucks."

"I know." And I wanted to tell him that it sucked a little for me, too, since I had wanted him for so long. But mentioning it really wouldn't help anything, so I kept quiet.

He stared into the fire again, as if still processing what just happened. Then he pushed himself to stand up. "I guess that's probably all you came here to say, then?"

"Y-yeah," I said. Was he going to kick me out now?

He must have seen the surprise on my face because he said, "A huge part of me wants to put up a fight and tell you that we could be amazing together and that you're picking the wrong guy." He sighed and rocked back on his heels. "But I'm guessing it would only make me look stupider and do nothing to change your mind."

"You wouldn't look stupid," I said. "But yeah... I don't think it would change my mind."

Even if Asher decided he didn't want to be with me after everything, I knew deep down that Nash and I would still be missing something.

"Well, I guess I should probably wish you the best," he said. "Because even if you and I aren't meant to be, I still want you to be happy." He gave me a sad smile. "Asher and I may have our issues, and I'll probably never be part of his fan club, but he must be doing something right if he won you."

I didn't know what it was but what he said kind of broke my heart. Because even though I was breaking up with him and hurting him, he was still kind enough to wish the best for me.

"Some girl out there is going to be super lucky to capture your heart one day," I said, meaning it.

Nash was one of the good ones.

But he just kind of scoffed like he didn't really believe it. "I won't hold my breath."

"It's going to happen." I stepped closer to touch his arm. "And she's going to find out that I did this tonight and probably tell the whole world that I'm an idiot for not choosing such an amazing guy."

He chuckled. "Then I guess I'm going to have to tell her that she's right because I'm basically the best."

I smiled, only realizing then that I had tears prickling at my eyes. He wiped them away with his thumb. And as I looked up into his ocean-blue eyes, I couldn't help the little ache in my chest.

If we had lived in a different world where Asher Park didn't exist, I probably could have been very happy with Nash Hastings.

"So, does this mean Asher is taking you to the debutante ball?" Nash asked.

"No," I said. "I, um, haven't exactly told him how I feel yet. Plus, I'm sure he already has plans with his aunt and uncle for the holidays." I shrugged. "I'll have to figure something out, since you probably wouldn't want to be my escort anymore."

"What?" he asked, sounding shocked. "You're trying to kick me out of that, too?"

"You'd still go with me?" I asked. "Even after all this?"

He shrugged. "We're still going to be friends after tonight, right?"

"Yes," I said. "At least, I hope so."

"Well, then I would still be just as honored to be your escort as I was before," he said. "I won't leave you hanging."

"Really?" I asked, not believing he was saying this after everything.

"Sure," he said. "I'll be there, anyway. Plus, Hunter and

Scarlett will be there together, so it's okay for people who are just friends to go together."

"That's really awesome of you," I said, still not believing this. If the tables were turned, I doubted I'd be okay going to a fancy ball with a guy who had just dumped me. I would tell him he could just go on his own.

But I guess this only went to show that Nash was a bigger person than me.

"Well, like we established earlier," Nash said. "I am basically the best."

## 37

## ASHER

I MADE it to Ridgewater around eleven and got a ride to my aunt and uncle's house with my cousin Logan in his Corvette.

My aunt and uncle weren't billionaires like the Hastings, but they had come into some money fairly recently and had a really nice home on the top of the hill with the other wealthy people of their small town.

After I got all settled in and figured out how to ship the journal to Bailee's parents in the morning, my cousins and I stayed up late chatting about everything that had happened in our lives the past month.

"I still can't believe the Cohen twins are going to your school," Jace said when I told them about Elyse and Ava. "It's such a small world sometimes."

"Yeah," I said. "Elyse and I were actually wondering if we went to some of the same parties this summer but couldn't remember seeing each other."

"We probably did," Logan said, running a hand through his shaggy brown hair that was always messy. "And you said you have a thing for Elyse?"

"I don't think I said anything about it..." I said, wondering how he'd even guess it.

"Ah, well, you may not have said it with your words, but your eyes totally did when you talked about her."

Had he suddenly become a mind-reader while I'd been away?

"I'm right, aren't I?" Logan prodded when I didn't say anything.

I could have denied it, but he was apparently a lot better at reading me than I'd like. "Okay, yeah. She's cute."

"Cute?" He raised his eyebrows.

"Fine." I sighed. "So she's amazing and I can't stop thinking about her. Are you happy now?"

Logan and Jace just looked at each other and laughed, like they thought it was so hilarious for me to like someone. I was the cousin who, growing up, never cared about what girls they wrote down for me when we played the game M.A.S.H. It was a game that their other cousin Lauren had taught them, and we'd never admit to anyone else that we ever played it during our sleepovers.

"Did Elyse tell you that we actually dated?" Logan asked once his laughter died down.

"Yes." I crossed my arms, feeling slightly jealous that my cousin had a more serious relationship with Elyse than I had. That he'd kissed her first. "But she says I'm way hotter and a better kisser."

"She did not," he said. "Elyse would never do me dirty like that."

"Fine, so I'm the one who said that," I admitted. "But she didn't disagree."

He laughed. "That's just because she's too nice."

"Did you say she's going to be at the debutante ball with another dude?" Jace asked.

"Yeah." I sighed. "She's going with that guy, Nash, that I've told you about before."

"The guy who got the part you wanted in the play?"

"That would be the guy," I said.

"Well, we can't have him getting the part *and* the girl," Logan said.

"I'm trying not to let him."

"Does she even know you're going to be at the ball?" Jace asked.

"Not unless my friends Scarlett or Hunter told her." I shook my head. "But I don't think they did."

"Well, then we're just going to have to find a way for you to steal her away from the prince at the ball."

<hr>

LOGAN, Jace, and I tried to come up with a plan for how to somehow sabotage Nash and have him miss the ball, so I could swoop in and save the day at the last minute. But since most of their ideas involved things like kidnapping or tying him up in a hotel room, I told them it was probably best that we just leave things how they were and try to keep ourselves out of jail.

The next few days were busy with all the holiday parties and traditions my aunt and uncle had planned for us. I tried to text Elyse a few times just to see how she was, but she was always busy doing something with her family whenever I texted her, and then I was always in the middle of something with mine when she finally responded, so our conversations didn't get very far.

She mentioned that they went snowmobiling with the Hastings one of the days she was still in Eden Falls with her dad, so I just hoped that hadn't been a chance for her and Nash to bond even more.

We headed to New York the day after Christmas since my aunt had a lot of last-minute things to do for the debutante ball and my cousins had their events to go to with their girlfriends before the main event. So while they all did those things, I just hung out in the hotel, watching TV or playing the piano in a cool lounge they had on the main floor, and trying not to worry about how things would go the night of the ball.

On the evening of the twenty-eighth, I was just changing into my tux and trying to figure out how to style my wavy hair in a way that looked neat but not too dorky when my cousin Logan called from the other room.

"Hey, Asher. Are you hearing this?"

"Huh?" I frowned and walked into the living area of our hotel suite where he and Jace were watching something on TV.

"Just watch..." Jace pointed at the screen, like whatever was on there was making it hard for him to finish his sentence.

A female news anchor was talking on TV, and the banner across the bottom read, "Breaking News: Vanderbilt heiress who went missing last April was found alive in Alaska."

*What?*

My whole body went tingly and weak. "Turn it up," I said, sitting down on the bed so I could listen properly.

"Our sources say that the FBI were given a tip that led them to the secluded town of Sitka, Alaska to search for a young science teacher named Elijah Hicks. He was one of the heiress' teachers at the private school she attended in Eden Falls, Connecticut. Our sources claim that he moved to the small fishing town after his hire this past June. His neighbors reported seeing a young woman go in and out of the house with him on occasion." The news anchor finished, and the screen switched to a reporter doing an interview in a picturesque town.

"They liked to keep to themselves." A woman who looked

to be in her sixties came onto the screen with the title of *neighbor* under her name. "Seemed like a cute young couple, though. She was a beautiful girl, and a couple times I thought to myself that she seemed familiar, like she'd been a model in one of my clothing catalogues or something. She looked like she'd be a good clothing model, back before she got pregnant, anyway. The teacher and his wife didn't get into no trouble, and my granddaughter said he was a real good teacher. But now that I know they weren't even married—" She shook her head, like that in and of itself was a huge scandal.

She blew out a low whistle. "Well, I'm sure glad I forgot to have my granddaughter take them over some baby clothes when I saw they'd had the baby. To think he's a pedophile and a kidnapper who could have hurt my sweet Talia. Oh no, sirree. What is this world coming to? Teachers having babies with students?"

The shot changed again to another news reporter standing on a crowded sidewalk in New York. He started talking about how Bailee had been found two days before and was just now returning home with her family after eight months away.

The screen shifted to show video footage of a girl with dark-brown hair and dark sunglasses climbing out of a black sedan with an infant car seat over her arm.

Bailee.

And her baby.

It was so surreal seeing her on TV. She was walking up near what I now recognized as her family's upper east-side penthouse. Cameras were flashing all around her, with reporters shouting their questions. Two large men who I recognized as her father's bodyguards flanked her and her baby. In front of her were her parents, with her older sister Alisha bringing up the rear.

The family all kept their heads ducked low as they walked

up the path to their house. I searched the screen to see if Professor Hicks was there with them, but he was nowhere to be seen.

Was he in police custody?

———

ELYSE TEXTED me as soon as the news report went to a commercial break.

> Elyse: I just saw the news. Did you? Did you see that they found Bailee?

> Me: Just saw it. It's kind of crazy how fast they found her and brought her home.

> Elyse: I know. Did you have any idea it was happening? Did her parents say anything to you?

> Me: No. I didn't even know if the journal made it to them.

> Elyse: Apparently it did.

> Me: Yep.

The conversation dots showed up on the screen, like she was typing another text, so I waited. But then they disappeared after a few minutes went by, so she must have gotten distracted by something.

———

"WANT us to help you brainstorm any other ways for you to

get rid of Nash tonight?" Logan asked as we rode the elevator down to the hotel's first level.

The ball would be held in the large ballroom on the main level. When the elevator doors opened, I saw that there were already dozens of people milling around in tuxedos and ballgowns.

"I think I'm just going to try my usual lie-low-and-look-hot method and hope it does the trick." I straightened my bow tie as we stepped out of the elevator. "If she wants to pick me, she'll do it because she likes me more. Not because I sabotaged Nash to get close to her."

I was done making an idiot out of myself because of my rivalry with Nash.

"Suit yourself." Logan shrugged.

We walked into the crowd and zig-zagged our way to the table that would be ours for the night. From what I'd heard, these tables cost close to twenty thousand dollars a piece, so even if I didn't get to dance with the girl I wanted tonight, I was at least hoping the dinner would be amazing based on that price.

My uncle was already at the table near the stage with Jace and Logan's girlfriends' fathers. The moms were apparently putting the finishing touches to their daughters' hair and makeup and would be down in a moment for Jace and Logan to take backstage and wait for their turn to be presented.

I was just about to take my seat next to my uncle when my attention was drawn to the back of the room. Mack Aarden was walking through the door with his father, and right behind him stood Elyse and Ava with their mom.

At first, I didn't know which twin was which—we were so far away, and their hair and makeup was done so similarly—but then I saw Elyse bite her lip in the way she did when she was nervous, and I knew it was her.

When I let myself really take her in, I had to swallow hard because she was so beautiful.

Stunning.

She wore a white ballgown like the rest of the debutantes had been instructed to wear, but while all the other girls simply looked nice in their dresses, it seemed like this particular dress had been made just for her.

Which it probably had been, since her mom designed fancy dresses for a living.

The dress was held up by thin satiny-looking straps, and the skirt was so full I wondered if it was heavy, with layer after layer of fabric underneath.

She wore white gloves that hit her just above the elbow and her hair was half up with the lower half cascading around her delicate shoulders in curls.

Logan nudged my arm and handed me a napkin, saying, "Here, you might want to wipe the drool from your mouth."

I felt around my mouth to see if I'd been drooling without knowing it.

I hadn't.

I elbowed Logan in the side.

"You should go up to her," Logan said. "At least let her know you're here."

"You think I should?" I asked, feeling like I had a jackhammer in my chest.

"Sure." Logan shrugged. "I mean, you're friends, right? Friends say hi to each other."

Yeah, they did.

But then, if I was going to just go and say hi, I probably should have told her I was going to be at the ball a long time ago.

We hadn't actually spoken about it in any sort of depth. She'd noticed that I'd seen the text from Nash that night in her room. And she'd mentioned coming to New York for the ball. But that had been all. I'd never said anything about coming myself.

As far as she knew, I had no idea what a debutante even was.

"She's going to see you later. Just say hi so it's not so weird when you suddenly show up at her side later tonight, asking her to dance."

"I'm allowed to dance with her even if I'm not her escort?"

"I think so," Logan said.

He turned to Jace and asked him.

Jace shrugged. "I think that's okay. Our mom already made us promise to dance with her."

Okay. Maybe I should at least let her know I'm here...

But before I could make my way across the room, Scarlett suddenly showed up at their side, wearing a white dress of her own, and was beckoning for them to follow her backstage where the debutantes were probably lining up with their escorts.

I sat back in my chair again. I'd just have to figure out a way to approach her after dinner. This thing was going to last for several hours.

I'd have a chance later, right?

# 38

## ELYSE

"NASH IS COMING, RIGHT?" I asked Cambrielle and Carter who were standing in a circle with our friends backstage at the debutante ball.

One of the women helping to put on the event came to announce we'd be starting in a couple of minutes. And even though all of my friends had been standing back here with their escorts for the past twenty minutes, mine was still nowhere to be seen.

"He said he just had an errand to run before this," Cambrielle said, looking just as lost as I was about why Nash hadn't shown up yet. "He said he'd be back with plenty of time to spare."

"Well, hopefully he's almost here," I said, checking the clock on the wall for the fiftieth time tonight. "Because if he doesn't get here fast, I'm going to have to escort myself."

I never should have let my friends and Ava talk me into doing this. This wasn't my kind of thing. I didn't care about all the high-society stuff.

"Do you think he's just trying to get back at me for breaking things off with him?" I asked Cambrielle in a low voice.

"You broke things off with Nash?" Cambrielle's dark eyebrows knitted together.

"Yeah..." I said the word slowly. "Like a week and a half ago. I told him I just wanted to be friends."

Since I have feelings for someone else.

I searched her heart-shaped face for signs that she'd heard of this before, but she just stared at me with shock in her blue eyes. "He didn't tell you?"

"No?" She said it like she wasn't sure now and was trying to think back and remember a conversation she might have forgotten having with her brother. She turned to Carter, who was just walking back to the group with Ava, and asked, "Did Nash ever tell you that Elyse broke things off with him?"

Carter's lips puckered as he considered her words, but he shook his head. "Last I heard, you guys were going strong and he was excited about tonight."

Had I just imagined that whole conversation in his library then? The one where Nash said he was sad but understood and still wanted to be friends?

I'd been amazed at how well he'd taken it. Had he not really heard me?

Had I not been clear enough?

Did he somehow think tonight was another romantic evening where he could convince me to choose him?

I shook my head. "Well, if he's trying to win me back, he certainly has a weird way of going about it." You'd think he'd be here by now if he wanted to impress me.

Then another thought occurred to me. Was it possible that he hadn't told his siblings about us breaking up because he was actually planning to ditch me tonight and didn't want them to have the heads up?

Was that his plan? To make me look stupid in front of everyone because I fell for the guy he's had a stupid rivalry with since elementary?

Ugh.

He was supposed to be the sweet guy.

"Does anyone have a way to call him?" I asked my group of friends, looking to see if any of them had their cellphones on them since I'd left mine with my mom.

Mack and Hunter patted their jackets, but Carter slipped his phone out of his breast pocket. He looked at the screen and said, "Ah, looks like Nash sent me, like, ten texts in a row."

He squinted his blue eyes as he read what was on his screen. Then looking at me, he said, "He's stuck in traffic. His text from five minutes ago says he's been stuck in the same place for forty minutes and is still about ten minutes away."

So maybe he wasn't trying to be a jerk tonight after all. Maybe he simply had poor planning skills.

And if his time estimates were right, it didn't sound like he'd make it here on time since the ball was going to start in about two minutes. And because my last name started with a C, I'd be called near the beginning.

"I'm so sorry," Cambrielle said, pulling me into her arms for a hug.

I wrapped my arms around my friend and tried not to cry as I wondered what I was going to do now.

Should I run and ask Brendon to be my escort? Most of the girls back here were being escorted by guys much younger than my dad—most guys being in their late teens or early twenties. But at least I wouldn't have to go out there by myself.

Except Brendon didn't know the choreography for the dance we were all supposed to do together.

Maybe I should just go sit at the table with all of our parents and pretend like I was wearing a white dress and gloves because I liked white—and not because I was supposed to be a debutante tonight.

"Maybe we can go out there together?" Ava suggested. "Each of us on either side of Carter. We're twins. I'm sure people would think it was fine. Fun even..."

"That's sweet of you to offer," I said, looking at my sister and her boyfriend. "But you deserve to have that special moment together without me being a third wheel."

"You wouldn't be a third wheel," Ava said. "It's fine. Right, Carter?"

"Uh, sure," he said, not looking particularly interested in the idea but willing to do it for his girlfriend. "We could do that."

Mack stepped forward. "Or maybe I could take you first since there will probably be a few people in line between you and Cambrielle. I can help you do that weird curtsey thing we're supposed to help you do, and then hurry back here to escort Cambrielle."

"That might work for the first part," Ava said, seeming to consider our half-brother's idea. "But we're all supposed to do that dance together once we're all out there, and that might get tricky..."

Yeah...that wouldn't work very well. I would look like an idiot doing the dance by myself.

"It's okay," I said. "I'll just sit this one out."

Scarlett, who had been having a whispered conversation with Hunter, got a look in her eyes that told me she might have an idea. She said, "Hold on. Hunter and I just realized something."

"What is it?" I frowned as I watched Hunter run off through the crowd and to the doors that led back to the ballroom.

"We just remembered someone who said he'd be here."

"Is it someone I know?" I asked, not super comfortable with the idea of going out there with a complete stranger.

Did Hunter have an older brother?

I didn't have much time to worry about it, though, because Mrs. Carmichael appeared at the front of the group a few seconds later to tell us that it was time to line up. We were about to start.

Wait—

Jace and Logan's mom was here?

Asher's aunt was here?

I frowned and looked around the room filled with debutantes and escorts. Then I noticed that Jace and Logan were standing at the far end of the line with their girlfriends Raven Rodgers and Alyssa Turner who they'd started dating last year.

If the Carmichael twins were here, did that mean...?

Almost as if I'd conjured him up in my mind, Hunter came around the corner again with a tall guy with dark hair and the most handsome face I'd ever seen following right behind.

*Asher?*

I blinked my eyes a few times, wondering if I was hallucinating. But no. When my eyes focused again, I was face to face with Asher.

"Hunter said you needed a last-minute escort?" he said in a low voice that made my stomach flutter when he stepped up beside me.

"Yes...I do..." I said, still not believing my eyes as I studied him. He had his hair combed to the side in a way I'd never seen it combed before. It was different and new, and yet I loved it on him.

But then, I'd probably love his hair any way he did it because I was just so happy to see him. It was like I hadn't known just how much I'd missed seeing him the last week and a half until now.

"H-how did you get here?" I pulled my gaze away from his face to take him in. He was wearing the exact type of tuxedo that the escorts were supposed to wear. Tails. White vest. White bow tie. White gloves. "D-did someone from Ridgewater ask you to be her escort?"

*Please say no.*

I knew it was super hypocritical of me to hope he'd come here alone since I had asked someone else, but I really didn't want to know if he had found a rich heiress to spend his time with over the break. I was pretty sure I'd seen Kelsie Perkins here. She was a neighbor to the Carmichaels, and I'd seen on social media that she'd recently broken up with her boyfriend. So there was a chance Asher had come with her.

"No," he said, searching my gaze like he wasn't sure how I felt about him being here. "My aunt was worried she'd need a backup escort for one of the debutantes and had me dress like this and learn the dance just in case."

"You know the dance choreography?"

He nodded. "She made me practice it with her all last week." He narrowed his brown-eyed gaze. "I probably should have said something about it when you told me you'd be here this week."

"I wish you had," I said.

If I'd known he was going to be here, or that getting the tux wasn't going to be a problem for him, I could have asked him to be my escort when I realized I wanted to be with him.

I would have called him as soon as I ended things with Nash and begged him to come with me.

"Are you mad I didn't tell you?" he asked, a worried look in his eyes.

"No, of course I'm not mad," I hurried to say. "I'm just shocked. And I—" I shook my head, my brain still trying to catch up to everything. "I could have done things differently, if I had known."

"You would have done things differently?" He looked hopeful for a moment. Like, he would have wanted me to ask him to be my escort. "I was going to tell you about it that night I came to your room. But I got all weirded out about being in Bailee's room. And then, I saw that text that said you were already going with Nash so—"

"Hey, you guys probably should tell the lady in charge that Asher is your new escort," Scarlett said from behind us, interrupting whatever Asher had been about to say.

"Oh right," I said. "Of course."

I saw Mrs. Carmichael walking toward the front of the line, like she was about to walk onstage to start introducing the debutantes and our escorts.

"Hey, Mrs. Carmichael," I called, walking as fast as I could in my heels to catch up to her.

She turned and looked at me. "Yes?"

"I need to change the name of my escort."

"You do?" she asked, a flash of anxiety crossing her face as if worried I was going to cause a hitch in her plans for the night.

"Yeah, it's—"

"Hey, Elyse," a familiar voice said from behind me, sounding out of breath. "I'm here. Is it time to go on?"

*What?*

I turned and found Nash standing right behind me, dressed in his tuxedo, his blond hair slicked back and his jacket lightly dusted with snow.

"Sorry, I'm late," he said. "I was stuck in traffic. There was an accident. I tried to call you, but you didn't answer." He took a deep breath. "But I just ran the rest of the way here."

"What was your name and the name of your escort?" Mrs. Carmichael interrupted Nash, clearly in a hurry to get started.

"Oh, there's no need for a change anymore," Nash told Asher's aunt. "I made it."

But wait.

No.

Asher was here.

Asher was going to be my escort now.

I could still make the change, right?

But Mrs. Carmichael un-clicked her pen and said, "Perfect." She took a step toward the stage, and with the wave of her hand, she said, "If you'll get to your places, we're going to start."

Instead of moving, I just stood there frozen in place. I could tell Nash that he'd been replaced, right? That because he was late, his position had been filled.

But then Mrs. Carmichael disappeared through the curtains, and a minute later, her voice sounded through the speakers as she welcomed everyone in the audience to the event.

"Come on, let's get in line," Nash said, tugging on my arm.

As Nash and I walked back to where I'd left Asher, he explained that he was late because he had to pick up something for tonight and he was sorry for cutting it so close.

And though it sounded like his late arrival had all been a mistake and not payback for choosing Asher instead of him, all I could think of was that I didn't care.

I didn't freaking care how much of a close call it had been or how important his last-minute errand was and how lucky he was to make it here in the nick of time, because I didn't want to be here with Nash anymore.

I wanted to be with Asher.

I wished Nash was still stuck in traffic so I could tell Mrs. Carmichael of the escort change—I wanted to spend the evening with the guy I actually wanted to be here with.

I wanted to have not been so stupid that I hadn't even thought to ask Asher if he could be here tonight.

Why had I just assumed that he couldn't make it? Or that he wouldn't be able to get the right outfit for the night?

Even if he hadn't been able to afford a tux without dipping into his college savings, I could have gotten the tux for him. There would have been a way to make it happen if I'd been thinking creatively at all.

We were about ten feet away from the spot in line where I'd left Asher, when Asher seemed to notice Nash for the first time. And it only took a second for realization to dawn on his face and for his expression to fall.

*No.* He was going to bolt.

He was going to think that I had chosen Nash over him.

I knew he would. He always thought that's what the people in his life did.

Choose someone else.

I quickened my step to rush over to him and explain what was going on. But before I could say anything, he put on what I knew was a forced smile and said, "Looks like your escort made it and my services aren't needed after all."

"No, it's not—" I started.

But before I could get any more words out, Nash slipped his arm behind my waist possessively and said, "Thanks for being willing to stand in, but I'll take it from here."

What?

Was Nash actually doing this?

He knew I'd picked Asher. I'd told him so, like a week and a half ago.

But he must have known that Asher didn't know I'd picked him, because he just looked at Asher in a way that said, *I won the war, bro.*

Ugh. Their beef with each other was so stupid.

I wanted to tell Asher that I had most definitely *not* picked Nash, but before I could, Asher slipped back into the cluster of debutantes and escorts behind us and was heading toward the exit that would lead back to the ballroom.

"Asher, wait," I called, hoping that he'd stop. But he either couldn't hear me over the buzz of voices around us, or he didn't *want* to hear me because he just kept on going.

I started pushing my way through the crowd, but I only made it a few feet before I heard Mrs. Carmichael announce Ava's name over the speakers.

*No! Not yet.*

I stopped and looked back to the stage entrance, then back to where Asher's head and shoulders were about to disappear through the double doors.

Mrs. Carmichael would be calling my name in a few seconds. There was no way I could make it to Asher and then drag him back here in time.

*This freaking sucks.*

A second later, Asher was gone, and I knew that I really had to do this without him now. So I begrudgingly marched back to where Nash was waiting.

"Something wrong?" Nash asked, like he really didn't know that I was an emotional wreck right now and that he had probably just ruined any progress I thought I'd made with Asher tonight.

"Everything is perfect," I lied through my teeth.

As he led me out onto the stage, I forced a smile on my face and decided that I would pretend like I was happy to be escorted by Nash, that being at this stupid ball was exactly where I wanted to be right now.

He and Asher had said themselves that I was a good actor and could have been pretending to enjoy being with either one of them. I hadn't been acting with Nash before, but I was certainly acting now.

I would get through the next few hours, play the part of a bashful debutante who was having the time of her life since everyone would be watching, and I knew how much my mom had been looking forward to tonight.

But once I got Nash alone, I was going to make sure he knew without a shadow of a doubt that we were over.

My chance at a future with Asher was not going to be a casualty of their stupid war.

---

## 39

## ASHER

HOW MUCH LONGER DID I have to stick around and watch the girl I was in love with dance and smile and seem altogether enchanted to be at this stupid party with Nash?

Five more minutes? Ten?

I'd already sat through the part where she'd been presented and had him help her with the weird curtsey that was apparently customary for the debutantes to do.

Then I had to watch their stupid dance with the other debs and escorts. And as they sat next to each other at their table, I had to watch him lean over every so often to whisper whatever sweet nothings he had to tell her in her ear.

Was she enjoying this?

Was this her idea of the perfect night?

Was she hoping to have many more fancy balls and ballgowns in her future?

Because if that was the case, it was probably good that I found out now. Though I was here tonight, I didn't belong in this world. I didn't belong in the world of glittery chandeliers, fancy orchestra music, and dinners that cost more than a used car.

No, I was the guy who had always been on the edges of high society. Always watching and interacting with the rich and famous.

But never one of them.

And even when I was here, actually invited to sit at the fancy table, I couldn't even enjoy my stupid overpriced dinner because Nash and Elyse were right there at the table across from me, in my exact line of sight.

"Do you think your mom will notice if I just head back to our room after dinner?" I asked Jace as the chocolate raspberry dessert was being served to our table.

"She might," he said as he poked his fork into the dessert. "But before you go, you should at least try to talk to her."

"To your mom?"

"No." Jace nodded toward Elyse. "Talk to the girl you've been staring at all night."

I sighed and looked back at Elyse. And almost like she'd sensed we were talking about her, she turned her head over her shoulder and looked back at me.

Our eyes locked, and my chest tightened as I met her gaze.

Even though I'd been staring at her all night, I still couldn't get over how beautiful she was.

Her perfectly shaped eyebrows were knitted together, and I tried to interpret what might be going through her mind. Was she looking at me because she felt sorry for me? Was she trying to figure out how to tell me that she had chosen Nash after all, that I'd never really had a chance with her in the first place?

Or was she looking at me with her light-brown eyes all sad and longing because she wanted to be sitting next to me?

I sighed and pushed the thought away. I was just making

up the longing look in my head because I wanted her to wish she was with me.

Jace leaned closer again and said, "If she wanted to be with that other guy, she wouldn't be looking at you like that."

Nash tapped Elyse on the arm, to bring her attention back to him.

I tossed my napkin on the table. "I can't watch this anymore."

I was considering sneaking outside for some fresh air when my phone started vibrating in my jacket pocket.

Thankful for the distraction, I checked to see who was calling. And when I looked at the screen, my heart stumbled to a stop.

The name and photo of someone whom I hadn't received a call from since last April showed up.

It was Bailee.

## 40

## ELYSE

IS *Asher going to come back?*

I looked back at the doors where he'd disappeared through thirty minutes ago. He'd been holding his phone, as if taking a call. But was that just a prop to help him pretend he had a reason to leave early?

I'd been watching him all night, and from his frustrated expression, I could tell he wasn't having the time of his life. But I was hoping that he'd stick around. Dinner was the last part of the night where I *had* to stay by Nash's side. I wanted to at least dance a few songs with Asher.

But if he never came back, that wouldn't be happening.

The slow song that had been playing ended, and Nash finished dancing with his mom. He looked around the room as if searching for me. I considered slipping out the back before he could, but he spotted me too quickly and started walking toward me.

"Hey, sorry about that," he said. "My mom has been talking about dancing with me here ever since they signed Cambrielle up."

"It's fine," I said.

Really.

I had already spent over an hour by his side tonight wishing I was with someone else. I would be fine if he danced with all the other debutantes here if he wanted.

He didn't know that, of course, since I'd been putting on the performance of a lifetime and making it look like I was just dying on his every word.

But maybe it was time to remind him that I didn't like him that way.

So I said, "Actually, would you mind stepping out in the lobby with me for a minute so we can chat?"

"Of course," he said. "I was actually hoping to give you something."

He was hoping to give me something?

*Please don't be another kiss.*

We walked out of the ballroom and found a cushioned bench against one of the walls. My feet were sore from wearing heels all night, so even if I didn't want to be here with Nash, I was grateful for the chance to rest my feet.

Nash sat down beside me. I was trying to think of a way to bring up our conversation in his library again when he reached into his jacket and pulled out a small box.

The type of small box that usually held jewelry.

What was he doing?

He cleared his throat, his cheeks tinged with pink like he was nervous.

"So, uh, I had planned to give this to you before the ball started tonight," he said, his blue eyes lifting to mine like he was back to the bashful Nash that I knew. "It's actually the reason why I was late. You see, when you asked me to be your escort, I thought it would be nice to get you something to show how grateful I was for the opportunity. And well..." He opened the box to reveal a necklace with a simple gold chain and a pendant in the shape of a long-stemmed red rose.

And though I'd been annoyed with Nash all night long, I couldn't help but gasp at how beautiful this necklace was. I'd never seen anything quite like it.

"That's for me?" I asked, unable to keep my jaw from hanging open.

"It is." He nodded. "I had my family's jeweler custom-make it. It wasn't ready until this afternoon, which is why I was late." He pulled the necklace from the box and held it out for me to hold and get a closer look. "It's to symbolize the roses The Phantom gave Christine after each performance."

I took it in my hand, my fingers trembling slightly, as I examined the rose pendant that seemed so small for how detailed it was. How did someone even make something like this?

"The rose is made out of rubies," Nash explained. "And the thin row of black diamonds around the stem are supposed to be like the black ribbon The Phantom tied around the roses." He pointed to the tiny detail. "I wasn't sure if you preferred gold or platinum since I've seen you wear jewelry with both, but I thought the gold would look nice against your skin." He lifted his gaze to mine, a tentative look in his blue eyes. As if he was worried I wouldn't like it.

And I knew I'd been so mad at him before. But for him to do something so thoughtful like this...

I guess I could understand why he wanted to pick it up and make sure I got it.

"It's beautiful," I said before he could think I didn't like it.

It was exquisite and possibly one of the most thoughtful gifts I'd ever been given.

"Glad you think so." He licked his lips. "And I know you said you don't feel the same about me anymore, and that this could be potentially very awkward. But I'd already ordered it before winter break. And since it was literally designed for you, I figured I'd give it to you, anyway."

A custom-designed necklace made from rubies, black diamonds, and what had to be very high-quality gold?

It probably cost a lot of money.

"Are you sure you want to give it to me?" I asked. "Because it's beautiful, but I don't... well..."

"You don't want to give me the wrong idea?" he guessed, a flash of sadness crossing his expression.

I nodded.

He sighed, as if a part of him had hoped I was still open to the possibility of us. But then he said, "I'd still like you to keep it, if you don't mind. It might not mean the same thing I'd been hoping it would when I ordered it, but it's kind of even more symbolic this way. Because just like Christine didn't choose The Phantom who gave her all those roses in the end, you're not choosing me."

Well, now I felt really bad...

He must have seen the worry in my face because he chuckled lightheartedly and said, "It's okay, Elyse. You don't need to look at me like that." He shrugged. "Believe it or not, you're not the first girl who hasn't picked me. Yes, it might sting a little, but I'm sure I'll eventually get over it. My mom always says I fall too hard too fast, so this isn't the first time it's happened to me and I'm sure it won't be the last time, either."

"Yeah?" I asked, hoping it was true that he'd be okay.

He nodded. "In fact, if you take Asher off the market for me, I think my chances will get better since he's usually my biggest competition."

"You two usually fight over the same girls?" I asked.

"I might have tried to win over Bailee before they started dating."

"Really?" I asked, genuinely shocked.

"Didn't work, obviously." He shrugged again. "But it seems to be how it is for us. Always wanting the same things." He made a face. "I mean, people. You're a person and not a thing, of course."

"Yeah…"

"Anyway…" He cleared his throat and pointed to the necklace. "Want me to help you put that on?"

"Sure." I handed him the necklace and then swiveled around on the bench, so my back was to him.

I pulled my hair away from my neck, and he was just in the process of hooking the chain through the tiny clasp when Asher appeared out of the corner of my eye.

He had just stepped out of the elevator down the hall and seemed to stumble a little when he noticed Nash and me.

I looked at him with wide eyes, worried that he might think this was something more than it was. But instead of meeting my gaze, he just trained his eyes on the ballroom doors ahead and walked right past us.

Of all the things for Asher to see tonight, this was probably the one that looked the worst.

"I know I was a jerk to Asher backstage," Nash said under his breath as he finished with my necklace. "But I promise I didn't plan for him to see us doing this."

"I know." I sighed.

I just had the worst luck in the universe tonight, apparently.

"I'll leave you here to talk to him," Nash said, eyeing Asher who had just opened the ballroom doors and was peeking inside as if looking for someone.

"Thanks," I said.

Nash walked through the door Asher was still holding

open, but Asher didn't even seem to care. He just continued to run his gaze around the room.

"Is something wrong?" I asked, stepping up beside him, realizing only then that he wasn't wearing his tuxedo anymore. Instead, he wore the puffy black coat he'd let me wear during the fire alarm and a pair of dark-wash jeans.

Was he going somewhere?

"I'm just looking for Jace and Logan." He pulled his gaze away from the ballroom and looked at me. "I wanted to tell them where I'm going, but it looks like they're busy." He shrugged. "I'll just text them."

"You're going somewhere?" I asked.

"Yeah." He let the ballroom doors shut again and pushed his hands into the pockets of his coat. "I got a call from Bailee a little while ago, and she asked if I could come see her."

"You're going to see Bailee right now?" I asked. "As in, *tonight?*"

It was close to nine-thirty.

"We're leaving early in the morning for Ridgewater, so I figured this was my chance to see her."

*Oh.*

He eyed my necklace for a second. "And since I was just a backup, there's not much for me to stick around for."

Did he think I saw him as a backup?

"Anyway..." He glanced toward the front doors of the hotel. "Bailee said the car would be here to pick me up any minute. Could you just tell my cousins where I went? And that they shouldn't wait up for me?"

They shouldn't wait up for him?

What was he planning to do with Bailee?

When I'd watched the news report, I hadn't seen her with a guy that could be the teacher she'd run away with. Was he out of the picture then? Was she hoping to get back together with Asher?

He'd been in love with her before. Did he want to pick up where they'd left off?

It was a crazy idea, but this whole thing with Bailee was pretty crazy so it was possible.

The doors opened, and Jess Brooks, a guy who graduated from Ridgewater High last year, suddenly burst into the hall like he was running away from something inside the ballroom.

Was all of Ridgewater here tonight? Because this was just getting weird now.

Jess stepped back when he saw Asher and me, a somewhat frantic look in his eyes. Then with a shake of his head, he said, "Sorry. I didn't know anyone was here." He darted down the hall like he couldn't get out of the building fast enough.

"Is there a fire?" I asked, wondering what the heck was up with him.

Asher opened the ballroom doors so we could take a look at what might be going on inside, but everything looked normal.

Maybe Jess was just *really* done with the ball then?

Was it possible someone was having an even worse night than me?

Asher closed the doors again, and we both took a couple of steps down the hall, in case Jess's date tried chasing after him.

Asher cleared his throat. "So anyway, do you think you can tell Logan or Jace where I'm going?"

"Oh, um, sure," I said. Then shaking my head, I said, "I mean, I guess I can do that."

Not that I wanted to. I didn't want him to go see Bailee.

Not tonight when things were so weird between us.

"Okay, perfect." He studied my face for a moment, and it almost seemed like he wanted to say something. But then he shook his head and said, "I'll see you later, Elyse. Enjoy the rest of your evening with Nash." His gaze flicked to my necklace again, like he thought it must mean something more to me than it really did. "I'll see you back at school next week."

Then he turned toward the front doors and left.

And as I watched him leave, I had the feeling that if I didn't do something now, I might miss any shot I had at a relationship with Asher Park.

## 41

## ASHER

"ASHER, WAIT," I heard Elyse's voice say from behind me as the hotel doorman was about to shut the door of the black sedan that Bailee had sent for me.

"Yes?" I asked, holding my arm out so the doorman would keep the door open.

What did she need to tell me?

That she'd picked Nash?

Because I was pretty sure I'd gotten the memo after watching them all night.

"I—" she started to say, before shaking her head and seeming to rethink the direction of her words. "I know tonight has been bad. And nothing went the way I wanted. But please don't go back to her."

"What?" I asked, poking my head farther out the door to hear her better.

Did she just ask me not to go back to her?

Like she thought I was going to hook up with Bailee?

But the street was busy and loud with traffic, so maybe I'd heard her wrong.

Elyse stepped closer, visibly shivering on the hotel steps as snow lightly fell on her bare shoulders. "I didn't choose Nash," she said through chattering teeth. "I know everything looks bad, but..." She sighed and rubbed her arms. "I didn't pick him. W-we're just friends."

They were?

"Hey, are you getting in or not?" Bailee's family driver asked. "There's a break in the traffic, and I need to pull onto the road."

"I need a minute," I said.

I needed a minute to think. Which was really hard to do when my mind was trying to figure out a million things at once.

Elyse must have seen me hesitating because she said, "Don't pick Bailee." She shivered again. "Please."

"Are we going or not?" the driver asked impatiently.

"Yes," I shouted back to her. "Just...one second."

I shook my head. Before the driver could say anything more, I bolted from the car and ran up the two steps to Elyse.

"Can we talk about this in the car?" I asked, taking her arm in mine, my heart racing. "I have to go, but I want to talk to you, too."

"You want me to come with you?" Elyse frowned. "To see Bailee?"

"Yeah." I looked at the car behind us and yelled to the driver, "She can come with me, right?"

"I don't think the Vanderbilts would like that very much," the driver yelled back through the open back door.

"Well, since she's the reason the Vanderbilts even knew where to find Bailee—" I pointed to Elyse. "—I'll just lead with that if they have a problem with Elyse joining me."

The driver's eyes widened, but she lifted a shoulder in a shrug that said she wouldn't stop me—a gesture that was probably also sign language for: "Your funeral."

So I pulled Elyse with me down the snow-covered steps and helped her into the back of the car.

---

I THOUGHT Elyse and I would have time during our drive to talk about what she'd said about being friends with Nash and how she didn't want me to pick Bailee. But we barely had time to text everyone back at the ball the details on where we were going, because we had pulled up to the towering stone building that I'd seen on the news report this afternoon.

"We're already here?" Elyse asked, bending over to look up at Bailee's building through my window.

"I guess?" I slipped my phone into my coat pocket. "Somehow, that was a lot faster than I expected."

"Yeah," she said. "I don't know if I've ever gotten somewhere so fast in New York."

"Me either."

Not that I came to New York on the regular or anything.

"Here, you can wear my coat." I started shrugging out of it, realizing I probably should have given it to her when we first got in the car.

"Thank you," she said.

I wanted to help put it over her shoulders, since I had been craving a chance to touch her for the past two weeks, but the doorman for the Vanderbilt's building opened my car door and I had to explain why I had brought Elyse with me and why she was someone they could trust not to run to the gossip magazines.

For a long moment, it looked like the doorman wasn't going to let Elyse inside the building. But after a quick call up to the Vanderbilts, he said that she could come up with me.

I took Elyse's hand in mine and held it tight as we rode the Vanderbilt's private elevator to the top floor.

"So what are you here for, anyway?" Elyse asked in a quiet voice as the elevator started climbing floors.

"I think Bailee just wants to talk." I still wasn't really sure what this meeting would entail. "She called me at the end of dinner. When I told her I was in town, she asked if I could just come over. Maybe she just wants to tell me what she's been up to these past eight months."

"Or maybe she knows she needs to apologize for leaving you to deal with the mess she made by disappearing." Elyse sounded like she might not be Bailee's biggest fan right now.

Which I definitely understood. Knowing that Bailee had planned this whole thing and let everyone drag my name through the mud was something I was still trying to decide how I felt about.

Like, had she seen any of the news reports that named me as a person of interest in her case?

Had she just sat back in Alaska, or wherever she'd been at the time, and laughed at how far off everyone was in figuring out where she went?

Maybe she had. She'd laughed about a lot of things when we'd been together.

"Maybe I don't want to do this," I said as I watched the floor number in the elevator climb, a surge of anxiety hitting my chest. "Maybe this was a bad idea."

"We can leave if you want." Elyse hugged my arm, stepping closer to me. "But it'll be good for you to get some answers, right?"

She was probably right.

Before I could be mentally ready, the elevator doors opened to reveal the entryway of a beautiful home with light-blue walls, a shiny gray floor, and extremely expensive-looking decor.

A short woman wearing a gray pantsuit came to greet us, and she led us into a formal sitting room with two couches and four chairs arranged in a square.

Elyse and I sat on the white couch while the woman left to go get Bailee.

"So I'm guessing Bailee's family is, like, super rich?" Elyse asked after taking in the surroundings.

I nodded. Leaning close to her ear so no one else would hear, I said, "Last I heard, her parents are number twelve in the United States for wealthiest families."

"So not quite as rich as the Hastings," Elyse said, a playful smile on her lips.

"Not quite." I laughed, grateful for the slight break in the tension.

Footsteps sounded on the floor behind us, and when I craned my neck to see who it was, I found myself looking at the brown-haired, brown-eyed girl I'd last seen face to face in The Italian Amigos eight months ago. A whoosh of nerves flooded my chest and my hands instantly felt tingly when our gazes met.

But she was here. She was right in front of me. The nightmare really was over.

"Hi, Bailee." My voice shook slightly as I stood to give her a hug.

"Asher!" she said, rushing forward and wrapping her arms around me.

And once I had her in my arms, I was instantly taken back to the time when we'd been putting on our ruse.

A lot of time may have passed and things had changed a lot since then, but she still felt and smelled the same.

Well, almost felt the same. She was slightly softer—probably a product of becoming a mom. And while my heart had started racing every time we'd gotten close that last month we'd been together, I didn't have the same reaction to her now.

Those kinds of butterflies only happened with Elyse these days.

We pulled away from the embrace, and Bailee seemed to noticed Elyse.

"Hi," Bailee said, walking over to Elyse to shake her hand. "I was told you're the one who found my journal."

"Yeah," Elyse said, glancing at me as she shook Bailee's hand—like she wasn't sure exactly what she was supposed to say or how much I might have told Bailee about her in our brief phone conversation earlier.

"And I guess you probably read it, too." Bailee scrunched up her nose, like she was embarrassed about what she'd written.

Elyse nodded. "People thought Asher killed you so..."

"Yeah, I'd probably read it, too," Bailee admitted. "And man, I was an idiot, wasn't I?"

Elyse and I looked at each other, not sure how to answer that.

Bailee just laughed. "Sorry, I haven't been around people for so long that I'm super socially awkward right now."

"It's okay," I said. And then, since she'd brought it up and I was crazy curious about what she'd actually been up to for the better part of a year, I asked, "So we know what happened before you disappeared, but what happened after that?"

"It's actually not super exciting," Bailee said, taking a seat on the chair diagonal from us. "Basically, a lot of sitting around in a cabin and then a house by myself."

## 42

## ELYSE

I STUDIED Asher as Bailee told us about what she'd been up to since her little disappearing act.

Did he seem like he still had feelings for her?

Was he looking like he wanted to pick up where they'd left things and be best buddies again?

Or was he upset that she'd just disappeared and left him to deal with the fallout?

I'd read her journal and had felt the confusion and desperation she had felt as she'd written her entries, so I didn't think she'd even really thought about how it would affect Asher. Because she was never actually in love with him, she probably didn't even consider that people would think she'd been killed in a crime of passion.

But I was a bit protective of him and hoped that she knew just how bad her choices had made things for him.

"I was just kind of stuck in the cabin for the first two months and had no idea what was going on," Bailee said. "I left my phone and laptop and basically everything else in my dorm room as you probably found out. There was no internet. No

TV channels. No connection to the outside world, really. It honestly felt like I went back in time to like the early nineteen hundreds."

"Did you ever leave the cabin?" Asher asked.

"Not until we drove to Alaska," Bailee said. "So it felt a lot like I was in jail. Or that I'd just been stranded on a desert island—you know, an island that looked like the forest."

"That would be quite the change," Asher said. "Going from constantly surrounded by people at school to never seeing anyone."

Bailee nodded. "There were actually a couple times when a truck or car would drive by and I'd think about chasing it down just because I was going so crazy from being alone all the time. I mean, Elijah would come visit me on the weekends and bring me books and movies that I could watch. But that was it."

"Did you have any idea what was going on in Eden Falls?" I asked, curious how much she'd known.

"Not until we moved to Alaska and I had the internet and TV again," Bailee said. "Elijah told me a little. He said that people were worried and looking around for clues of what might have happened. But I didn't know that they were blaming you for anything." She looked at Asher.

"You didn't?" he asked, sounding as skeptical as I was.

Bailee shook her head. "I asked Elijah how everything was and he said you were fine." She shrugged. "I guess maybe he didn't want me to worry and feel guilty enough that I'd ruin the plan." She sighed. "Anyway, I didn't see anything until the end of June, and by that time, the police had stopped investigating you so I figured it was fine."

"It only became fine because I left Eden Falls," Asher said, his jaw flexing and un-flexing, probably upset that she'd just let people believe whatever they wanted about him. "But it didn't go away. In fact, when I came back to school last month,

I still had people looking at me like I was going to chop them up."

Bailee flinched. "I'm sorry. I didn't know how bad it was. I honestly thought everyone would know you well enough to know that you couldn't have hurt me."

"That would have been nice..." Asher said.

"I'm sorry. I really am. I know I don't deserve to be forgiven for what I did, but I really am sorry, Asher." She blinked a few times and wiped at her eyes. "You were my best friend, and I was so selfish and only thinking about myself and Elijah and our baby." She wiped at her eye again. "So if you hate me now, I really don't blame you. I kind of hate myself for doing that to you."

"I don't hate you," Asher said, his voice sounding froggy, like he was getting choked up. "Am I frustrated about what happened? Yeah." He wiped at his eyes, as if fighting back tears, too. "But I don't hate you."

And gah, the way they were both getting emotional was making me feel emotional. Because I was starting to get it now. I'd sensed it a little when Asher had told me about Bailee, but even though they had been apart for so long and were frustrated with each other, I could still feel the bond between these two. It was a palpable thing.

Though I only sensed friendship between them now, they had been thick as thieves—they still clearly had a bond that didn't come around every day.

It was kind of like how I felt about Ava.

The room was silent for a moment, as we all seemed to need time to gather our thoughts. But then Asher asked, "So is Professor Hicks still in the picture? I didn't see him with your family when the story broke this afternoon. Is he in New York?"

Bailee shook her head, her eyes filling with tears again.

"He's with the FBI right now." She inhaled deeply, and her chin trembled like she was trying very hard not to completely lose it. "Sorry." She blinked her eyes a few times before giving us a watery smile. "It's just kind of a disaster right now. I, um, I'm trying to talk my parents out of pressing charges, but..." She drew in a shaky breath. "But I don't know what's going to happen with him or with us."

"I'm sure it's confusing," Asher said.

She nodded. "Like, I love him still and he's such a good dad, but I don't know. It's just..." She drifted off. "It's just been stressful and hard, and I guess we just made a really big mess for ourselves."

That they did.

Asher asked Bailee a few more questions, but then the sound of a baby crying came from one of the rooms down the hall.

"Sounds like Emmy has had enough grandpa-and-grandma-bonding time," Bailee said. "I should probably get her to bed."

"So you had a girl?" Asher asked. "Emmy?"

"Short for Emmelyn." Bailee nodded. "She's two months old." She bit her lip and looked down the hall before turning back to us and asking, "Do you want to meet her?"

Asher looked at me, like he wasn't sure what to say. But then he shrugged and said, "Sure."

Bailee headed in the direction of where the tiny human cry was coming from, and a minute later, she was back with the cutest little pink bundle in her arms.

"Here she is," she said, gently bouncing the baby as she cradled her in her arms. "Emmy, meet Asher and Elyse."

Asher and I both stepped closer. And I couldn't help but smile because she was literally the cutest baby I had ever seen. She had lots of dark hair with the biggest green eyes.

"She's beautiful," I said, looking at her tiny body dressed in a pink sleeper with cartoon foxes printed on it.

"Thank you." Bailee gazed down at her baby with such love in her eyes. "She's the reason I kept going when things were hard."

"You had times when you wanted to give up?" Asher asked, his voice suddenly tender.

"Yeah..." Bailee looked down, as if ashamed for having her low moments. "It was...really hard sometimes."

"Well, I'm glad you kept going." Asher rubbed Bailee's shoulder in a comforting way. "Not all of us have moms who would sacrifice so much for their baby. She's lucky to have you."

It was a seemingly little thing the way Asher comforted and accepted her—reckless choices and all. But the way he said it just made me love him more because it showed how much he'd experienced in his life and how strong he'd become through those hard things.

He knew from experience what it was like to not have parents around. One from a terrible accident. The other from stupid choices.

He'd had to do a lot of growing up all on his own.

"Most people would say that what I did was crazy," Bailee said with tears in her eyes. "But I did do it all for her."

The baby seemed to realize we were talking about her, because in that moment, she giggled and smiled the biggest, gummy smile I'd ever seen.

"Does she always smile like that?" Asher asked, returning Emmy's smile with a big one of his own.

"Yes," Bailee said, proud mom written all over her face. "She just started smiling a couple weeks ago."

"Talk about lighting up a whole room with a smile," Asher said, holding out one of his long, piano-playing fingers to

Emmy. Her hand was gripped in a tight fist, though, so it just bumped against Asher's hand.

But it was kind of the cutest thing watching him be so sweet with a baby.

Yes, I was totally the type of girl who melted when a guy was good with babies and kids.

We ooohed and ahhhed over Emmy for another minute, but then she started getting fussy. I grabbed Asher's coat from where I'd left it on the couch so we could leave, and Asher helped me put it on.

"Thanks for answering my call and coming over," Bailee said, holding Emmy over her shoulder and patting her gently on the back to soothe her. "I know you might not want to, but I hope we can talk more some other time."

"I'd be happy to talk again sometime," Asher said. "Take care."

"Thanks," she said. "You guys have a good night."

43

———

ASHER

ELYSE and I were quiet on the drive back to the hotel, each lost in our own thoughts. Like before, the ride only took a few minutes, and then the driver was pulling up to the curb where she'd picked us up earlier.

The ground was slick when we stepped out, so I helped Elyse out of the car and held her hand as we walked up the steps and into the hotel.

Anyone watching might think I was just acting the part of a gentleman helping a beautiful girl in a fancy ballgown. But it was purely selfish on my part. Holding someone's hand may seem like a small thing to lots of people, but tonight, it was everything. Because if Elyse was willing to hold my hand, it meant I might have a chance to really win her heart.

"Did you want to go back in there with everyone?" I asked when we made it to the doors that would lead into the ball-room. "I'm not dressed for the event anymore, but I understand if you want to go back in."

She shook her head. "I was done with that ball way before it even started. Is there somewhere else we can go? To talk?"

"I think I know a place," I said. "Hopefully, it's still unlocked."

"Is it your room?" Elyse asked, not following me quite yet.

I looked back at her and smiled. "I was thinking of somewhere else, but if that's what you prefer…"

"No." Her eyes widened, as if embarrassed for even bringing it up. "I was just making sure."

I chuckled. "Don't worry. I'm taking you somewhere else." I tugged on her arm, and she started walking beside me again. "It's a room I found yesterday while everyone else was at the cocktail party."

"What kind of room?" she asked.

"A room with a piano."

"Oh, that sounds nice," she said. "Did you play it?"

"For like three hours."

"Really?" she asked, seeming surprised. Which made sense since I was pretty sure the only time she'd heard me play had been that first time we'd met, at the Hastings' house on Thanksgiving. "That's a long time."

"I might have been trying to distract myself from how good of a time a certain girl might have been having with a certain classmate of mine."

"Yeah?" she asked, like she really hadn't expected me to be thinking about her so much when we weren't together.

"She's kind of amazing, and so my jealousy was totally warranted." I gave her a cautious smile, my heart beating faster since telling a girl how I felt about her wasn't exactly something I had a lot of success with. I squeezed her hand. "In fact, every guy at the party was probably jealous of her escort."

"I doubt that." Elyse slipped her free hand onto my forearm. "But I bet she would have preferred to listen to you play instead of being at that stuffy party."

"I guess I should have crashed the party to let you know I was having a concert," I said.

"You should have." She leaned closer as we walked down the empty hall. "Guys who play the piano are basically one of the hottest things on my list."

I laughed. "I thought it was 'bad boys.'"

She shrugged. "Fine, so it's actually bad boys who play the piano that are my real weakness."

"You have a very specific taste," I said, my heart fluttering. I licked my lips. "Which tells me I should probably play the piano more often so you can remember how hot you think I am."

"You totally should," she said. "Though, I don't think I've ever had a problem with remembering that."

"No?" I arched an eyebrow, not recalling if she'd ever said she found me attractive before.

"Come on." She playfully shoved my arm. "You know you're the hottest guy at our school."

"Well, of course I know it." I winked. "I just didn't know if you'd realized it yet."

She rolled her eyes but smiled to show me that she liked talking about this. "Pretty sure it's one of the first things I thought of when I saw you."

We came to the lounge area that I'd found the day before. The grand piano was visible in the corner through the glass doors. There was a beautiful water feature in the center of the room, and various couches and chairs were placed in clusters here and there.

"Looks like we have the place to ourselves," I said, opening the door and pulling Elyse inside with me.

The lights were off, but there were several windows along the far wall that let the moonlight in, casting the room in a soft glow.

"Think we're allowed to be in here?" Elyse whispered, as if afraid we were doing something wrong.

"The door was unlocked, so..." I shrugged.

"So no breaking and entering for us tonight. Dang it." Elyse snapped her fingers, like it was a missed opportunity. "I was really hoping this was my chance to have a night of mischief."

"I should have pretended to pick the lock, huh?" I said with a smile. "Then I'd look like a true bad boy."

She laughed and leaned her back against the wall just inside the door. "I guess we'll have to save the lawbreaking type of stuff for another day."

"Ah yes," I said, leaning my shoulder against the wall beside her. "Gotta keep dangling that carrot over your head, so you'll want to keep hanging out with me."

"Pretty sure you don't have to bribe me to want that." Her eyes lifted to mine in the darkness.

And when she looked at me in that way, instead of making me feel all jittery and nervous like it had the first few times we'd hung out together, it just made me feel warm. At peace.

Like I was exactly where I needed to be right now.

We just stared at each other for a long moment. And I was pretty sure it was probably time for me to kiss her again—it'd been almost two weeks since the last time I'd done that. But before I could, she started pulling off my coat that she had been wearing and asked, "Do you feel like you got to say everything to Bailee that you needed tonight?"

She wanted to talk about Bailee right now?

When we were finally alone in a secluded room, and she was looking gorgeous in her white dress? The skin of her shoulders and collarbone begging for me to touch them?

But then, of course she would ask about that. I had told Elyse that the last time I'd been with Bailee, I had fallen for her. It was only natural for Elyse to wonder if any of those feelings had come back tonight.

"I think I said what I needed to say." I took my coat from Elyse and tossed it to the piano bench behind her, so I could take her hand back in mine. "Tomorrow morning, I might be wishing I'd chewed her out for running away and leaving me to deal with the mess, but..." I shrugged. "I think she realizes how much what she did affected everyone and that she wishes things had been different."

"I think so, too." Elyse let her fingers curl around mine. "Though, a tiny part of me does think you shouldn't have been quite so nice."

I chuckled and lifted my other hand to trace my thumb along her cheek. "Is this your way of saying that sweet and innocent Elyse Cohen likes to get revenge?"

She laughed her cute little laugh that always made me smile. "Maybe I just pretend to be sweet and innocent sometimes."

"I guess I can see that." I shot her a half-smile. "Since I've had the pleasure of seeing your bad-girl side come out once before." The memory of how she'd kissed my neck and unbuttoned my shirt on that couch backstage came to my mind.

Her eyes flashed wide open for a second, like she was remembering the exact moment that I was.

"That only happens every once in a while."

"Yeah?" I raised an eyebrow. "Has anyone at Eden Falls Academy besides me experienced that side of you?"

Nash had said their ride home after their Broadway date had been epic.

But she shook her head and said, "Not even close."

"Really...?" And since it was right there staring at me, I lifted the rose pendant on her necklace and said, "Not even the person who gave you this tonight?"

She pressed her lips together. Then meeting my gaze with soft brown eyes, she said, "I know I was at the ball with someone else tonight. But..." She glanced down for a second before looking back up at me. "All I could think all night was that I wished I was with you."

"You were really thinking that?" My heart caught in my chest, suspended with the hope that she had actually felt the same way as me.

She nodded. And my heart, instead of falling back into position, just grew to fill up even more space.

Man, I loved this girl.

It was crazy how much.

"Well, that's interesting," I said, releasing her necklace so it could drop back in place. "Because that's exactly what I was thinking all night, too."

"You weren't just glaring at me because you've always secretly wanted to dance with Nash and I was keeping you from him?"

I laughed. I slipped my hand up her arm, along her shoulder, and up to cradle her neck, and then whispered, "You're way more my type."

"Well, that's good," she said, angling her head back against the wall and licking her lips as if anticipating what was coming next as much as I did. "Because you're exactly my type, Asher Park. Everything about you is exactly my type."

And with that settled, I bent my head down the rest of the way to kiss the beautiful girl I could never get enough of. Her lips parted, and she seemed to sigh into the kiss, like she'd been waiting just as impatiently as I had for this moment.

But even though I'd been dying for this moment and hoping it would happen again, it was different from the last time we'd kissed.

When I'd kissed her backstage, it had felt like I was racing to kiss her. As if I was fighting against time and only had one chance to hold her in my arms and show her how I felt before something came and snatched the moment away.

But now?

Now we took our time. We kissed each other slowly. Savored each touch, each taste. Let the moment linger and grow and take on a life of its own.

And when Elyse slipped her arms behind my neck to pull me close, I had that unexpected feeling that I'd had the last time she'd been in my arms.

The feeling like I was home.

I hadn't felt like I'd had a home in such a long time.

I'd had places where I'd *lived*. Places that I could go to hide from the rest of the world.

But they'd never felt like a home that was actually mine. Those homes had always belonged to someone else.

My aunt Vivian's home had gotten close. And when she'd told me I could call it home and be the place where I could spend my holidays and summer vacations, it had felt right.

But it still wasn't *quite* there.

In this moment with Elyse, I finally realized why.

Because home didn't always have to be a place. It wasn't always a specific location that you could mark with an "X" on a map.

Sometimes, home was a feeling. A rare moment in time where you were wrapped in a cocoon of safety and love and acceptance from someone else you cared deeply about.

Someone you loved.

It was having someone know about the good and the bad parts and not just loving you in spite of them. It was having them love you because of the person they had shaped you to be.

Elyse and I still had so many more things to learn about each other—I had so many things I wanted to share with her.

But I knew that I *could* share those things with her because of who she was as a person.

She was the girl with a heart of gold, who had a weakness for loving broken things.

Which wasn't really a weakness at all in my book.

It was her strength.

## 44

## SCARLETT

"DO identical twins run in your family or something?" I asked Elyse after poking my head through the curtains to look out at the audience. It was opening night for *The Phantom of the Opera*, and as the head of the school newspaper, I had a backstage pass to interview the cast before the musical started.

Not that I'd needed to come backstage to talk to them really, since they were all my best friends and we had already talked about everything earlier. But it was fun being back here and soaking up some of the high energy everyone was putting off as they rushed around to make sure everything was ready for the performance.

"Why do you ask that?" Elyse glanced at me briefly. She was helping Asher put on the gray beard he had to wear while he played the aged version of Raoul at the beginning of the musical. She was already dressed in a red dancer's costume—a corset leotard thing with long gold fringe for the skirt, with her hair half up and curled.

"Because there are two super hot guys sitting next to your mom and dad that I've never seen before." I opened the curtain a crack and pointed toward the two boys our age that I didn't recognize.

"My grandma was a twin," Elyse said, frowning as she stepped up beside me to take a peek through the break in the curtains. "But my mom was an only child, so I don't have any cousins on that side."

Asher put a top hat on his head and came to see what we were looking at, draping his arm behind Elyse.

A few seconds later, they both seemed to notice the two guys at the same time because they smiled and said, "That's Jace and Logan."

"Jace and Logan?" I asked, not recognizing the names.

Elyse nodded. "They are actually *Asher's* cousins." She pointed toward the right. "Which is why they're sitting with Asher's brother and his aunt and uncle."

"So identical twins run in *both* of your families?" I asked.

"I guess?" Elyse said, glancing up at Asher who was still looking out at the audience.

"Well, you guys better just plan on automatically having twins when you get married because those are some crazy odds."

"We've been dating for a month and you're already planning our wedding?" Elyse asked with a laugh.

"Seems pretty inevitable." I shrugged and looked at the way Asher still had his arm around Elyse's waist, despite having his attention focused on the audience.

When they'd come back from winter break and told everyone that they were dating, I hadn't been one bit surprised. Sure, Elyse had been distracted by Nash for a while. But I'd known from the first time I'd seen her and Asher walk into the library together for that study session, that it was only a matter of time before they got together.

Hunter and I had even made a bet that night that Asher

and Elyse would be together before opening night of the musical, since we knew how much time they'd be spending together.

Hunter had bet they'd get together before New Year's. I'd bet it would be more mid-January since I was more of a realist.

And of course, as what always happened in the bets I made with Hunter, he had been right, and I'd had to take him to dinner at The Italian Amigos.

Again.

If I were smart, I would stop making bets with him since he always won. He was way too good at reading people.

But since I was way too competitive for my own good, I just couldn't resist the chance to beat my best friend and have bragging rights until we made our next bet.

"Five minutes until showtime," Miss Crawley called from behind us, rushing through the sea of students wearing their late 1800's get-up.

"Well, I guess I better go find my seat," I said to my friends, picking up my notebook from the chair beside me. "Break a leg."

"Thank you." Elyse smiled, giving me a quick hug. "And if I do anything embarrassing, please just leave it out of your article."

"Okay, fine." I returned her hug awkwardly since I sucked at showing affection—initiating hugs or saying *I love you* being something I just didn't know how to do. "I guess I'll just go with my other plan of writing about how real the chemistry seemed between Christine and Raoul. How it felt like they were actually in love."

"Yes, it's totally not real at all." Elyse laughed as she pulled away from the hug. "We're just *super* good actors. Right, Asher?"

"Huh?" Asher turned away from the curtains, and I had to

do a double take because it kind of looked like he was having an emotional moment.

"What's wrong?" Elyse asked, noticing it, too.

"Ah, this is embarrassing," Asher said, wiping at his eyes carefully and trying not to smudge the stage makeup that was supposed to make him look like an old man.

"Was I not supposed to say 'break a leg?'" I asked, trying to make them laugh because I always felt awkward when people were emotional.

"No." He chuckled. "That's how the saying goes." He blinked his eyes a few times and looked at Elyse. "I just... I saw my aunt and uncle and cousins out there in the audience with Owen and Rosa and..." He blew out a low breath, like he was fighting another wave of emotion. "Well, I've never had anyone besides Owen in the audience for me before."

"Really?" Elyse asked.

He nodded.

"Well..." Elyse stepped closer and wrapped her arms around him. "I wish I'd been here for all your other performances. But you have a lot of people here for you now."

"I know," he said. And when he kissed the top of her head and she snuggled closer to him, I suddenly felt like I was intruding on a moment.

I was also reminded of just how long it had been since I'd had someone hold me like that.

Approximately two hundred and eighty-two days, seven hours, and two minutes...

But who was counting?

Certainly not me.

I definitely never regretted telling Hunter that we should just be friends...

You know, except for basically every time I saw him talking

to another girl and wondered if she was going to be the one who stole my best friend from me.

I sighed and glanced back at Asher and Elyse who were now holding hands as they walked to the corner where the rest of the cast was gathering for a pre-show pep talk.

Why did all my friends have to be so happy and in love right now? First, it was Carter and Ava. Then Mack and Cambrielle. Now Elyse and Asher.

Didn't anyone want to stay single these days?

I sighed. Okay, so maybe I didn't actually want to be single, either.

I started walking toward the stage exit so I could find my seat before the show started. Nash walked away from the hair and makeup station, wearing his Phantom mask and suit, and when he noticed Elyse and Asher join the circle, his shoulders drooped.

So maybe I wasn't the only one of our friends who was feeling utterly single two weeks before Valentine's Day.

Though, knowing Nash, once the show wrapped and he had time to focus on something other than being the best Phantom a high school drama program had ever seen, he'd probably find another girl to crush on.

I didn't know if that was a good or a bad trait—to fall in and out of love so easily. But it kept him from pining after someone he was constantly around but forbidden from dating for the past nine months.

Yay for having a dad who kept too close of tabs on what might or might not be happening in my dating life.

I swore he had a spy at the school, watching and reporting my every move.

I exited the stage and went into the auditorium through the side doors. I looked around the audience for a few seconds before my eyes caught on a brown-haired boy wearing a maroon hoodie waving at me.

I waved back at Hunter, so he'd know that I saw him. Hugging my notebook to my chest, I walked down the aisle to take the seat he'd saved for me between him and Mack.

"Get some good stuff for your article?" Hunter asked in a hushed voice, holding my seat down so I could sit.

"Yeah," I said. "New York Times, here I come."

"You know it." Hunter chuckled.

The lights in the auditorium dimmed and the overture the orchestra had been playing ended just as the curtains opened to reveal a scene on the stage that looked like an auction.

As the scene started and Asher's character placed a bid on a music box, I took off the jacket I'd been wearing and settled into my seat.

And as my friends and classmates put on the show they'd spent months perfecting, I tried to keep my focus on the stage instead of looking at the way Hunter's hand rested on the arm rest between us.

I forced myself not to think about how easy it would be to slip my hand into his and pretend like we were more than friends, and that my dad wasn't set on arranging a marriage between me and the son of the wealthiest man in his congregation.

If I could just not think about any of that for one night and enjoy the musical, then maybe I could have at least one night where I didn't feel like I was trapped living a life I didn't get to choose for myself.

# EPILOGUE
## ELYSE

"TIME TO WAKE UP, MRS. PARK," Asher whispered after the alarm on my phone went off for the third time.

"Just a few more minutes," I said, snuggling even closer to my husband who had curled up behind me when my alarm went off the first time. "The wedding doesn't even start until five. We still have like seven hours until then."

"Yes," he said next to my ear in the low voice that I absolutely loved. "But your spa day starts in twenty minutes."

*Ugh. He was right.*

I sighed and turned around to face Asher. I couldn't help but smile whenever I looked at him because even after being married to him for two years, he was still my favorite human in the whole world. And waking up next to him was one of my favorite parts of the day. "We can just tell everyone we got in late last night and needed more sleep."

Asher chuckled and brushed away some of the hair that had fallen over my eyes. "We're at your dad's house. Everyone already saw us get here last night. And they know we went to bed at nine."

"Well, we didn't actually go to sleep until eleven, so I'm still tired and deserve to stay in bed a little longer."

"You gonna tell your dad and Mack about why we were up so late last night?" He arched an eyebrow. "Because I think your dad still likes believing that his little girl thinks boys have cooties."

"He knows I don't believe that."

"That's debatable," Asher said. "We haven't gotten pregnant yet, so maybe he thinks we're still just best buddies."

"Or, maybe he knows that I wanted to graduate college and do a show for a couple of years before I started having kids," I said. "When there's a high possibility of having twins, you don't just make babies for fun."

"Really?" he asked, a half-smile lifting his lips. "Because I thought making a baby was the most fun part of the whole process."

"Asher!" I said, covering his mouth before realizing *I* was the one who had actually been loud.

He just laughed, so used to me getting all flustered at the slightest innuendo. Yes, my husband loved whispering naughty things in my ear when we were in public way too much.

"So, are we going to tell everyone the good news then?" Asher asked.

"That we're good at staying up late and not making babies?" I raised an eyebrow, not quite sure what we were talking about anymore.

"I was thinking of the call that we were celebrating last night." He chuckled. "But if you want to brag about how attractive you still think I am after two years of marriage, that's fine with me."

"Pretty sure everyone already knows that you're still hot,

Asher." I patted his bare chest and smiled up at him, thinking that I was so lucky to be married to him.

And not just because he was good-looking. Yes, he was still the most attractive man I'd ever laid eyes on—one who somehow got better looking every year we were together.

But he was also just an amazing human. He was my best friend and the best husband a girl could dream of having. He was always the first person to volunteer when a friend needed help. And when he loved, he loved so hard. It was a beautiful thing.

Some people loved with their hearts or their heads, but Asher loved with his whole soul.

And I was grateful every day that I was the lucky girl who got to be on the receiving end of that love.

"I'm glad you still think I'm hot." He rubbed my arm. "But in all seriousness, when do you think we should tell everyone the news?"

"That you'll be playing the Beast and I'll be playing Belle on Broadway later this fall?"

He nodded, his brown eyes full of the same excitement I'd been feeling since we got the news last night.

I was going to be on Broadway.

And I didn't just get to have that dream come true, but I got to have it come true with Asher.

When we'd auditioned together, we thought it would be amazing if they just cast one of us. Even getting a minor role would have been a dream come true.

We never expected in a million years to *both* have the life-changing opportunity to be the leads in one of the greatest fairytales of all time, on one of the most popular stages in the world.

I still wasn't quite sure I believed it was real. Probably

wouldn't believe it was until I was in costume and actually on stage in front of the crowd with Asher.

"Well…" I smoothed my hand up his chest and behind his neck so I could comb my fingers into his hair. "I was thinking we should probably wait until after the wedding. Let Cambrielle and Mack have their big day today, and then maybe tomorrow at breakfast we can tell everyone the good news."

"Sounds good." Asher kissed me gently on the forehead. I was about to direct his lips to mine when the alarm on my phone went off again.

I sighed. "Guess I better get up for real."

"Yes, you should." He laughed and reached across me to turn off the alarm for good.

I climbed out of the bed and put on a comfy tank top and shorts, trying not to get too distracted by Asher's amazing abs and biceps when he climbed out of bed and pulled a shirt on over his head.

Yeah…seeing those every day was also a nice perk of being married to him.

"You guys doing anything fun before the wedding?" I asked as I slipped my feet into my sandals.

"I think Carter, Hunter, and Nash wanted to take Mack on a hike to Eden Falls to say goodbye to his bachelor days," Asher said with a laugh. We both knew what that waterfall had been to Mack before he and Cambrielle got together. "But I'm pretty sure we'll end up playing video games until it's time to get dressed in our suits."

"Sounds about right." I smiled.

Even though we were all in our twenties, the guys still loved their video-game nights.

Which I actually loved.

I loved that even though we were all starting our careers or finishing college, our group of friends was still close and got together a couple of times a month.

Sure, it was probably easier to do when a bunch of us were related. But it was cool to see the bond we'd made in high school stick. Even better to see that after Asher and Nash had apologized for all the things they'd said and done in the past, that Asher had become one of their brothers again. That after years of being at odds with the guy who had been his childhood friend, they'd been able to mend their rivalry and become the kind of friends who texted each other daily.

I grabbed my phone and slipped it into the pocket of my shorts. Then walking over to give Asher one more hug, I said, "Don't have too much fun without me today, okay?"

"I'll try not to." He gave me a quick kiss. "I'll see you at the wedding."

"I'll be the girl wearing pink."

He smiled. "And I'll be the guy begging to dance with you all night."

---

Don't Miss Scarlett and Hunter's book:

**Grab it here:** https://www.judycorry.com/the-confidant

---

TO STAY up to date on news, sales, and releases from Judy, join her newsletter here: https://subscribepage.com/judycorry

DEAR READER,

I want to thank you for taking a chance on *The Ruse*, and for giving me the opportunity to share this story with you. I couldn't do my dream job without you!

I would also be so grateful if you could take the time to leave a review. It's amazing how such a little thing like a review can be such a huge help to an author! Even a sentence or two counts!

Thank you so much!!

-Judy

# ACKNOWLEDGMENTS

I can hardly believe that I'm here, writing the acknowledgements for my seventeenth book! When I started writing my first book way back in 2012, I don't think I expected to write this many books. Would I have thought it was super cool? Yes! I totally would. But since my first two books took me five years to write, I figured I'd probably be eighty years old before I got to this point.

But what a ride it has been. I feel so lucky that I get to have my dream job and that there are readers who love my books and characters as much as I do. (Some of you have read them even more times than me, which amazes me every time I think about it!)

Every book is a labor of love, and this one was no different. But I couldn't do it without the support of so many people.

First and foremost, I need to thank my husband Jared, who helped out a ton with the kids and everything that comes with having a big family so I could finish this beast. The Ruse is my longest book to date, and if he hadn't had so much time off work this winter to run kids to all the activities they have going on, there is no way that I would have finished this book on time. (Okay...so even then I was 2 weeks late. Thank you, Elyse and Asher, for never wanting your story to end.)

I also need to thank my wonderful kids, James, Janelle, Jonah and Jade, for being so supportive of my career. Thanks for being excited about my books and for letting me talk about my characters like they're real people and not looking at me like I'm a crazy lady.

Thank you so much to my editor, Precy Larkins, who has been part of this journey since I published my first book. You are so amazing at what you do and there is no one else I trust more with my book babies. Also, thank you for the much needed pep talks when I was doubting my story. You are the best!

Thank you to my developmental editor, Cara Seger, for always seeing my books from a different angle and having great insights for how to make them better.

Thank you to my awesome beta reader, Sofia Simpson. I'm so thankful we happened upon each other last year. Your feedback has been so helpful, as well as your encouragement. Knowing my book has your nod of approval is more helpful than you can know.

Thank you to Wastoki who once again did an amazing job on the cover illustration. I am obsessed with your work.

And as always, thank you to the readers, bookstagrammers, booktokers, bloggers and reviewers who read my books and share them everywhere. I appreciate all the care you put into your posts and reviews. It truly means so much to me.

And lastly, thank you dear reader for taking a chance on this book. I feel so grateful that I get to write books for a living and I know a huge part of that is because of your support. You are the best!

If you enjoyed this book, I would appreciate it if you left a review on the retailer site you bought it from, and/or on Goodreads. Thank you so much!

-Judy

# ALSO BY JUDY CORRY

## **<u>Eden Falls Academy Series:</u>**

The Charade (Ava and Carter)

The Facade (Cambrielle and Mack)

The Ruse (Elyse and Asher)

The Confidant (Scarlett and Hunter)

The Confession (Kiara and Nash)

## **<u>Kings of Eden Falls:</u>**

Hide Away With You (Addie and Evan)

Say You Remember Me (Maddie and Ian)

Wish You Were Mine (Lucy and Owen)

## **<u>Rich and Famous Series:</u>**

Assisting My Brother's Best Friend (Kate and Drew)

Hollywood and Ivy (Ivy and Justin)

Her Football Star Ex (Emerson and Vincent)

Friend Zone to End Zone (Arianna and Cole)

Stolen Kisses from a Rock Star (Maya and Landon)

## **<u>Ridgewater High Series:</u>**

When We Began (Cassie and Liam)

Meet Me There (Ashlyn and Luke)

Don't Forget Me (Eliana and Jess)

It Was Always You (Lexi and Noah)

My Second Chance (Juliette and Easton)

My Mistletoe Mix-Up (Raven and Logan)

Forever Yours (Alyssa and Jace)

## **<u>Standalones:</u>**

Protect My Heart (Emma and Arie)

Kissing The Boy Next Door (Lauren and Wes)

# ABOUT THE AUTHOR

Judy Corry is the Amazon Top 12 and USA Today Bestselling Author of Contemporary and YA Romance. She writes romance because she can't get enough of the feeling of falling in love. She's known for writing heart-pounding kisses, endearing characters, and hard-won happily ever afters.

She lives in Southern Utah with the boy who took her to Prom, their four awesome kids, and two dogs. She's addicted to love stories, dark chocolate and chai lattes.